YO-ACE-585

Dance TOUGH GUYS

Osmund **JAMES**

©2007 Osmund James
First Edition
10 9 8 7 6 5 4 3 2 1

All rights reserved. No part of this book may be reproduced, stored in a retrieval system, or transmitted, in any form or by any means, electronic, mechanical, photocopying, recording, or otherwise, without the prior written permission of the publishers or author.

If you have bought this book without a cover you should be aware that it is "stolen" property. The publishers and author have not received any payment for the "stripped" book, if it is printed without their authorization.

All LMH titles, imprints and distributed lines are available at special quantity discounts for bulk purchases for sales promotion, premiums, fund-raising, educational or institutional use.

This is a work of fiction. Names, characters, places and incidents either are the products of the author's imagination or are used fictitiously, and any resemblance to actual persons, living or dead, events or locales, is entirely coincidental.

Edited by: Nicola Brown and K. Sean Harris
Cover Design by: Sanya Dockery
Text Design and Layout by: Sanya Dockery

Published by: LMH Publishing Limited
7 Norman Road
LOJ Industrial Complex
Building 10 -11
Kingston C.S.O., Jamaica
Tel: 876-938-0005; 938-0712
Fax: 876-759-8752
Email: lmhbookpublishing@cwjamaica.com
Website: www.lmhpublishing.com

Printed in U.S.A.   ISBN: 978-976-8184-97-9

CHAPTER 1

DECEMBER 1991

It is a hot and windy Monday morning in capital city Kingston. I'm in my neat, spacious, richly furnished workroom, labouring at a second novel which I hope will be an even bigger international success than the first. The clock on the wall facing the huge mahogany desk says ten bulls eye. I am feeling like a king, mind flicking to the reality of being the first and only Jamaican to top the International Bestsellers lists. A debut novel that's also the all time bestseller by an Afro writer and one of the twenty fastest selling novels ever — I who didn't go to college.

My panicky wife has taken our ten month old son to the doctor. The little prince of mine has a cold, certainly nothing to worry about, but I can afford his mother's penchant for unnecessary visits to doctors.

Ahh, Jah bless that delightful son and only child of mine who I love more than all else, although his mother used him and my religious view against abortion to enchain me in matrimony. For his sake, it appears that I must remain handcuffed in marriage to his neurotically shrewd mother for at least another fifteen years.

I set aside the unruly thoughts, lean back in the swivel chair, tapping my pen and reading over the paragraph I wrote before the mind drifted aside a minute or two ago. This last paragraph appears stiff, flat — no melody.

The girls next door turn up their stereo full blast. The hit song they're blasting is one of the first I wrote years ago. I put down pen and paper, then move to stand at the windows looking down on the two-storey home next door — my home is three floors and my workroom is on the third floor. Since I moved here over two years ago, the three teenage girls next door have been making bold eyes at me, as if competing against each other to see which one of them can become my lover. Unfortunately the mother is a housewife who dislikes Rastafarians and is almost always at home; the father a friendless, anti-social accountant. Plus, for the past year-and-a-half, there has been my wife — I got married when she was twelve weeks pregnant. Still, quite likely someday I will bed one of those three girls next door, most likely the eldest sister, who is nearly nineteen. Of course, I might escape my addiction to sleeping around and become faithful to my wife — I honestly would like to be a more upright Rasta man in the year at hand.

Suddenly, I am gripped by another heady bout of pride because added to my success as a writer, I'm married to one of Jamaica's most popular and successful beauty queens and we live in one of the loveliest homes in the mansion-dotted hills of Beverly Hills, Kingston. I'm only twenty-eight years old.

I flash my neck-to-near-shoulder-length locks and begin rocking to the music blasting next door. Seconds dance by. A taxi stops at my gate. My wife's younger sister pops out of the cab and glides up the gently inclined driveway. Her mini-skirt couldn't be any shorter. Her blouse is a tiny thing. I frown, flooded by the strong suspicion that she would like me to become one of her lovers, possibly even her only lover. But although I occasionally think I hate my wife, and though I'm a bit of a playboy and my sister-in-law has a pretty face and the kind of remarkable curves that I adore passionately, there's certainly no intention to break my religious view against sleeping with sisters.

My lusty sister-in-law Sandra now disappears out of sight, gone on to the veranda. One of the two maids will welcome her into the house. With a troubled sigh I return to sit behind my large, glossy, mahogany desk. It doesn't take Sandra long to come up the two flights of stairs and float into my workroom without knocking. Damn me for not bolting the door. Her smile is jaunty and her hips are dancing all over the place. There's no denying that she's a hot number — at times like this I must labour to keep from lusting at her.

"Hello there, sugar-writer," she purrs, coming to a dramatic stop in front of my desk. Like her tall nails, her mouth is blood red and goes well with her rich, bronzed mulatto complexion. The long, thick, false lashes framing her sparkling grey eyes are fluttering seductively, and today those manufactured lashes are the same shade gold as her short, wavy, dyed hair. Her face and figure resemble her only sibling, my wife, Janice, but she is a bit shorter than Janice's five-feet-eight-inches, and her eye-catching hips and remarkable rear-end are slightly richer than Janice's.

"Hello, Sandra," I say in bland tones, tapping my pen and glancing at my writing, hoping to discourage her against lingering. "Janice took the baby to the doctor."

"I know." Her tone and the fluttering of her false lashes are definitely meant to be provocative. I steel myself against lust. She's four years younger than Janice's twenty-five and not half as widely travelled, but is certainly the bolder and worldlier sister where flirting and the battlefields of sex are concerned.

"Labouring at the next novel," I declare kindly, hoping she'll get the subtle hint and leave quickly.

"No more work now," she says, wagging a finger suggestively, a tongue-swinging grin splitting her pretty oval face. "You see, dear sugar-writer Charlie, today I claim my share of your famous manhood."

CHAPTER 2

I am shocked beyond words and movement. Her bold, shameless declaration is beyond anything I would've expected, even from her.

She laughs lustily and declares, "I always take a share of Janice's men; not that she's had many. Today I take my share of you, sweet Charlie baby."

Anger now replaces shock — my past is clouded with too many women who saw me as a sex tool to be used according to their whim. I leap up and snap: "Please leave. I may be an unfaithful husband and a less than upright Rasta man, but I still have some decency. And my wife, your sister, is a lady of high morals."

Calmly, she turns and goes towards the door. But instead of leaving, she bolts it. And then, with her back to me, she deftly steps out of her micro-mini, wags her lovely ninety-five percent naked bum, and whips around with her pelvis thrust forward like a precious gift. "Mr. Rasta writer who rarely uses Rasta talk, my puss-puss gonna get you. Gonna juice you today, sir."

My lips and throat are suddenly on fire, the old weakness for beautiful females leaping up to battle Rastafari's rule against sex with sisters. Instantly, ballooning lust clogs my larynx, accompanied by a soothing buzz in the ears and maddening heat in the balls, while the eyes are pegged to her lovely mound. The thick tufts of hair overflowing her minuscule black bikini are curled and rinsed gold. "Sandra, please go," I manage to croak, knees trembling.

Advancing slowly at me, she purrs: "Dear Charlie, I'm sure you've known for quite a while that I want you inside me. And, baby, I always get any man I desire." Her strong, trim, shapely light-brown legs are waxed and now appear to be the world's loveliest sight.

In desperation I am thinking: You must not allow her to lead you astray. She's an agent of the devil. Resist her. You are a Rasta man...

Touching her gyrating crotch, she whispers: "It's yapping for you."

I am lost. My carnal side overwhelms the desire to be true to Rastafari. Lust and carnality bury the religious tenets. Instantly, my erection becomes a battering ram.

As if from outside my lust-flooded body I hear myself snarl, "I'll teach you a lesson," and then see myself clawing at my pants.

At the sight of my thick eleven-inch long black pole, she gasps greedily, no hint of the tiny fear displayed at the first sight of my live spear by all the other sex-mad ladies I've had since attaining this grand size. I quickly discard my clothes. The powerful passion is now totally in control of me.

"What a glorious sight!" Sandra finally exclaims. "At last, the answer to the dream of a live one that's as big as my favourite vibrator!" Her eyes are alight with wondrous expectations. I stride to the windows and close the drapes. Then I stretch my robust body up to its full lofty height, rush over to the horny bitch, push her to the narrow divan under the bank of windows and rip off her blouse and bikini; there's no bra. She doesn't complain — she's grinning. I intend to be as rough as I can be with a woman.

Time and space become over-loaded with our energetic caresses and movements. I get caught up in a truly amazing and unique ecstasy. Greedy passion and carnal desire rule the room.

It turns out that she loves the roughest sex I could ever give a woman. She's an exceptional lover who gives as good as even a man of my huge size and great vigour can dish out — only a sadist could cause her fear and pain. We're in the timeless man-on-top position. I'm riding hard and deep; and I realize that she's exciting me as no other woman has done in many years. Then in the throes of intense ecstasy she begins talking dirty: "Sock it to me big dick! Maul me!...Haarder...you prick! Fuck me...harder...you big beast...kill me!" Her noisy climax arrives fairly quickly, while I am forced to kill the original intention to withdraw my erection after her climax — our awesome passion overwhelms the will.

5

As I begin firing the great juice deep inside her, she locks her strong legs around my waist and sinks her teeth into my neck, as her nails rake my back. It takes all my willpower to remain silent. Thankfully, her bite and nail raking are brief. She then releases me from her arm-and-leg-lock with a powerful shake of her hips and hard push of her hands. I am caught unawares and tumble over the edge of the narrow divan onto the thick red carpet.

"Shit!" I am indignant. But it's a very brief jolt of indignation — within two or three seconds, this emotion is overcome by guilt at having fallen prey to my sister-in-law's charms and temptation. I have sinned against Jah — the Most High God — and His Son Rastafari, and my own son . . .and, yes, against my scheming wife.

With eyes closed, I groan anguish and regret. Moments drum forward. I open my eyes and sit up on the carpet. Sandra is still on the divan, now reclining on her side with chin in hand, a satisfied leer on her lips, which have traces of my blood. The blood reminds me that we didn't use a condom. But, strangely enough, for a safe-sex devotee like myself, I feel calm about this condom oversight.

Her bite and nail rakes begin aching — I welcome the pain as a reminder of how great a sin and folly I've just committed with her.

With a resigned sigh, I look around the room, feeling like a stranger. It's a big workroom for a writer, twenty feet by eighteen, but it now appears small. The high glass-front bookcase, the two wing chairs, desk and swivel chair, the blue wallpaper, thick drapes, coffee table, ottoman, three hassocks and mini bar, all appear unfamiliar. My eyes go to the pink divan where Sandra is now hugging two of the purple cushions, still reclined on an elbow. She's gazing at me with a triumphant half-smug-half-amused look. And weak sinful fool that I am, there's a unique magnetic pull in the brain and a pleasant stirring in the balls; a remarkable feeling of satisfaction permeates me, proclaiming the knowledge that willpower won't save me from an affair with this lusty, sex-mad sister-in-law of mine. Her sexual proficiency, pretty face and voluptuous body, have swiftly taken control of my senses, maybe largely because her sister is not big on sex and even thinks that regular orgasms ruin a woman's complexion. For quite a while to come, this totally immoral sister-in-law will be able to get me to betray Rastafari's religious view against sex with sisters.

Her voice breaks into my thoughts: "Honestly, I've always sampled Janice's lovers." Her tone is easy, calm. I recognize the truth and find it distasteful. But this distaste cannot free me from her powerful spell. I sit there on the carpet chuckling self-disgust. After a few seconds she calmly declares, "I'll tell you the story before we make love again." A grin fills her face. "Janice won't be back before evening, as you should know. She's going to visit Mom after the doctor, and Aunt Joy will be there." She sits up on the edge of the divan, a cushion clutched to her naked chest. My eyes move to her amazing legs and a euphoric desire takes hold of me at the little glimpse of her glistening cunt. She grins at me knowingly and executes two tantalizing crossing and uncrossing of those amazing thighs, ending with them closed.

Dragged forward on my bum by a magnetic force, I'm about to leap up and jump her, but she kills the notion by saying: "Janice has always been afraid of me; while she has always been," — an edge of resentment now enters her tone — "the greater beauty and luckier one. Anyway, during our early years we were the same size, but I was stronger and more agile. At fourteen she began getting taller and when she turned sixteen, our parents began allowing her out on infrequent dates, while I had to sulk at home. But I got even by bedding her boyfriend long before she gave him her virginity after her seventeenth birthday. She broke off with him when she found out that he was my lover too. Thereafter, I bedded the two men she took as lovers before you, but I made certain she never found out about this sharing, just as she will not find out about us."

I move my eyes from her pretty face to the carpet — I'm still sitting naked on the carpet, she naked on the divan. I feel a surge of pity for my wife. With a sister like Sandra, it's no great wonder that Janice is such a muddled soul about sex. In any case, for now I am hooked on Sandra's beauty and greater sexual skills. I'm a horrible creature but hopefully this affair with Sandra will be brief and also be the last great carnality of my life.

Sandra gets to her feet. Her marvellous breasts jiggle invitingly. My dick jumps to attention. She laughs and says, "Come fuck me again, mister big stuff. Honestly, I'll keep our affair secret. I'm no longer a jealous thirteen year-old. And I do love my frigid sister more than I love anybody else. Come fuck me again."

Lost totally lost. I've no choice but to obey.

About thirty minutes later we're lying on our backs beside each other in clammy fulfilled silence on the carpet, having just won a remarkable simultaneous climax that arrived relatively quickly — there was nothing rough about this second bout of sex, no bites and scratches by her, while I operated in tender mode. Now the bites and scratches from our first stint begin hurting. I rise to my feet and leave the room silently, suddenly feeling eighty-two instead of twenty-eight. She follows. We are both naked, carrying our clothes. Our naked walk is no great risk, as my wife won't be back before early evening; and on my order, to be able to write with the least disturbance, the two maids never venture up to this floor of the house after ten in the mornings, unless summoned. Sandra and I go through the master bedroom, which is dominated by three full-length mirrors. We enter the adjoining bathroom, which has two full-length mirrors to suit the wife (my wife loves mirrors so much, I often wonder what she'll use to smash or cover them when her international beauty queen looks begin fading away). One of the bathroom's full-length mirrors shows that the bite on my neck is ugly. I snap: "Sandra, what the hell am I to tell your sister about the damn teeth marks and nail scratches?"

Sandra shrugs her naked shoulders. "She'll think it's the work of a young fan of yours. Loosen up lover; we both know she expects you to have lovers. But it might be wise not to let her or the maids see my vampire bite before tomorrow." I sigh, flashing my locks. Where will this sordid affair lead us? Why am I such a carnal creature?

Sandra and I are at my desk having celery tonic, cheese sandwiches and cassava pudding for lunch. She's really devouring the sandwiches and pudding. I have no great appetite. We're fully dressed and refreshed from a shower together, after which I came to my desk and did a bit of writing, while she napped in her sister's matrimonial bed before going downstairs to fetch lunch from the maids.

When we are through eating, I say: "Sandra, we mustn't take this thing any further. It's immoral."

She places her elbows on the desk, gazing at me as if at a mad man, clasps her lovely hands and rests her dainty chin on her fingers. The silence balloons until I manage to gush: "It's against my Rastafarian tenets." Her silent half-reproving, half-questioning gaze instantly has me feeling like a mad man and besotted schoolboy weaved in one.

Her response is to lean back in her chair and lock her hands behind her head, causing her prominent bosom to rise majestically, and causing yours truly to smack lips. Then she declares: "You religious dicks are all alike; whether Rasta or Christian. How can something pleasurable that's no threat to anybody's health and freedom be wrong?"

Just about two years ago, I came to the knowledge that it's never wise to argue religious morals with a passionately non-religious person. Better to argue from a social perspective. "Think what even just gossip that we're lovers could do to your sister and nephew, and your parents. The press would holler if word gets out that there's strong reason to believe we had sex even just once."

"Nobody will suspect us, unless we get stupid. Even if I had a best friend, other than the priceless pussy-cat between my thighs, she wouldn't know." Fluttering of her long, manufactured lashes fills the pause. "You're too much of a man for me to be satisfied with just this one day." She grins. "Plus with me you won't need to do much sneaking around behind Janice's back — she'll never fuss about your affairs as long as you're discreet. The poor soul is one of those women who find all types of sex tiresome."

She certainly knows her sister.

"My dear, big sweet Charlie, you and I must be lovers for a while. I must have more of that big, beautiful, black dick." Her sugary tone is hypnotic.

"I'm scared of AIDS. In the past two years you're the first girl I've had without a condom, and I often insist on a HIV test. That's a major reason why Janice is willing to turn a blind eye to my discreet affairs."

"Since last year I've been insisting on condoms as well, although HIV is rare here in Jamaica — it might explode in '92; certainly will be fairly common by 1994. But you're special, definitely worth the risk. Still, you can use condoms if you so desire. I won't need other men while you're my lover. In any case, they say what drops off head drop on shoulder — Janice doesn't like sex, so I her sister, who truly loves her, is justified in giving you all you need for a while."

She gathers the lunch utensils and crumbs onto the tray, then kisses my cheeks and says: "I'll go now and leave you to work. I have a few clients to see." She owns a little highbrow fashion boutique and also has a moderate income from a trust fund set up by her departed grandfather. "Come by my apartment tonight."

"Not before nine." I sound weary and sullen to my own ears.

"That's fine." She goes, her remarkable rear-end wagging promises.

I get up and pour a shot of whiskey, my first strong drink in three days. I'm now chained up by two sisters — handcuffed in matrimony to one by love for my son; tied to the other by a unique overwhelming lust.

Dear Jah, if only my mother hadn't died due to a botched abortion when I was nine years old, my life would've been better, less disgusting. I wouldn't have suffered the horror of being seduced by a stepmother, which in turn led to...

Why am I standing here weeping and thinking such thoughts? It's a waste of time and energy to brood on past horrors... but there is so much to be ashamed of — abuse by vain, hard-hearted women in my youth, my later vengeful behaviour with innocent girls and women, all rooted in Momma's early death and my step-mother's cunning seduction.

CHAPTER 3

CHARLIE LOOKS BACK

Momma was a kind, high-spirited, independent-minded twenty-two year old when she gave birth to me in June 1963. All I've heard of her backs up this glowing description of my memories of our short time together. I clearly recall that the big smile present in the photographs I have of her, was almost always lighting up her attractive, fleshy, black face. To be in her plump embrace was to feel a rich sense of security. Because I was her only child, it's possible that her naturally kind, gentle spirit overindulged me somewhat. Up to my eighth year, I got great comfort from sitting in her soft, warm lap with my head against her large bosom, and she was given to kissing me regularly. When relatives and friends chided her for hugging and kissing me too frequently, she'd smile, hug and kiss me again and say something like, "This little man soon don't hav' much time fo' me, so mek we enjoy we time before him begin looking at pretty girls, yuh see?" And although I was certain of always having a lot of time for Momma, some inborn instinct would keep me from protesting.

Momma and I shared a room in the home her deceased parents had built, a five-room board house, which also housed Momma's older sister, Flo, and Flo's common-law husband and their three children, a girl my age and two older boys — we shared the drawing room and dining room like a big family. The room I shared with Momma was small and crowded with a double bed, dresser, night table and wardrobe — Momma said she was saving to buy a small house. Her parents had died before my birth, and her brother had migrated to England the year before she got pregnant.

Momma and Aunt Flo were plump and of medium height; but the resemblance of their fleshy faces wasn't strong because Aunt Flo was as grim and quick to anger as Momma was merry and peaceful. Aunt Flo ruled her little mate with fiery looks and a cutting tongue — on paydays he had to give her his sealed pay envelope, then she'd give him pocket money according to her whim; he was a drinker who rarely got drunk because of the tongue-lashing Aunt Flo gave him for days after each bout of drunkenness. The house we lived in was at the top of a minor road on the outskirts of our small town. Our yard was grassy and flat, with a small plot of bananas and plantains in the backyard behind the kitchen, which was roomy and separated from the house by a twenty-foot covered walk way. There was an abandoned outhouse in the banana-plantain plot, a modern bathroom having been added to the house not long before my birth. Highgate was a very small town with a handful of shops and a tiny market. Its newest pride was a "young" high school, which would quickly become nearly as important to the town's economy as banana-cocoa farming and the chocolate factory just outside the town.

My tall, broad-shouldered Daddy lived on the other side of our town, and I was his only child. After my birth, he and Momma ceased to be lovers but were — in their words: "The greatest friends." Two years older than Momma, he was a skilled mason and dedicated father. Most days he always found time to visit me; and every Sunday morning, rain or shine, mud or dust, he visited to give us money, or occasionally, to tell us he had no money that weekend. Then we three would sit and chat for a while, he playing with me most of the time. Momma was never upset when he had no money. Her sales-clerk job was steady and earned her enough for our basic needs; she was a young woman not given to fancy clothes, jewellery and partying. Daddy's Sunday morning visits often ended with me getting dressed and going off with him to spend the day with him and his parents. I didn't grow up with much church going, as Momma and Daddy, and his parents, tended to mutter against all churches, although they all believed in the God of the bible. Momma's deceased parents hadn't been much for church either, I was told.

Grandfather Joe, my paternal granddad, was a tall near-totally-bald headed man who taught me to revere Marcus Garvey and be proud of our Afro heritage.

Unlike most of his generation; he knew a lot of facts about African history. Grandfather Joe's fat wife, my grandmother, Granny to all and sundry, was a witty old lady who shared her husband's glowing Afro pride and great respect for Garvey. She smoked a clay pipe and literally cooked all day — she had stopped washing clothes many years before my birth. In those first years of my life, two of their children, including my father who was their youngest child, and five grandchildren and one great-grandchild, were living with them in their decades-old, half-board-half-brick eight-room house built on a level stretch of land on a major road that ran down on to the town's Main Street. When she was a young cane cutter, Granny had found a "bag of money" lost by a Backra (plantation owner). The nice leather bag of money had fallen from the Backra's buggy on a deserted stretch of road. Granny and Grandfather Joe wisely buried the small fortune and kept it secret for a few years before spending any of it. Part of that bag of money had built the house, wisely constructed over a number of years.

Granny had a story she was fond of telling, and I never grew tired of hearing it. She had learned this story from her grandmother, who had been born in the days of Jamaican slavery. As the story goes, back in slavery days there was a slave fresh from Africa who refused to eat salt-fish or any food cooked with salt, and it was clear to all that this tall, handsome, muscular, proud, jet-black-skinned young man — said to be in his mid-twenties — who kept to himself, had been a learned, celebrated warrior- prince or medicine-man back in Africa. He spoke more than one language and was given to using charcoal to write ancient calligraphy; his eyes appeared powerful and his bearing so regal that the slave-drivers treated him with grudging respect and the overseer was edgy around him. Eventually, on an overcast afternoon while cutting cane in a field by the sea in Robins Bay, in our parish of St. Mary, he flung down his cutlass and began booming an African chant that stupefied the other slaves and the slave drivers; then chanting his mystical chant, with all eyes locked on him, he strode towards a large tree. At the base of the tree, he roared out an eerie cry that chilled all persons within miles around, and then in the echoing silence, he swiftly climbed up to the tree-top where he again roared the eerie blood-chilling cry and immediately flew out of the tree like a bird, headed towards the sea, and due east across the sea he flew.

I never doubted this story. A power in my soul has always told me that Granny's grandmother's father had truly witnessed this awesome happening, a great African warrior/medicine-man flying like a bird across the sea, preferring to chance death rather than live in slavery.

Like Daddy, Grandfather Joe, Granny, my great-great-grandmother, and the great-great-great-grandfather who witnessed the marvel in the presence of many other persons, I have spent many nights wondering if the man-bird had made it back to Africa.

CHAPTER 4

Other vivid memories of life before Momma's death in my ninth year are few. One of these few clear remembrances is Granny's death just before my seventh birthday. Granny's funeral was huge. For weeks after, people talked about the feasting, hymn singing, dinky-mini folk music, and dancing at the set-up and nine-night. Grandfather Joe took Granny's loss with mournful dignity. Granny's death was my first poignant lesson on the great change called loss.

Just before Granny's death, Daddy had moved from his parents' home to "begin a life" with Monica, a shapely brown girl from Kingston, who he had met while visiting a friend in the city. It appeared that Monica was eager to leave the city, a reality that pleased Daddy, who has always viewed city living as inferior to small-town life. They rented a small, three-bedroom house that was fairly near the home of Daddy's parents, and Monica trucked her two sewing machines and a nice array of furniture from Kingston (her brothers were furniture makers). Monica was a good dressmaker and immediately became the most sought after dressmaker in our little town, partly because she was from the capital city — she and Daddy had rented the little three-bedroom house with this business success in mind; the bigger of the two small bedrooms was ideal for her work. The little board house was also perfectly located for a dressmaking business — it was just two doors away from the market and town-clock square, which was the heart of our little town.

Almost immediately, Momma developed a great liking for Daddy's choice of common-law-wife. "She is a nice independent girl," Momma said without malice. "Real sensible of yuh father to choose one like her to settle down with."

The future would prove Momma partly wrong, and dispatch me into a life loaded with sexual horrors.

Monica was a pretty, large-eyed, voluptuous brown girl. I didn't resent her sudden queenly role in Daddy's life. From a tender age my dear mother and father had drilled into my head that they were not suited for living together, and that one of the major reasons for being together was to produce me; I loved and accepted them as they were.

Within five or so months, my mother and Monica became friends. Obviously, Monica was quick to recognize my mother's warm honesty that declared the absence of any sexual/romantic ties with Daddy. When this friendship came to life towards the end of that year, 1970, Monica was five years younger than my mother's thirty but was clearly more experienced in some areas.

Yes, the world was wonderful until the Saturday evening in my ninth year when Momma left for an "overnight stay with a friend" in our parish's capital town, Port Maria. She didn't return home alive. She died in the home of an old quack who was widely known as a good abortionist.

I became a confused, motherless nine year old.

Memories of the hours, days and three-to-four weeks after Momma's death have always been blurred and foggy in my mind. Now that I'm older, I realize that this obscure memory of that poignantly sad time is due to a subconscious fear of thinking much about what I've always seen as Momma's one rash action — having an abortion, and by a quack at that. Of course, in those days, abortion was a much bigger crime and a far greater sin (religiously and socially) in Jamaica, so finding a doctor to do it back then was harder and more expensive than it is now. Strangely enough I have never tried to discover who Momma's lover was or what happened to the accused abortion quack. My thoughts of Momma have always been overwhelmingly of our happy times and the conviction that if she hadn't died young, life since my thirteenth year wouldn't have been loaded with exploitations at the hands of lecherous women who saw my way-above-average-size dick as a prize for their egos, and conflictingly, also a reason to try humiliating me.

CHAPTER 5

Two or three days after Momma's death, Daddy moved my life to his home, and for many days I cried oceans on Monica's bosom when he wasn't around. When he was there, he kept reminding me that I was a man, born to suffer, and that too much crying weakened a man. In his presence I forced back the tears and became a nine year old man, hating the thought of disappointing him, wanting to be strong. It's almost certain Monica didn't tell him how I cried alot when he wasn't around, how she'd take me on to her lap and hug me to her bosom, and caress my head and coo soothing words. There were also the long soothing baths she clearly enjoyed giving me.

So I settled in with Daddy and Monica in the centre of town, roughly quarter mile from my former home on the outskirts. The little house was mostly board — the small kitchen and tiny bathroom were concrete. I had a small room to myself — the rest of the little house was comprised of the modest master bedroom, Monica's crammed workroom, the living-dining room and a small veranda. Slowly I returned to normal, began smiling and playing again.

Monica was a good cook and had a good sense of humour. My regard for her grew each day and I spent hours with her in her workroom listening to the music of her electric sewing machine; she had a pedal singer as well, which was used by a girl she employed on weekends.

Within weeks after Momma's death, my gland abnormality began heralding itself— suddenly my little willie ballooned into a dickie, was much bigger than those of other boys my age, and bigger than half the boys who were up to three years older. The rest of my body remained at being simply one of the taller and heavier in the nine to ten year old age group. I saw the new much-bigger-than-average size dickie as a thing of good luck, which was what Daddy and other adult males said: "Boy, yuh born lucky!" or something like "Girls a go rush yuh, an' nuff man goin' grudge yuh!" This would be the standard reaction of my poor and lower- middle income relatives and friends; nobody thought it might be an abnormality a doctor should see. So, of course, I was given to flashing the good luck for friends to envy.

My first sexual romp was with the daughter of one of Monica's customers. This momentous event occurred roughly seven to eight months after my mothers' death, and shortly before my tenth birthday in 1973. It happened on a Saturday.

The mother was the first customer to arrive that morning. She came to see Monica about a new dress, and her eleven year old daughter was with her. The mother was Indian; the daughter was half-Afro-half-Indian.

"Joan, yuh an' Charlie go play while I settle this style problem with Monica," the mother said crossly when Joan persisted in peeping at the fashion book and offering unwelcomed advice. Monica nodded agreement. Joan and I left the workroom and entered the crowdedly furnished living-dining room. Two more women entered the house and headed for the workroom — they were regular customers. Daddy was out working that day.

"Let's see," I said to Joan, labouring to appear and sound manly. Since entering our primary school three years previously, I had been admiring her, but she was two classes ahead of me at school and didn't live near me, making it hard for us to become friendly at school. Now with visions of my dickie's first voyage, I said, "Come see my room first."

"Yes, show me yuh bed," Joan said, fluttering her long lashes, and causing my little heart to race excitedly.

Feeling very much the cunning man, I led her across the living-dining room to my room. I was thinking: Sex was what she wanted.

Was her pussy hairy? Or was it bald as those of the two girl cousins in my age group, the only ones over baby age I had seen? (I had heard bigger boys talking about hairy ones. Hairy or not, she was eleven, two years older than me, so although her body was smaller than over half the girls of her age group, and looked puny beside mine, her pum-pum must be big enough for my special dickie.

CHAPTER 6

The moment we entered my little room, she skipped around me and launched her thin body on the little single bed, bouncing on her butt; her long, raven-black, half-Indian plaits flying about.

I gently closed the door behind me, suddenly feeling quite nervous. Still, determined to have her, I boldly stepped forward, eyes riveted on her, anxious but proudly conscious of the stirring in my balls. She said: "But is why him lookin' at me so? Never see me before, eeh?"

"Yuh. . .yuh so pretty an' is the first girl to go on me bed," I blurted, standing over her. She was now perched on the edge of the bed, gazing up at me from under fluttering lashes. Then I heard myself saying: "Show me yuh pum-pum an' me show yuh my dickie that bigger than all my friends."

"Here this little boy." But she was grinning and instantly added, "Yuh show first."

I quickly had my shorts and underwear down enough for her to get a clear view of the half-erect Mr. Dickie.

"Wow," she gasped, eyes popping. "Yuh is only nine but yours bigger than Ha..." She didn't complete the name. But I didn't care a fart about the partly spoken name, for her open admiration had pumped Mr. Dickie to a size and hardness that filled me with boyhood wonder and manly pride.

More than ever I craved the first taste of sex. I said, "Your turn now."

After a slight hesitation, she lay back on my bed, raised her thin legs, and drew up her tall green skirt. It's certain that by that point I must have been tilted forward on my toes, tongue and eyes popping out of head, erect dick in hand. She pulled down her green panties a bit.

I gulped all the air in the room — her little pussy with its mat of short glossy black hair was the loveliest sight I had yet beheld. Dickie made a throbbing jump that dragged me up and forward on to the very tip of my big toes, my head and upper body way over the bed. But the tantalizing sight was brief — she quickly snapped her panties back in place and sat up.

"Let's do it?" I pleaded, throbbing dick in hand, shorts and underwear almost down to my knees, bent over the bed. As I'd heard bigger boys say, I wanted her so badly I'd have eaten a mile of her shit to get in her pussy.

"No. Momma might soon call. One day we'll do it. Kiss me."

With a little groan of manly agony, I drew up my clothes in the best possible way, sat down beside her on the bed and launched my first real kiss, hoping that the kiss would quickly lead to sex. One of my hands snaked between her thin thighs and she allowed me my first real fingering job, while she also guided my other hand to her budding bosom. But just as I had her groaning and writhing with pleasure, lying back on the bed with her arms around my neck, her mother's voice called from the living-dining room: "Joan! Ah ready, girl."

I got my first sanity-threatening stab of man-deflating frustration, and mumbled: "Shit." I released Joan. She jumped out of the bed, hastily straightened her clothes, calling out: "Comin', Momma." She ran from the room. I lay there with a maddening ache in the groin, trying to console the anguish with the memories of our kisses and petting, and the fact that she had promised me sex soon. When the time came for us to have sex, I was going to fuck her real good.

The ache in my groin lessened. Dickie dwindled. I sighed with relief, having heard that petting and failing to get sex can cause a young boy to have a painful erection for up to four to five hours.

Before long, there came the thought to go by her home just before dusk that very evening to try getting her to sneak off with me. This idea quickly became a dedicated plan. But about an hour before I was to set off on this hopeful quest to her home on the outskirts of town, I heard the horrible news that Grandfather Joe had died suddenly in his backyard.

Grandfather Joe's sudden death from a heart attack distressed me more than it would have if it hadn't happened less than a year after my mother's untimely death — for years he had been telling us he wanted to go in a quick sudden manner before his head or body became feeble. I didn't cry much but felt too dejected to pay Joan much attention at school during the two school weeks between his death and funeral.

Which close relative would die next, and how soon? What if Daddy died?

The Thursday night set-up of feasting, music and dancing for Grandfather Joe; and the Friday funeral were big and grand as Granny's had been three years before. But because of the lingering sadness over my mother's death, Grandfather Joe's set-up didn't ease my dejection as Granny's set up had. Still, when Grandfather Joe's funeral ended, I suddenly began feeling much better; most of the weighty gloom and foreboding began falling away in the sunset like a burden borne to its destination. So at the nine-night merry-making and feasting at Grand-father Joe's "dead-lef'" home the following night, my spirit rocketed sky high when Joan sought me out with a most inviting smile.

She approached me at about 8 o'clock when several older cousins and I were in one of the bigger front bedrooms having a chat. In a chirpy voice, Joan said: "Charlie, ah hav' a secret for yuh." She was alone, her dark-brown face glowing in the softly lit room. I jumped up eagerly, certain that the secret was fulfillment of her erotic promise made two weeks ago. I led her from the room, grinning at my cousins' teasing.

Without a word, I led Joan to a small bedroom at the back of the house — the handful of adults and children we had passed in the livingroom had appeared deep in gossiping; we had avoided the kitchen, which was the only other place inside that held eyes. Joan giggled when I bolted the bedroom door behind us. A few weak streaks of light flowing in around the edges of the thick curtain from outside were the only illumination. The darkness felt perfect. To the low hum of the hymn singing in the front-yard and laughter in the backyard, we tumbled to the big bed in pre-teen frenzy, removing only what garments had to be removed. I was excited beyond words, although now a bit nervous about finding her sweet road in the dark — I'd always pictured the first taste of sex in bright lights but now thought the darkness was better. Thankfully, she wasn't a virgin eleven year old — she skillfully guided the head of my oversized soon-to-be-ten year old dick into the moist gates of her hot core. Then I was gleefully sinking myself deeper into her and she began moaning what sounded like: "Lord, Charlie, yuh big...big...tek time...nuh do...it so hard."

Of course, with my boyish glee I was driven to going as deep and as fast as possible. And, as is to be expected, that first ride of mine didn't last long — after just two-to-four minutes I was shuddering and gasping, spurting weak juices deep inside her.

A mixture of satisfied joy and triumphant pride filled me. Restful seconds floated by. Then her little hands pushed at my chest. I rolled off her.

"Boy, Charlie, yuh thing big fi true," she said respectfully. Then she added a bit irritably, "But yuh go too hard an' fast. Next time a hope yuh do it right."

I didn't respond, was busy hauling on pants, feeling very much the man of the moment.

A minute later, I opened the bolted door to peep into the adjoining bedroom and found myself gazing into a rage-filled face.

CHAPTER 7

Whey yuh a do with my girl, little boy?" growled eleven year old Trevor, one of Joan's classmates. Rage made his brown face red in the bright overhead light. Trevor wasn't seeking answers. He was in war mode.

I wasn't afraid of him. He was a bit thicker but we were the same height. I stepped into the room and snapped: "Joan is not your girl!"

Joan walked around us wordlessly and stood off in silence. Her face appeared to be a mixture of anxiety, curiosity and pride. But I didn't have time to be certain of this reading of her face, as Trevor glanced at her and immediately rushed me with fists extended. I lashed out my right foot to his shin. He grunted but leapt at me. We toppled over, hitting aside an armchair and a night table. In a mad tangle we rolled to and fro on the gleaming floorboards and a rug, flailing ineffective punches. Then just as I managed to pin down the fool and was hammering a fist firmly into his jaw, two of my aunts and several cousins and Monica burst into the room. Instantly, just as I hammered a second devastating fist downward, hands hauled me up.

Someone said: "Them fightin' over Joan!" My eyes found Joan across the room — she was easing out of the room, glancing back over her shoulder, her dark-brown half-Afro-half-Indian face radiant with pride.

"But see here!" said one of my aunts, her tone and face tinged with amusement. The other aunt intoned more sternly: "Charlie, boy, ah can't believe yuh fightin' over girl already."

"So yuh turn man already," Daddy said next morning over a late and light breakfast — the previous night's music, dinky-mini dancing and feasting at the nine-night had remained at full blast till near dawn, which was when we had stumbled home. There was nothing amusing about Daddy. "Fightin' over girl. Well? An' she older than yuh."

I hung my head, worried about getting the first flogging from him. In the months since he had moved me to his home he had only slapped my shoulders lightly two or three times for general boyhood misconduct. He now added: "Charlie, what yuh an' Joan was doin' in the backroom alone?" His tone was firm, his eyes hard. He and Monica were sitting beside each other across from me at the dining table.

Monica shot him a disapproving look, but her tone was soothing when she said: "Ah, Wesley, don't be so hard. Charlie is only nine years old..."

"Almost ten," he injected, pointing his teaspoon at her, but his tone had softened, "an' they know a lot these days."

Monica said in placating tones: "Trevor attacked Charlie because he found Charlie and Joan havin' a talk away from the noise. It's (Daddy was grunting disbelief) really so silly for a little boy like Trevor to think he owns a girl."

At that moment I loved Monica nearly as much as I had loved my departed mother. I knew Monica was labouring to save me from a possible flogging, a favour she would do quite a few times over the next few years. Now our eyes met across the dining table, she winked and said with a grin: "Me proud a Charlie for teachin' him a lesson."

"Yuh two think I fool-fool," Daddy said around a mouthful, voice and face holding sternness and resignation.

"Honey, we know yuh smart," Monica said, squeezing his arm, her pretty brown face beaming a smile at him, "an' we love yuh."

I nodded solemn agreement at him. He sipped his coffee, took up a slice of bread, and that was the end of the matter. It was my first lesson that love, backed up by soothing words and caresses, will soften even men as rough and strong-willed as Daddy.

Because Trevor was an only child with no close male relatives attending our primary school, he didn't dare try to fight me at school, for I had several older male cousins at our school. He had to endure his friends' teasing that a younger boy had taken away his girl and beaten him.

But although Joan was one of the smallest girls in her age group, I was sensible enough to resist trying to claim Joan as my girl, seeing that she was older and obviously a bit wild. So, while I was a bit of a hero among my age group, the only one who was quite friendly with an older girl, and a girl pretty as Joan, I kept reminding friends that Joan had other boyfriends. Meanwhile, Joan's friends were somewhat amazed that she paid me so much attention, although she paid an equal amount of attention to a few other boys, including one who was three years older than her. The prevailing whisper among her age group and mine was that, yes, she had given Charlie sex. Anyway, because Joan lived a mile away from me, and her parents didn't allow her much freedom, we weren't able to see much of each other outside of school. Three years would flirt by before I was able to get a second go at sex; of the half dozen girls in the nine-to-twelve age group who lived near me in the town centre, only two were willing to allow me even just quick kisses and hurried caresses. Showing my prized dickie to these girls just didn't work as it had with Joan, for the ones who were not terrified by the size were obsessed with the common girlhood tendency of not having sex with a boy who wasn't at least three years older.

Boyhood sexual frustration became a part of my world.

Life rolled along quite nicely until I was twelve years old, which was when Daddy's mason trade got real slow and he made his first "farm work" trip to the USA, and sexual exploitation at the hands of older females entered my life.

CHAPTER 8

At age twelve, I began feeling embarrassed about allowing Monica to wash Mr. Dickie whenever she insisted on giving me a "proper bath". These proper baths had been occurring about once a week during the three years since I had moved to live with her and Daddy; I knew other mothers/guardians who gave boys of up to thirteen the occasional "proper bath" (some of these boys would sometime grumble about a sore neck or "knee-back" after such baths). Other than feeling that I was bathing appropriately enough, the great problem with Monica's proper baths was that within two weeks after Daddy left for the USA as a farmworker in July, 1975, she began taking far too much interest in washing my dick, and these baths suddenly increased to two and three per week.

"Why yuh drawin' away?" Monica asked airily during one of these newly frequent proper baths at the end of July. One of her hands was moving the foreskin of my dickie back and forth slowly, her big glittering eyes gazing up at me from under lowered lashes, brown cheeks flushed and her mouth in a pleased smile. "What wrong, Charlie?"

I was in the bathtub, standing shin-deep in bubbled water, and was too embarrassed to meet her eyes squarely or to try answering her.

Silence filled the bathroom, echoing in the young night — the long summer evening had briskly turned to night in the past ten to fifteen minutes.

Monica was sitting on a chair beside the bathtub, clad in a floral housedress, her low Afro hairstyle covered by an old beret. She resumed moving my soapy foreskin back and forth. I became greatly afraid that Mr. Dickie might soon get erect in her hand.

In the past few years since moving to live with her and Daddy, allowing her to wash my dick had always appeared acceptable, and having her wash Mr. Dickie was not the least bit arousing because she was Daddy's live-in love and my mother was dead. But, this was the first time she was moving the foreskin back and forth more than once or twice. Now I was worried about becoming aroused. She cracked the agonizing silence with a cool: "Yuh think yuh is big man eh?"

A quick glance showed me an enigmatic smile lurking at the corners of her painted, cherry red lips, while her eyes held amusement. I stared at the ceiling.

She tugged my dick hard and said, "Answer me. Yuh sex Joan or other girls since the night yuh beat Trevor?"

I was taken aback. She had known that I had dicked Joan! A quick glance at her brown face suggested that her amusement had been replaced by excitement.

"Monica," I blurted, "Mission Impossible soon start." In fact, I knew that the popular television show was roughly half hour away. Then I heard myself gushing: "Yuh know ah think Momma woulda did love Mission Impossible, too."

She gulped, released Mr. Dickie and began scrubbing behind my knees. Relief flooded me. But instinct told me that was not the end of the matter.

CHAPTER 9

Watching TV in our softly lit living-dining room after that unforgettable bath, I focused most of my mindpower on trying to believe it was wrong to have been thinking that Monica was interested in me sexually. I was slouched in an armchair, only half my mind on the movie. Monica was curled up on the sofa. She was still wearing the housedress she had been wearing from before nightfall.

We hadn't exchanged a word since leaving the bathroom.

When the show ended, she got up and went to her room. Roughly twelve minutes later, she returned smelling as sweet as a garden. Now dressed in a sheer white negligee, her big nipples and red bikini clearly on display in the soft light, she commenced a mysterious stroll around the living-area room, caressing each piece of furniture.

I began feeling afraid. It was obvious to even my reluctant twelve year old brain that Monica was attracted to my huge dick and was determined to try it while Daddy was away.

Two terrors banged and staggered around inside my head while Monica was making her leisurely stroll. Firstly, she was Daddy's woman, which meant that it would be a grave sin to even think about sex with her. Secondly, she was thirty years old; old enough to be my mother, so most likely she would "strain" me if we had sex. I would've gladly fucked just about any female up to age twenty, as eight years older was not enough to be my mother; older boys and grown men had warned us younger boys that if a woman was old enough to be a boy's mother, she could strain and stretch him beyond repair, leaving the little fool with a life-long bad-back and useless dick.

Monica ended her mysterious stroll by coming to a wide-legged stance in front of my armchair.

It was impossible to keep the eyes from moving to her plump love mound, which curved forward majestically from inside her red lacy bikini and up to her lightly rounded belly. Her belly had fattened a bit these past weeks in an attractive manner. Self-disgust and interest battled in the soul.

"Charlie," she said. My eyes jerked upward to her pretty, large-eyed, brown face. There was an alluring smile on her lips. I glanced aside — she was blocking the view to the TV. She added, "Six months from now yuh will be getting a brother or sister. I am three months pregnant."

A little bolt of joy killed some of my guilt and fear; causing me to meet her eyes with the thought that perhaps it really was wrong to have been thinking she wanted to seduce me.

"Glad?"

I nodded vigorously, sincere, and even managed to grin. A baby brother or sister would be a lot of fun.

She said, "I not afraid of thieves troublin' us while yuh Daddy in America. But I just cannot sleep good alone, an' pregnant woman need plenty sleep. Yuh Daddy said yuh should sleep with me, (I stiffened) if I have difficulty sleepin'. An' believe me; ah don't get a good night sleep since him gone. So come let's go to bed. It gettin' late." She moved to turn off the television. And, once again, I became near totally convinced that her aim was seduction.

Still, I got up and immediately focused all brain cells on the thin hope that the gut feeling about her true intentions was wrong. The hope thickened. But when I went to my room and was changing into pyjamas, I instinctively fell to repeatedly telling myself that a female couldn't rape a male. Monica could not seduce me if I didn't allow lust to give me an erection. And if she tried seducing me, I'd simply refuse to sleep in the same room with her.

When I emerged from my room, she was still in the living-dining room awaiting yours truly, standing by the floor lamp, which she immediately turned off. Then she floated out of the dark room ahead of me. I followed her with a heart drumming to the hasty replaying of the thought that she could not seduce me if I didn't get an erection.

The overhead light in the master bedroom was on, it all appeared new to my eyes. The bed was ready for sleeping or seduction — two pillows but only one big sheet for covering.

It was a typically hot Jamaican summer night but apprehension had me chilled.

Avoiding my eyes, she said: "Get in bed Charlie, so I can turn off the light." There was a sugary edge to her voice, her brown body was swaying to some mystical tune, and she was pointing at one of the green pillows.

I moved on to the bed without saying any prayers. Instead of a prayer, I repeatedly wondered if she usually went to bed wearing lipstick. She turned out the light and got in bed beside me. I stiffened and drew the thin cover up to neck level, although the room was too hot for covering above the waist. Her perfume flooded my nostrils. I found the will to turn away from her — the bed was close to one of the room's two sets of windows, and turning away from her placed my face toward this set of windows, which faced the road; the floral curtain allowed a dim glow of streetlight to filter into the room, and I fancied that this dim glow was some kind of protection.

I felt her moving up closer to me under the thin coverlet.

Her breath burned the back of my neck, then her hands seized a shoulder and a thigh. "Charlie, face me," she cooed huskily, forcing me around.

I wanted to run, but lacked the power to even move away on the bed — simply could not resist her efforts, although I wasn't the least bit aroused. She embraced my stiff powerless body to her softness, face against her bosom, one of her legs thrown commandingly over a hip, her hands caressing my neck and back, her breath burning an ear. Still, although my body was powerless in her grip and caresses, the brain was blasting. Certainly like everyone else, she must know it would be a great sin for us to have sex, so either she had gone mad or the pregnancy and Daddy's absence had rendered her a little crazed and in need of someone to hold close.

That's it, my brain decided; the pregnancy and Daddy's absence had made her desperate for someone to hold close and caress. She wasn't after real sex.

"Relax an' hold me my little man," she purred, running fingers through my hair. "I'm so lonely, and can't get a good sleep. Holdin' yuh will help, especially if yuh caress me all over...kind of...like I'm your girl. Jus' that."

We were lying on our sides. It appeared the darkness added power to her hands.

Telling myself she wasn't after sex, I began caressing her back and bum. She sighed with pleasure and said: "That's right, my little man." I continued caressing her back, bum and thighs, until I felt one of her hands enter the front of my pyjama pants. Her hand on my limp dick brought back the dread that she was after sex. I ceased caressing her.

"Charlie, yuh is a special little man, yuh thing already big enough for big woman." And she began pumping, caressing, tugging — but dickie remained limp as I wanted it to, for I had no intention to plummet into the dual horror of sinning against Daddy and risk getting "strained" by a woman old enough to be my mother.

After wasting a few minutes in futile effort trying to get my dick erect, she moved her hand away and said: "Charlie, why yuh don't want me?" Her voice sounded on the verge of tears. She still had me in a tight embrace, and she guided one of my powerless hands to her crotch. "Why yuh don't want me, eeh?"

I was too scared and confused to answer. But the brain whispered that if I didn't do something instantly, she might make matters far worse by getting up to turn on the lights and go completely crazy. So when she guided my hand into her panties and eased down that little lacy thing, I commenced to caress her hot, plump, hairy pelvis. I was telling myself that caressing and fingering her wasn't a great sin, and that giving her some kind of pleasure was the best way to prevent her from going crazy with hatred for me.

Quickly, she removed her bikini and positioned my hand so that two fingers slid into her hot, wet core, and then she instructed me to use my thumb on her stiff clit. She then began riding the fingers. It was all a most enlightening lesson for a boy to use on girls, and she was soon groaning with pleasure. I obeyed her when she commanded me to kiss her breasts. Again she tried using a hand to get Mr. Dickie hard, but quickly gave up to concentrate on riding my fingers — I was now certain that she'd never be able to get my dick erect; I was her robot programmed to caress and finger and kiss her below her neck, nothing more.

After a while, her breathing grew rapid and she groaned: "Bite me nipples." I obeyed her. She cried out in the throes of ecstasy and entered a long shuddering climax.

I thanked God that the room was dark, and I prayed that she'd go to sleep now. I remained quietly in her embrace. Many seconds tiptoed away. But instead of falling asleep, within a minute she asked:

"Why yuh don't want do it with me?

CHAPTER 10

I gulped a ton of air, taut with a clutch of dismay and a stab of fear. But the knife of fear was brief. I guess the fact that she'd just had an orgasm made me bold enough to give her the truth in fairly calm tones. "Yuh so big, an' is Daddy's woman."

"Yuh is no ordinary boy, an' I wouldn't hurt yuh," she responded soothingly. "An' because yuh father away, an' I pregnant an' lonely an' not yuh mother, it wouldn't be wrong — what drop off the head drop pon shoulder. But I won't try forcin' yuh. Now go to sleep." She released me and moved away a bit.

Strangely enough, within seconds I was asleep, and slept away the rest of that unforgettable, poignant, character-shaping Friday night.

I awoke next morning from dreamless sleep to rosy Saturday morning sunlight dancing through the half-open windows over the bed. I was alone in the big, rumpled bed. The clock on the night table said minutes to seven. Music from the radio in the living room and rich smells from the kitchen were flowing in through the open door.

Feeling a bit weary and slightly dazed, I sat up just as Monica entered the room smiling and looking fresh in a pants suit. Her brown face was aglow. I avoided her eyes.

She sat on the bed, kissed my cheek and said calmly, "Today goin' be very busy for me. Customers soon begin arrivin'. What yuh want to do?"

I shrugged and mumbled: "Don't know."

"Tell yuh what, after yuh eat I give yuh a money to go enjoy yuh-self on the town." Her voice was calm as if nothing unusual had taken place between us in the night. "But remember to stay away from bad company." She hugged me; then left the room humming merrily.

I had decided that it was best for me to humour her by fingering and caressing her whenever she wanted. Refusing might make her completely mad or cause her to give Daddy "bun" with another man, even several men.

After I completed the prodigious attack on that wonderful break-fast of eggs, bread, chocolate, cornmeal porridge, orange juice and fry dumplings, Monica gave me two dollars, which was a whole lot of money for a twelve year old boy back in 1975. "Don't squander it," she said calmly, smiling, "but hav' a nice time." I was using reserve will power to match her cheerful gaze with a forced smile. I thanked her and bounced out of the house, feeling manly in long pants and T-shirt, and rich with a dollar bill in one pocket and one dollar in coins in another.

Fourteen year old Joan was flirting in my twelve year old mind. I was determined that very day would witness my second bout of real sex, obsessed with the idea of ending the three year drought ruling Mr. Dickie since the first and only taste of sex; and it appeared that the best possible second fuck would be with Joan, who had given me the first. Humming and whistling, I headed down towards the nearby clock-tower-market-entrance square on Main Street.

The main street of our little town was already fairly busy, although it was just about fifteen minutes after eight. The market was already loaded with food higglers and other types of sellers, and early shoppers were arriving in a steady colourful flow. I met two friends by the clock-tower. We bought peanuts and stood listening to a group of the town's young men airing remarkable tales — one of these arresting narrations reinforced the thought that Monica was experiencing a bout of temporary sex madness. Still, interesting though the remarkable narrations were, roughly every two minutes I would wonder if it was too early to go by Joan's house, which was just outside the town.

When the clock tower said 8.45 (it was working correctly that week), I saw Joan's mother and father entering the market, which meant that most likely Joan was at home with her three younger siblings, two sisters and a brother. I hastily bought eight packs of peanuts, gave my friends two, crammed the other six into my pockets, and hurried away from my puzzled friends.

Since that night three years ago at my grandfather's nine-night, Joan and I simply hadn't been able to meet for sex. She had begun attending high school a year ago but we were still good friends and in the three years since we had sex, we had only managed to have hasty petting bouts at my house on a few of the many occasions when she came by to visit Monica's dressmaking business. I was now hurrying down Main Street with two heads loaded with the hope that she was home and I'd be able to fuck her in the bushes behind her house before either of her parents returned home. Why hadn't I seen the use of those bushes before this Saturday morning in August 1975?

I hurried to the little community. Her three-bedroom home was on a rise overlooking the railway line that skirted our town, and her father had a little banana-plantain-coconut field adjoining their back lawn. She was at home with her three younger siblings, the oldest of whom was eight. She looked good enough to make any boy crazy with lust — in the last two years her body had moved from skinny to a slight plumpness that was rich with fascinating curves. At first, she teased me that she wasn't interested in sex with a boy two years younger, even if he had an over-sized dick. But shortly after, she fell in with my plan. We gave her siblings sweets and three packs of my peanuts and got them glued to cartoons on the TV. Then we crept off to a clump of wild berry that was within sight of the house and atop a steep banking flowing down from one boundary of her father's little farm to the railway line. And there, in the middle of that blessed thicket of wild berry, we had a merry fuck on an old blanket. My climax, which erupted immediately after her gasping orgasm, was a wonderful thing of laughter and tears.

When Joan regained her breath she said: "Boy Charlie, yuh mustn't bother with girls younger than me. Yuh wood too big! Yuh can get big woman!"

I laughed, wondering how she'd react if she knew that Daddy's woman, dear Monica, was already interested in my remarkable dick. "Girl, yuh pum-pum truly sweet."

She giggled and said: "We can't leave them kids alone long." Shortly after, we returned to the house. I went to their bathroom with a rag Joan gave me to clean my dick — she knew her parents wouldn't be back till after noon. Then we watched television and drank lemonade with the younger kids. Of course, it wasn't long before I got horny for another fuck. But she wasn't game.

The sun was scorching when I left Joan's home just after eleven-thirty. I felt strangely energetic, but didn't relish the thought of walking the mile home in the roasting heat. I took the first bus going towards the town centre, and got off at the clock-tower market square. Feeling hungry, I hurried across the noisy, crowded square, rejoicing that home was just about a hundred metres away. But just as I was moving beyond the square, I was hailed by Lorna, the heavy breasted sixteen year old who shopped at the market for my home on Saturdays — Monica's dress making business was busiest on Fridays and Saturdays. For some reason, when I turned to acknowledge Lorna's louder-than-necessary shout, I was hit by a vivid fleeting picture of last night with Monica, and immediately the hunger for lunch turned into an obsession to fuck Lorna that very midday.

CHAPTER 11

I strode back into the crowded square and Lorna gave me one of the two big shopping bags containing goods for my home. Then we moved off in silence, the brain busily weaving a plot to seduce her within the next hour or two.

She was a plain face girl with lank hair. But her dark-brown complexion had a lovely, silky, even tone glow, and her tall, trim figure was blessed with a magnificent bosom. She would be entering her fifth year of high school after the summer holidays. She lived next door to me, so over the past few years I had done a fair bit of lusting at her; but because she was four years older and tended to be loud and foul-tempered, I had always retreated from making a pass at her.

"Monica, I am back," Lorna hollered out as we entered my home, "an' Charlie is here, too!"

"Thank yuh, my dear," Monica called above the dim of the two sewing machines in her small workroom. "If Charlie hungry let him get something out of the breadbox and fridge."

"Boy, yuh hungry?" Lorna asked as we entered the little kitchen.

Her haughty tone made me both angry and more determined to ride her within the hour. My dickie went iron hard. A glance through the window showed me the fat washer lady in our little backyard hanging wet clothes on the line, her back to the kitchen. Without thought, I stepped back from Loma and in one deft movement I had my stiff dick free and waving at her.

She gasped, and then froze in a wide-eyed, flared-nostril gape. Her dark-brown cheeks flushed purple.

Her reaction was obviously a thing of awe, and this made me bolder. I said: "See how big Mr. Dickie is? Big enough for yuh."

Seconds danced by without any response or movement from her, her protruding eyes riveted on Mr. Dickie. Obviously she was intrigued.

Finally, just as I was beginning to wonder if she had become a lifeless figure, she closed her gaping lips, sucked in a huge breath, moistened her lips and murmured: "An' yuh is jus' twelve." Her eyes were still chained to my oversized pride. "When yuh turn man it goin' be..." She broke off and met my eyes with an embarrassed half-grin.

I immediately knew that she had sampled one or more dicks quite a bit bigger than mine. "Any puddin' over yuh house?" I asked, forcing the iron-hard Mr. Dickie out of sight, then zipping up and belting down. The pudding question, of course, was just a boy-wise manner of moving closer to jockeying her — Lorna and her mother were forever baking a wide variety of puddings; and I knew that no-one would be at her home at that time. "A piece of puddin' would be the best lunch. None here."

"Yes, we hav' puddin'." Her voice was husky, and without looking at me she led the way out of the kitchen. In the living-dining room, she popped her head into Monica's workroom and said: "Charlie say he not in the mood for bread, bun or biscuit. We goin' over my yard fo' puddin'."

Monica's response was lost in the female and sewing machine chatter in her workroom. But Monica had no reason to be suspicious, for all the kids in the area went to Lorna's home regularly for a taste of their scrumptious pudding.

Lorna's crammed home was identical to mine. I began fondling her the moment we were through the front door. She said: "Charlie, behave yuh self. Let's go eat lunch."

I grinned and kept my hands to myself. She avoided my eyes while serving us cassava and sweet-potato pudding, and ginger beer in the kitchen. We sat on stools at the kitchen counter. She ate as fast as I did, all in silence. Being wise enough to know that she wanted my dickie but was still uncomfortable about the age difference, when we finished eating I tactfully said: "Long time ah don't see inside yuh room."

"Nothing new there."

"Let me look at yuh scrap books."

"Alright." She led the way to her room, the smallest of the three bedrooms. And, of course, I was all over her the moment I closed her door behind me. She didn't resist. Quickly, we were both naked.

I was brimming with pride over the fact that she was my truly older conquest, and having had sex just about three hours ago, I now had greater than normal control over the boyhood tendency to climax quickly. After a nice battle, she grunted, groaned and thrashed through an orgasm just before I squirted weak boy-water deep inside her. A minute later, our sweaty, naked bodies lying beside each other, she said: "Charlie, yuh really special. I never dream that a twelve year old could be so big an' strong. But I not goin' give yuh more than one time a week. Yuh hav' other girls, an' too much will mek yuh grow up weak. Listen up. Don't do it more than two times a week, an' better if only once most weeks. Yuh hear me?" I grinned, and she declared: "Yuh better take warning! Now, come let's go bathe quick. I have work ah mus' do before Momma come home."

True to her word, thereafter she was willing to give me sex only once per week, although we could've had sex almost every day during the rest of that summer holiday. I quickly came to realize this limitation on our affair was partly due to her policeman lover who lived half mile away. When school reopened in September, we had only Saturdays for sex and we missed out only when her period was on or if she managed to go off with her cop lover.

Anyway, after that first fuck of ours, Lorna and I had a quick shower, and then I returned home and headed straight to bed. Within seconds the afternoon faded out. The sun was disappearing when Monica shook me awake.

"Wake up, my little man," she cooed. She was in a fresh roomy dress and smelling of her favourite perfume. "Ah finish work earlier than usual for a Saturday. So tonight we're goin' to the movies. The new cowboy show, my boy."

Instantly, I sprang to life — a cowboy movie on the big screen was pure ecstasy.

"Go bathe and dress while I fix a quick dinner. I want us to catch the first show."

There was no need to ask her which theatre and the time of the first show. Our town's only theatre must be the place, and when Saturday night's attraction was one movie, the first of two showings began at seven-fifteen. I raced to the bathroom, took a quick shower, then dressed and went out to the kitchen. Monica was there adding the finishing touches to dinner — leftover rice from the refrigerator and tinned beef. "Sir," she remarked cheerfully, "I'm afraid there's not much of a dinner tonight."

"Madam, even biscuits would do," I responded sincerely, "when we're goin' to a cowboy movie!" She laughed. Before long we were eating the tasty meal of hot rice and tinned beef with tomato and lots of onion. We ate quickly — dusk was thick on the land, seven o'clock was near, and it would be unwise to arrive at the cinema late when the offering was a cowboy movie that had just ruled the island's capital city, Kingston, for weeks. We managed to leave home a few minutes before seven, pointing our toes and noses down toward the brilliant lights of the clock-tower market square.

We hurried behind the teenagers and zipped through the lively square to the nearby theatre on Main Street. At the theatre, there were long lines of movie fans on the sidewalk. But, Monica and I managed to get in quickly, thanks to one of her dressmaking customers allowing us to join a line just in front of the ticket windows; nobody complained because Monica's obliging customer was there with one of the town's most feared and liked rude boys.

The theatre was half full when Monica and I took our seats upstairs, after having bought cokes and popcorn in the lobby. The movie turned out to deserve its great reputation, and this was most likely why sitting beside Monica in the dark did not cause me to wonder what she'd ask of me when we returned home.

After the show we met Elaine, who was one of Monica's few close friends, and Elaine's man in the theatre's lobby. The four of us went across the street to a little restaurant-lounge, and the jukebox was quickly drowned out by the many voices talking about the movie we had just seen.

"Charlie, yuh old enough for half a beer?" Monica asked shortly after the four of us sat down at one of the small round tables.

"Yes," I replied eagerly, while also feeling a bit indignant, despite never having drunk half a beer. Simultaneously, I buried the budding thought of what Monica would require at home that night.

Monica's friend, Elaine, cheerfully said: "My eleven year old son can drink a whole beer without gettin' even tipsy." And her man intoned: "That boy get him grandpa tough head and iron stomach!"

I got the half a beer and took manly sips, running my eyes around the crowded restaurant-lounge, listening to my adult companions without speaking. When my half a beer was finished, Elaine kindly gave me quite a few sips of hers. The alcohol made it an easy task to kill all thoughts of what Monica would ask of me when we arrived home.

After just about twenty minutes, our group left the restaurant-lounge, and strolled up the lively Main Street. I was feeling tipsy and floated through the fairly short walk that saw us arriving at my gate just about ten minutes to ten. Monica and I said good night to our companions, who were going to the reggae dance further up the road. I could hear that the dance was now in full swing and thought it'd be nice to go dancing. But before I could air this dancing interest, Monica yawned and said to Elaine: "If I wasn't so tired I would come look for a while."

I didn't expect Monica to allow me to go to a dance at that hour without her present; plus there had been a note of finality and sincerity to Monica's avowal of being too tired to go up to the dance for even just a short visit, considering that she'd laboured all day and was pregnant.

I kept silent and followed her into our home.

But, despite feeling tipsy, I noted that the moment she locked the front door behind us she lost her air of fatigue. Her brown face brightened in the brilliantly lit living area of the living-dining room, and she gave me a quick look that was lustily appraising.

CHAPTER 12

She literally bounced ahead to the kitchen. I felt compelled to follow. She fixed two cheese sandwiches in record time, humming merrily and flashing me bright smiles. I was resigned to giving her a repeat of last night — the minor sin of caresses, breast kissing and cunt fingering. I was smugly confident that she'd never be able to get my dickie hard. With the sandwiches, she presented red wine, saying airily: "We're goin' to bed so no harm if yuh get a bit tipsy."

I was still tipsy from the beer I had at the restaurant but I nodded. In any case, I was glad for the wine, although aware enough to realize that she was trying to get me half-drunk. I was inclined to believe that her intention was to use alcohol to make me less uptight about petting her to climax. Anyway, it seemed a waste of time to muse deeply on the matter, as the bottom line was that she'd never be able to give me an erection; and would never be able to get me to fuck Daddy's cunt.

We didn't linger over the sandwiches and wine — I drank the nice little glass of wine as if it was fruit juice. Then we retired to her bed, and I did not hesitate about falling in with her desire for caresses and kisses to her breasts. But the wine, on top of the lingering effect of the beer, quickly made me so high I faded out and would have no recollection of what went down after the first few minutes .

The following morning I awoke clasped in Monica's soft arms. She was dead to the world. The sun was already up but hadn't been on our town for long. The morning felt cool. Within a few seconds, my nose began sensing an odour of sex. My groin felt sticky but I feared putting a hand down there. And, although I also felt weak, my brain began churning up alarming thoughts.

Could it be that Monica was evil enough to have given me some kind of drug that had made it possible for her to get my dickie erect after I had faded out? Was it the effect of a drug why I had no memory of what happened after the first five or so minutes in bed? Dread permeated me. The room spun and tilted.

For some unclear reason, I simply could not put even one finger to my sticky-feeling front. Instead, I began trembling and twisting out of Monica's arms. I was convinced that if she had used a drug to get sex from me, God would still charge us both because I was a man — Daddy had taught me that because man was stronger and ruler of the earth, man's sin was always greater.

Monica awoke, automatically trying to hold me in her embrace. I resisted her. "Charlie, what's wrong? What's wrong, honey?"

Our eyes locked. She didn't look evil in the soft morning light. She looked what her tone suggested — concerned. After a few hushed seconds, I gushed: "Last night, did we...?" I was beginning to wonder if I had imagined smelling sex. But what of the sticky feel to my front? "Did yuh give me...something that cause us to...to sex?"

"Charlie, I would never do such a thing." Her voice was as calming as the hand caressing my neck. "We didn't have sex. It was just like the night before, but yuh were a bit drunk, so yuh forget."

Still afraid to touch my private, I asked: "How come my...my front...sticky?"

After a fleeting stillness, she chuckled and declared: "Mus' be a wet dream. First yuh havin' one?" She ruffled my head.

Now embarrassed and certain she was speaking the truth, I broke our eye contact and responded sincerely: "Yes. But I know what it is." I was no longer trembling or trying to escape her embrace.

"All boys hav' it till they begin havin' sex regularly. But yuh mustn't let wet dreams cause yuh to begin tryin' to get sex from any an' every girl. An' I won't pester yuh about sex if yuh wet dream don't change yuh mind about us."

Still avoiding her eyes, I mumbled: "We mustn't." I was telling myself that sex once a week with Lorna should keep away wet dreams.

"Anything yuh say." She rose up on an elbow, beaming at me and added. "Remember, by sleepin' with me an' caressin' me yuh doin' me an' yuh father a great service, though we can't tell him. The thing is that I love yuh daddy so much I can't bring mi-self to have sex with another man; but at the same time the young belly ah hav' cause mi nature to raise up so high I need somebody to give me relief till yuh daddy return. Honestly, if I wasn't pregnant I wouldn't ask yuh to touch me. An', in any case, if our pettin' is a sin the fault is all mine. Understand?"

I nodded, having quickly convinced myself — as only a young boy could have — that she was speaking the honest truth.

She kissed my brow and got out of bed, saying: "I'm goin' to fix us a real grand breakfast." She left the room humming. She was not a sleep about, I mused, but I must watch her closely to be certain she didn't have sex with another man before Daddy returned from America.

But although totally resigned to sleeping with her every night I hoped she would never ask for this little sin every night. I began watching her movements and body language for any hint that she was giving Daddy "bun" with another man — I never saw any hint of this.

It was a smooth August week that followed that first Saturday night of me going to bed half-drunk. The following Saturday night, I again allowed her to get me half-drunk before we retired to bed, and I awoke next morning with vague images of us embracing — nothing alarming about this. But when I left the bed and was changing my clothes I had a moment's unease that my dickie and groin appeared strangely clean. I instantly dismissed the thought without wondering what it implied. This troubled reality was to be the case many Sunday mornings till Daddy returned from the USA.

CHAPTER 13

The start of the new school year that September meant extra lessons in preparation for the Common Entrance High School Examinations in January. I was one of the brighter students in my primary school class, and was determined to conquer this dreaded exam and move on to high school. This would be my second and final go at the exam, having failed it in the previous school year; a failure that had caused my teachers and myself to say it was just another case of inadequate spaces at high schools. So the places went to those with the highest marks and older students with average pass marks. Extra lessons for the exams didn't dampen my manly sexual quests; neither did the fairly busy sex life affect my schoolwork.

The most interesting development of the first term of that fresh school year was the relationship that developed between a new, petite, brown-complexioned teacher, twenty-two year old Miss June Simpson, and me. Back then, I didn't have the slightest idea why by the end of the first week of that school year, I was obsessed with the idea of bedding this new teacher from Kingston. In later years, I would come to realize that this seemingly uncanny obsession was a subconscious reaction to my confusing, unholy relationship with Daddy's woman.

Miss Simpson's spectacled face was not pretty — at best it was plain. Her only attractive curves were those of her hips and rear, but even these marginally appealing curves and her passable legs appeared too generous for her sadly flat chested top half. Her mouth was too wide but a lovely set of teeth added a quaint charm to her smile. Perhaps her best physical attributes were her delicate little hands and feet. No more than five feet three inches tall, she appeared weaker than many of the sixteen year old girls in our little town — certainly weaker than my next-door lover Lorna.

Miss Simpson was one of two teachers for Grade One, the youngest class at primary school level — the other Grade One teacher was a fat, middle-aged married lady. It took two weeks to come up with a workable plan to become Miss Simpson's lover.

Although she wasn't one of my teachers, there was no reason for her to have doubted the sham distress with which I approached her on the unforgettable afternoon that I launched the bold plot of seduction. Guided by some inbred male power, this approach was crafted to ensure that there would be no reason for her to think it odd that I should approach her with a problem instead of one of my teachers.

My class had extra lessons after regular school hours Mondays to Thursdays, none on Fridays. After school, on the third Friday of that new school year, I approached Miss Simpson just outside one of the two wide doors of the teachers' staff-room. My shoulders were slumped, and with downcast eyes, I said in subdued tones: "Good afternoon, Miss Simpson." She responded with a bright good afternoon. I forged ahead in my most polished English, eyes still downcast, timid voice low against possible eavesdropping: "Miss, I have a problem I need to talk to somebody about." I paused and guided her aside from the few teachers standing nearby, then resumed in the timid half-whisper: "If my father wasn't away on farm-work in America I'd ask him. I think that yu...you're the best person to talk to now — because you're new and from Kingston, and the youngest teacher here at school." Movements of other teachers and students caused us to move further away from the staff room door but we remained on the covered corridor, which adjoined an asphalted parking area in the school yard. I continued in timid half-whisper, "It's not about school work, and I live further up Main Street from you, so it'd be nice if I could walk home with yu...you and tell you there."

Her immediate response was in cheerful tones: "I'll be glad to help if I can. What's your name?"

"Charlie, Miss." I was fighting to keep triumphant excitement from my voice and face. "I'm in Grade Six."

"Okay, Charlie. I'm about to go home. Carry some of my books. Your bag looks light!"

I took some of her books, and off we went.

During our short, brisk walk to her home, I was barely able to keep my excitement under wraps. In a fairly good projection of a nervous boy, I told her about Daddy, Momma's death, and Monica's skill as a dressmaker.

Phase one of the bold plan had gone off without a hitch, and I was confident that phase two would be equally successful if I said "the lines" convincingly. The dangers of failure didn't enter my thoughts. I am amazed that at that age I could've been so cunning and bold. What devil guided me?

Miss Simpson lived in a rented room at the back of a house that was near the bottom of Main Street. She had her own bathroom (a tiny thing) but had to share a small kitchen with the two ladies who occupied the rest of the three-bedroom house. These two young working women didn't arrive home until after six o' clock in the evening Monday to Friday, which meant that Miss Simpson was relatively free from disturbance and prying eyes and ears until then.

The room Miss Simpson rented was of medium size but appeared small because her big bed, a modest dresser, small buffet, an armchair and a little round table with two chairs crowded the room. "Charlie, welcome to my crowded home," she said when she let us into the room. "I'm so glad it has a wall closet, as I don't see how I would've fitted in a wardrobe."

"It's nice, Miss." I was now a bit nervous.

"Thank you. Sit." She was all good-natured big-sister charm. I sat down at the table. She asked, "How about a drink before telling me your trouble?"

I nodded and croaked: "Thanks." I was getting more nervous each minute but was determined to go ahead with the plan.

"Can't afford a refrigerator as yet." She took two small cokes from her icebox and offered me one. I thanked her. She sat down in the other chair at the table, putting us in a face-to-face position, and began leafing through a magazine on the table. While I gulped down my coke, prangs of doubt floated through my mind. What if she laughed at my next act? Suppose she reported me to the headmaster? Was she a true Christian? What if...

But the plan had already become part of reality. There was no turning back now. I gulped down the last of my coke, took a deep breath and with downcast eyes said: "Miss, the problem is that the boys...and some men say...I...my...private is...so big doctor will" — I glanced up and saw that her face held no hint of dismay or righteous horror, and this killed most of my nervousness, — "they say doctor will...hav' to operate...on it."

Her brown face was flushed, eyes popped behind her glasses, her generous mouth frozen in a large 0, all of which suggested fascinated surprise. While I, no longer nervous, was holding her incredible gaze, aware that I was putting on a marvellous act, and was now certain the bait had hooked the fish.

After several hanging seconds, it appeared best to break the eye contact. I looked aside. Silence ruled a few more expanded seconds, and I sensed her eyes boring into me.

Finally she spoke: "Pull...pull your...pants...let me see...it." Her voice trembled. "Wait, let me draw the curtains." She sprang up, closed the curtains and bolted the door. "Okay...now."

I was mostly excited. There was almost no fear or doubt that victory would be mine within ten-fifteen minutes. I stood, half-turned away from her, pulled my belt, drew down pants and briefs, and then turned to face her with my eyes on her face.

She gaped at my half-erect dick, her popping eyes glued to it. She gulped a bucket of air. "It is...big for your age," she said huskily, without moving her eyes from Mr. Dickie. Her tongue wetted her lips. "As a man...you'll be...bigger than most."

It was now certain that I had her. "Miss, see if yuh feel anything wrong wid it." The standard of my English was weakened by smouldering passion.

She glanced up into my face, which was supposed to be projecting boyish anxiety without any hint of the passion bubbling inside me. Instantly, her eyes returned to my growing manhood and she came at me like a sleepwalker — this was one of my first lessons that the average sexually active girl or woman cannot resist a big one. It appeared fairly certain that she was dreaming of how big I would be six to eight years time. She reached out one of those delicate hands and gently caressed Mr. Dickie. Ecstasy made him jerk to iron-hardness in her lovely hand.

"Yes, it is big," she whispered throatily, and her other hand instinctively went to my balls. Her eyes were glued down there. "And so beaut...But I'm sure you don't need to see a doctor. Some men"— her hands were still caressing Mr. Dickie and his balls, her eyes glued on her delicate task, while I was having a hard time standing fairly steady and suppressing groans of ecstasy and keeping my hands off her — "I've heard and read that some men have real big ones." Here there was a pause in her throaty whisper and she looked up into my face, her hands still caressing below. She added: "You're special...so we're going to do something and you mustn't tell anybody."

"Uhhh, I won't." I was trembling with pleasure. She moved back, briskly undressed me, and then led me to her bed. Then she turned on her radio, took off her glasses and tore off her clothes. Her breasts were very small and her figure certainly wasn't a thing of wet dreams; but the hair on her front was a thick glossy black and horny sexually active boys do not refuse pussy because the lady lacks the sexy figure and/or pretty face that they worship.

The moment she joined me on the bed, my actions told her that, although my presence in her bed was by her invitation, I was not an inexperienced lad. I moved to fondling and kissing her tiny breasts and fingering her moist cunt. Before long, she was muttering little gasps of ecstasy, her eyes closed, her hands caressing my neck and shoulders and back — before long, I shafted her with one aggressive bull-like thrust. She vented a startled cry, and then crushed me to her bony chest.

Strengthened by mental triumph over my first adult conquest I was able to subdue boyhood excitement and ride her at a slow steady pace for many minutes till her eyes widened in a crazed look and her legs circled my waist and she began a series of ecstatic huffing, puffing and groaning. I felt my juices rising, and rode her faster. She vented a long gasping cry as the vast thrill of an orgasm seized her petite body. Then, before her gasping cry and shuddering ended, ecstasy overwhelmed me and I burrowed deeper when boy-water rushed forth— it was my sweetest climax to date.

For quite a few contented seconds I lay there atop her, avoiding her eyes, enjoying the soothing caresses of her delicate hands and the self-esteem building sounds of her contented sighs. Then, sensing that my big twelve year old frame was getting too heavy for her petite body, I rolled off her. She turned towards me, propped herself on an elbow and said: "Charlie, you're a special boy." Her tone was solemn, her heavy lidded eyes screwed-up thoughtfully. "How old are you? Twelve?"

"Yes, Miss." Some instinct made me realize that the best way to ensure a regular long-term place between her thighs was to continue addressing her at all times with the respectful student-to-teacher "Miss".

"You're a twelve year-old man, and not just in size, strength and sexual skill." Her face was a great admiring grin. "That's why just now you said the usual Miss. And although I want us to continue being lovers, you must always address me with the normal Miss, so that nobody will ever guess we are lovers. I would lose my job and reputation if we don't keep our love secret." She paused, one of her lovely hands began caressing my chest, and then she declared: "So it's best that even when we're alone like this you must always say Miss."

Lying there on my back, I took hold of the hand caressing my chest. "I understand Miss. Honestly." I was back to trying to speak Standard English like her.

"And you must not tell even your best friend about us."

"Miss, I would never tell anybody about us." This was a sincere avowal. "I know even the very best friend would soon tell another friend."

Smiling her trust, she remarked, "You're truly special," and then asked: "How long since you've been having sex?"

It appeared best to sweeten the fact a bit. "Not so long, Miss. Use to do it with a bigger girl. But she gone away since last month."

She kissed my cheek and cooed: "Come let's go get a shower."

It appeared that women and girls loved to have me in the bathroom, one way or another. This shower turned out to be a mighty exceptional pleasure. In the midst of it, Miss Simpson introduced me to the joy of getting a blowjob but she didn't show the least interest in getting me to give her head — of course, back then in the 1970s, Jamaica, it was rare for males to give head and even most women viewed it as a revolting act.

Next day, a Saturday loaded with wind and sun, Miss Simpson came to see Monica about getting a new dress made and they became instant friends — of course, according to plan, Miss Simpson and I pretended that we didn't know each other well.

Two weeks later, Monica — whose pregnant belly had suddenly leapt to a great size — told me I was to go home with Miss Simpson on Fridays after school for additional extra lessons. I had enough cunning to mask delight behind a frown and grumble that more extra lessons was not necessary, while allowing Monica to coax me into verbal agreement. So I began spending Friday evenings with little Miss Simpson and we did do school work, but half our time together was spent in bed; I continued addressing her as "Miss" even in her bed. At school and at my home I was just another polite student to her. I never thought of telling anyone about our affair.

CHAPTER 14

Alongside the merry affair with Miss Simpson, the energetic Saturday romping with my sixteen year old neighbour Lorna continued to help balance the stress of the unholy relationship with Daddy's woman. I also saw these two welcomed sexual diets as the best medicine to keep me from having another wet dream in Monica's bed. By the end of that September, Lorna became very attached and dear to me — lover, good friend — and I learned to live with her moments of loud quick-tempered behaviour. She fed me foods that were said to be good for the male libido (Monica and Miss Simpson were doing this, too). She took a keen interest in my schoolwork and dreams for the future. She told me about her plans for the future with her policeman lover, who she met illicitly most Saturday and Sunday evenings and occasionally after school hours, I, of course, didn't even think of telling her about the wonderful affair with Miss Simpson or the sinful relationship with Monica. Lorna was also good for helping to install certain wisdom a boy needed, like her thirst for success in a chosen career. On one occasion when speaking of a future with her cop lover, Lorna said:

"Despite the dream of marrying him, I'm not so dumb I don't realize he an' I might drift apart. The one thing I really certain of is that I shall become a nurse an' be good at it."(She did enter nursing school the following year and she and her cop lover would split up while she was in nursing school, largely because she'd embrace lesbianism there.)

Of course, Lorna's parents and brothers, and my guardian Monica, noticed how close we had become by the end of that September of 1975. They believed her when she said: "I always wished one of my brothers was younger than me. An' Charlie is the type I'd want."

Needless to say, the conviction that I was superior to my age group had ballooned after I became Miss Simpson's lover. No doubt this feeling of superiority was the major reason why I never had a best friend in the first four to five years after I started having sex.

Back then in my thirteenth year, I even lost friends because most Fridays I'd avow that I didn't want any visitor the next day that wasn't wearing a skirt — most Saturdays were for Lorna.

The fellows mostly stayed away on those Saturdays that I warned them not to visit; but most Saturday mornings and evenings, we met down by the town's clock-tower square, at the bakery or one of our homes. I was certainly the unofficial leader, and felt like a great president — after all, I was certain none of them had a dutiful sixteen year-old lover. I was also convinced that I was the only boy under fifteen in Jamaica to have such a dick and a teacher lover.

Although I didn't have many chores at home and was obviously blessed with superior stamina, my hectic sex-life and determination to pass the high school entrance exams in January meant that I had no time for sports at school, although I liked cricket and football. Instead of sports, I tended to sleep a lot, and I ate like a weightlifter. I was a famous drinker of milk by the quart and fabled eater of thick oats and cornmeal porridge.

On a windy Sunday afternoon in November, Daddy returned from his first farm-work trip to the USA. We'd been expecting him at any moment during the past week — in those days, the going and coming of farm workers was erratic and often sudden. When the taxi that he and two fellow farm- workers from our town had hired at the airport in Kingston halted at our gate, Monica and I were sitting on the veranda. At the sight of Daddy in the taxi, Monica leapt up like a lithe ten year old, her face radiant like a hundred watt bulb, and with her huge six-and-a-half months pregnant belly leading the way, she dashed down the walkway to throw herself into his powerful arms. Her intense joy had me choked up; and Daddy's great delight in her welcome was a knife in my balls. I couldn't do more than walk slowly towards them with a face made heavy by a plastic smile. Their love was tangibly brighter than the sunny afternoon, and I began feeling a gut wrenching guilt about the nights in their bed. Immediately, this guilt was so powerful that it took reserve willpower to force a few welcoming words for Daddy. I was thinking that I must shoulder most of the blame for having allowed Monica to coax me into touching her. That first night when she took me to her bed I should've overruled her and returned to my bed after forcefully advising her to get a girlfriend or teddy bear to keep her warm at nights, and thereafter warn her that I would be watching her movements with all males.

Aching with this vast guilt, I was barely able to force laughter at the three or four brisk stories Daddy told us after we had carried in his luggage. During the telling of these brief tales of his farm work experience, he and Monica were in embrace on the sofa, she devouring his every word, their faces clouded with desire for each other. I was in an armchair pretending interest.

"So how yuh two get on?" Daddy asked after we'd stopped laughing at the last of his jokes.

"Ohh... like house on fire!" Monica exclaimed, actually grinning at me.

Guilt killed the desire to utter a nice little lie like Monica's. But I managed to give Daddy a passable grin and nod of agreement.

"Good." His tone and face were pure pleasure. "Well, Charlie, brother or sister yuh want from Monica?"

"Any one welcome," I replied sincerely, "but a brother would be a little nicer."

"Yuh might get both," she giggled.

Daddy exclaimed: "That would be something!" His eyes flicked down to her face glowing up from his shoulder, one of his hands caressed her big pregnant belly.

At that point I simply had to get away. I jumped to my feet and lied: "I did promise to check two friends about some homework this evenin'." Monica said: "Don't let night catch yuh out because I not alone this evenin." Her tone was even, her face beaming at me as if all was perfect between us.

"Yuh hav' money can buy ice-cream or such?" Daddy asked.

"Yes, I okay. Monica give me pocket money Saturdays." I had no intention of downplaying her good points, just as I certainly wouldn't give even a hint of her lust crazy side, and didn't want Daddy to get the slightest feeling that something was wrong. Anyway, I was truly cashy, as Miss Simpson was handing over pocket money every Friday evening as well.

"Alright," he said. I hurried away under the burden of guilt. The line of thinking was this: Now that I was witnessing the power of his love for her, my time with Monica no longer appeared as a minor and necessary sin. And I had failed Monica, although she wasn't blameless in the matter. I should have killed her sinful advances. I had failed her, just as I had recently heard one old Rasta man explain that when Adam ate of the forbidden fruit offered by Eve he had failed Eve and caused man to become a slave to woman's beauty.

CHAPTER 15

Laboured steps tugged me down towards the town square. The windy afternoon was flowing into a cool evening. There were roughly eight adults and a few small groups of girls and boys of all ages enjoying pastries, ice cream, packaged snacks, oranges, cold drinks and peanuts. More boys and girls and adults were arriving to add mass, lust and fun to the square — it will be lively Jamaican gaiety until after nightfall if there was no rain. I was Mr. Gloom and felt fifty instead of just twelve years old.

"Charlie, wha' happen?" asked Anne, a thin, flat-chested eleven year old classmate who lived near me; she and three of her friends were standing at the gate of the empty market, eating ice-cream cones and looking happy. Twice in the last two months, Anne had given me hasty sex under the cellar of her board house, but she had lost her virginity before me and I knew she was involved with at least one adult man. Anne now added, "Charlie, how yuh lookin' so sad, an' yuh father jus' come from US?"

"Ee-eh," intoned one of her friends, a fat moon-faced twelve year old.

I forced a smiled, patted Anne's sparse plaits and said: "I not sad. Yuh girls seein' doubles."

"Anyway, buy me some peanuts," Anne said, a promising smile on her pretty black face, batting her lashes and sticking out her thin bosom.

"Yeah," I said, digging into the money pocket. I gave her some coins. "Buy peanuts fi yuh an' yuh friends. I goin' check a pal down bottom a Main."

They beamed at me. I walked away down Main Street, pretending not to see two friends and a few girls of our primary school class inside the ice cream and pastry shop on the other side of the square. I was glad they didn't see me. I wanted to be alone for a while, or be able to go by Miss Simpson. This Sunday evening had nothing of the grand light heartedness common to Sunday evenings.

Trudging down our mildly twisted Main Street, hands buried in pants pockets, not seeing the locked stores, barely aware of the other scattered pedestrians and the few vehicles on the road; I began nurturing a great dislike for Monica.

I sighed regret and self-disgust, then altered my thoughts a bit. Monica was kind, wasn't coarse, she'd soon give me my first brother or sister, and Daddy loved her. Also, perhaps she will be faithful to him. So I couldn't hate her. But I no longer liked her one bit; didn't hate, didn't despise her, but disliked her and wished I could stop living with her and Daddy.

I must find a way to leave before next summer, so that if Daddy went on US farm-work next year I wouldn't be alone with her. The basic depraved streak in her character might cause her to try getting me into her bed if Daddy went away on farm-work next year, even if she wasn't pregnant and half-mad. Although nothing could cause me to ever touch her again, if she should ever again try to seduce me, I might become enraged and attack her. I must immediately begin seeking a way to move away from her.

This thought echoed.

I was now near the bottom of Main Street, where there were more homes than shops. I lifted my eyes from the sidewalk and beheld Miss Simpson a chain ahead, standing alone at her gate. My spirits soared. My steps quickened towards my blessed adult lover, who was in a modest red dress and looked more like a coquettish fifteen year old instead of the petite twenty-two that she was. The slight touch of make-up and a new curly Afro hairdo added a nice aspect to her plain brown face.

"Hello, Charlie," she said, her smile engulfing me and sweeping aside all gloomy thoughts. I quickly learned that she was at her gate hoping to see me, as the two ladies who occupied most of the three bedroom house were away visiting relatives and weren't due back before nightfall. We strolled to her rented room at the back of the house and immediately had a nice romp in her bed. Next we showered. Then she served up ice cream, jelly and cake. While we ate, sitting across from each other at her little round table, a question flooded me, and I asked it timidly: "Miss, will yu...are you...will you stop giving me sex...love...if you find a man." Though feeling a bit timid, I was gazing into her heavy lidded bespectacled eyes.

She reached across the table, squeezed my hand and cooed: "I'm not in any hurry about finding a man."

Her answer was good enough for me. Pride and joy swelled in my heart. I said: "I love you, Miss, an...and want to marry you when I grow up." At that moment the words were sincere — it didn't matter that she didn't have the pretty face or curvy figure of a dream bride, I was in love.

"That would be grand!" A far away look graced her face. "There's really nothing wrong if a woman is ten years older than her husband." She returned to the present, grinned and said: "But, dear Charlie, you must first do well in school and enter college."

"Yes, Miss, I think a...like to be an engineer or writer — perhaps both, like the star in a library book I read last month." This was my earliest interest in writing.

The idea of being her husband and a writer-engineer felt perfect. Tranquil seconds drifted by before she lost her dreamy look and her spoon dipped to her nearly empty ice cream dish. Then she smiled across her little table at me, her brown face flushed. She said: "The first step is to pass your Common Entrance exams."

"Miss, I shall pass it; can't wait for January to come to tackle it!" Confidence bubbled through me. Then, smiling across what little was left of our ice cream and cake; I began thinking how wonderful it'd be if within the next five to seven months Miss Simpson rented a two room place and I got Daddy to allow her to become my guardian. That'd free me from Monica, and allow Miss Simpson and I freedom to truly be lovers.

But I sensed that the time wasn't yet right to share this wonderful dream with her. Just as I knew I mustn't tell her of the sinful acts with Monica.

The sun was near setting when I reluctantly left Miss Simpson's room and headed home. I skipped and hummed up Main Street, thrilled by intermittent thoughts of finding a way to become Miss Simpson's ward within the next seven months.

In the clock-tower market-entrance square, I spent a few minutes chatting with friends before moving on towards my home. The cool November sunset glowed and glittered magnificently, as if rejoicing in my hope to become the ward of my blessed adult lover.

But in bed that night — after a quick supper, some talk and TV watching with Daddy and Monica, both of whom were caught up in starry eyed romantic lust — I realized that nothing could get Daddy to allow Miss Simpson to become my guardian there in our town. I saw that the only way to escape Monica's depraved presence would be to convince Daddy that it'd be better for my future if I could attend one of the old prestigious boys' high school in Kingston and reside in the city; no sense thinking of the two first-rate boarding schools further away at the other end of the island, as I hated the idea of boarding school.

If I could get Daddy's agreement towards trying to get accepted at a top boys' high school in Kingston, I mused excitedly, perhaps Miss Simpson would be able to get a job in Kingston and become my guardian. But it appeared best that I should not suggest this great idea to her until a week or so after the Common Entrance exams, by which time I'd be able to convince her that I would get high marks in the exams. It was now November and the exams would be in January. I must pass my exams.

With or without Miss Simpson, I now intended to enter a top boys' high school in Kingston next September, preferably Calabar High School or Kingston College. But how wonderful it would be if Miss Simpson and I could live together in Kingston while I attended C-bar or K.C.?

I fell asleep in this fantastic thought.

Unfortunately, less than two weeks later, cracks began appearing in the dreams about living with Miss Simpson in Kingston while attending high school. I became aware that an ugly young dentist who worked and lived in our parish capital, Port Maria, was wooing her. Still, our after-school Friday evening extra lessons and sexual romps at her home continued, and she smothered my mumbled jealousy by repeatedly swearing that the dentist was just a very good friend, and that dating him would keep her neighbours from suspecting that I was her lover. I lacked the guts to ask if she and the damn bug-eyed, buff-teeth dentist were lovers. In any case, just after the Common Entrance exams in January, she would stride out of town and my life, and I'd develop a deep-rooted mistrust of dentists.

CHAPTER 16

Meantime, I claimed my first virginity three days after Daddy returned from the United States. Her name was Carol. She was an eleven year old classmate. I got her virginity thanks largely to help from Anne. The three of us stopped by Anne's house after extra lesson class that Wednesday evening. Anne's housewife mother was away visiting a sick relative and wouldn't return until later that night and her father never arrived home from work before nightfall.

Carol was reluctant to give me her virginity. Good-natured Anne helped me clinch the deal but it turned out to be more trouble than fun. Carol bled badly, then fought and wept, and had difficulty taking my man-size dick — perhaps at that time I lacked the finesse to take such a young virginity. Carol's weeping and struggling was such that after just about two minutes inside her, I gladly withdrew from her tight, bloody cunt without discharging. Instantly, I grabbed welcoming Anne and rode her to a pleasurable climax, with Carol looking on in silent awe. Thereafter, Carol avoided me like a plague, and I developed a jaundiced view of the excited to-do about "picking a cherry."

In the two weeks following Daddy's return from the USA in November, I managed to keep Monica ignorant of my new intense dislike for her. Of course, I had no intention of allowing Daddy or anybody else to see this dislike, and there were occasional moments when I wasn't completely certain that I disliked her to any great degree. It was a delicate two weeks for me.

On the Sunday at the end of this touchy two week period, after dinner I went to sit with Monica on the veranda. The early December evening was cool, and the sun was about to disappear.

"Monica," I said calmly enough, "I know I goin' pass the Common Entrance exams, an' I already tell the Education Ministry I want to enter either Calabar or Kingston College." She turned in surprise. Our chairs, both facing the fairly quiet street, were about five feet apart on the tiny veranda. I continued: "Yuh an' Daddy can afford it, an' I'll repay yuh someday. It's jus' for yuh to get him to agree, or ah goin'... (here my courage fell down a bit), or I'll blow up everything by tellin' him an' my aunts what yuh forced me to do while he was in the US."

Her brown face paled. "Charlie, I..." These two words were loaded with anguish and dread. Her lips quivered. In her lap the hands trembled and wrung each other. Her eyes fell from mine. I regained lost courage. In a less choked voice she said: "But why yuh want to go away to a Kingston school when we hav' a good one right here in our peaceful little town? Gun violence gettin' worse an' worse in Kingston. Plus to travel from here to school in Kingston would tired yuh bad, so yuh would have to live in Kingston, an' boardin' homes usually unpleasant."

"You're from Kingston, (I felt forced to move into the Standard English I talked with Miss Simpson), so you know that schools like Calabar and Kingston College have better equipment and staff. Plus, I don't want to be alone with you again when Daddy goes away."

She looked at me with such anguish that I couldn't help feeling a jab of compassion, began wondering if I was coming down too hard on her. This modest feeling was kept alive when she said: "Charlie, I'm sorry I talked yuh into doin' something yuh didn't want to do." Her voice trembled a bit. "But please believe me, I truly love your Daddy. An' the sin is mine if what we did was a great sin."

Growing compassion forced me to say: "Ah know yuh love Daddy. Let's jus' forget 'bout the past. But ah still want to go to C-Bar or K.C. I willin' to board with a family that would charge less in exchange for mi doin' yard work an' such." I forced aside the compassion and made her see my determination in the matter and the great dislike I had developed for her.

She sighed defeat, her pregnancy heavy bosom and belly heaving. "Alright. I will talk to yuh Daddy."

My triumph was slightly tinged by a tiny feeling of having been too hard on her. I got to my feet and said soothingly: "If Daddy go on farm work next year, when I go to Kingston yuh will hav' the baby, plus Lorna or Delrose to stay with yuh at nights."

She forced a smile and nodded. I hurried inside to my room, convinced that attending a high school far away from her would be best for everybody. I was pleased that I'd accomplished the first step by getting her agreement to talk to Daddy on my behalf. But I sort of wished I hadn't won her agreement partly by threatening to expose her depraved behaviour towards me while Daddy was away. I sat on my bed and vowed to thereafter act in a nice forgiving and gentle manner towards Monica, despite the strong dislike for her lustful side.

Two days later, Daddy and I were in our little backyard admiring a young orange tree when he said: "Monica think we should send yuh to one a them top boys' high school in Kingston. I know yuh hav' better brains than mi, an' people who go those schools get good jobs easier. So send up yuh name for the two yuh like best."

"Calabar an' Kingston College!" I gushed, and resisted the urge to confess that I'd already requested a place in C-Bar or K.C. "Gee! Thanks, daddy. An' I willin' to help by boardin' with a family that will charge less in exchange for me doin' yard work an' such."

He ruffled my low Afro and said: "Jus' pass the exam. I can swing the boardin' fee, an' in an area away from the crazy political violence."

After this conclusive declaration by Daddy, it became easier for me and Monica to be amiable towards each other like true friends, whether we were alone or not. Before long, I was able to truly forgive her. Then, again and again I asked God to forgive us as I forgave her, beseeched The Almighty to overlook the fact of her having said that we hadn't committed a great sin. The intense dislike for her quickly shrank to a reasonable wariness and mistrust of her lusty side. I did my best to let her realize that I wasn't nursing any great dislike towards her, that I cared for her quite a bit and wanted her and Daddy to be happy, and that I appreciated her kindness and gentle ways. I now saw her as a person with one manageable depraved stripe, not really an immoral person.

In that same December, she and Daddy made our home happier by announcing their intention to marry the following April. I was pleased.

There was a powerful gut-feeling that she wouldn't sleep about when Daddy was away.

By this time — middle of December — I had become aware that the toothy bug-eyed young dentist from Port Maria was visiting Miss Simpson more regularly at school and at her home late evenings and Sundays. She continued telling me he wasn't the type of man she wanted. But, although I didn't see any change in our after school sex on Fridays, I knew that perhaps she was lying about him. I strongly suspected they were lovers and that because he had a respectable middle-income career, there was a chance he'd take her away out of my life and dreams. I kept these fears unspoken, was wise enough to realize that my age was a great threat to her position in life.

To keep boyhood jealousy in check, I repeatedly told myself that I had other lovers, wasn't living with her and was many years away from being able to support or help support a woman, and that she wasn't a great beauty. Realizing there was a chance of the dentist or some other man destroying the dream of becoming Miss Simpson's ward in Kingston; I began preparing for boarding with a family of strangers. And, hoping to be able to get a place with a nice middle class family by way of doing yard work on top of what boarding fee Daddy could afford to pay, I began making a greater effort to speak standard English most of the time. I also started paying more attention to table manners and taking more interest in becoming good at lawn cutting, fence pruning and garden weeding.

The Christmas-New Year season of 1975 found me preoccupied with sex and studying. There wasn't enough time to focus on the feasting and partying. January came and the Common Entrance high school entry exams rolled in. I found the exams much easier than on my first unsuccessful attempt the previous January. I was certain of getting marks good enough for the Education Ministry to give me a place at the prestigious Calabar or Kingston College boys' high schools in the capital city. I didn't get a chance to tell Miss Simpson about the dream of us together in Kingston.

Two days after the Common Entrance exams, she announced her engagement.

CHAPTER 17

"Charlie, I'm delighted you feel certain you passed the exams," Miss Simpson declared on the late afternoon of that second day after the exams. Her voice was tense. It was a Thursday, we were in her room and fully clothed. Before noon, during the lunch period at school, she had summoned me to the staff room and told me she wanted to see me when classes ended that afternoon — after school extra lessons had ended with the exams. At the end of the school day, we had left the schoolyard together and things had been a bit strained on the short walk to her home. Now we were sitting on her bed, and she continued: "I'm confident you'll pass. Anyway, ah...well, I have news you must accept in manly fashion and wish me all the best." She paused and then hugged me, but her eyes didn't meet mine.

My back stiffened, getting ready for the disagreeable jolt of unwelcomed news.

She said hurriedly: "Calvin asked me to marry him. I said yes. It's not a great love, but it might be the best offer I'll ever get." She still wasn't meeting my wounded eyes; I felt crushed, despite the fact that her declaration was not a complete surprise. Her hurried avowal continued: "You're young. I'll be old and unattractive when you reach your prime at thirty." Here she met my eyes. Her eyes pleaded for understanding and blessing. She embraced me closer. There was a feeling of betrayal but part of me recognized the truth of her words, especially seeing that I already had a powerful desire for great beauty. "I'll be moving to his home Saturday and I'll stop teaching at the end of next month."

I hung my head to hide disappointed gloom. "I'm going to miss you," she cooed, half-lover half-mother. Then she became all lover. She pushed me to lie back on her bed, drew down my pants and briefs, and gave me a wonderful blowjob.

By the time I fell asleep in my bed that night, I was inclined to think the dentist had saved her and I from a great blunder. So I wished them well, despite a gloomy ache in the heart and lingering resentment against the dentist.

Thereafter I've always remembered Miss Simpson in a tender manner, have been happy to see her marriage surviving quite happily and productively, but never could get rid of the strong dislike for her husband.

The morning after Miss Simpson announced her engagement Monica went to the hospital and quickly gave birth to a healthy baby girl, who came into this wonderful depressing world of joys and horrors with an amazing resemblance to Daddy's departed mother. This problem-free birth immediately relieved most of my heartache over Miss Simpson.

For many days after Monica and the baby came home, Daddy and I were like two clowns. Monica and my next-door lover, Lorna, made Daddy and I realize that we had taken to constantly grinning, jigging and nudging each other like a pair of merry madmen, marvelling at every move and sound baby Natasha made. Daddy and I ignored this enlightenment about our crazy male bonding. It took quite a few more days before we were able to begin restraining ourselves. I couldn't help feeling a vast love for my half-sister, and Daddy's delight in his second offspring was spiritually uplifting.

Baby Natasha, Daddy's joy, Saturday sex with Lorna and occasional fucks with a few girls nearer my age of twelve, all helped to make Miss Simpson's move from our town, and then from our school, a change of little pain.

Monica and Daddy got married on a bright Saturday afternoon in April. It was your typical sizeable, festive, lower-middle income small town wedding — folks in Sunday best or newly made attire, the usual multi-tiered wedding cake, along with an assortment of other delectable, mouth-watering items. After the official toasting, feasting, chatter and brief dancing and the departure of the newlyweds, there was a sound system dance for all and sundry, free entry, but refreshments were on sale. I was pleased with this wedding. I felt confident Monica would be a good faithful wife for Daddy but the great joy was that the newly-weds went to the north coast on a three-day-two-night honeymoon, leaving the baby with an aunt, while Lorna was to be my guardian for the two nights.

Two nights with my main lover!

I thought — still do think — that Monica had arranged this juicy interlude for me as a gesture of goodwill, having either come to suspect Lorna and I were lovers or decided I deserved a chance to try bedding Lorna.

In any case, just before midnight, Lorna and I left the wedding dance at the basic school and walked the short journey home with her parents — Lorna's half-drunk Dad saw us to my front door, then he and his wife moved on to their home next door. Of course, Lorna and I — grinning like merry cartoon figures — raced straight to bed. This was our first night fuck, and ahh, what a grand double chapter of fucking we had that night. It was the greatest Saturday night of my life.

The following night we were able to retire to bed early, and spent half the night trying out eight to ten positions illustrated in a sex manual Lorna had borrowed. Half of these positions caused more giggling, muted laughter and muscular aches than sexual delight.

Less than three weeks later, my school was informed that twenty-two of its students had gained passes in the Common Entrance exams. I was among the twenty-two, and I had been granted a place at Calabar Boys' High in Kingston.

Then, in early June, just as Monica and Daddy were about to begin seeking a place in Kingston for me to board, there was an ad in the newspaper that sent my pulse racing with hopeful glee. The ad said:

An Anglican family with sixteen year old twin girls is seeking to share our home with a rural boy who was successful in these last Common Entrance exams and wants to attend high school in Kingston. He doesn't have to be Anglican. Interested parents/guardians please bring son with references to…

We saw this ad on a Thursday. Nine o'clock Saturday morning, Monica and Daddy and I were in Kingston, standing at the gate of the given Fairfax Drive address in Havendale, a nice peaceful middle-income neighbourhood. We had references from an Anglican priest, three teachers and the headmaster of my primary school. Two sleek Alsatian dogs stood in the carport barking.

The tall, trim, elegant mulatto Mrs. Chen and her half-Chinese twin daughters came to answer the gate. All three had engaging smiles and greeted us cheerfully. They led us up the short level driveway to the roomy flower-decked veranda. The twins, Debbie and Debra, were tall for half-Chinese girls and looked quite sophisticated. I was preparing myself to live amongst them without ever having any great desire for their bodies.

CHAPTER 18

DECEMBER 1991

Yesterday I got a call from my stepmother, Monica. She and Daddy and their three kids are happy over in my home parish, St. Mary — they are now living a mile outside my hometown Highgate, settled in the nice four bedroom house I helped them build a year ago. I also had a pleasant chat with sixteen year old Natasha, the oldest of my three "half siblings." Dad and the boys were out on the twenty acre farm behind the house — five years ago Dad stopped going on the U.S. farm-work program, gave up his mason trade and became a fulltime citrus and vegetable farmer. Monica and I have maintained a cordial relationship over the years. She has been a good enough wife to Daddy — over the years her home-based dressmaking business has paid a big part of their bills, and there have never been any whispers of infidelities by her.

Today is a sunny Tuesday and I'm in my comfortable workroom in the Beverly Hills area of Kingston. It's now just a few minutes after two in the afternoon but I've stopped writing for the day. I've written alot since early this morning — the eyes and brain need a break till tomorrow. The novel is going well, the words flowing fast and gloriously. It's pure pleasure. Life is dancing on happily. My one trouble is that I appear to be totally hooked on sex with my uninhibited sister-in-law, Sandra.

This errant affair is just over two weeks old, but it feels like I am sexually chained and enslaved to her more than with any other woman I've known. I want to end the cursed carnal affair, but lack the power to stay away from her. She's a potent drug, an irresistible sin. What am I to do about her uncanny power over me?

I get up from the desk to go stand at the bank of windows looking down on the immaculate front yard of my three-storey home. In bed, Sandra is every man's dream — skilful, imaginative, climaxes easily, can sometimes have multiple orgasms in half hour, while her pum-pum appears to have extra muscles of which she has amazing control. Sex with her is always exotic, wild and stimulating. Out of bed she's an expert at using sexy attire, cosmetics, gesticulation, laughter, smiles, eye contact and words to make men willing to risk their lives and positions for a chance in her punany. She's the opposite of her sister, Janice, my wife.

Still, I must not fall into the common devilish trap of trying to justify that which the bible repeatedly says is an offence. Sin is sin and I'm guilty of enjoying carnality with my sister-in-law. Admitting your misdeeds means you're still within Jah's grace, even if just barely; on the other hand, trying to justify transgressions means you're outside Jah's grace, thereby spiritually dead.

Dear Jah, creator of all things, source of life, forgive I-man.

Sighing, I force aside thoughts of this latest carnality of mine, covering up the uneasiness it has planted in the soul. With another sigh, I move the mind to the greatest delight of life — my wonderful son and only offspring. The afternoon begins regaining nature's sunny glow. I leave the workroom and stride down the short passage into the large, airy, predominantly white master bedroom — my wife loves white almost as much as she loves mirrors; I'm indifferent to mirrors and adore many colours. I freeze just inside the doorway of the master bedroom, caressed by a warm soothing feeling produced by the spiritually uplifting view on the king-sized bed.

Janice, my beautiful low-sexed wife, is lying on her back, her long, glossy raven-black hair spilling over the edge of the bed. She's laughing and cooing with our delightful ten month old prince, who is sitting on her firm, flat, light-golden-brown belly. They make a glorious picture. How I love my son!

I'm grateful to Janice for bearing this loveliest and brightest of sons. I wish it were possible to love her — there's no overlooking her low-sexed nature, and I cannot downplay how she used her pregnancy and my religious horror of abortion, a horror partly due to Momma's death by a blotched abortion — to force me into this delicate marriage. She should've given birth to Jason without marriage and I'd have gladly raised him, in addition to giving her generous payment for giving birth to him, if she had desired.

"Jason, look, Daddy is here," Janice says, ending my thoughts. Her exceptionally pretty mulatto face is exquisitely made-up in quiet hues — her face is prettier than her sister's and she also has a stunning figure and a remarkable complexion. She beams a fond smile at me via one of the three full-length minors in the room. "Hello son," I call, bouncing across the thick carpet to stand over them with one arm on the white headboard. He beams, holding out his chubby arms. I scoop him off his mother's belly. He gabbles happily. I kiss him.

Janice gracefully rises to a sitting position on the edge of the bed — her training and success in beauty contests and modelling have given her graceful movements in all areas. She says, "Through writing for the day, darling?" Her voice is melodic. "Yes; did quite a lot since morning." (For the sake of a peaceful home I speak mostly Standard English in her presence at home, leaving the Jamaican patois and Rasta talk for the streets; she gets wordlessly uptight about patois and Rasta talk when we're alone together.) I throw Jason high. He squeals delight — he's a fearless bundle. I catch him, and dance us over to sit in one of the two cream-coloured bedroom chairs by the door leading to the balcony. I coo at Jason: "Little prince in blue, how are you." He smiles, emits baby talk and pushes a hand inside my shirt.

"This new novel of yours is going to shake up the world," Janice says, coming to a graceful stop in front of me.

I'm pleased — I don't love her, sometimes think I hate her, but she's the wife and will remain the wife at least until our wonderful son is fourteen. "I think it should do as well as the first."

"It'll do even better" she declares confidently, "and silence those local critics who think you cannot make it to the international bestsellers lists a second time."

And gain her more of the international spotlight she's comfortably addicted to, I think, grinning at Jason. I say: "My agent wrote to say the sample chapters and outline I sent her are a sure indication of a hit. She showed it to two publishers and both are offering contracts; my present publisher already willing to put up a US half million advance. Jane thinks we can get at least twice that when the manuscript is complete — Jane is an expert at playing publisher against publisher for a hot manuscript."

"Charlie! When did all this happen behind my back?" She's now in a wide-legged, hands on hip stance, her lovely pink mouth prettily pouted, her brown eyes sparkling with delight and dreams of a fresh wave of hectic international limelight.

Lovely, that's her always. Now standing here in tight shorts and T-shirt, she would arouse any man. The oval face is perfectly pretty as a face can be, firm ample breasts, a small waist and firm, flat belly ninety-nine out of every hundred young mothers can only dream of, curvy hips and an exquisite rear end; and those enchanting golden-brown legs. I now remember the first time I saw her and was roped by beauty as never before or since — so damn enchanted that during the many weeks between becoming her lover and the day she forced me into a marriage agreement, I failed to detect her overwhelming obsession with the international limelight, and was blind to her pretence that sex was a great delight to her.

Despite the awkward aspect of this memory, my manhood awakens.

"Charlie, please answer the question?" she prompts.

I reply: "After finishing the first draft and doing half the second, I mailed Jane the first three chapters and outline of the rest. Yesterday I got her response..."

She interjects: "How could you keep such news from me for a whole day?" Her voice trembles with hurt. Frowning at me, she sits down in the chair next to mine. Jason is silent. "And why didn't you tell me about mailing her a sample?"

Fearful of one of her anxiety attacks that I'm planning to seek a divorce, I say soothingly: "Darling, I'm sorry. Mailing the sample appeared unimportant. Then yesterday you weren't home when the surprise response came, and somehow it just slipped the mind to tell you." I'm speaking honestly but, of course, I cannot tell her that lust and anxiety over her sister caused the lapse in memory. "Come on, forgive your devoted husband."

Her face relaxes. "You're forgiven." She crosses those lovely long legs, beaming at me. There'll be no neurotic attack. The baby grins and sleepily lays back in my lap. Janice says: "I'm sure Jane is right about getting better terms when it's complete."

"Whatever Jane says; she's one of the best lit agents. Anyway, I should soon be able to give her the manuscript."

"Charlie, since our marriage you've come to know I do love you?" Her velvety voice trembles a bit. She's leaning towards me gracefully. One of her lovely hands reaches out to touch my knee.

I know that in her own warped way she is earnest. "Yes, love. I know." Eager to change the subject, I declare: "Seems that Jason wants to nap."

"Let's put him to bed." Her voice is warm.

Thank God she is off the touchy subject of her twisted love for me, a subject I always labour to keep her from, seeing that it's likely to lead her to ask if I love her — to this question I must lie with a yes, which I hate doing. Now she leads the way across the thick carpet to the big grand cradle at the foot of our bed. I follow with our son in my arms. Lowering Jason to the cradle's quilted mattress, I avoid his mother's eyes, fearful of reviving the subject of love.

Jason is asleep. His mother gently rocks the cradle. Her eyes are gazing down at our sleeping prince. Her mouth is a proud smile. Her face glows with love. I know that leaving the room now is the best way to avoid a return to the prickly subject of love but I feel compelled to stand there watching her rocking our son's cradle — the blissful picture of it, my love for our son, a sense of compassion towards her, and the power of her beauty. She looks up and beams at me. Before I can find the will to break the eye contact and say something casual or create an excuse to flee the room, she glides up against me and cups my chin. Instinctively, my hands grip her waist.

"My life," she murmurs, "my love." She pulls off my beret and ruffles my locks. "My handsome lion, king of my heart." She glues her lips to mine, pressing her body closer.

The joyful surprise of experiencing one of her extremely rare physical initiatives floods me with raw lust. Our kiss is short and hungry — I am ready for action; of course, Jason may soon awake, so making love now will be a bit awkward although he's only ten months old. "Tonight," she coos when our lips part and I don't try stopping her move out of my arms, "we'll have wine and some fun." Her attention is already returning to our sleeping son.

"Sounds good," I say honestly, although disappointed that just this once she couldn't simply let us hop into bed spontaneously. It has been two weeks since she last allowed me her beautiful body (has since used claims of headache and back pain to turn down the two or three advances I've made), and our last fuck was bland, which is what our infrequent love making is usually like. I move to sit on the bed, watching her rock our son's cradle.

Before the chilling day when she coolly forced me into agreeing to marry her, she willingly gave me sex often as I desired it, night and day. I was so taken with her beauty that I didn't even suspect she was faking orgasms most of the time by way of an inbred acting talent. There was also the fact that I was limiting sexual intercourse as much as possible because I didn't want to hurt her with my oversized dick and reputable stamina in the sack. After agreeing to marry her, I quickly learned that she cannot climax if she isn't tipsy. Needless to say, there was an uneasy truce between the forced marriage agreement and the honeymoon. And surprisingly enough, the honeymoon turned out to be a time of mostly drinking and highly passionate sex that caused me to have actually begun wondering if it might be possible to grow into loving her. But immediately after the honeymoon, she declared that she didn't like sex and she avowed that she had no intention of allowing me her body regularly — of course, this attitude killed my tentative thoughts of trying to find true love with her. Still, seeing that we were sharing the same bed and she occasionally allowed us a highly passionate night, I simply couldn't stop desiring her. Now after roughly sixteen months of marriage, I'm pretty much resigned to the fact that the only time I can get good sex from her is when she drinks enough to be highly tipsy, which happens only occasionally — like me, she isn't a lover of alcohol.

So her proposal of wine and fun tonight is highly attractive. It takes just two or three small drinks of any strong alcoholic drink to get her tipsy enough to enjoy sex.

Night has fallen long ago. The December air is now still, no hint of the "Christmas breeze" that dominates this time of year. Janice and I have just tucked Jason into his cradle. We're now out on the balcony adjoining our third floor bedroom, listening to love songs, drinking wine and nibbling wonderful French cheese. We're sitting across from each other at the small, round, wicker table. Soft light from our semi-dark bedroom and from our well-lit back yard below is providing the right level of illumination needed for this "romantic date" of ours. The view of the city's lowlands and sheltered harbour are beautiful from up here in the hills. An enchanting and beautiful view, but not as much as my wife in a short, thin, body-hugging, shoulder baring silk dress; her shoulders are covered by an exquisite scarf and she's a twinkle with matching diamond necklace, earrings and bracelet, and her diamond studded wedding ring; silk stockings and high heel slippers complete the get-up. She loves getting all dressed up every evening, whether she's staying home or not. I'm in a necktie, although I dislike all ties — wearing one tonight is a signal to her of my great appreciation for her promise of physical joy this night. Her body is swaying to the lovey-dovey music flowing from the tape deck on the floor. I'm already aflame with desire but she hasn't yet drunk enough of the wine to move into her passionate mode.

This warm intimacy reminds me of our previous weeks together; I hate to admit it but those weeks before our marriage were a great joy to me. Now I smile and raise my wineglass at her in silent salute. Her response is a beautiful smile across the rim of her wineglass, provocative fluttering of her tall lashes, and a slow tongue-flicking drink — all of this reminds me of the fact that she does know how to get a man going, although not as accomplished as her younger sister, but...

Damn it, Charlie, forget about the sinful affair tonight.

Lionel Richie's mellow voice washes away the unwelcomed thought.

"A lovely night, dear husband," Janice purrs.

"Yes, truly a lovely night," I agree. "But not half as lovely as you, dear wife, the most beautiful lady in the world."

"Mmmm. I'm not completely sure you're the most handsome man in the world."

I chuckle and pour us more wine. Ah, how a lusty man who isn't cruel must work hard for a little pum-pum.

"Trying to get me drunk, huh?" Her remarkable brows arch gracefully.

"That wouldn't do," I say sincerely — highly tipsy is where her passionate self lay; at drunken level, sleep rules her. "This is only your second little drink." I lean forward to feed her a bit of cheese. She bites my fingers. "Eat them if you wish."

Grinning, she raises her glass. "To us and Jason." Her voice is a bit thick. She's getting tipsy. We touch glasses and drink.

If only she wasn't so reserved and odd where sex is concerned, I muse wistfully; I might have grown to love her since our marriage, and wouldn't have fallen prey to her lusty sister. It...

Shit, Charlie, this is no time for musing. Here is your beautiful wife getting ready for one of her rare times of lusty passion.

I drain my glass. Silently she copies me. I pour us another drink, drain mine immediately, get up and move to stand behind her chair. I remove the expensive scarf from her shoulders. Then I begin massaging the lovely shoulders — her dress has very thin straps. Her hair is like velvet against my hands. She sighs pleasure, leans back against me and quickly finishes her drink. No doubt about it, she's now ripe for a fine time in bed. Still, I must not simply drag her off to bed. A bit more work before bed and pum-pum joys.

"Would my lady care to dance?"

"Gladly, my lord."

She rises up into my embrace and we waltz off across our softly lit balcony to the love song purring from the tape deck. She is a good dancer to any and every type of music. During the many weeks before marriage, we spent many nights on the dance floors of various highbrow parties and the best clubs in New York, Miami, L.A., San Francisco, Washington, Toronto, London, Paris, and here in Jamaica. Now I waltz her around our Jamaican balcony and into our semi-dark bedroom to bed.

CHAPTER 19

I awake to soft morning light. The radio clock on one of the two elaborate night tables reads minutes after eight. The window curtains are still closed. Janice is seated near the bed in one of the two antique, British wing chairs, which she bought to replace the two sturdy Jamaican wicker chairs I used before our marriage. She's bottle-feeding our son. Obviously, she has already taken her morning shower — now looking fresh like a lush garden on a bright morning. Memories of our satisfying night dance up. She smiles at me. I fear that my responding smile is a bit bewildered — as always, after each of our rare satisfying nights I feel a bit embarrassed and, paradoxically, wistful that there won't be a repeat for weeks.

She purrs: "Good morning, my love."

I sit up. "Same to you, my wife." Then immediately, I hop out of bed mumbling truthfully that I planned to begin writing early.

"My dearest, you looked so at peace I refrained from disturbing you."

I wave at Jason. The greedy little fellow ignores me. I hurry to the bathroom and hop into the shower stall. What a confusing, delicate and uncertain thing your marriage is? It's like...damn it, Charlie, start thinking about the day's work at hand. It's to be a productive Wednesday.

Friday night. The December night is chilly, a steady breeze flowing from the city's harbour, and the city is now truly in Christmas groove with sparkling Christmas trees all over. There are three fancy Christmas trees in my mansion (a huge one on the veranda, one in the living room, and another on the balcony adjoining the master bedroom) — my wife's doing, of course. Carols are flowing from my house. I am going to see my outrageous sister-in-law; insatiable Sandra. I-man honestly wishes for the power to end the sordid affair, but I'm at her mercy for now.

I simply must obey Sandra's directive to report for new delights tonight.

My Rolex says 7:25 as I drive my Mercedes out of the carport. There's no need to worry about the safety of Janice and our son. The house and yard feature a sophisticated security system that's linked to a private security company, and I never go out for long at night without getting Mr. and Mrs. Boots to spend the night in one of our guest rooms.

The Boots are now inside the house. Mr. Boots is a tough fifty year old ex-soldier who'd rather give up his life than part with his German 9mm pistol and British bayonet for even one second — he left the Jamaican army a few years ago due to bad blood with a high ranking officer. Mrs. Boots is a lively middle-aged lady who can shoot as well as her husband. They're diehard fans of my fiction and songs, adore Janice and Jason, and are glad for the comfortable high-paying task of staying with Janice and Jason while I prowl the town at least two nights a week. When Janice and I are out of the city for more than a day, or travelling abroad, the Boots occupy the house at nights.

Memories of the first night with Sandra jump in and out of my head — it was one of those incredibly wild night of sex that leave you swinging between total exhaustion and amazing vitality. Since that unforgettable first night, we've had other glorious nights at her apartment, but all just a bit below the remarkably thrilling first night. Now there's a strong gut feeling that tonight will be comparable to the amazing first night of this almost-three-week-old affair.

I enter one of the elevators and ride alone up to Sandra's floor, get out and stride down the carpeted corridor. I ring Sandra's doorbell. Many seconds thud by before one of her eyes fills the peephole. Then she opens the door.

I freeze, gulping a ton of air, dazzled by the sexy reality in the door way. She's in a plastic see-through, high-necked, short-sleeve body-suit. No underwear. Her large nipples are rouged a brilliant red. The curled hair on her crotch is dyed red. She's surveying me through long, sooty, false lashes. Under the clear plastic suit, her waxed mulatto skin is like golden velvet. Her pretty hands cover the front of her waist — are they hiding a special surprise?

"Well," she purrs, "aren't you going to enter before someone walks by?"

I enter the tiny entrance hall and close the door, saying: "Pardon me, Madame loveliness."

She turns, displaying her amazingly shaped bum, skips ahead of me to the well-lit living room, makes a dramatic turn to me and says: "Lover, without further delay you better take a closer look at my new play-suit."

I now see what her hands were hiding in the entrance hall. The sturdy zipper down the front of her bodysuit is fastened to a little iron ring at the waist, and held in place by a small combination lock.

I frown at the lock, feeling a touch of despair. But I am also conscious of the birth of a remarkable glee. Trust Sandra to come up with the most amazing fantasies — this lusty ability is a major reason why I'm under her spell.

"Yes, yes!" she giggles, bouncing up and down on the thick round purple rug in the middle of her colourful living room. Her pretty feet are bare. "Yes Mr. Rasta! To fuck me, you'll have to find the combination that opens the lock or weep tears for me to open it! I won't mention the third way now."

Focusing a half-hearted glare into her twinkling eyes, I am wondering: What's the unmentioned third way through the cursed but fascinating combination lock? "Sandra, damn it, that's not fair. Down right uncivilized of yuh." I don't want her to realize that already I am aching for her.

"Fair or not, that's the fact." Her grin is ecstatic. "Anyway, champagne first."

We sit down on the sofa. On the coffee table before us, there are two glasses and a silver ice bucket with a bottle of champagne. She fills the glasses, hands me one and moves away to curl up at the far end of the sofa. "To a joyous night," she toasts. My erection lurches, and I shift to mask it. We drink.

"No Charlie," she purrs, "the third way into me tonight is the easiest and tastiest way — if you be a good boy and promise to eat my pussy tonight, I'll open the lock. I'll add chocolate, cherry or strawberry flavour to make the eating tastier to you. If not, you'll have to find the combination or weep tears for me to open up." Her brows go up over her wine glass.

"Damn it, Sandra, I told you I don't expect you to give me blowjobs, for I don't eat pussy. You insisted on doing me the one-sided oral honour. Sorry, I will not pay what I don't owe."

Instead of responding, she moves into a mode of grinning sexily and sipping her drink with much provocative tongue flickering. Finally she breaks the silence. "Why should kissing pussy be wrong? I once had a Rasta lover who enjoyed it."

"Not this one." I sip my drink, thinking how good it is that my wife isn't into oral sex. "Seems best if I simply leave." I begin rising, half bluffing. "Certainly not?" She jumps to her feet, turns on her stereo and begins a sexy dance to a reggae hit. My dick instantly springs to attention. She says:

"If you won't eat you must labour to open the lock, and if you cannot find the combination I'll open it when you begin weeping."

I must stay and challenge that damn combination lock on her clear plastic playsuit. Must die trying, or weep the tears she'd love to see.

CHAPTER 20

Two o'clock in the morning. I'm just returning from Sandra's apartment. We had some wild unforgettable hours together — left her abed without her plastic bodysuit. I failed to open the lock, and she eventually had me so crazy with lust I really tried weeping the tears she insisted on seeing for her to open the cursed combination lock; but the tears just wouldn't come. To get her to open the damn lock, I had to grovel on my knees and pay her a string of poetic compliments about her beauty and skill in bed, followed by a promise to dedicate my third novel to her, and further enhanced my case by promising her a diamond necklace.

The things a man will do to satisfy a vast lust. Blessed is the man whose lust is modest.

Based on my sexual history, it appears best to add: Blessed is the man whose dick is of average size.

Before leaving Sandra's apartment I had to take a real good shower to get rid of the great stink of our remarkable sex.

As is the norm whenever I'm out after her bedtime, Janice has left one of the bedside lamps on, the frill pink shade allowing just a soft glow. I undress, take a good look at my sleeping son in his cradle by the bed and turn off the lamp and edge under my coverlet. Janice awakes and asks the usual question: "Had a good time, dear?" Her voice is even — this question is always asked in even or cheerful tones.

"Okay," I murmur. That little question always fills me with a mix of irritation and reluctant guilt — she knows that I fuck other women.

Shortly after our marriage she told me she was not big on sex and wouldn't try stopping me from having affairs. All she asked was that I use protection against sexually transmitted diseases and do nothing that would distress her, so no long-term mistress, because that'll certainly lead to embarrassing gossip, and the other woman might take it into her head to stage a confrontation.

Yes, she encourages my infidelity, and thereby feels justified in her determination to avoid sex regularly.

Now she says: "Goodnight, dear."

I mumble a response and drift towards sleep worrying about the possible hysterical horrors that would unfold if she finds out that my latest lover is her sister.

The Saturday noontime is bright and bubbling with the hectic, festive Jamaican spirit of the final days before Christmas and rich with vivid memories of last night's romp with Sandra. I'm in a crowded upscale department store in one of the smaller and more exclusive shopping plazas on Constant Spring Road. The store is loaded with Christmas decorations. Carols are anointing the crowds. Since entering the store minutes ago, I've been getting a lot of smiles and greetings from fans, along with requests for autographs. Now I'm looking at a nice display of socks, aided by a fairly attractive, heavy- breasted, young sales clerk.

Two sexy and fairly tall part-Chinese women in tight pants suits pop through the crowd on my left. Simultaneously and hesitantly they say:

"Hello there, Charlie." They are both wearing plastic smiles — no hint of teeth.

I am transfixed. I couldn't fail to recognize these two females, although we were high school students when I last saw them; Debbie and Debra. I quickly regain my wits. "Debbie and Debra, good day." Willpower has my voice civil enough, for a public show of displeasure might eventually reach the ears of their nice parents, plus it'd be a waste of energy and bad for my reputation. I'm certainly not thrilled to see this pair of twins, even though now that they're just into their thirties, they look sexier than when I was the boy their kind-hearted parents had taken into their home. Their pale, yellowish-brown faces have hard lines that make them look years older than their early-thirties.

"I'm Debbie," one of them is gushing, all smiles. "So wonderful to see you, our favourite author."

Debra intones: "The best." Her head nods vigorously, smiling madly, glistening shoulder length black hair dancing.

"Kind of nice to see you two," I say in slightly harassed tones. I turn aside, selecting socks and reluctantly declare, "Saw your parents in New York last year, and have spoken to them by phone twice this year."

"We heard."

"Nice of you to treat them so well."

Without looking at them, I say: "They were good to me as a boy, unlike some people." Here I give them a quick harsh look. Discomfort flushes their faces. I smile and comment: "They said you ladies were living in Canada. No doubt that's why you're looking much paler."

"Yes. But a few months ago we convinced our husbands — our boyfriends who you knew — convinced them to return and set up business here. We're really just settling in now."

I think: Ordered the husbands, no doubt, for as teenage boys they were great wimps.

"Got tired of North America," Debra is announcing. "Found out we're islanders to our core."

I select a sixth pair of socks, thank the clerk and turn to my old twin enemies and say: "That's my shopping for the day."

"We're through too," Debbie gushes. Debra nods. Clutching their few items — appears to be local T-shirts and skincare products — they troop behind me towards the cashiers. We do not speak again until we're out in the plaza's busy, sunny carpark. I rudely head straight for my car. Debra says, "Charlie, we owe you an apology. Forgive us for our bad behaviour."

I think: Wicked and evil are truer words. "Sure," I say, for their parents' sake.

"We were young and mad," Debbie says.

"Forget it," I declare calmly and give them a right grin. We're now at my car. Curiosity makes me comment: "So, your old boyfriends are now your husbands." They nod, and I venture: "Did they take up Kung Fu seriously?"

"No," Debbie responds with a guarded grin.

Debra intones, "Too busy with studies and building a business, and laziness."

I chuckle ironically, pitying those two poor chaps. As teenagers, Debbie and Debra were very good lifelong Kung Fu students who ruled their boyfriends like evil witches. Well, perhaps those two boys loved to be dominated by girls, and are now happy wife-ruled husbands.

Grinning lustily, Debra says: "Charlie, we owe you ah...some real...good times."

"Together or singularly," Debbie adds coyly. "We live next to each other in Cherry Gardens. You can..."

I interrupt, "Thanks for the offer, ladies. But I'm married and avoid married women." My voice is pointedly sarcastic, for I simply wouldn't touch them even if they were single and the only attractive women alive. "Don't think I fear your Kung Fu — I'm now an expert too, and also a legal gunman."

I hop into my car, leaving them speechlessly embarrassed. With a jaunty little wave I drive away.

CHAPTER 21

CHARLIE LOOKS BACK

The evening was cool on Kingston city. It was September, 1976. Mrs. Chen and I were seated on the roomy back veranda watching Mr. Chen and their twin daughters, Debbie and Debra, at the habitual Sunday evening Kung Fu practice on the neatly trimmed back lawn. Mr. Chen, a full-blooded Chinese who had loved Kung Fu from before his birth, was a damn good fourth degree Kung Fu black belt expert, while sixteen year old Debbie and Debra weren't far away from getting their black belts; Mrs. Chen was a mulatto who wasn't into Kung Fu or any type of martial arts. That day was my second Sunday in the Chen household, and it had been pleasant living on all levels. The parents were kind, outgoing, gentle and appreciated humour; and they were pretty laid back about their Anglican faith, a fact that went well with my religiously uncommitted upbringing. The girls were witty, daring, sophisticated sixteen year olds. On top of the great vibes in the Chen's home, there was the wonderful fact that the neighbourhood had a merry liveliness to its broad middle class respectability. Almost all the homes in the community were one-storied four bedroom affairs, each on its own modest lot, while style was of a wide variety.

My first school term in high school had begun the previous Tuesday, and I was already in love with the school, Calabar Boys' High. I was also overjoyed to be away from my lusty stepmother, Monica.

Before the school term had begun that September, and after Daddy had gone off to farm-work in the USA, I had had to endure spending the last month of the summer with Monica and the baby. Those weeks alone with Monica had been a time of nerve-wracking tension. Every night rattled down with the worry that she'd try seduction. Thankfully, she made no attempt to get us to repeat the sins of the previous summer, but being alone with her and the baby those last weeks of summer 1976, bombarded me with the wretched unwelcomed memories of our sinful nights together. So when the day came for me to begin life with the Chens in Kingston, I was the happiest boy in Jamaica.

The Chen family gave me such a warm welcome that I began feeling at home from day one, didn't feel odd about living with a mulatto lady and her Chinese husband and their daughters, didn't feel more than a bit strange about moving from a lower-middle income small town background to an upper-middle income city life. I immediately fell in love with my comfortable room and Mrs. Chen's good cooking. During the first week with the Chens, I often wondered if Monica would take a lover before Daddy returned and I prayed that the baby would keep her from cheating on Daddy. This thought was the only discomfort to my new city life; but by the eighth or ninth day in the Chen household, I was able to stop worrying about Monica giving Daddy "bun".

The girls' baggy white martial arts suits were wet with sweat pouring from their bronzed skin, their heart shaped faces solemn, their long, glossy, black plaits dancing about their heads and shoulders. On a day to day basis, the twins were ordinarily attractive, easy-going, candid and fairly quick to smile, but somehow, when doing Kung Fu, they always looked beautiful, deadly, devious and grim. I was too young and inexperienced to grasp the possible dangers of this metamorphosis.

Mr. Chen, a relatively muscular Chinese, was in a black Kung Fu suit. He was by far the tallest Chinese I'd seen up to that fourteenth year of my life, although he was two or three inches shorter than his wife's five- foot-nine frame.

The girls ejaculated fierce sounds with almost every kick, slash, chop, punch, block and stab. Their dad rarely made a sound. Mrs. Chen was watching the Kung Fu with a fond smile on her attractive mulatto face. I was enjoying the scene, often overwhelmed to the point of nearly kicking and punching — Mrs. Chen and I were seated in the two armchairs of the three piece patio suite at one end of the roomy back veranda, which was dominated by an expensive tennis table. The low walls of the back veranda were packed with a wide variety of potted plants, similar to the low walls of the front veranda; the family was big on sports and plants.

The fingers of dusk were touching the neighbourhood when father and daughters made the traditional bows that brought the Kung Fu practice to a close. Sweaty and grinning, they strode to the well-lit back veranda. There was a big jug of iced cherry juice and drinking glasses on the small table beside Mrs. Chen and I. Jumping to my feet, and no doubt grinning madly, I began pouring juice for the sweaty trio.

"Charlie," Debbie said with a grin, "tomorrow evening Debra and I will begin giving you Kung Fu lessons."

"You'll get lessons whenever time allows," Debra intoned, nodding a smile and accepting a glass of cherry juice from me.

I nodded my eagerness to begin. Yesterday they had bought me a white Chinese martial arts suit.

"Good," Mr. Chen said, sipping his cherry juice. "A wife who knows no Kung Fu isn't too bad." He grinned at his wife, who gave him a mock-glower. He smiled at me and said: "But a son who knows no Kung Fu would be terrible to bear."

I blushed. They were all beaming fond smiles at me. It'd be quite awhile before I'd stop feeling overwhelmed by the parental warmth with which he and his wife treated me. Although I had been with them less than two weeks and was only a temporary member of their household, they acted as if they had adopted me years ago. They had even ordered the young maid, who came in on weekdays, to address me as Mr. Charlie, just as the twins were Miss Debbie and Miss Debra. The twins and I addressed each other by first names, and I addressed their parents using Mr. and Mrs.

Since moving into their home, I had been willing myself to think of the girls as sisters. No thoughts of sex with them, I had been musing regularly. This was no easy challenge — their identical heart-shape faces were attractive, their tall, sleek, pretty-legged sixteen year old bodies were well developed, and they used make-up and appeared highly mature. After the first four to five weeks in their home, I would be able to begin appreciating their good looks and charm without much lust, a fact that was quite likely due largely to knowing that each could use Kung Fu to whip me in a fight. Plus, the day after I moved into their home, Mrs. Chen had said to me in the girls' presence: "Debbie and Debra are now your older sisters, and you must think and act towards them accordingly, just as they too, must act in similar fashion." I nodded my understanding of the subtle message of her words, eyes and tone, which was that she'd ship me back to the country if she found me guilty of any lustful move towards the girls.

Thankfully the weeks would roll by without the twins showing any sexual interest in me. Nothing they did could've been termed flirting with me and they had steady boyfriends. I was just a humorous younger unofficial brother, and would remain as such until the unholy day they found out I was no ordinary thirteen year old boy in my pants.

Meantime, I lusted at the twins' girlfriend but none showed any interest in the younger, poor country boy and the few younger sisters of the friends gave me similar treatment.

Learning Kung Fu proved to be tougher than I'd expected. Most days one or both of the twins were able to give me some form of Kung Fu lessons, but muscular aches dictated that there wasn't much fun to the lessons for the first few weeks. Then, after the daily and nightly muscular aches disappeared, I had to contend with the twins' grim impatience with mistakes — where Kung Fu was concerned, they were not their usual witty easy-going selves. But my great passion to learn the Kung Fu art, and the determination to remain in Mr. and Mrs. Chen's good book, made it fairly easy to ignore the girls' cold impatience during Kung Fu lessons. The moment I changed from Kung Fu attire, the girls became their usual nice, patient selves and never mentioned the mistakes I made during the Kung Fu lessons. After three months or so, the lessons became mostly pleasure.

I was disappointed that Mr. Chen's expanding business concerns caused him to rarely have time for Kung Fu at home; the twins said that up to the previous year he used to tutor them Kung Fu at home three or four times a week; now the regular Sunday evening workout with the girls was his only steady Kung Fu time at home. I preferred to sit with Mrs. Chen and watch his expert moves coupled with the highly competent twins; the girls were close to getting their black belts and no longer needed regular tutoring, so they didn't bother taking classes with any other expert. Unfortunately the Kung Fu lessons would become infrequent after the girls found out I was exceptionally "well-hung".

I was enjoying Kingston's clannish, high-spirited boys' high school world — each school held a passionate belief that it was Jamaica's best in an all round manner, above the younger co-educational high schools, and deserved the prettiest girls from the girls' and the co-ed schools.

Meantime, life in the Chens' comfortable four-bedroom bungalow flowed along equally merry. The family had a good sense of humour and loved all kinds of music and foods; and they also enjoyed watching a wide range of sports. Mrs. Chen was a great housewife who loved cooking, especially baking, including wholesome things like real whole grain breads and muffins, made delightful by a rich mix of local fruits and spices.

Mr. Chen was a successful businessman from a wealthy US Chinese family. Mrs. Chen was a mulatto of the Jamaican upper-middle class. They were both in their late-thirties but had the wisdom of open-minded older folks, coupled with the charm of cheerful optimistic twenty year olds. Mrs. Chen and the twins were confirmed Anglicans and we all went to early morning service two or three Sundays a month, but that was about it where religion was concerned in the family — the twins insisted that Kung Fu and their school work were more important than other church activities. Mr. Chen was essentially non-religious, and he was fond of saying he respected Rastafarians for daring to see God in terms of themselves. Mrs. Chen viewed the Rasta movement as a quaint product of harmless emphasis on the history of European enslavement of Africans while the twins were indifferent to Rastafarians but had quite a number of reggae songs by Rastafarians in their record and tape collections. The girls' nerdish boyfriends were free to visit and came by often enough, while the girls visited the boyfriends' homes occasionally. Fairly regularly, the four of them went to parties and movies.

My chores at the Chens were easy; watering the outside plants, occasionally helping Mrs. Chen and the girls to water the potted plants on the two verandas, trimming the shrubs and fences, and putting out the garbage. A man who did gardening jobs all over the neighbourhood cut the lawns. Mrs. Chen loved seeing to the flowerbeds.

The first Christmas of my high school life was spent with Daddy, Monica and my baby half-sister. I got a great welcome from the small town friends and old lovers, and was able to work off some of the sexual energy that had built up during the sexless months in Kingston. Two days before New Year's Day of 1977, I returned to the Chens bearing the chopper bicycle Daddy and Monica had given me for Christmas. This bicycle meant that I could now go riding with the twins and their neighbourhood pals (the twin's rich bookish boyfriends lived over ten miles away across the city), but being that I was three to four years younger than each member of this predominantly female group, they tended to act condescendingly towards me when we went riding. This attitude irritated and amused me, for I was as tall as them and I knew I could give any older school girl hell in bed. Before January ended, I began doing most of my riding alone or with a few boys of my age who lived close by; none of my friends from school lived near the Chens, but one friend and several schoolmates of my year were scattered within a half-mile radius of our sprawling community, so eventually I'd sometimes ride to their "corners" or they'd ride by the Chens, who always welcomed my friends.

When the Easter holidays arrived I had managed to alter my speech and manners enough to comfortably pass as one who had lived for years in the city's upper-middle class. I was passionately focused on remaining in the upper-middle class world or rising even higher, and was determined that there'd be no return to my poverty-line lower-middle class origins.

Life was bliss until a Saturday morning four to six weeks before the end of my first year in high school. On this earth-shaking morning, Mr. and Mrs. Chen went out leaving the twins and I alone at home, which was often the case on most Saturday mornings. Unfortunately, Debra barged into our bathroom through the improperly closed door and the size of my dick filled her eyes.

CHAPTER 22

Debra exclaimed: "Debbie! Come here! Quick, girl, quick!" As I stood there blushing and trying to finish the pissing job I'd just began — your sisters shouldn't see your dick if you're nearly fourteen years old, right? Debra's eyes were glued to my limp pissing dick, her bronzed cheeks flushed. She was rooted in the doorway. Part of me wished she wasn't an unofficial sister. I said: "Why are you calling Debbie?" Then I turned my back on her, but piss was still flowing out, as if I were a beer drinker returning from a drinking bout. "Debra, you shouldn't be standing there."

She chuckled in a most bizarre way. A second later, Debbie burst onto the scene asking, "What's up?"

"Charlie is big like the men we saw in the magazine at Cherry's house!"

"You mean his dick?"

"What else, Miss dumb-dumb?"

Having finished pissing and a swift zipping up, I turned towards them. Debbie said: "This I must see. Show it, Charlie."

I began feeling a chill of fear, was getting a powerful feeling that this scene would lead to their parents asking me to leave their home long before I was anywhere near to completing high school. I stood there not knowing what to say or do. The girls suddenly looked alien and evil in their short skirts and T-shirt. "Debbie and Debra," I finally managed to croak, "please remember what your Mom said about us living like brother and sisters."

Their responses were identical grins and a menacing advance into the bathroom. I was rooted and wanted to beg them to put aside their obvious intention, which would certainly lead to one great folly or another, but my throat felt clogged with gravel. If the bathroom had two doors I'd have fled.

"Come out with your amazing dick," Debra commanded.

Debbie said: "No harm in giving us a look. We won't chop it off, you know."

"Girls, it...it's not right." I was scared of intimacy with them because I didn't want to lose the comfortable place in their parents' home, under normal circumstances I would have gladly showed them Mr. Dickie. "No, it'd be wrong."

"Come on, Charlie, Debra saw it, so be a sport for me," Debbie said. They were now planted just three feet away. Every part of me knew they could use Kung Fu to strip me naked. The bathroom shrunk, the sunny morning went chilly.

While the mind filled up with a dismaying vision of having to leave this comfortable home to complete high school while living in one of the city's violence-prone, lower-middle class or ghetto areas, I tightly clamped my hands over my trousers front. Dear God, I prayed, please let Mr. and Mrs. Chen or some friend arrive now.

The twins grinned at each other and then nodded. Immediately, Debbie's left foot was on my right instep, while simultaneously Debra's right foot pinned down my left foot; and each of them delivered a powerful rap of knuckles to my upper arms — all done before I could've blinked. My forearms and hands became dead, lifeless things, and fell away from my trousers front. As for my poor feet — they were dead under the girls' smaller feet that were now out of their sandals.

I know not if I'd cried out or made any kind of sound. In any case, before I could plead or try moving, my Kung Fu teachers hammered knees into my thighs, and I was twisted around to face Debbie, my useless hands now pinned behind by Debra, whose knees then turned my legs to useless jelly. They had to hold me upright.

"Girls please, don't," I managed to plead, as Debbie's nimble fingers began unzipping my pants. I was unable to offer the slightest resistance.

"Wow!" Debbie exclaimed when she hauled my limp dick into view. She stroked Mr. Dickie. "It's man-size!" Her voice echoed in the bathroom.

"I told you so," Debra said. "Wonder what it'll be like when pumped up, eh?" Then they released me and stepped back. I slumped against the nearest wall. The sunny Saturday morning felt like a cold night.

"Now listen, big dick," Debbie said. "You ain't no ordinary boy so you're going to provide us with some fun. You do as we say or you endanger your stay here. Simple."

"Understand?" Debra said. Her hard tones filled the bathroom.

I understood well enough. Although their parents were wonderful and intelligent, the cursed twins could get me shipped out of their comfortable world. Despite indignation and the conviction that it'd be best to avoid any kind of sexual link with them, it was obvious that the best thing was to go along with them and hope their parents would never suspect. If I refused to cooperate and then complained to Mr. and Mrs. Chen about this assault, the girls would be punished; but all round embarrassment and the twins' anger would almost certainly force their parents to ask me to leave. The thought of having to return to live with my lecherous step mother and perhaps transfer from Calabar Boys' High appeared as terrible as death. Burning with the zeal of a happy new convert-soldier, I was convinced that a high school education at Calabar would make me much wiser than education at any other high school, including the one in my hometown. I was willing to do just about anything to remain in the Chens' comfortable middle-income world, which was no cost to my struggling Daddy.

"Alright," I said, and filled the bathroom with a sigh. "But nothing that might cause your parents to suspect."

With an ugly grin, Debbie chilled my bones by saying: "No real sex. We'll masturbate you. Sometimes you will do yourself."

"And you'll have to tongue us," Debra intoned.

I stood there gaping, wondering if they had gone crazy. Although the lack of sex in Kingston had caused me to begin masturbating once a week in the months since the feast of sex in my hometown during the Christmas period; allowing them to masturbate me without any real sex was certainly not a pleasant prospect. But it would be tolerable. On the other hand, masturbating in front of them seemed impossible; and if Debra meant me kissing their cunts, that was a terribly dreadful prospect, although I'd do just about anything to remain in their comfortable home.

"Let's go begin right now," Debbie said. Like a dumb lamb being led to the slaughter, I walked behind her to their room. Debra was behind me. I was hoping that they'd been joking.

Their bedroom was large, airy and luxuriously furnished; my smaller but equally comfortable room was across the passage. High twin beds and large posters of Kung Fu movie legend Bruce Lee dominated the girls' room. Debra drew the thin curtains. The room remained bright enough with sunlight. I was pushed onto a bed. Then while Debbie hauled down my pants and briefs, Debra commented with a far-away gaze: "We are feminist virgins and intend to remain virgins until we complete fifth form and graduate next year summer. You see, our virginities are to be rewards and the foundation for the way we shall rule our boyfriends when we marry them. We think it's the best way to begin our life as the new woman who shall someday rule the world; any son we have shall be raised to be the perfect husband who will not sleep about and won't be too jealous if he learns that his wife has lovers." Here she grinned lustily. "We'll have our fill of various men after we marry. If we sleep about before marriage we'd be risking our reputations and might lose our perfect boyfriends, the type of boys who are now rare but will be common in a feminist-dominated world. So sad that Mom and Dad will be misfits in the feminist ruled world."

I now saw that they were truly evil, had somehow come under the influence of some fanatical minority in the feminist movement. They were not the nice girls their parents thought they were — no, not mad, just plain evil like cruel men who brutalize their wives and kill for power; but, I had to try enduring their sexual torture.

Debbie had completed her task of removing my clothes — I was reclined on my elbows in the middle of the bed. She and her twin sat down on either side of me; and, lustful creature that we males are, their hands soon had me tingling with pleasure. Mr. Dickie quickly swelled to iron-hardness in their hands — instantly, it was obvious that they gave their boyfriends hand jobs, which kept me from feeling any great fear that they might mistakenly cause injury to my dick or balls. I closed my eyes and lay back, but was very aware of their exclamations and comments of delight. I, at least, managed to keep a bit of dignity by remaining silent and relatively still. How could I not be aroused, despite the fact that I was a reluctant participant? They caressed, stroked, pulled, squeezed, massaged and tugged at my dick and balls — all done gently and competently enough.

"Whoo. So wonderfully big for a boy not yet fully fourteen."

"Real man-size. Uhh!"

"Will our boyfriends ever be this big?"

"Five years from now this should be a giant!"

"Bigger than ninety-nine percent of all men, I should think."

"Hold the towel ready! He'll soon spurt!"

Sure enough, seconds later I was ejaculating. When Mr. Dickie had spent himself in the towel, one of them giggled: "That was really more fun than wanking my boyfriend."

My eyes were closed and remained closed in bitter embarrassment.

"Huh-uh. Certainly was."

I opened my eyes and they were both now kneeling on the bed, grinning down at me. Debra said huskily: "Big boy, I'm sexy. Debbie, go and stand guard at the window while he tongues me. Next time you'll get it first." Debbie sighed displeasure but moved off the bed. Debra stood and removed her panties, and my depressed spirits sank below earth when she commanded: "Now you eat my hot virgin pussy, big-dick boy. Let's see if your tongue is better than my boyfriend's. Remain on your back; I wanna ride your mouth." She bunched her little skirt above her waist and stepped over me.

A mixture of dismay and indignation robbed me of the delight I should have felt over seeing her golden brown thighs, lightly haired pelvis and glistening cunt — this gloomy anger was due to having grown up hearing that pussy eating was a nasty European habit that causes a black man's lips to get pink or blood red and overly fleshy. But it was now too late to disobey Debra and her twin. The matter was clinched by Debbie's snarl from across the room: "Big dick, don't think of biting or anything funny." Wasting her breath; as if I was stupid to risk having my dick twisted off.

I placated indignation and lightened the heavy dismay by reminding myself that the girls' rich older boyfriends gave them head without getting any real sex.

Debra kneeled lower, saying huskily: "Obviously this is your first time. Just lick it like a cone; suck gently, and kiss it like a mouth."

Her odour overwhelmed me and wasn't really awful, but the taste was most unpleasant. I almost gagged. I had to marshal reserve willpower by telling myself that millions of men did it.

Having to give both of them head one behind the other was a very arduous task; I didn't feel the least bit aroused. It was pure humiliation. The moment Debbie climaxed, I left the bed, dressed in clumsy haste, stumbled to the bathroom, and briskly caused myself to vomit. Then came brushing of teeth and a shower. My tongue and jaws began aching. Part of me was indignant towards the supposedly unofficial sisters, but the greater part of me was resigned to being their toy, unless they tried something that was a real health risk. The Chens' spacious home was much better for studying than any boarding house my Daddy could afford. Hell, no boarding house would feed my vast, inherited appetite half as well as Mrs. Chen was feeding me, and a great diet made learning easy.

I began feeling less humiliated. The bathroom was brightened by thoughts of a bright prosperous future that jumped to life while I dried off and got dressed.

Coming out of the bathroom, I saw the twins on the sofa in the living room. I rushed to my room to put on clean underwear, then strode out and turned down the passage towards them. There was a need for me to set a certain limit now. I sat down in the armchair closest to them. The radio was on. Without delay, I met their eyes and said: "Girls, you know your parents will send me away if they find out." My tone was calm as I wanted it. "I'd hate to leave here, but I'd rather leave than masturbate while you look."

With eyes narrowed on me, Debbie said: "We'll make certain our parents don't even suspect. Nothing risky. You masturbating? Mmm."

Debra intoned, "Oh I'm willing to forget about watching him masturbate." She giggled.

"Yeah," Debbie agreed, "that'd be a bit gross. Forget about that."

This was a sweet victory. I immediately tried for another. "If I am to continue ah.. tonguing your cunts you should give me blow jobs."

"Oh no!" bristled Debbie.

Debra snarled: "Certainly not! This is the age of the liberated woman, boy! A liberated woman will blow her main man, who must eat her regularly, but her minor lovers must eat her without getting any blow job."

"Correct," Debbie said. "Our boyfriends eat our cunts a lot more often than we blow them. We give them mostly hand jobs and after we marry them our temporary lovers will have to eat without getting blowjobs. See?"

The twins refusal to give me sex and blow jobs, while forcing me to eat their cunts and endure their toying with my dick, was a bitter reality. But enduring their prankish wanking wasn't completely bad — it did ease some sexual tension, although in a bittersweet way. My first year in Kingston was coming to a close and I still had not been able to get a city girl to bed, despite chatting up quite a few in and outside the Chens' neighbourhood. On the other hand, giving the twins head remained as distasteful — physically and emotionally — as it had been the first time. Thankfully, they didn't try anything as risky as applying their torture treatment at night after their parents went to bed. They limited their abuse to when their parents were out for quite a while and we were alone.

Mrs. Chen didn't go out much, so the girls' tortures were applied mainly on Saturday mornings, a time their parents often went out together to play golf, and the twins' friends almost never visited before noon on Saturdays (the maid didn't work on weekends). Twice I arranged to have friends pop by on Saturday mornings but the twins immediately realized what I was up to, and they put an instant end to these visits by threatening to have me thrown out of their home.

Occasionally on weekday evenings, Mrs. Chen would go visit a friend or relative outside our neighbourhood, and the minute the maid left for home one of the twins would order me to her bed, while the other did lookout duty.

Then there were those rare nights when Mr. and Mrs. Chen would go out together leaving the twins and I alone. On a more regular basis, Mr. and Mrs. Chen went out singularly at night with friends. The twins' night tortures were always a bit less humiliating than the more regular daylight torments, for they didn't use bright lights for the night scenes.

Those damn twins were insatiable in their delight in masturbating me and getting my head between their legs. I despised them but had to pretend otherwise, especially in the presence of their parents; it appeared best not to let the twins see more than half the depth of my intense dislike for them. Meantime, being genuinely fond of Mr. and Mrs. Chen made it possible for me to be truly happy enough whenever one or both of them was home with the devious twins and I.

My sexual tormentors continued giving me Kung Fu lessons whenever time allowed and we were not alone at home. Their sexual abuse
of me made the lessons bittersweet — bitter to have them teaching me
something I truly wanted to learn; sweet to think of someday knowing
enough Kung Fu to whip their butts.

When my fourteenth birthday arrived that June, the twins gave me
generous gifts but this didn't ease the secret contempt for them — I
would've refused the gifts if it were possible to do so without having
their parents know. The gifts I delighted in came from their parents
and my Dad; the nice gift from my stepmother wasn't a great delight
although I wasn't nursing any contempt towards her like that which I
had for the twins. I truly had forgiven.

The end of June meant the end of my first high school year. I'd
enjoyed every hour at school. The twins were to go spend the first
weeks of the summer with their US Chinese grandparents and other
relatives. Two days after the last day of the school year, they flew out
of the island. That same day, I journeyed to my hometown for the long
holidays. It was a journey of both joy and wariness — I was happily
looking forward to lots of real sex with Lorna, Joan, Anne and several
other girls; but I was worried about the appearance of my lips and I was
also uneasy about the weeks to be spent with Monica after Daddy went
away.

Near the end of the bus journey from Kingston to Highgate, I
began praying that even if I had to continue giving the twins regular
head during the four years I had left in high school, there would be no
worsening in the new pinkness and fleshiness I thought my lips had
began acquiring — although not a religious boy, I sensed there was a
God and that requests by prayers were often granted. I also prayed for
the hopeful possibility that the twins might go off to a US college
anytime after the end of the coming school year — their parents had
said that if this happened the twins would reside with their US
relatives. But if the worse happened, my Kung Fu and a good lie would
make certain that absolutely nobody teased me about my lips. When I

got off the mini-bus at the clock-tower market-gate square in Highgate, the immediate worry was if Monica would try to seduce me during the two to four weeks I'd be with her after Daddy went off. Last summer she had refrained from trying to lure me to her bed. But that was no guarantee against her renewing her sinful efforts this summer, especially if she was pregnant, as she'd been that wretched summer when she lured me to bed. Would she have tried seduction last summer if she'd been pregnant?

CHAPTER 23

The first couple days in my hometown rolled by without any comments about my lips. Neither did I notice any funny or sly looks directed at my mouth. Relief pumped up the spirits. I began wondering if it was mind over matter why I thought my lips had acquired a slight pinkish hue and a touch of puffiness in the previous weeks. Were my eyes playing tricks due to anxiety?

By the fifth day, I really began enjoying the holidays. It was good to laugh, chat and wrestle with Dad. It was a great joy to be amongst old pals, and not mainly because they were in awe of my minute Kung Fu skills. I was a bit like minor royalty about town — being a resident of Kingston was something to rural folks back then in the 1970s; and Calabar Boys' High was one of the island's oldest high schools; one of the best in academics and a giant in the top Jamaican sports of athletics, cricket and football; plus, Kung Fu was viewed as the king of martial arts and there wasn't any place in our parish to learn it. Also, my tall frame was beginning to take on the sleek, muscled look of a strong sprint athlete, thanks to bicycling and Kung Fu, and quite a few older women described my face as dangerously handsome.

Lorna, Joan, Anne and several other girls, welcomed my big dick with open legs; no hand jobs or oral sex, just plain good fucking. Ah, that summer was one great feast of sex. What a great joy after the many sexless months throughout my first high school year in Kingston; I'd be somewhat drained when I returned to the Chen household at the end of August.

During the weeks before Daddy's departure, there wasn't much tension around when he was out and I was at home with Monica and my baby half-sister (it was a great delight that he wasn't flown out in July, as in the previous two years). The day he left the island, I began feeling uneasy at nights. Within a few nights came nightmares of the twins chasing, capturing and tying me up for Monica to "rape". These nightmares came most nights during the two-and-a-half weeks I was alone with Monica and the baby. I was spending as much time as possible away from the house. But I was only fourteen and not an unruly boy, and my sex romps occurred mostly during daylight while parents were at work and/or out shopping, so most nights I was home by half past eight. Thankfully, Monica didn't try luring me to bed.

Between regular sexual exploits, bicycle riding, hanging out with friends and relatives around the small town and nearby villages, and a few visits to relatives further away, plus the tension between Monica and I, there wasn't much time that summer to think about the Chen twins and their sexual abuse. August quickly drew to a close and I returned to the Chens for the new school year.

The first day of the new school year was a few days away when I returned to Kingston. The twins had returned from the US over two weeks ago, and they had just spent time with their maternal grandparents on the island's tourist oriented north coast. Debbie gave me a good camping knife and a valued pair of jogging shoes, while Debra served up a smart leather windbreaker, mementos of their US trip. With empty smiles and thanks, I accepted the costly gifts. But after a while I'd find myself actually valuing their luxurious gifts, although my contempt for them remained strong — there at age fourteen, I was becoming highly materialistic.

By the end of September, my behaviour and performance at school began deteriorating, and I began having sadistic fantasies about the twins and their girl pals and any girl who refused to talk to me. Before October ended, my grades dived from good to average and my conduct became bold and somewhat reckless in class. But I was never a bully, although I was one of the biggest and strongest in our class, in addition to being the only martial arts student. Still, because I did my homework promptly and was getting passable marks in all subjects, was never late for school and never even thought of hiding from any class, I was able to use smiles and charm to disarm the teachers most of the time. So instead of many detentions and reports to the headmaster, I escaped with mostly a string of half-hard searching looks, warnings and reports to our form teacher, a cheerful thirty-odd year old math teacher who did no more than try talking gentle sense into my head. In those first two months of the second high school year, I became the most popular figure in our class, and was certainly one of the "Top Rankings" in the five classes of our year — big wit, acceptable academic performance, feared and respected as a fighter, kind with the generous flow of cash and goodies from the prosperous Chens. Also, it was now common knowledge that I had a man-size dick, which earned me the nice name "Charlie Man".

But I didn't do anything outrageous enough for a report to be made to the Chens, in whose presence my behaviour remained excellent.

Towards the end of that November, my sex life in Kingston took a change for the better, at long last.

CHAPTER 24

After school, on the last Friday of that November, I stopped off with a new friend at his home, which was less than half a mile from the Chens. It was wonderful to have a school friend living less than half a mile away; he was a new face in our class but in the few months since his inclusion, we had developed a tight friendship that felt years old. On our walk from the bus stop to his home, we had to pass the home of his girlfriend, who lived four houses away on his street. She was already home from school on that clear, late afternoon.

"Mark!" she called from her veranda. Mark and I turned into the open gates and strode up the short driveway.

"Her Mom car not here," Mark mumbled to me. "But you can bet Natalie is."

There was no need for him to say anything more. Days ago he had told me that over a week ago, Suzanne had agreed to giving him her virginity now that they were both fourteen (he was months older than her, and a month older than me), but so far they'd been unable to find the privacy to blast away her ignorance. I now murmured: "I'll handle the older one." Mark gave me a dubious grin that said Natalie was not interested in boys three years younger than her seventeen, even if he was big dick Charlie Man.

Suzanne stood when Mark and I walked on to her veranda. "Hi Charlie," she said pleasantly, having met me at Mark's home, but her smile was for Mark. She was a short, plump, light-brown complexioned girl. "Let's go have a drink," she said and led us by arms into the living-dining room where her older sister, Natalie, was curled up on the sofa with a romance novel. The girls were truly home alone — Mom was out shopping and visiting, and the helper didn't work on Fridays. I was introduced to Natalie — she appeared bored with her romance novel. Mark sat down in an armchair. Suzanne bounced out of the room to fetch cokes. Instead of sitting down I got to work instantly, sensing that this was the best opportunity for a fuck in Kingston — Natalie appeared bored enough to humour me.

"Natalie," I said boldly, "the best thing now is to come let me show you why they call me Charlie Man. You won't have to do more than look if that's all you wanna do."

A surprised frown graced her plain, light brown face. She was a big, tall girl, but her fleshiness wasn't the flabby sort. She put aside her novel and sat up before responding: "You one of those overgrown boys who think height and a little muscle make you a man, huh?"

Mark had a surprised grin and cocked ears.

"Lead me somewhere private and you'll see," I coaxed. "No need to fear me."

"Ha," she snorted, "the day I fear a younger boy. Really...surely you couldn't be thinking to...She leaped to her feet. "This mystery I must solve."

She sailed off across the room into a passage without another word or a backward glance. I winked at speechless Mark and trailed Natalie to her room, a spacious, comfortably furnished room splashed with bright colours. The louvre windows were half closed.

She sat down on her bed and declared: "Nothing funny. Just stand and show what you have to show."

Without delay, I said: "Girl, I wanna be your lover. That's why I'm going to show you that I'm more man than any boyfriend you have." I immediately closed the door behind me, then unbuckled and unzipped Mr. Dickie.

She gasped and sprang to her feet. Her face was flushed, mouth gaping, popping eyes glued to my rock hard dick. She huffed, puffed and licked her lips. I had been correct in assuming she was not one of the rare seventeen year old virgins.

"Am I not more man than any boyfriend you've had?"

She glanced up at my face but didn't respond. My erect dick was a magnet. Her eyes returned to it. She gulped, pressed her heavy thighs together, her fists clenched at her sides. Her mouth was now a little smile of wonder and lust.

Still standing by the door, I declared: "I have condoms in my bag. I'll go get one and give one to Mark."

She glanced up and huskily said: "You're an unusual boy." Her head bobbed.

I grinned, zipped in Mr. Dickie and hurried from the room, rushed down the passage to the living room where Mark and Suzanne were on the sofa holding hands. He eyed a big silent query to me. Suzanne said: "You want the drink? What's Natalie doing?"

"No drink," I said, taking up my school bag and digging out two condoms from the pack I had been travelling with for the past two months, in hope of an unexpected fuck in the city. I tossed one of the condoms to awestruck Mark and said: "You two go have some fun, while Natalie and I tackle a big problem."

With a huge wink I left them in incredulity: he beaming, she gaping.

Natalie was in bed when I re-entered her room. She had closed the thin curtains and the bottom half of the bank of louvre windows. I joined her on the bed, and noticed that she appeared a bit nervous. She said anxiously: "We can't stay long. Mom might be back soon." So without further delay I got down to business. No long kiss or fondling — shafted her within a minute and began a hard pace that promptly made her whimper for me to go easier. I reluctantly eased the pace, although her whimpering appeared to stir a powerful thrill deep within me. Resisting the voice urging me to try making her scream, I rode her at this easy pace until the throes of orgasm sent her thrashing and huffing. Then I went into a harder ride and quickly spent myself in her depths.

When I rolled off her, she was panting and groaning. She said:

"Charlie, your thing big bad, and you're strong, so you must be gentle. Otherwise I won't allow you inside me."

"Sorry if I hurt you, love. Honestly. From now on I'll be gentle as you want." I was sincere, and would always be gentle with her, no matter how the beast inside urged me to try making her scream. Although I didn't feel, and would never develop, any great love for her, it was fairly easy to treat her well because she was my first Kingston fuck and the sister of a good friend's number one girlfriend.

Mark and Suzanne had already blown away her virginity when Natalie and I joined them in the living-dining room.

"Suzanne, the soda would be good now," I declared, breaking the sisters' tension.

Thereafter I became a regular visitor to Mark's home, and together we'd go visit the girls frequently as possible. Of course, because Natalie was three years older than my fourteen, it wasn't possible for us to declare ourselves a couple like Mark and Suzanne. The girls' mother, Mrs. Jones, was often home when Mark and I popped by. Mr. Jones, of course, was your typical middle class father — never home before six on weekday evenings. To Mrs. Jones and everybody else, except Mark and Suzanne, Natalie and I were "good casual friends" due to three reasons: Mark and I were best friends, Suzanne was Mark's girl, and Suzanne liked me like a younger brother.

Mrs. Jones was a highly tolerant open-minded Christian housewife. She was one of those wiser humans who didn't place too much emphasis on looks. Deeds and words were what she mainly noticed and I was an angel in her presence. She was an energetic lady who liked doing much of her housework herself instead of hiring a full time helper or overworking the part-time one she used. But she often found time to make charitable visits to the sick and elderly in the late afternoon to evening period after collecting her two daughters from school. Mark and I were able to bed the girls on many of these afternoons; luckily, the sisters didn't have any good friends living nearby to intrude, and Natalie had broken off with her last boyfriend over the summer holidays.

Despite good honest intent towards Natalie, I often found myself tempted to try out on her some of the sadistic fantasies that were becoming more prominent in my dreams and thoughts, especially after one of the sexually torturous bouts at the hands of the cursed Chen twins. Of course, these fantasies featured mainly my so-called unofficial twin sisters, but also included were girls who acted stush (standoffish) with me on the streets and famous women I didn't like.

After a while, Natalie began walking or riding to visit me at the Chens, roughly once or twice most weeks. Generally she came alone and always in the late afternoon to evening period, other times she came with Mark and Suzanne. Whenever she came by alone, it was slyly done to avoid having her parents and friends knowing that she was visiting me by herself. After our affair was a few months old, we began to have the occasional movie and party dates in the company of Mark and Suzanne — here again we had to avoid any show of public intimacy if any friends were present. Neither Natalie nor I ever referred to "falling in love" — our affair was a sexual friendship; Mark and Suzanne accepted this.

Of course, after Natalie's second visit, the twins began pestering me about how close Natalie and I were. Although Mr. and Mrs. Chen would never appear to find anything odd about the older sister of my best friend's girlfriend stopping by to chat with me for a while, the damn twins quickly smelled a rat. When Natalie made her third or fourth visit by herself, I craftily asked her to try visiting me mainly on Saturday mornings — I was hoping that her coming by then would at least save me from a few of the unpleasant cunt tonguing I had to give the twins. Natalie, of course, didn't know about my unpleasant sexual ties with the damned twins.

Natalie phoned before her first Saturday morning visit. Her call came minutes before Mr. and Mrs. Chen left home for their regular Saturday morning golf. Minutes after the golfers left, I told the twins that Natalie was on her way to visit me. Of course, the news of Natalie's coming angered them.

"You asked her to come because you don't want to tongue us, right," Debra snapped, glowering from her seat, a statement, not a question. We were sitting on the veranda. I denied the truth of Debra's assertion.

Debbie said, "Think he's smart. But it won't do."

I willed aside the fair measure of fright in my guts, a stab of the old fear of their Kung Fu skills and power to have me evicted from the comfortable life their parents were giving me. Then my nice slice of indignation ballooned enough for me to say evenly: "You have your boyfriends, and there must be a few boys about here who would gladly give you girls head. I need real sex, and you girls won't even give me a blasted blow job."

Instead of further show of anger, their faces brightened and they grinned at each other. Debbie said: "Okay, big dick. You're free to sex her here this morning."

"Should be an interesting show," Debra intoned.

I retorted: "Don't expect me to allow you to watch."

They scowled, and Debra said: "Either we watch or scare her away." They sprang up from their chairs into Kung Fu stances.

"Plus a special punishment for you," Debbie said with a sadistic leer.

There was no sense in further resistance, and I was truly hungry for some sex. "You two are witches," I growled.

"The devil's favourite," Debbie mocked. "Trust us; we'll make certain she doesn't suspect you're on show."

From more than one angle, that Saturday morning should've taught me that not all that glitters is gold. Instead, I would become even more prone to lusting after every glitter on the horizon. Nearly a decade would bob pass before I began seeing this important and simple lesson; and even now I sometimes wonder if my life isn't still full of lust for fool's gold.

CHAPTER 25

Natalie rode her bicycle on to the scene. I was waiting at the gate. She looked uptight. Her smile was tense but her eyes held hints of sexual desire, and she looked damn sexy in jeans and a skimpy blouse. I immediately sensed what her problem was: she wanted sex that morning but was apprehensive that the twins would think little of her for bedding a boy three years younger, and would gossip about it to friends, gossip that could reach the ears of her friends or parents.

"Baby girl, I crave you," I whispered, as we started up the short drive way. I was pushing her bicycle.

"Should we?" Her whisper and eyes were a mix of misgivings and desire. "The twins..."

I interjected: "Lover, they are not like most schoolgirls. Trust me. They're more like you — mature. They'll keep it secret for me." I was feeling a bit awful about what I had agreed to with the twins. But lust and my obsession with remaining in the Chen household made it fairly easy to meet Natalie's gaze without any show of guilt.

"I don't know...we'll see."

The twins were in the living room playing records on the stereo. "Natalie, dear, how good to see you," Debbie said with a large smile when Natalie and I walked through the front door.

Natalie said: "Hi, both of you."

"Hi yourself," Debra said, wearing an ear-to-ear grin. "You know, Debbie and I are already planning your wedding to our little brother."

Natalie's brown face flushed to her hairline and neck. I was a bit alarmed.

Debra added: "It's stupid that people think a girl shouldn't get involved with a younger boy."

"Believe me," Debbie intoned, "in view of Charlie's unusually big size in body and other parts, I'd have been after him if he wasn't our unofficial brother and I didn't already have a big boyfriend."

"Debbie!" I exclaimed, truly alarmed, afraid to look at Natalie, who was rooted beside me just inside the front door. The twins were dancing on the big rug in the centre of the room.

Debra said: "Debs, it'd have meant war between us after the day we barged into his room and beheld his third leg, although my boyfriend is just as big."

For some reason beyond my male brain, this made Natalie giggle along with the twins. I glanced at her and saw that her worry was almost completely gone.

When the giggling subsided, Debbie said airily: "If you two want to be alone together, you best go now in case Mom and Dad return quickly."

"Yeah, Nat, I have a few things to show you," I said and grabbed a coke from the tray of iced cokes the twins had nearby, and took Natalie's arm. She came along without hesitation. I led her to my room. We gulped down the coke and fell on to my bed in a blaze of frenzied teen lust.

My room looked out on the roomy back veranda, and it was from there that the twins would be executing their cursed peeping via two neat openings they'd arranged in the half open louvre windows and the thick curtains where there was a group of big potted plants.

At first I felt uneasy with the knowledge that the twins were peeping. But before long, the pleasures of the flesh took over and the twins became nonexistent. Natalie and I moved through three different positions before I climaxed less than a minute after her orgasm. A minute later we went to the bathroom for a quick shower — she had to hurry back home, and I knew the twins might do something stupid if I delayed too long.

The twins pretended indifference when Natalie and I joined them on the front veranda. They really were good at deceit. I was tempted to try outsmarting them by announcing that I was going to accompany Natalie home, but Debra killed this plan by saying: "Charlie, we better go tackle the backyard before Mom returns." Her eyes flashed a deadly promise if I failed to fall in line.

"Yeah," I said.

A minute later, Natalie mounted her bicycle and rode away.

It wasn't yet ten o'clock so the twins immediately ordered me to their room — they literally frog marched me inside. Both of them tore off their clothes and jumped into the bed with me, instead of the usual act of one standing guard. For the first time I had to tongue both of them simultaneously, flicking my head from one to the other every few seconds until Debra was able to convince Debbie to let her climax first — that's how much they'd gotten turned on by watching me fuck Natalie. It was easily the hardest head job they'd ever demanded of me.

Debra climaxed noisily and Debbie immediately hauled my buzzing head to her crotch.

The moment Debbie climaxed I began leaving the bed to go wash and gargle my mouth in the bathroom. Debra, who was now dressed and sitting on the edge of the bed, stopped me by grabbing my wrist and saying: "Oh boy you and Natalie were wild. Get her to come regularly on Saturday mornings."

Debbie, sighing through the lingering ecstasy of her drawn out orgasm, purred: "Charlie, you were amazing for a fourteen year-old. Where did you learn so much?" Her brows froze in the elevated position.

I shrugged, pretending indifference, even though I was feeling proud of having impressed them; and although I was in the usual hurry to go scrub the disagreeable taste of their cunts from my mouth, I said: "Why not just try me?"

"No, not until after high school."

"We made a vow on our Kung Fu and feminist honours."

I hissed my teeth and said: "Both of you scared of the real thing."

"After high school, you'll see," Debra said. "A Kung Fu-feminist vow must stand."

At that moment I saw that they'd really stick to their vows and would execute their devious plans for married life to their wimpy boyfriends. I tried to escape Debra's hold on my wrist. She resisted and said: "One question, brother. Don't you and Natalie do oral sex?"

"Never," I replied truthfully, literally sneering. "We don't need that."

Debbie said: "Natalie is a fool."

Debra nodded agreement and released me. I rushed to the bathroom for the overdue mouth scrub.

Thereafter, between the twins' liking for peeping at live sex and my own delight in sex, I helped Natalie to concoct a variety of lies to trick her Mom and friends for her to be able to visit me alone fairly regularly on Saturday mornings.

Natalie, not suspecting that the twins and I were using her as a show piece and bargaining chip, grew genuinely fond of the twin witches. I wasn't proud of deceiving Natalie; but, in addition to the reality that Natalie wasn't in any physical danger, I soothed the guilt by reminding myself that she wasn't in love with me. I felt that there was a strong chance of getting sex from them soon after they gave up their virginities, and was dreaming of giving them some hard rides before they got engaged.

The rest of my second high school year flowed on in this manner; and the ensuing summer holidays was much the same as the year before.

After spending the summer in the hometown, it was back to the Chens in Kingston for the start of my third high school year that September of 1978. The twins were now lawful adults, eighteen years old. During the summer holidays they'd attained their Kung Fu black belts while in the USA, had cut their hair into bobs, and they'd received good results for the GCE O' Level exams they had sat in June. On my first day back in Kingston, they proudly told me that they'd given their boyfriends their virginities during the summer and were unofficially engaged — their wimpy boyfriends did appear more enslaved and happily resigned to the twins' rule.

Towards the end of September, two weeks after the start of my third form high school year, the twins began their high school's two year sixth form GCE A' Level class, and they did look swell in the sixth form jacket and tie styled uniform. Of course, since my first week back in their home at the beginning of September, they had resumed torturing me in their bedroom, continued refusing to give me real sex, insisting that I'd have to wait until after they became officially engaged at the end of the two year sixth form GCE A' Level program. Their wanking of my dick and the taste of their cunts were no different now that their virginities had been blasted away. I was no gloomier about all this than before. In fact, I was more upbeat than I had been before the summer, for I now sensed that they would give me real sex long before the end of the two years of sixth form.

Natalie had done very well in the GCE O' Levels of that year, good enough so that instead of going on sixth form, she was able to enter the University of the West Indies. We continued to be lovers but her heavy first year university workload caused a great drop in the frequency of our fucking. By the end of October, I was desperate to find a new lover in the city to make up for the big fall in the regularity of sex with Natalie; regular bouts of real sex made it a hell of a lot easier to deal with the twins' humiliating demands. Fittingly enough, at the beginning of November, it was Natalie who set me on the track to finding another lover in the city.

CHAPTER 26

Late in the afternoon on a weekday in the first week of that November, Natalie and I were taking a leisurely walk after one of our newly rare sexual encounters — this one had occurred in her bed, as that day she wasn't buried under school work and her mother was out on a charity visit. Mark and Suzanne, had chosen to remain at the house enjoying their own sexual after glow. When we were roughly quarter mile from her house, she pointed her chin at half the house we were walking by and said with distaste, "A lesbian couple occupy that side." Instantly, as if on cue, the front door of the lesbian-nest opened, and out stepped a mightily voluptuous young lady of medium height. Natalie added in a whisper, "There's the wife."

I pretended disapproval of the lesbian lady but I had long had a strong fantasy about bedding a lesbian, although I had never met one. "How you know they're lesbians?"

"Well, lover boy," Natalie said, "up to about five months ago they were living next door to one of my friends in Cherry Gardens. I know their faces well, and, guess what, the so-called husband, a white Ad executive, kind of resembles a man. A few days ago I was passing by and saw both of them getting out of the she-he's car."

"Silly women." I shrugged. But I had to look away from Natalie to hide excitement at the thought of bedding that sexy, black, young lesbian and then charm her into getting her white lover in a three-some.

In one of life's incredible twists, the following afternoon dished up a remarkable hand of luck that still amazes me now, over a decade later.

As was usual, Mark and I left school together. We didn't linger after the last bell, and were lucky enough to get a bus within minutes after school ended in the mid-afternoon. I didn't bother to get off with him at his bus stop, knowing that Natalie would be on campus until evening and Mark was expecting a cousin to visit. Then, on a spur of the moment impulse I got off at the next stop, which was two stops before mine, and turned up the avenue on which the black-white lesbian couple lived. The November afternoon was overcast. There were large displays of dark clouds drifting in from over the northeast mountains looming beyond the mansion-dotted hills over-looking the city. Those clouds and the slight breeze heralded rain. Well, a taxi pulled up at the gate of the lesbian nest when I was three houses away, and out popped the sexy "wife" with a big shopping bag. The taxi sped away. My heart and mind went into high speed. Should I hail her immediately?

I moved faster towards her just as the intended prey opened her gate, and there was a sudden jarring roar of thunder and a blinding flash of lightning. The lady was severely frightened — she jumped backward, the paper grocery bag slipped downward, and in her unsteady effort to prevent the bag from falling, she tore it. Vegetables, yam and meat hit the pavement of the gateway. Then there came rain roaring towards the city off the distant mountains.

With a heart singing praises to fate, I bounded forward to help her pick up the foodstuff. I jumped to the task with a hasty hello and my most boyish grin. She neither spoke nor smiled, but there was no indication that she felt anything but gratitude at having a strange, schoolboy helping in her hour of need. Then the rain was bearing down on us in a mighty roar.

Holding a chicken and a cabbage in one hand and a long leg of yam in the other, with my school bag over a shoulder, I jogged beside my scurrying prey up the driveway. She had the torn grocery bag clutched to her venerable bosom. The rain, a fairly thick downpour, caught us halfway up the short driveway. Our clothes were damp when we reached the safety of the empty double carport — obviously, half was for each of the two similar apartments that made up the big one storey house. There was a veranda on each side of the carport. The young lesbian stepped up onto the veranda to our right. I followed.

"Thank you," she panted and smiled. It was a lovely smile that displayed strong, even, glistening white teeth. Now I saw that she looked no more than twenty-one, younger than I had first assumed. "You'll have to stay till it holds up, and that may be a while," she remarked, her lovely bosom still heaving.

I, of course, was pretending to be a shy boy, but my heart was drumming joy and praying for the rain to keep pouring down for a long, long time. She, clutching the torn grocery bag, fished a key from her little purse. She opened the front door. "Come on in. You deserve a drink."

This boy hunting more than that, I thought, entering the semi-dark living room. She flicked on the big chandelier hanging from the centre of the ceiling. Brilliant light flooded the long room. I followed her to the small kitchen, admiring her brisk, hip swinging walk and the lovely black legs flowing from under her mini-skirt. She flicked on the kitchen light. Her short, brownish, rain-wet hair glittered in the brilliant light. I placed my burden on the spotless yellow counter. Outside the half-open louvre windows, rain darkened the afternoon.

"I'm Charlie. I live over on Fairfax Drive." I smiled into her pretty black face that, added to her remarkable figure, made her an awesome beauty.

She smiled in return and declared: "I'm Melody." Something about the prominent, wide-set eyes of her luminous face, told me she was a bold, passionate, impetuous young lady who wouldn't refuse any reasonable challenge. My original intention had been to build a strong friendship with this young lady before trying to become her lover. Now the bold, horny impetuous aspect I saw about her killed that original plan for a friendship start.

"Recently," I said with a racing heart and a grin, "someone told me that you and the lady you live with are lesbians."

Her face flashed surprise and defiance. I hastily added: "Not that I disapprove. It's just that I've heard some contrary things about lesbians."

The rain roared in our silence. The three feet of space between us vibrated.

Her searching look quickly became a grin. "To think I had you down for a shy boy. How old are you?"

"Fifteen."

Her brows flicked way up. "Is it that you're a homo? Perhaps only by fantasies?"

"No. Nothing of the sort."

She shrugged: "I'm not ashamed of what I am." Her tone was even. "I tried several men and none were as caring and understanding as my lady."

"Why not try me?"

"You're a boy," she laughed. "What good could a boy be?"

"Depends on the boy."

She chuckled. "You certainly fooled me, not the big shy boy I saw at first! Anyway I'm not interested in sex with males at this point in life." She turned to the refrigerator, her back to me.

I pulled my belt, opened the pants zipper, and, praying that I was correct in my assessment of her, I eased out my erection. Lightning flashed modestly across the backyard outside the window. There was a low distant rumble of thunder. The rain continued pouring down heavily but the afternoon brightened somewhat.

Melody turned from the refrigerator with a big bottle of orange squash in hand. She gasped and froze. Her eyes got as round as saucers.

Grinning, I asked: "Afraid, or just surprised at my man size?"

"Why would I be afraid?" she replied a bit huskily glancing up into my face; instantly her eyes returned downward to the erect dick. Alongside a few nods she said: "It truly is very, very impressive for a boy. Never knew a boy could be that big."

"I say you're afraid" — she looked up into my face — "of it. But no harm would befall you. Try me if you're not a softie."

"Of all the cheek!" She stepped forward and slammed the bottle of orange squash onto the kitchen counter, then turned to me and said saucily: "I'd teach you a lesson if I had a condom."

"I've three!"

"Well, let's go see who is the boss, huh?" She strode off and led me directly to what she said was the guest bedroom. She closed the slightly open louvre windows and turned on the overhead light. It was a dull and sparsely furnished room, the opposite of the rest of the flat — obviously she and her lover weren't big on stopover guests. Rain continued washing the afternoon. She began undressing. Her medium height body was full of lush curves in the right places. Her even-toned skin was like the best black silk.

Pulsing elated triumph, I was tearing off my khaki school clothes. At last, I'd have my first lesbian. It didn't matter much that she'd had men before me. I wanted to experience a wide variety of women.

We tumbled on to the bed. What followed was the clash of two passionate competitors who initially were wary of hurting the other — I wanted to show her I was more than just an unusually big-dicked boy and I was hoping for a long affair with her. After about three minutes of caressing and kissing, she sighed, concerned about the strength of my back. At the same time, I was so excited that my first lesbian was also a great beauty and over nineteen years old, that it took a lot of willpower to resist the strong urge to plunge into her instantly instead of showing her what I knew about foreplay. I held this fierce brutish impulse in check and kissed and caressed her for quite a while, all in the style I used with Natalie, no kisses below the breasts.

Melody's kisses and tender caresses were a lot more skilful than Natalie's, or any of the many lovers I'd had in my hometown. Twice she tried forcing me on to my back but I resisted in a loving manner — my arms were somewhat stronger than hers. When I shafted her moist cunt I didn't last as long as I'd wanted to and she didn't climax. But when I rolled off her, she sighed and said: "You really are some boy. Huh-uh. Somewhat better than most of the men I've tried."

"I'm not through yet," I said, and dragged her back down from the sitting position she'd just risen to.

She didn't resist. "Greedy," she said. Her lips sought mine and I knew this was the beginning of a long-term affair. "Greedy, naughty big boy."

The quick reawakening ability of teenage hormones took effect swiftly. Our second time began as tenderly as the first, but a minute after I shafted her, our rhythm became hectic as I now knew she wasn't afraid of a hard enough man-ride; and I was confident she now realized that my stamina and back were manly like my dick. I gave a better account of myself. This time she climaxed; an intense body-rippling orgasm that fired me into a panting explosion.

"That was great," she said when we lay spent beside each other. "No male can take the place of my lady, see? But you're such a unique boy I wouldn't mind having you come by one or two weekday afternoons; that's if you're willing to be discreet so that my lady Nancy doesn't find out."

Thereafter, I visited Melody one or two afternoons between Mondays and Fridays. Most times I went there straight from school, both of us reasoning that my school uniform would lessen the suspicion of neighbours. One of the greatest joys of our steamy affair was that she didn't show the slightest interest in oral sex with me; of course, I knew oral sex was a major force in lesbian life. We usually spent at least an hour in the guest bedroom. She refused to allow me into the bed she shared with her ladylove, Nancy.

Melody was a big talker, and even way back then I was a great listener, so naturally, I learned a lot about her life.

Twenty-one years old and not college educated, Melody was from an upper-middle class family in the island's famed tourist city, Montego Bay. Her sexual experience had begun with men. She lost her virginity just before her fifteenth birthday, then had sexual affairs with several males of her age and older, before meeting the man she married after her eighteenth birthday. She had met him three weeks before her eighteenth birthday, and months later she abandoned a college education to marry him, a business executive from a wealthy Montego Bay family. He was ten years older than her. The marriage lasted only six months.

Shortly after the honeymoon she found out that he was a great cheat, and a week after she confronted him about his infidelity, he battered her over an absurd claim that she was having an affair with a retired, widowed dentist living nearby. Then, just over a week later he gave her a second beating, this time accusing her of sleeping with her cousin. She returned to her parents' home the next day. Not long after this, she was on a beach just outside Montego Bay and was approached by Nancy, who briskly seduced her into lesbianism and instantly whisked her off to Kingston. When I entered the picture they had been living together for over one and half years.

Nancy was a college educated, American blonde in her middle thirties who had always favoured voluptuous Afro girls of all complexions. She had fallen in love with Jamaica on her first visit to the island twelve years before meeting Melody, and had migrated to the island over a year later. Shortly after her move to Jamaica, she got a job in Kingston. Her private life rolled forth with a Jamaican girl popping in and out every few months or so. When she met Melody she had just lost her first long-term live-in Jamaican lover to a man.

I saw only pictures of Nancy until an unforgettable afternoon in late March 1979 — by this time, Melody and I had been lovers for over four months — when she came home unexpectedly and caught Melody and I in bed. To my honest regret, youthful zest and the powerful bottled-up sadistic fantasies about the tormenting Chen twins, led me to commit one of the most disgusting acts of my life.

CHAPTER 27

I was deep inside Melody's moist, meaty cunt doggy fashion, one hand on her plump love-mound, with a finger on her clit, my other hand massaging her solar plexus. Both of us were kneeling on the bed. One side of her face was buried in a pillow, her mouth turned sideways and emitting a near-continuous flow of dog-like sounds. Occasionally I added a growl to her erotic humour. Both of us were buck-naked — at times she liked us to have sex partially clothed. As usual we were in the guest bedroom.

There was a loud gasp, followed by a low heart-tearing "Noo! Oh God, no!" My head snapped around and got the first flesh-and-blood look at Melody's Euro-American lover, Nancy. She was transfixed in the doorway, her bronzed face drained, eyes on the verge of leaping from their deep sockets (quite likely she was remembering how she'd lost her only other long-term Jamaican live-in lover to a man). She was in a well-tailored, plaid, three piece pants suit, that, along with close cropped, mannish-styled blonde hair, low heels and thin figure, made her look like a weak little man of medium height. Her plain face and the fact that she didn't pluck her bushy eyebrows further enhanced her male appearance. Melody had forgotten to lock the front door, an extra precaution against any unexpected and highly unlikely happening like the touchy reality now exploding on us. "Nancy!" cried Melody.

Seconds continued floating by while Nancy gaped at the bed scene. Melody and I were still locked in the doggy sex position but unmoving and staring over shoulders at Miss-Mr. Nancy. Then suddenly, Nancy was pure rage. "Get away from her, you beast!" she snarled, eyes blazing, and stalked across the room.

I flew backward out of Melody's cunt to stand by the bed. I felt no fear; a unique excitement was in my gut and expanding rapidly, the condom-sheathed Mr. Dickie returned to iron hardness. I grinned at the fake-man. She halted about four feet from me and took a little step backward — my defiant posture and grin were sapping her anger rapidly. Still, she pointed at the door and snapped: "Get out!"

A part of me knew it was best to leave. But I stood and served up a mock glower. On top of the uncompleted fuck with Melody, there was the sudden powerful crave to fuck Nancy. But, before I could respond to Nancy, Melody's sexy naked body sprang between us.

"Nancy, please, no violence," pleaded Melody. "He's just a fifteen year old school boy."

Nancy's face flashed a fleeting look of surprise, but the anger returned and she immediately delivered two hard slaps to Melody's face. Melody stepped aside and sobbed in an open-eyed fashion that hummed indignation: "So now you're going to be like my ex-husband."

A surreal anger flooded me but I still had enough wisdom and self-control to keep my voice somewhat even when I said: "Melody, what she wants is a good fuck. Come on; help me give her a nice little fuck. That will make her return to being loving towards you, and a friend to me; a happy three-some ending." My bizarre anger vanished, leaving me pulsing sheer lust.

Nancy turned to me. Her face was showing the first big hints of fear but she snapped: "Get out of our home!"

Grinning at her but without moving, I coaxed: "Don't be afraid of the size of my thing." Mr. Dickie lurched at her. "I'll be gentle. Be a sport."

A weak smile lit Melody's tear streaked face and she said: "I think it's true that she's never had a man, though once in a long while she allows a small vibrator or dildo to be used on her. Plus, she is thirty-five, so a man fuck won't kill her."

"And," I intoned, "it'll make her accept me as a pal. We'll be three the loving way. Hey, hey, hey!"

Nancy was backing up, her eyes now glued to my mighty erection. Her fear had swiftly ballooned to terror that rendered her speechless. Melody said: "Go ahead, grab her."

I grabbed the fake-man just as she turned to flee the room. Her little frame was no match for my burning, oversized, country-bred, fifteen year old body. Two powerful shoves propelled her to the bed. She landed face down. I dived in and rolled across her thighs. Melody imprisoned the hands and dragged them above the thrashing head.

"Melody, no," pleaded Nancy in low terrified tones, "don't do this to me. I'll die."

"No, you won't, darling," coaxed Melody. "Just relax."

"Please, no, don't," the prey pleaded and whimpered. Melody continued helping me to hold her on her belly, while I peeled off her clothes. Melody was using soothing words to downplay Nancy's pleas and whimpers and futile struggling. I knew she wouldn't back down now. Quickly we had Nancy naked as ourselves — the moderate patch of hair on her front was similar to the cropped blonde hair on her head. But just as her face couldn't be called pretty, her body wasn't what could be termed sexy. On the other hand, she was the first naked Euro woman I was seeing in the flesh, and I was about to be the first man to fuck her. She had a large clit and she was definitely pure female.

Well, I was far too excited to try calming her with foreplay. Her drained face, terrified whimpers and useless efforts to escape were boosting the new excitement bubbling within me. With Melody still holding the hands above the head, it was easy for me to spread the thin thighs and use my shoulders and one arm to pin the knees to the little breasts. My sheathed erection found the target instantly. I jammed. But, although the condom was a lubricated type and was also coated with Melody's love juice, I just couldn't enter Nancy with that first thrust. Before I could make a second attempt to enter, she released a piercing scream that knocked me to my senses. I leapt off her, horrified that I had come so close to doing a truly evil deed.

Nancy began weeping the moment I eased away from her. Rising shame forced me to avoid her eyes. I began dressing.

"Oh God!" Melody cried. "I almost helped you to rape her!" She looked as ashamed as I felt. Then she actually snarled at me: "You dirty prick! I don't want to see you again! Ever! You hear!"

Resisting the urge to remind her that she'd been an eager accomplice, and that it was I who broke the evil spell when Nancy screamed, I hurried from the room, filled with self-disgust, part of which was due to a lingering little touch of the sadistic delight I had felt during the near-evil deed just done. Hurrying out of the house, I tried soothing twisted emotions by reminding myself that I hadn't raped Nancy, and I vowed that thereafter I'd be extra kind to true lesbians like Nancy.

I would see Melody and Nancy a few weeks later at their gate but they walked away when I began declaring a sincere apology. Thereafter, the few times I'd see them singularly or together, they'd refuse to give me a second glance, and it appeared best to leave them with their hostility.

Hopefully, someday I will be able to get Nancy to accept my burning apology.

Life returned to normal after the horrible assault on Nancy: sex with Natalie occasionally; the humiliation of being the twins' toy; happy times with Mr. and Mrs. Chen; a jolly school life; fun with my city pals at house parties, sport events, reggae dancehalls and movies. A great new aspect to life was that, at last, I was now friendly with a few girls in the city who appeared willing to give me some sex — unfortunately there was no convenient place to get into these tender, choosy, middle class schoolgirls. The truly big new difference to my life was that, despite remorse over mauling Nancy, the sadistic urge that had been born out of having to endure the twins' humiliating sexual torture, was now a true force nagging me to get into some sadistic experimenting with females who "deserved it".

That third high school year ended. Summer was pretty much the same as the two preceding ones. September meant returning to the Chen household in the city to begin the fourth high school year at Calabar, and to continue being the twins' toy, while still having a hard time finding somewhere to get sex from my would-be city lovers. Then 1979 ended and 1980 began with strong expectation for national elections before December. This anticipation caused a bloody, sharp increase in political violence in the ghettoes of Kingston, further fuelling my ambitious country bred dislike for those crude areas.

In the first week of January 1980, the Chens served up an announcement that turned the world upside-down, and brought a change for the worse.

CHAPTER 28

The Chens declared that they had decided to move life to the USA at the beginning of February. But they had a plan to help me. Unfortunately, their plan would turn out to be a time bomb fashioned like a bouquet of roses.

Mr. Chen's wealthy US parents and other close relatives had made him a sudden business offer he just couldn't resist. The offer meant he'd have to begin residing in New York by the first day of March and the twins would enter a posh US college that the Chen clan favoured.

"But, of course, dear Charlie, we couldn't leave you hanging," Mrs. Chen was saying to me after announcing the family's migration plan. It was a Wednesday night. The family and I had just finished a light supper of sorrel and ripe banana and cornmeal muffins. We were still at the dining table. With her maternal smile, Mrs. Chen continued: "Miss Fraser has offered to give you a home for as long as necessary."

"We'll continue to help you, my boy," intoned Mr Chen.

I forced a smile for the adults but ignored the twins.

Mrs. Chen added: "As I told your Dad on the phone today, we simply had no control over the suddenness of this move. Anyway, Miss Fraser is already assuming you'll be with her up to university level. As you already know, she likes you. A dear soul she is. I'm certain you'll both get along real fine."

I knew I'd miss Mr. and Mrs. Chen, and my ego would suffer a great cut to have the twins go away without a chance to fuck even one of them. But, seeing that I knew Miss Fraser as a nice, decent, generous, middle-class and open-minded young Christian lady, I was glad that I'd soon be free of the twins' humiliating tyranny.

Miss Fraser was an active member of the Chens' church and a fairly regular visitor to the home. Mrs. Chen visited her in similar fashion. The younger sister of Mrs. Chen's life-long best friend, who had migrated with her husband and kids to the US almost three years before, Miss Fraser with whom I'd soon be living, was a young, single, junior business executive, one of the new breed of college educated middle-class Jamaican women, who placed high-powered careers firmly ahead of the traditionally more important acquisition of husband and children. She was of medium height and trim figure, and had a lovely, luscious, dark complexion. Her regularly straightened hair was short, thick and a glowing black. She had a narrow face with bold features. Her whole aspect oozed confidence.

I was certain we'd get along fine. To enjoy the comforts of her middle class home, while completing high school, I was willing to be a dutiful, charming, Christian boy in her world. I'd keep my carnal side far away from her.

On the Saturday afternoon after I learned of the Chen's impending migration, Miss Fraser paid us a visit. Not long after her arrival, I was called away from homework to join her and Mrs. Chen on the front veranda.

"Well, Charlie," Miss Fraser greeted me with a fond smile, "I'm real pleased that you'll soon be my unofficial son. I'm only thirty, just fourteen years your senior. But all over the world there are thirty year old mothers with sixteen year old sons — not the best thing for a woman but life is like that!"

I was returning her smile from my standing position facing the veranda chair she and Mrs. Chen were on. They laughed. I beamed brighter and nodded.

Miss Fraser continued: "My boy, all I ask is that you continue behaving as well as you've been doing with Mrs Chen and do your best at school. Like dear Mrs. Chen, I won't force my religion on you. I'm not rich but my parents need no financial help so I can afford a son.

"Mrs. Chen tells me you're good at Kung Fu. Wonderful! With you in my apartment, I'll feel a lot safer than I now do by my martially unlearned-self!" The three of us chuckled at her wit. She resumed: "Also, I assure you that if I should meet an eligible husband next week, next month, or whenever, there'll be no wedding if he cannot accept that my home is yours until you complete your education and start on your chosen career. All we need now is your father's permission."

Of course, four days later when Daddy met Miss Fraser, it didn't take him ten minutes to decide she was a perfect guardian. Right in my presence, he let it be known he was glad she was a strong Christian woman who wouldn't allow me to do as I pleased. She said he was what all fathers should be. With a disarming smile, she waved aside his asking about the cost of feeding me, declaring that food and utilities would not be a burden to her and that my companionship would be more than worth it to her.

It was decided that I should move to Miss Fraser's chic Constant Spring Road apartment ten days before the Chens were to leave the island. The twins bid me special farewell two days before I changed residence.

"We shall truly miss you," Debra said with a lengthy sigh.

Debbie intoned: "A lot." The three of us were sitting on the front veranda. It was a Thursday evening. The tropical winter sun was about to leave the city. Mrs. Chen was next door. Mr. Chen hadn't arrived home as yet. "Sorry you can't emigrate with us."

"Yeah," I said acidly, "and I shall miss your humiliating usage of me."

"A pity you didn't learn to enjoy tonguing us."

I snapped: "Maybe I wouldn't have minded it much if even one of you were honest enough to even give me head. Anyway, why not try real sex with me before we part?" I was holding back the urge to vent the full weight of my bitterness towards them — they had a bit of power over the comfortable middle class life I wanted to continue in with Miss Fraser.

"Forget about any of that," Debra said. "And believe me, the wanking of your dick and riding of your tongue aren't the only reasons we shall miss you."

Debbie said: "You are good company, and a good Kung Fu student."

"I understand, dear sisters," said I ironically.

"Anyway, little big brother," Debra said, "here is our farewell gift." She held out an envelope with money. A part of me wanted to tell her to stuff it up her cunt. I took the envelope, telling myself that it was the perfect thing to begin the serious saving plan I'd been thinking of in the past few months. There was five hundred Jamaican dollars in the envelope, a lot of money to a sixteen year old in 1980, especially one from my background.

That Saturday afternoon I moved to Miss Fraser's comfortable apartment. She had prepared the spare bedroom with all the middle class comforts a sixteen year old boy needed. And from day one, she was generous with food, money and everything in her comfortable home. The first week was pleasant, as I'd expected, but on the evening of the eighth day — a Sunday, two days before the Chens flew out of the island — she gave me a chat that was to broaden my horizon, providing an uneasy view of a new, and a peep at the real, Miss Fraser. This shockingly unexpected eye-opening chat, was to be the first step into another distasteful chapter of my tortured youth.

CHAPTER 29

Miss Fraser's two-bedroom apartment was on the second floor of a relatively new apartment building in the middle sector of Constant Spring Road, one of Kingston's major uptown arteries, a road of varying width that was lined with a mix of commercial and residential areas. This new home of mine was less than a mile from school. The four-storey, U-shaped building, had three small lobbies with elevators and stairs, and it overlooked a rectangular courtyard that faced the backyard. There was a modest sized pool towards the open end of this courtyard, with a tennis court beyond in the backyard lawn, which was dotted with little circles of shrubs and fringed by a scattering of young fruit and hardwood trees growing close to a nine foot high concrete fence topped by barbwire. Most of the sixty apartments (a balanced mix of one, two and three bedroom units) were occupied by childless, unmarried, young professional couples and married ones with young kids — it was obvious that the majority of these college educated folks were of solid upper-middle income background. The building was fronted by an open car-park that extended to a narrow strip of lawn running along the base of the front fence. In the centre of this fence was the twenty-four hour manned security post at the sole entrance-exit to the grounds.

Miss Fraser said her two-bedroom apartment was more than a home: "It's an investment," she said, "bought with the help of my parents and the bank." The tiny entrance hall led to a L-shaped living-dining room that had French doors at the elbow, providing access to a small balcony overlooking the building's courtyard; there was a similar balcony on the master bedroom. Like the bathroom, the kitchen was a little wonder, constructed efficiently to appear bigger than they actually were.

"You've been here a week," Miss Fraser said on the unforgettable Sunday afternoon. "Time now to lay down certain facts, which should begin the process of broadening your horizon." Her tone was cool like the end-of-January late afternoon breeze caressing us in our comfortable arm chairs on the balcony adjoining the living-dining room. We'd just finished a pleasing version of the usual Jamaican Sunday afternoon dinner. As usual, the lady was looking chic, now wearing a floral dress and sporting a modest coat of carefully applied make-up: I was having a successful go in the endeavour not to lust at her, viewing her as an attractive aunt or older sister. She continued coolly as she'd begun: "I'm a real feminist who knows it's my duty to do all I can to make the next and all future generations of men," (my flying soul began falling, and I broke our eye contact), "recognize women as their equal in all things. That's why I jumped at the chance to take you on. I'd like to see you become a man who truly appreciates women — knowing that we aren't sex objects, cooks, maids and reproductive machines."

I now did what appeared best for the dream future: fix the finest possible stoical expression and flick eyes up from the sexy females in the pool below at ground level to meet Miss Fraser's appraising gaze. The little second floor balcony suddenly felt crowded and ten stories above the pool.

She continued: "I do hope it isn't already too late. In my heart I'm almost certain it isn't, seeing that for the past three-and-a-half years you've been with Mrs. Chen, who — although a housewife — isn't backward on women's rights. And, of course, her daughters are true little teen feminists."

I managed to swallow a gasp but my eyes must have shown part of the shock and dismay, causing Miss Fraser to smile complacently before saying: "Yes, I expect Debbie's and Debra's immaturity made them a bit erratic in their desire to have a positive influence on you." (I now remembered how the twins had always appeared extra jaunty after visiting Miss Fraser without their Mom along.)

"Anyway," she was saying, "you shall not support music, books, magazines and movies that present women in a degrading light. I shall guide you in these areas." She paused to give me a searching look. For a few heavy seconds I laboured to meet her gaze and then I smiled shyly and looked off at the near cloud-free sky.

Of course, I didn't like the direction of her lecture. The prudent thing, it seemed, was to remain calm and stoical. Besides, in any case, I knew that throughout the ages women had been harshly treated in most societies, and I truly believed they deserved equal career opportunities and pay. But what did most erotic movies, music and literature have to do with women's rights?

In a more passionate voice, she ended the little pause by saying: "Charlie, I'd like you to be bold enough to object when your friends and older males you know air dirty jokes. Think carefully and you'll see that a man telling dirty jokes about women is encouraging cruelty in society. Strong men avoid that kind of behaviour. Begin moving towards becoming a truly strong man."

I gave her a studious look and a couple of thoughtful nods. But I was wondering where the hell all this was leading to, if she wasn't aware that dirty jokes mock men, too.

"Women are the main foundation of life," she stated passionately. "We are the ones who have the greater control over the life and death of each and every child. And because a man can impregnate many women in a year, while a woman can have only one pregnancy per year, the survival of the human race is more dependent on an abundance of female children. Then there are the facts that we are more cautious, compassionate and loving than men. Put all that together and it's obvious that if either of the sexes should be boss, woman is better equipped. But I'm not for women ruling men, or trying to get revenge for past male tyranny. Equality in all things is the issue." She paused briefly as if to gather her thoughts, then she pressed on:

"Until women enjoy equality in all areas there'll be no chance for lasting peace on earth. Thousands of years of male rule have delivered nothing but wars and crude societies. When women get hold of anything near half the power in this world, you'll find that peace and truly humane societies will stand a great chance of becoming a reality." She paused. I turned a sincere admiring smile on her, as this last statement had a ring of truth to my sixteen year old ears. Her face showed delight in my open admiration. She said: "Perhaps the hardest challenge facing women is sexual exploitation at the workplace." Then she appeared to drift away, her face taking on a hard aspect, as if remembering unpleasant experiences.

I wondered if she'd ever received sex-for-promotion offers at her workplace, and had she accepted or refused? Had she ever attempted to try using her beauty to advance in her career?

She returned to the present, grinned at me and got to her feet saying: "Enough lecture for one day, I'm for an afternoon nap. You amuse yourself with TV, a walk or ride or whatever. But remember the Chens will be phoning this evening."

For the following six to eight weeks, Miss Fraser would deliver similar feminist lectures roughly two or three times a week. But she wouldn't say or do anything to push me beyond moderate unease, although at times these lectures were quite passionate.

Half dozen or so male friends in the twenty-five to forty age group popped in to see her fairly regularly and there were three in this lot who occasionally spent a night or weekend. All of these men proclaimed support for feminist goals. I didn't really see anything wrong with a young single Christian lady having simultaneous sexual affairs with a few men, but it made me realize that perhaps she was more of a radical hard-nosed feminist than what her lectures to me presented. She and the three men who made overnight stays executed absurd efforts to have me believe they weren't involved sexually — she never took the one spending the night to bed before I retired, and they pretended that he spent the night on the sofa. I never saw two of these dandies together for more than a short while in her apartment, and they were cordial to each other. Towards me, these lover men appeared torn between friendliness and masked resentment. Still, all of this appeared mostly harmless — I down-played the possibility that three lovers was a sign-post of deep dishonesty in Miss Fraser, seeing that she was such an active church member. Of course, it never entered my head to tell friends or Daddy about her lovers.

In any case, life with her was comfortable and easy. At first my few chores on weekdays were light sweeping, a little dusting and some of the dish washing. After a few weeks, I made her realize that I was good at cooking rice and other staples and vegetables, and I began doing this job some evenings. She worked nine to five and didn't like to eat refrigerated cooked meals, preferred to cook meat early mornings or late evenings. Usually one of us fixed vegetables most evenings or sometimes we dined on take-out meals from two restaurants close by. On weekends, the only difference was that I did all the dish washing. A day's worker washed our clothes.

Miss Fraser went to church almost every Sunday morning (mainly the 11.00 a.m. service), regularly on Sunday nights, plus occasional weekday night meetings. Regularly, I happily practiced what Kung Fu I had learnt at the Chens' home. But I didn't bother thinking about learning more, as it'd have been an expensive hassle. Life was pleasant enough until I found out that in addition to her male lovers, Miss Fraser was also into the flesh with a few of her girlfriends.

My esteemed young Christian guardian was bi-sexual. Did her heterosexual friends — male and female — know this?

CHAPTER 30

Miss Fraser's two most regular visitors, including overnight stays, returned home with her from partying that Saturday night (she was given to leaving me alone at home until after midnight on weekends, as our apartment building had twenty-four hour security). I was watching television in the living-dining room when they trooped in after midnight. They hailed me in tipsy, friendly fashion. I responded in the usual respectful way. Shortly after the movie I was watching ended, I went to bed leaving them having a snack at the dining table. But, although it was after midnight, instead of sleep there came mocking thoughts of the sexual drought that had been squeezing me since the move to this new home just over two months ago. I must have been lying there sleepless in the dark bedroom for nearly an hour when I felt a strong urge to go take a piss. I snapped on the bedside lamp, went out into the softly lit passage and turned towards the bathroom. Slow-paced music was seeping from Miss Fraser's bedroom. Were her friends gone or spending the night? Well the king size bed was big enough...

Miss Fraser's door burst open as I drew alongside it. Impulsively, my head turned towards the room. Shock froze me. Coming out was one of the visitors, naked and lovely in a little robe that yawned open to reveal a dildo strapped to her trim waist. Beyond her, the room was bathed in soft, pink lights. My eyes caught a clear enough view of Miss Fraser and the other visitor frolicking naked on the bed inside.

The robed, dildo-enhanced friend in the doorway, April, frowned at me.
Most likely I was gaping, on top of being rooted for those few incredulous
moments. Then she realized that her little robe was open. She clutched
it together, hiding her light-brown quadroon loveliness and the dildo
at her waist. I returned to life and scurried off to the bathroom, shaken
and worried that Miss Fraser was going to ask me to leave her home.

It took quite a while to begin pissing.

On the way back to bed, Miss Fraser's door was closed and there
was no sign of April. Low music was still purring from within the room.
I plodded on to bed, cursing myself for having wanted to piss. How I
wished for the lost ignorance of the lesbian half of Miss Fraser's bisexual
world. It was possible that she'd be afraid to ask me to leave before
quite a while went by for her to arrange a good excuse that'd make it
appear reasonable for her to kick me out without fear that most people
would believe me if I aired her sexual secrets publicly.

The dominant thought was this: Whatever her reaction, I mustn't
lose this comfortable home.

The following morning, I ventured out shortly after eight o'clock
and found Miss Fraser and her two lover-friends having breakfast. My
head felt a bit giddy, due to anxiety and lack of sleep. The three ladies
looked fairly fresh and energetic. I faltered.

"Charlie, come along, sit and eat," Miss Fraser called. "No church
this morning."

Her bright tone and attitude suggested hope that I'd be able to
remain in her home for the rest of my high school days. Avoiding all eyes,
I plodded forward to sit at the extra place awaiting me at the dining table.
It was like being under the eyes of three guns that could fire at any
moment. I wished we were going to nine o'clock service that morning. If
only last night's shocking eye-opening view had been a bad dream.

April poured me coffee. "Aren't you going to tell us good morning?"
She was mostly humour but there was a distinct edge of wariness about her.

"Sorry," I mumbled, realizing it was best to appear as near as possible
to my usual respectful self. With a forced smile I said: "Good morning,
ladies." But I just couldn't meet their eyes for more than a second.

April sang: "Morning, Charlie."

"Fine morn to you, Charlie," Diana said, and commenced to dish
me some liver.

I wondered if it was all kindness before the axe.

Miss Fraser said: "Charlie, look at me." I looked and beheld a smiling face that appeared free of any hint of malice, fear or trickery. Hope and suspicion warred within me. She added: "My boy, there's no need for you to be glum because of what you found out last night. That is, unless you think I'm horrible and want to stop being my ward." Everything about her appeared honest.

Relief poured forth, and hope booted away suspicion. The dining table was suddenly brighter. I gushed: "No, Miss Fraser. I still think you are a kind, wonderful person. Nothing about you is horrible." We beamed at each other. I truly meant the words I just uttered, and did love her like a kind aunt.

"Or is that pure tact?" April interjected. She was a trim beauty with curly dyed blond hair, and was a few years younger than Miss Fraser's thirty. "Level with us, youthman."

Meeting all three pairs of eyes, I said: "Well, women are so sex...lovely, you know, I don't think it's strange for them to...love...desire each other."

"Correct," Diana said. She was a curvy dark-brown, the most beautiful and the youngest of that lovely female trio.

Miss Fraser said: "Glad to hear you say that, Charlie. But you must realize that most of the ladies who come by are straight heterosexual. And what do you think about the fact that I'm a church member, seeing that churches claim lesbian love is a sin, huh?"

I met her appraising gaze and said with honesty: "I grew up among relatives who don't fancy church, and I think the bible has been muddled up by men. So I see nothing wrong with a smart lady or man using a church for social and career progress. And I'd never tell anyone whatever I know about your private life. Plus in the laws given to Moses there was a law against homo men but none against lesbianism."

The smile that my guardian beamed across the breakfast-laden table glowed with relief and joy and trust. I felt a rush of the same happy mix.

However, the matter didn't end there.

After April and Diana left later that morning, Miss Fraser called me to sit by her on the pale pink sofa in the living area of the living-dining room. She said: "There are a few points I want to raise. As you said, in view of our beauty, it isn't strange for women to be attracted to each other. I expect you know I'm bisexual?"

I nodded, meeting her searching eyes with a stoical face.

She smiled and continued: "Anyway, there is another reason why every liberated woman should go in for lesbian sex, even just temporarily: it helps us to a truer understanding of ourselves and frees us from having to hunt sexual satisfaction from chauvinistic men, and thereby it strengthens us for the hard march to equality for all women. So the bottom-line between you and I is this: I'm a bisexual feminist who wants to do all I can to help you. Just be obedient, accept the facts I show you and ignore the influence of the macho pigs on the streets.

Thankfully, your Dad is a man who knows the sexes are equal in abilities, and deserve equal opportunities and rewards." (It was true that Daddy treated Monica as his equal, and he believed women deserved equality in careers and pay.) My guardian continued, "I intend to make certain you grow up to be more civilized than your Dad, even if I must break a dozen whips across your Kung Fu trained back."

We grinned at each other. All was back to normal, I thought, not realizing that I was really one step closer to a special hell.

So I was happy to continue being Miss Fraser's ward, although I was a bit uneasy about having regular contact with at least half a dozen women who were lesbians and bisexuals. They kept their doings of the flesh out of my sight, but knowing that they were slapping flesh in Miss Fraser's bedroom made me maddeningly horny, especially seeing that a few of them were truly beautiful and I now had no lover in the city to turn to. The girls' high school in the neighbourhood only added to the maddening need for sex. This frustrating condition swiftly forced me to make a less than cautious all out attack on Nicola, a brown complexioned fourteen year old in our apartment building who was alone with a younger brother and younger sister after school hours, Mondays to Thursdays. I took Nicola's virginity on my bed, taking great care not to give her tight fourteen year old pum-pum more than half the manly sixteen year old nine inches of erection, and in gentle fashion. The major aim was to make certain we'd be lovers in the months ahead, and it was a huge help that coming up shortly was the Easter holidays for me to visit the country. Still, it took some ninety percent of the willpower arsenal to be gentle with Nicola's plump virginity. And, despite the gentle picking of her cherry, the following

afternoon she refused to sneak off to be with me. This depressed me —
hadn't I been gentle enough with her virginity? She continued in this
fearful mode in the days left before I eagerly went off to my hometown
for most of the short Easter holiday. I returned to the city sated from
lusty sex. Then to my delight, Nicola sneaked off to be with me on the
afternoon of the first school day of the new term. Once again I was
gentle. Next day, I bought her a nice gold bracelet out of my growing
savings, most of which was the money those devious Chen twins had
given me as a departing gift, and money their wonderful parents had
sent me since the family's migration from Jamaica. (Of course, to be
able to wear the bracelet openly, Nicola had to arrange a lie with her
best friend, who resided miles away across the city.) Thereafter, Nicola
began sneaking off for sex in my bed two or three afternoons each
week, and within a few weeks I was able to give her nearly all of my
great man-size length and a brisker pace. I was wary of losing her, as
she was my only lover in the city, and the sadistic urges had receded
after the abusive Chen twins' exit from my world.

The weeks now flowed by in a fairly gratifying manner with Nicola,
until the Monday afternoon when Miss Fraser made an unexpected
early arrival home. Nicola was there when she arrived.

CHAPTER 31

In a tight embrace, Nicola and I left my room, grinningly contented after a quick shower that had followed nearly an hour in my bed. In our pleased grinning silence we passed through the living-dining room, and entered the tiny entrance hall just as the front door swung open. We froze. Miss Fraser gaped, obviously seeing sex painted on us. Nicola and I flew apart. My guardian took on the look of an angry judge in a padded-shoulder pants suit. Foreboding twisted my gut, and most likely shrunk the prized third leg; in my second week in her home, Miss Fraser had calmly asked if I were a virgin and it had appeared best to lie; during the months since this lie, she had been sternly exhorting me to avoid sex until after age eighteen, and I had been acting the role of a reluctant virgin willing to try taking her advice.

"Young lady, aren't you supposed to be with your younger brother and sister?" It was really a crisp statement. Without a pause she continued: "It's clear what you two are into. Girl, your parents shall hear about this. And you young man…"

Nicola wailed: "Miss Fraser, we did nothing wrong. I just came here minutes…"

"Don't waste your breath!" snapped Miss Fraser. "Let's go view Charlie's bed." She gripped Nicola's hand and dragged her off inside — Nicola had gone dumb and limp. I was speechless, and stood there in the entrance cursing my luck and praying that the lady wouldn't ask me to leave her home.

After five or so minutes that, paradoxically, appeared to be both hours and just moments, a Sergeant-Major looking Miss Fraser and a tearfully subdued Nicola returned.

Miss Fraser said: "I'll soon be back." And she led Nicola pass me, out of the apartment. I closed the front door and shuffled inside to the sofa. Quite a while crept by — had no idea how long, but it must have been more than fifteen minutes. Then the lady returned. I went rigid when she came to a hard stop over me. "Stand," she ordered. I stood. My attitude was that she was the Commander, as her action could have a great effect on my dream future.

"Nicola told me all," she said in cold tones. We were standing just a step apart on the rug in the middle of the living area. My eyes were on the rug. "You came close to spoiling a girl who is roughly three years younger than you. She's just fourteen!"

A glance upward showed her filling the pause with a look I couldn't read. It appeared best to return eyes to the rug.

She said: "You'll either have to toe the line by accepting the punishment I decide on or leave. And please don't think you can affect my career by telling people I'm bisexual."

Eyes still heavily downcast, I avowed: "Miss, I don't want to leave. Forgive me. I'll do anything you say." I was close to going down on my knees in tears.

"Okay. It seems you aren't completely ruined." Her tone had softened. "Very well, we'll just have to increase our efforts to shape you into the right model young man." She moved to sit in an armchair and said: "Take off my shoes."

I leapt to this new task and freed her feet from the open-toe, high-heeled shoes. I then stood.

"Sir, sit," she ordered, pointing at the sofa. I sat; thanking God she wasn't going to turn me out of her home. She crossed her nice knees, gave me an intense gaze and declared: "We both know you can use Kung Fu and your above average strength to break my arms."

"I'd never do that," I gushed sincerely.

Her brows danced upwards. "You'd surely end up in prison if you ever allow the devil to fool you into hitting me. Anyway, I can help you a lot, and I am resigned to having you here at least until you leave high school." Her tone was now cucumber cool, and each time I glanced at her during this statement, and for the rest of this reproof and interrogation, her eyes were on me in a calculating manner. "As I said, Nicola told me all. However, I won't tell her parents you two were lovers. But I must tell them enough so that from now on Nicola will spend all her weekday afternoons under the supervision of an adult. Look at me and answer this: Was Nicola the first?"

I met her eyes long enough to mumble the lie: "Yes, Miss Fraser."

With a finger pointed at me, she instantly said: "I'm not convinced that's the truth. However, I'm glad you had the good sense and concern to use condoms."

"As I've told you again and again; boys and girls should refrain from real sex until after high school, especially boys. Male-female sex earlier than that can weaken the body and intellect, and also cause ill health later in life. Masturbation is okay. Boys should think only clean thoughts about the female body, and must not get involved in homosexuality. Male homosexuality is loaded with serious health risks." She paused, her eyes narrowed, and I wondered if she had just suggested that girls should engage in lesbian sex. She resumed: "From now on there'll be eyes watching your every move. You must keep away from sex until after high school, certainly none in our home. And tonight we'll begin what should've already began — lessons to help you control your lust."

The lessons turned out to be an emotional torture, a psychological war that almost reduced me to a nervous wreck.

That night, the moment the television news we were watching ended at eight, she rose from the sofa and announced that it was time for the first lesson in her bedroom. Instinctively, I knew there'd be no sex. What was her intent?

On the momentous walk to her bedroom, I forced aside all speculative thoughts as to what lessons were about to enter our world. I sensed that we were about to begin what was, perhaps, the greatest test of my life.

Time and space disappeared.

We entered her colourful room. She flicked on the bright overhead light. The room was spacious and dominated by a king size bed that had tall, thick, dark carved posts. She pointed at a bedroom chair. "Sit."

I sat in the chair, scared but determined to endure whatever she'd planned. Gazing at me through narrowed eyes, she said in flat tones: "As of tonight we shall commence to teach you how to love and admire the female body in a respectful way." She began pulling the buttons of her housedress. Astonishment and confusion choked me, but was quickly kicked aside by a curious mix of lust and anxiety. She took off the dress and stood there in pink bikini panties and slippers, dazzling and enchanting, her beautiful dark skin gleaming in the clear bright light, the nipples of her moderately sized breasts proudly aloft, the lovely sleek thighs apart and commanding my eyes. Then she stepped out of her panties, exposing an alluring mound of thick, glossy hair and the hint of a plump gateway to her paradise.

This was beyond anything I'd have expected. She said: "You're to keep your eyes on me without lusting. Enjoy the view just as you'd enjoy looking at a lovely flower or painting set behind a glass window. No sexual thoughts."

My eyes jerked to hers, but once again I wasn't certain what they suggested. Had her last words meant that she'd give me sex after I turned eighteen?

"Boy, you understand?" She sounded arrogant, and now appeared totally stern.

I nodded, although I didn't truly understand, and then broke the eye contact, conscious of a two-thirds hard erection and an oily little voice suggesting that I should either attack her or show her my dick. But instead of either action I sat there with downcast eyes and willed Mr. Dickie to remain below full hardness. It appeared best to obey her command.

"Charlie, you must keep your eyes on me." Her tone was commanding. She sat down across from me on her dressing stool, just five to six feet away, and crossed her lovely, naked thighs to expose a marvellous little glimpse of her rich punany. Her hands moved to cup a knee. Her nipples drew enchanting aims at me. She said: "That's it, my boy, keep your eyes on me and let them roam freely. But you must remember that the female body is more than a sex object. Sex is only one of its functions, it is governed by a mind, just like your body. Has strengths, deserves fulfilment, feels pain."

Flicking eyes between her feet, knees and glowing face, I now told myself: Charlie, you mustn't allow lust to overcome. Sit and enjoy the view. If she ever sees my dick it'd be at her desire. If we ever have sex it must be her wish.

Thankfully, I was wearing roomy pants and my dick receded to near limpness, for she now leaned forward with an intense gaze at my pants front and pointed a finger at the zip. She coolly asked: "Are you lusting? You must not."

"No, Miss," I mumbled. Our eyes met, hers proclaimed self-satisfied triumph. I broke the eye contact, and instantly began feeling an increasing flow of indignation and contempt for her. But I had enough control of the emotions to stay focused on the aim of keeping in her good grace. This contempt made it possible for me to keep eyes on her without feeling aroused during the rest of the roughly twenty minutes that she kept me there in her room, her lovely naked body moving about while she reeled out feminist views.

During the remaining three weeks before I'd leave Kingston to go spend the summer holidays in my hometown, quite a few nights witnessed me spending at least half hour in Miss Fraser's bedroom, gazing at her nakedness while she expressed her feminist views and gossip and dreams; and her twisted hope for me to become a kind of educated trophy son-lover-minion-bodyguard in her life. Sometimes, one or both of her two best friends, April and Diana, would also be there parading naked or partly naked, and at some point one or more of them would do a bit of erotic dancing. On each of these sordid occasions (whether only Miss Fraser was present or not) I was filled with the brooding contempt I now had for her and her two best friends, and this contempt made it possible to remain detached from the sexy enticing nakedness on parade in bright clear lights.

Perhaps the saddest thing of it all was that some nights I'd have nightmares of being abused by any combination of the Chen twins and the three adult females now tormenting me.

The terrible reality of life in Miss Fraser's apartment wasn't helped by the fact that once again I now had no lover in the city. Still, to me, this harsh reality was better than my other two options.

Hiding my contempt for Miss Fraser and her two bosom pals was no easy task. Daily, I had to repeatedly remind myself that the present school year would soon end and then there'd be only one more year to endure in Miss Fraser's apartment. Focusing on my schoolwork helped a lot, too.

The beginning of the summer holidays meant an end to roughly three or four weeks of torment. I gladly rushed off to the country. My little hometown was the same as usual and I was ecstatic to be there.

When Daddy left in late July for farm work in the USA, my step mother was about to enter her last two months of pregnancy and she became prone to intense fatigue that caused one of my aunts to spend the nights with her — so there was no threat of her incestuous inclinations towards me.

As usual, throughout the holidays there was a bellyful of home-town sex. At the end of August, I returned to Miss Fraser's home in the city determined to immediately get down to some serious studying for the GCE O' Level that'd come the following June.

I quickly found that Nicola had become close to Miss Fraser and had no interest in even trying to renew our affair. Obviously, during the summer Miss Fraser had seduced the fourteen year old. Of course, I was jealous and indignant, especially when the two of them were in Miss Fraser's bedroom — sometimes April and/or Diana would make it a trio or foursome. But I swallowed the anger. None of us mentioned Nicola's new sex life. A curt greeting was the only verbal acknowledge-ment Nicola ever showed me, and she never came by the apartment when Miss Fraser wasn't at home. The whole ghastly matter was made worse by the fact that the weeks flowed by without me being able to find a lover in the city. I was too scared to try sneaking a girl into Miss Fraser's apartment and there was no other convenient place to bed the few girls who now appeared willing to give me sex. Furthermore, in the first week of that new school year, Miss Fraser cramped my romantic prospects by declaring that because of the danger of political violence and the fact that the all important GCE 0' Level exams were right around the corner, she wouldn't allow me to do any dating beyond early Saturday evening movies and if I got invited to parties in our neighbourhood, I'd have to be home by midnight.

After the first two to three weeks of that fifth high school year, much of my resolve to remain on top of the grim reality that was life in Miss Fraser's comfortable, secure, cost-free home, was overwhelmed by the cruel parading of flesh by Miss Fraser, Diana and April, plus Nicola's depressing visits. I was still able to act docile at home but at school and on the streets I became one angry young man. My schoolwork suffered a bit. Friends, male and female alike, became wary of the snappish, impatient, bigger-than-average-size seventeen year old that I now was outside of Miss Fraser's apartment. Again and again Mark, my best friend at school, and the only friend who dared snap at me, would say something like, "Charlie, why the man so quick to temper now? You getting mad or what?" or if we were alone he might mumble, "You still don't find a girl in your new area to replace Natalie and the little thing in your building?" A cold stare was the most I could ever give Mark; thankfully, the jab of a finger to the chest or forehead was the worse I ever did in anger with other friends.

Meantime, I also lost most of the moderate interest I'd had in sports — athletics, football, cricket, and boxing. I continued practising Kung Fu though I didn't bother to even think about private lessons. Night and day I prayed for the school year to fly quickly, and for good results in the May-June O' Level exams, so that I could go about trying to get a university students' loan or find a good job that could pay for boarding in a nice middle class neighbourhood. Thanks to Jah, somewhere around this end of October to mid-November period, I began taking a keen interest in fiction and the effect of words in music. Suddenly, it appeared that all my spare time was going towards reading fiction and paying closer attention to the relationship between words and rhythm in music. Fiction and music became a balm to my troubled soul. By the middle of December, I was dreaming of writing fiction and songs, and started to hunt for information about fiction and song writing — it was an immense help that my History teacher was a fiction buff with a wide taste. Remarkable though it might seem, when the school term ended for the short Christmas holidays, I was far less uptight and had awakened to the fact that friends had been keeping me at arms length and justly so. Immediately, I began making an effort to re-strengthen my friendships.

The Christmas holidays in the country meant a feast of sex, and a welcomed break from the torments in Miss Fraser's bedroom. A few women over thirty threw themselves at me and were all impressed by my size and skill. But fiction and song writing were now the centre of my life and dreams, so the new female conquests were all one shot happenings. Daddy, other relatives, and friends in the hometown appeared a bit sceptical of my talk of writing fiction and songs. "Journalism is a good career," Daddy tactfully said. But, I knew what I was dreaming of, and English Language had always been one of my favourite subjects — English Literature in school didn't interest me much because of the poetry and the dull fiction on the curriculum.

When I returned to Kingston on the second day of 1981, I immediately began a more passionate search for a wider variety of novels, and any material dealing with successful fiction writers and songwriters of the twentieth century, plus any comments by literary agents, fiction editors and publishers. Once again, my History teacher's open-minded passion for a wide variety of fiction was a great help. His advice was that I should find a job that would allow me a lot of spare time, whether I went on to university or not, while avoiding fatherhood and marriage until I was a successful writer. In addition, it quickly became obvious that I favoured the type of fiction dominating the bestsellers lists. This recognition made me realize that a love for words and musing, a powerful imagination, heavy reading and intense observation of human nature were far more important to a would-be fiction writer than any kind of workshop on literature and writing that tried to go beyond the basics common to the writing of good essays and articles.

Also, in that first month of 1981, I began taking an interest in the Rastafarian faith; partly because Rastafarian glorification of the amazing list of hidden facts about African history was in tune with the vibes I'd gotten from my dignified grandparents in childhood. When this budding interest in Rastafarian reasoning was added to my passion for fiction and song writing, I was able to become a fairly sociable seventeen year-old schoolboy, in spite of having to live with the secret torments in Miss Fraser's bedroom.

I was preparing to sit five subjects in the May-June GCE O' Level exams — English Language, Math, History, Geography and English Literature. The preparation for these five subjects, the powerful interest in fiction and song writing, and the budding awareness of Rastafari took up most of my time and energies. But I still yearned for a lover.

It wasn't strange that towards the end of January I began taking a keen interest in a young housewife. Her name was Mrs. Ava Travels. She was a Euro-Jamaican, and was both the only Euro female and childless young housewife in our apartment building.

CHAPTER 32

She was a dark-haired, dark-eyed, native Euro-Jamaican in her mid-twenties, bronzed complexioned, with a supple long-legged build. Her angular face was handsome rather than pretty. Her husband, too, was a native Euro-Jamaican, but he was fifteen years older than her. They were both from rich merchant families. Their marriage was still relatively new, and was his second jump into matrimony — his first marriage had cost him a nice house and a heavy monthly cheque for years to come, and that was why this second marriage was housed in a fairly modest middle-income apartment building. The first step of my strategy to get between Ava's thighs was to feint shy friendliness whenever we met in the corridor on our floor, in either of the two lobbies we both used, in the elevators, on the stairs, and by the pool. She was engaging, friendly and curious. I began visiting the pool regularly at the times she tended to go there. Before long, we were having interesting chats by the pool, and I slyly began flaunting swim-trunk-erections under her nose, while pretending to be oblivious of the erections and her glances at my front. Then one late-afternoon on a weekday in February, a few days before Valentine's Day, while we were by the pool, she asked, "How about some fruit juice and cake at my place, huh?" We were in the shade of a beach-type umbrella on the tiled area surrounding the pool, she on a chair, I on a towel at her feet. "Or your choice of whatever I have."

"Okay," I said, masking elation, although I knew she knew that, like her husband, my guardian wasn't due home before another two hours. I wanted the real me to surprise her in her apartment. We got up, and minutes later when I emerged from the men's section of the pool house changing room, she was coming out of the female side, her nice body now in a modest housedress.

"Like my place?" Ava said when we entered her living-dining room. Her two-bedroom apartment was identical to, and just around the corner from Miss Fraser's.

"Yes, Mrs. Travels." This my first entry into her home, a luxuriously furnished place loaded with a wide variety of art works. "I like it. It's put together real nice."

"Glad you like it." She playfully punched my arm and added, "Come on, Charlie, call me Ava when we're alone. And it won't matter much if you say Ava when we're in company. Heck, you're seventeen, and I'm still quite a way from thirty." Our eyes were locked, hers calculating.

"Sure, Ava." I nodded, and was suddenly hit by a need to hurry the game. "You know, Ava, I've been aching to show you the biggest, strongest part of me."

Delighted surprise lit her face. "Show me," she said. Her grin brightened the room.

I was already pulling the front of my jeans shorts, fervently eager to experience having a willing Euro lover. Right there by her sofa, I stepped out of shorts and underwear.

"Wow!" she exclaimed, cheeks blazing, eyes popped wide and glued to the iron-hard Mr. Dickie. "I knew it would be big for your age but this is beyond expectation!" Her eyes rose to mine for a moment, then dipped again to Mr. Dickie, and she literally whispered: "Seventeen but bigger than my husband and the two adult black men I've slept with, and a heck of a lot bigger than the varied boys of my girlhood."

Needless to say, there was no mention of fruit juice and cake, or any thing else. In silence, she hurried me to her bedroom, a room dominated by wine-coloured drapes, plush carpeting, and an antique bed. We dived into the bed and were naked in seconds. I reined in excitement and gave her a nice interlude of foreplay, wanting to impress her enough to become her regular lover; but I firmly resisted her attempt to get my head between her legs, and prevented her from putting her mouth on Mr. Dickie. I shafted her and succeeded in getting her to climax before I began soaring towards the point of satisfied firing.

After filling her hot depths with seed, I rolled off her and instantly felt a little jab of alarm. "You're protected against pregnancy?" I asked. "Right?"

She turned to face me, smiled ruefully, caressed my chest and then said a bit wistfully: "Don't worry. I'm unable to conceive."

"Sorry to hear that," I mumbled, uncertain how to react.

"Sometimes it saddens me; but never for long. My husband has three kids from his first marriage, and it appears he loves having a younger woman to mother him. Perhaps someday we'll adopt." I nodded sympathetically and embraced her. She was still caressing my chest. "Tell me, is Miss Fraser a lover of yours?"

I managed to chuckle: "No, no."

"She's missing something!" Her laugh filled the pause. "I'm willing to bet she has no idea that you're already bigger than many, perhaps most, grown men."

"She doesn't, and I have no intention of showing her."

"Please, do keep her in ignorance. Now tell me, why didn't you kiss my twat and why did you stop me from kissing your cock?"

"Twat," I said thoughtfully, relieved to be free of questions about Miss Fraser but also wary of oral sex talk. "That's a strange name. Anyway, I don't like the idea of it. My Daddy and all my relatives are like that."

"That's disappointing but I know it's a common feeling amongst you black folks." She shrugged. "No problem. Each person has a right to their own likes and dislikes. My husband is good at it." Her eyes went down to my crotch, and she exclaimed: "Oh my, big boy, you're coming to life again! Ah, the teenage vitality. Well, there's time for more fun. But this time I wanna give you head. I love doing it, so don't worry that I'll ever pressure you to return the compliment." She immediately moved to use her mouth on Mr. Dickie and it was quickly obvious that she certainly knew how to give head and got pleasure from the act. Within a minute after her mouth began working on Mr. Dickie, she began emitting low sounds of pleasure, then one of her hands moved to her crotch, and she had an intense orgasm that began while she was drinking the mighty squirt of my eruption.

Thereafter, she gave me head regularly but she never bothered trying to get me to return the favour.

Now that I had a lover in the city to fuck regularly, life was richer and sweeter than it'd been during the months since the grim ordeal in Miss Fraser's bedroom had began.

Ava and I limited ourselves to one or two bouts of sex per week, and always in her apartment, as her husband was a virile man who wasn't likely to forgive her for cheating, and we didn't want to risk having a nosy neighbour carry talk of suspicion to Miss Fraser. To my relief, Ava was smart enough to avoid trying to move from pleasant neighbourliness to friendship with Miss Fraser.

I approached Ava's apartment only when she told me to come by and after our first fuck, most of our fucking was done in the cosy spare bedroom. I continued addressing her as Mrs. Travels when we were outside her apartment.

In addition to being a good energetic lover, Ava was also witty, a good pastry cook, and a source of generous gifts of cash that went into my growing secret savings in my room. She also helped my writing dream by getting current US bestsellers and fresh literary magazines from her sister who travelled between New York and Jamaica at least once every two months. I resisted the few weak urges to tell her of the torment in Miss Fraser's bedroom, as I didn't see how Ava could help me leave Miss Fraser's home without causing her husband to suspect that I was her lover.

My studies were now easier and friendships became stronger. Miss Fraser and her two tormenting cronies were less stress on my nerves, and Nicola's presence in Miss Fraser's bedroom stopped inspiring jealousy. The roughly two-thirds mile long journey between home and school, became more of a pleasure on foot and by bicycle. The dream of fiction and song writing grew. I literally stopped trying to get sex from any of the schoolgirls I was friendly with. The sadistic dreams and urges receded. The one negative was that my budding interest in Rastafarian teachings went into inert mode.

"I've a grand surprise," Ava said, her eyes a twinkle, when I entered her apartment one Tuesday afternoon towards the end of April. I'd arrived home from school fifteen minutes ago. She had just summoned me by phone. "You won't believe it!"

"Madam Ava, I'm certain it's gonna thrill me without killing me. A new sex position or some kind of sex toy, right?"

"You bet it'll thrill you." She was literally dragging me through the living-dining room. "But your guess is way off base, lover boy."

She hurried me towards the guest bedroom. When we arrived at our cosy destination, the surprise was beyond anything I'd expected.

There was an extraordinarily beautiful woman in a short white dress sitting on the bed, her jet-black skin alight in the brightly lit room. Her name was Kimberly. She and Ava had been best friends since high school. They became classmates in senior high at one of Kingston's exclusive girls' high school. Kimberly's father was one of Jamaica's best trial lawyers, and she'd chosen a law career. Ava had told Kimberly about my great size, teen vitality and skill. Now, within a few minutes after Ava introduced us, Kimberly and I were undressing each other. She was a truly awesome beauty — rich curves, satin smooth black skin, pretty face, wonderful smile, graceful movements, and velvety voice. Ava allowed us to enjoy a ride, which ended in a volcanic simultaneous climax, then changed the scene to three in bed.

Thereafter, Kimberly occasionally turned up at Ava's place to, in her own words, "Enjoy my man-boy." Thankfully, like Ava, she was an energetic lover and never tried to get my mouth on her crotch. She made life a much greater delight. She too, encouraged the literary dream, and became another source of cash for the secret savings.

Shortly after meeting Kimberly, a fourth tormentor joined Miss Fraser's group. This one was a blonde haired, blue-eyed, Euro-American attached to the US embassy in Kingston. But the delights I was getting from Ava and Kimberly, gave me the emotional power to remain detached from this additional parade of flesh. There was still no attempt to undress or touch me and their actions never excited me, so they didn't know about my manhood.

Consequently, I was able to settle down to a real sober final-stage preparation for the looming GCE O' Level exams, which began late in May and continued to the end of June.

For my eighteenth birthday that June, Ava gave me a fourteen carat gold pen and pencil set with my name engraved. Kimberly gave me a fourteen carat gold bracelet. I kept these presents away from the sight of Miss Fraser, whose birthday gift to me was a shaving kit and a feminist sex manual. A wonderful touch to this birthday was that the Math exam was in the morning and was relatively easy, then in the afternoon, Kimberly and Ava gave me a mind-blowing time in bed.

When I sat the last of the five subjects in the third week of June, I was confident of having done quite well in all but Geography, which I still expected to pass. But life became a dark depressed place because on the evening of the very day that I sat the last subject, Ava told me her doctor had just informed her she had cancer. She also told me that for years she'd been having yearly tests because cancer was a common curse in her family.

At the end of June, on the afternoon before the last day of the school year, I was walking home from school in a brooding mood, worried that I'd never see Ava alive again after she left the following day to undergo treatment at a private hospital in the USA. It also worried me that no matter how good my exam results were, it would be difficult to find a job because the island's economy was in a terrible mess, and jobs were very scarce. Plus, the latest news out of the government funded Students' Loan Bureau told of insufficient funds to help more than a small percentage of needy students. This meant that even if I was able to get a place at the university, I might not be able to secure a student loan.

Walking homeward on that afternoon, I was certainly a very dejected eighteen year-old when I stopped to piss by a weedy, vacant lot in the small enclave that began opposite my school. Just as I was finishing up, a luxury car going in my direction crawled by and stopped roughly thirty feet away. Naively, I didn't think that the bejewelled middle-aged lady had stopped because she'd seen the size of my cock.

CHAPTER 33

I thought you were my friend's son!" the lady exclaimed when I walked up alongside her car. Despite the unattractive obesity of her short stature, her fleshy brown face, which didn't have on much make-up, her smooth voice suggested a nice, cheerful, compassionate, middle-aged wit. "I was getting ready to have some fun by needling him for being so far away from home and school." While a few chuckles shook her three or four chins and huge bosom, I forced a smile out of my dejected heart. She reached out a hand decked with rings to open the door opposite her, and said: "Let me give you a lift."

"Thank you, madam." I got in.

She drove forward at a crawl and asked: "Where do you live?"

I told her.

"That's just a short ride with me," she said. The car was still crawling. "Are you a Sixth Former?"

"Fifth, ma'am."

"I'm Mrs. Barrett, widowed. You are?"

"Charlie."

"Nice name." Her fat and slightly wrinkled brown face flashed me a modest grin. She increased the car speed a bit. "So, Charlie, how did you find the O' Level exams this year?"

"Average, I think." Everything about her and her comfortable car was having a soothing effect on me, causing me to relax and lose some of the dejection over Ava's cancer and the immediate future, putting me in a talkative mood. "I expect to pass four of my five, perhaps all five."

"Good. Your parents, especially your Mom, must be proud to have such a handsome and brilliant son." She beamed a maternal smile that pulled to the point where I had a fantasy that if my mother had survived she'd have eventually been like this widowed matron in one way or another; Momma had been fairly plump when she had died at age thirty-one.

"My mother died long ago."

In a comforting voice she said: "Sorry that it's so, my boy; your Dad?"

"He and his wife live in Highgate, St. Mary," I related freely. "They have two young kids — one is just a baby. I'm from Highgate too, grew up there until I passed the Common Entrance exam." I was literally desperate to talk. "Wanted to attend a top Kingston high school, got accepted for Calabar, and a kind family in Havendale took me in as a sort of adopted son. Early last year the family migrated to the US, but they got me a place with one of their church friends, a single lady."

"Planning to enter Sixth Form in September?"

"Not likely." Everything about this Mrs. Barrett had me willing to confide fears, problems and dreams. "I intend to try finding a job here in Kingston and move to a boarding house or something. My guardian says I can stay until university, but we don't get along well in a...an important aspect of life, and same with my stepmother in the country. Daddy is great but can't afford middle-class boarding and university fees, while the student's loan situation is bleak, and I hate the political tribalism common in the poorer areas of the city."

Mrs. Barrett slowed the car to a crawl and, with compassionate glances, she declared graciously: "You certainly seem to be a honest, decent, intelligent young man. Most likely your guardian doesn't understand you. How old is she?" No other older stranger had ever shown such great compassionate interest in me.

"Thirty-one," I said and was seized by an overwhelming need to avow the whole sorry tale about Miss Fraser and I. "But it's not her age..."

Suddenly my voice broke and tears flooded my eyes. I just couldn't stop from breaking down into renting sobs, while simultaneously burning with the need to tell all. My head was bowed.

Mrs. Barrett stopped the car but she didn't touch me, two actions that appeared absolutely right. It also appeared perfect for her to say: "A good cry always helps. Never think it's shameful or weak for a man to cry."

For another minute, I sat there weeping, my head still bowed. When the tears ceased and I was drying my face, avoiding her eyes but not from shame, she made a statement that erased any qualms I might've had about avowing the facts on Miss Fraser. The incisive statement was: "Not being ashamed to cry is an asset, it's strong, like not being ashamed to admit when you're wrong."

I met her eyes and smiled in response to her revitalizing words and comforting smile.

"Want to tell me what's wrong?" Her tone inspired trust. "Or I could arrange for a counsellor. I like you."

Without delay I rushed into the telling, but had to avoid eye contact: "She's a bisexual feminist with several male and female lovers, and she has a number of horrible notions. For just over a year now she and two of her female lovers have been forcing me to sit and look at their nakedness while they talk about feminism; another joined them recently."

"Dear God! What horrible, wicked women!" Her voice had an odd timbre I couldn't place. Without moving from behind the steering wheel, she reached out to lay comforting fingers on my shoulder. I now looked at her but she wasn't looking at me. "Dear young man, I have an extra room at my home, and no children. God brought us together today. Why not come live there? It seems fated." She now looked at me, her eyes alive with excited hope that I wrongly read as maternal charity.

I gaped at her. What extraordinary luck. Now there'd be no need to stay on with Miss Fraser, and I could easily go to Sixth Form if by September there was neither a suitable job nor a place at the university. "Mrs. Barrett, that would be the answer to my dreams!" Feeling newly clean and wanted and protected, I fought the urge to hug her, although the car was still stationary.

"How old are you?"

"Turned eighteen this month." I was too excited to recall the exact date.

"Wonderful." She beamed at me. "Free to live where you please. How about coming to look at the room now? It's by New Kingston. I could drive you home afterwards."

"Yes, I'd love to see your home now. But I'll take a bus home."

She drove off, saying cheerfully: "Having you there will be no problem at all. In fact, although I'm not a Christian, I'm certain it's God's will. My departed husband left me several houses and other investments that earn me enough to live comfortably. I have no children, and never liked the adoption thing. So, considering that I don't relish the hassles involved in travelling or building a business empire, most of my time has always been spent alone at home reading and eating." She chuckled. "I have a few friends, but I was never one to sit around gossiping, while I have always loved reading." She now drove out of the enclave we'd met in. She headed her car down Constant Spring Road.

The afternoon traffic was light. Mrs. Barrett increased speed, whisking us out of my neighbourhood. After a comfortable silence, she said: "I'd gladly help you further your education. 'No sweat,' as your generation would say." Her head bobbed.

Her effort to show empathy with my generation was touching. "Most kind of you to be offering me so much, Mrs. Barrett. Something you should know now is that I want to be a top, world-class fiction and song writer; and I think a job and using spare time to research and practise writing is the best road to success."

"Sounds sensible." She nodded, then flashed me a grin and exclaimed: "Good Lord! You and I were truly meant to meet! I've always been crazy about fiction, just about any kind, so it'll be a great pleasure to help you set up a writing career! What luck that I met you today!"

"I'm the one who's lucky."

"Let's say we're both lucky."

We grinned at each other, and once again I got the intense feeling that if my mother had lived to Mrs. Barrett's age she'd have been like her in one way or another.

Mrs. Barrett said: "You know what I think? You should seek a job with a publisher."

"Mrs. Barrett, that's a great idea!" I exclaimed sincerely, wondering why I hadn't thought of it. "You're God-sent."

"So are you, Charlie. No doubt you're destined to be a great novelist, and God chose me to get you away from those evil women. It'll be an honour to see you get off to a good start. I might even be able to get you a job interview at a publishing house." She flashed me a youthful looking grin.

Excitement made me giddy.

Mrs. Barrett resided in New Kingston. Her townhouse was in the middle of a row at the centre of a town house complex of twenty homes surrounded by a concrete-and-mesh fence. The one entrance/exit had a twenty-four hour manned security hut and barrier. This upper-middle class enclave was one of the first gated communities built in Kingston, and it featured roomy two and three bedroom units. Mrs. Barrett had one of the two bedroom units. The two bedrooms were upstairs and each had a bathroom. She led me to a comfortably furnished bedroom that smelt of mothballs. Cheerfully she said: "It's used only when my niece comes from the US once every two or three years. In the future she'll share my room."

Excited to the point of glowing, I thanked her, and we agreed that I should move in that Friday. Twenty minutes later, after orange juice and nut-cake, and a chat about fiction in the living-dining room, I floated away in the highest of spirits, and took a bus to the home I'd soon leave with a happy heart. When I got off the bus there was a plan in my head to shake up Miss Fraser on Thursday night or Friday morning.

But, of course, when I walked into the apartment building there came the gloomy reality that Ava had cancer and would be leaving the island the following day to get treatment. Would she survive?

I shuffled to Ava's apartment to wish her farewell and good luck. A cousin was there with her. With a heavy heart, I bid Ava a hopeful farewell and then sauntered to Miss Fraser's apartment. That would be my last contact with Ava before cancer killed her a few months later; I wouldn't see Ava's best friend, Kimberly, again before a chance meeting in a store at year's end, and the two of us would miss Ava far too much to even think of ever becoming lovers again.

Thursday night, my last night in Miss Fraser's home, arrived quickly. And, as I'd been praying, there was no visitor present or expected after eight o'clock, fairly normal for Thursday nights. Perfect for the nice revenge I had planned.

CHAPTER 34

Labouring to camouflage mounting excitement, I allowed Miss Fraser to lead me to her room. Then, as usual, I sat in one of the bedroom chairs watching her undress under the bright overhead lights. But the moment she was naked, I changed the usual flow of things in her bedroom. Instead of continuing to obey the ruling order that I should remain seated and keep my eyes on her, I sprang up and leapt out of shorts and underwear.

As I'd expected, her initial reaction was to shrink in dread, her mind obviously shouting that I was about to use my Kung Fu skills and remarkable strength to rape her in a brutal manner. To help prevent her from going hysterical, I took a step backward instead of moving towards her, and kept my features composed.

My dick was only half erect, but rape was not the plan. My intention was twofold: if she showed any sexual interest I'd go along until she was all steamed up and then tell her my mind; on the other hand, if she didn't show any sexual interest I'd scare her by pretending that rape was the aim, and when she was truly in the grip of terror I'd tell her what I thought of her.

Now, her initial show of dread began evaporating when she beheld the size of my half erect dick. I stood unmoving. There was about eleven feet between us. Her eyes commenced to flick between Mr. Dickie and my stoical face, incredulity and interest quickly devouring her fear. The silent moments crawled by. Then, in a husky voice that purred out of a lusty little grin, she declared: "Charlie, my dear, I...ah I hope you aren't allowing the devil to tell you to...to hurt me. No need for that." She stroked her pelvis and a breast.

By this point I had managed to gain an iron-hard erection by focusing on her grin and husky voice and a mental picture of Kimberly. Now, the evil Miss Fraser sucked in a great mass of air, her eyes popped towards the iron-hardness waving at her. Her eyes gleamed and gaped wider, and her fear disappeared. She was now pure lust.

"Charlie, I never thought..." She paused and gave me what was meant to be a provocative grin. I forced a lustful looking smile — having her desire me was the plan I favoured. We were still rooted apart, her naked body now jutting towards me. She resumed: "You sure are a lot more man than I thought any eighteen year old could be. Oh, I always suspected you had a big one...but this is...well, deliciously incredible. Seems I chose quite well when I decided on you as a husband. Honestly, it was my intention to buy you an engagement ring soon and stop seeing other men. But we'd have to keep it secret until after you graduated from university, by which time my career will be established enough to withstand the shock our engagement may be to many. Then we'll marry and have two or three kids."

Her silly confidence amazed me. How certain she was that she'd enslaved my mind and lust.

She now began advancing at me with arms outstretched, saying:

"Tonight we begin loving each other, my dear."

I forced a smile and moved towards her. But when her hands touched me a great wave of revulsion roared up. I slapped aside her arms and shoved her away, no longer interested in either scaring her or getting her inflamed with lust before telling her my opinion of her.

With all my contempt, I said: "I wouldn't fuck you even if you offered all the money in the world. I just wanted you to see that I'm more man than the wimps and dildos and vibrators you deal with. You're nothing but a load of shit."

She was cowering where she'd fallen by the bed.

I hauled on my underwear and shorts. "I'm packed and will be leaving tomorrow. Maybe I shall tell your bosses, decent feminist friends and church folks what you and the other shits did to me! Plus inform Nicola's parents of the facts!"

Like a naked dead arising from a grave, she hauled up her trembling body from the carpet, drew a sheet around her nakedness and pleaded in a scratchy whisper: "Charlie, please, no, that...that might ruin me...I did help you... and I'll give you ten thousand dollars. Please, don't hurt my career."

The money was tempting. Ten thousand Jamaican dollars was a tidy sum in 1981— half the nation was earning less than that per year. But, I knew I wouldn't take a bribe from her, just couldn't stoop to blackmailing, and I knew part of her anguish was still due to the thought of losing such a big young dick without testing it even once. It seemed best to hand her a thread of hope for the night, to keep her from trying any kind of trick while I slept. I said: "You did help me, so we'll talk about it in the morning before I move out. You are a load of shit, anyway, so let me hear you acknowledge that now."

She gulped, and closed her eyes.

"Open your eyes, and tell me you're a load of shit!"

She croaked: "I'm a...load of...shit."

"Repeat it louder!"

She obeyed: "I'm a load of shit."

"See you in the morning, Miss Sewage." I strode out of her room without a backward glace. My heart was delighted by the thought of her reaction in the morning when I told her that instead of taking her money I'd be telling the world about her bisexuality and disgraceful actions towards me.

The following morning, I awoke feeling fresh and energetic. It was minutes before seven o'clock. "Miss Sewage" was already up, and she looked horrible — tinted bags under her bleary eyes, a tic at the corner of her mouth, her usually erect figure was bent, no trace of her usual confident facade. Dressed in a floral housedress, she looked like a confused refugee. Obviously she had no intention of going to work that day.

I stood in the kitchen doorway appraising "Miss Sewage", while she stood by the stove wilting under my gaze. One of her hands gripped the other and nails dug into a palm, while teeth bit into a lip. She looked so pathetic I began feeling the first pangs of pity.

Into my mind leapt these thoughts: Seeing that for roughly a year and a half she had given me a comfortable home, a good diet and pocket money, should I weaken her career and social standing? She was a nuisance to society, and might be a great menace if she made it to the top of the corporate world. But hell, many top male executives and wealthy employers were great menaces to society. Plus, time and fate might soften or crush "Miss Sewage". And one should show gratitude for all kindness, even if the person had also done you a great wrong.

I ended my musing and the silence by saying honestly: "Well, Miss Sewage, I'm undecided about reporting you to the world. In any case, I don't want your money. If I remain silent it'll be out of gratitude for the kind things you've done for me. But I must inform Nicola's parents of the facts."

She winced. But her face also showed a touch of relief and hope. The kettle began whistling. Absentmindedly, she turned off the stove. Then she moved to lean against the counter by the sink. "Charlie," she said cautiously, "you and I can...have...accomplish a lot together. Let's...give us a trial for six months." She paused. I leaned against the doorway, folded arms at chest and then gave her a nod and a steady go-ahead look. She resumed more confidently, "I'll give up lesbian sex, and won't look at another man. You see, well, my...my sex life, as you know it, was...well...just a pastime while awaiting the right man to marry. I'm now certain you're that man. Of course, (she now tried smiling but it came off as a pathetic mask) we cannot overlook the age difference between us, so I'd be faithful for the rest of my life but I won't mind you experiencing young ladies of your age group during the next three years and also later after I turn fifty."

At this point I couldn't help chuckling, amazed at her attempt to outsmart me.

My heavy chuckling and hard gaze made her tremble. But before either of us could speak, security buzzed the apartment to announce that Mrs. Barrett had arrived to fetch me. I turned away to go get my two suitcases, travelling bag, school bag and boxes of books. And, as I had arranged, the building's handyman turned up to help me carry down my stuff. I ignored "Miss Sewage", except for using cold glares and a few curt commands to keep her hovering about in silence. When I picked up the last box, I tipped my hat to her and said: "Miss Sewage, you great load of shit, tomorrow you'll get my decision."

I left her standing there in the little entrance hall, bent, rooted and dumb in her shattered expectation that money, her comfortable apartment and sex would've kept me under her thumb for years.

By the time I ate the huge breakfast Mrs. Barrett had prepared for my "homecoming" and unpacked most of my luggage, I had decided not to report my recent guardian tormentor. I owed her a good turn for the comfortable free board and pocket money she'd given me during my stay.

But I felt it was my duty to report her and her bosom cronies to the president of their feminist club, and to let Nicola's parents know that she'd been seduced into lesbianism by Miss Fraser and company. I executed both of these tasks that weekend; Nicola's parents believed me, but I know not what specific action they took beyond stopping Nicola from having any contact with Miss Fraser. The president of Miss Fraser's feminist club was so horrified by the report I made that she immediately phoned the vice-president to arrange a special meeting and I'd eventually learn that Miss Fraser and her close cronies got kicked out of the club to become isolated freaks in the eyes of the city's growing feminist movement.

Isolated from most of her former friends, with gossip of her evil hypocritical conduct spreading, Miss Fraser's career and social standing took a heavy blow, and she had to withdraw from her church. Within a year, she married a successful businessman who was about fifteen years her senior. Immediately after the honeymoon, he began giving her a less than easy life — it appeared that he was one of those odd easygoing and seemingly low-sexed men who turn into aggressive womanisers after marriage. Miss Fraser quickly gave up her career to become an upper-class alcoholic housewife.

Unfortunately, I began my stay with Mrs. Barret wearing blinkers, not suspecting that in her fleshy middle-aged body, there was a devious lust-filled heart nurturing a less than pleasant plan for me. Neither did I realize that I had become dreadfully enslaved by the ambition to become an internationally acclaimed writer of fiction and songs.

CHAPTER 35

FEBRUARY 1992

We are having another fine sunny day here in Kingston. I'm in a wonderful mood, undoubtedly one of the happiest men alive, pleased to be lounging in shorts and sandals at one of the umbrella-shaded tables by my pool, there's a clear view of the front gate from the whole pool area. Sitting across from me at the table is my wife, Janice. She's her usual lovely self in a one-piece swimsuit. Our one year-old son is on her lap, looking perfect in miniature swim trunks and vest. On the table between us, there are two tall empty glasses and a jug of cool orange juice. I'm smoking a spliff (a Jamaican term for a marijuana cigar); my neurotic wife doesn't smoke but likes — or alleges that she does — the smell of good marijuana, and I smoke nothing but the best; however, I don't do much smoking at home in her presence. Four weeks ago I completed the final hand draft of my new novel, and with Janice's help, the typescript is near completion.

Within the next ten days I expect to mail the complete typed novel to my agent, who's eager to get it. I'm confident it'll silence the Jamaican and overseas critics who think I cannot repeat the great international success of my first novel.

It's nearing dusk and Janice, Jason and I are in the family room. We came here roughly an hour ago, after cruising leisurely through the wonderful earlier-than-usual weekday dinner prepared by the cook. The wife and I are seated at the room's long card table playing a spirited game of ludo. Our son is on the table, sitting on a cushion that's beside the ludo board. At regular intervals he claps and squeals delight, a handsome little prince in tailored army styled jungle fatigues. I'm really enjoying myself— when in a good mood about writing and Jason is present, it's easy to enjoy simple relaxation with my beautiful wife. With a double six, Janice knocks away one of my tokens and drives another one of hers home. She cups the die, grins at me, shakes the die cup and rolls forth a six and four. This play sees her last two tokens safely home. I'm beaten, which is usually the case in any game with dice. Her triumphant grin makes her light-brown face sparkle like jewels. Jason caps the victory — he claps and squeals with more vigour than before.

Janice begins packing away the ludo game, pausing every few seconds to kiss our son. Her love for him is obviously as deep as mine.

She's now tickling Jason's neck, and beaming at me. With a merry humming, she gets up, moves to put away the ludo game and then skips the two or three metres to turn on the CD player on the expensive stereo system. Reggae music flows from the two speaker boxes. I scoop Jason off the card table to my lap. Will I ever experience true lasting love?

Janice returns to the table, sits in the chair beside mine and says: "You look thoughtful."

"Just thinking...nothing important." I begin making funny faces at Jason. Out of the corner of my eyes I see his mother flash a pleased wide-eyed smile. Then she picks up a fashion magazine. Jason pokes a hand inside my shirt but leans towards her and the magazine. They begin cooing over the fashion layouts. I like thinking that Jason will become a writer but his love for his mother's heavy supply of women's fashion magazines makes me wonder if he is to be a fashion designer.

Charlie, I wordlessly scold myself with inner amusement, damn it, you ass, he's only a baby.

Janice breaks my train of thought by looking up from the magazine and saying: "I'm looking forward to Sunday."

"Yeah, I hope it doesn't rain." We are to journey out to the country to spend the day with Daddy and his family. "No doubt Monica will be cooking all sorts of goodies."

"You and your deep belly," she laughs.

I laugh along.

Jason chirps: "Belliee."

"Yes, dear. Your Dad loves his deep belly. It's a good thing he likes to exercise and doesn't gain weight easily."

I chuckle at these home truths and say: "Today was a wonderful day."

She beams like a girl who's just won her heart's desire. I begin to regret having voiced delight in the day. She says: "Yes, darling, it was a wonderful day, which is why I hope you'll be staying home tonight so I can model the new outfits I bought Monday."

"That'll be great." I'm truly pleased, and now glad I avowed that this day has been fantastic. Modelling her recent purchases means she'll take more than one small drink of wine after the modelling, and then there'll be the good sex we have whenever she's tipsy.

I glance across my spacious workroom to where Janice is typing at the folding desk. Wearing a roomy striped dress, she's her usual extraordinarily beautiful self. She's a good enough typist, actually better than yours truly. I'm at my desk, also typing. We're typing the last pages of the final hand written draft of my new novel. My fingers move away from the typewriter, eyes fixed on her, the mind becoming possessed by memories of the erotic fashion show and wonderful sex she gave me Thursday night, over three full days ago. I move eyes to our son, who is asleep on the narrow divan. He's looking utterly at peace on this cool, tranquil Monday morning. Yesterday, the three of us spent a nice day in the country with Daddy, Monica and their cheerful children. Monica has gained some pounds since I last saw her a few months ago, and Daddy's beard is showing the first touch of grey. They're truly middle-aged now.

The phone on my desk rings. It's the lusty sister-in-law, Sandra. Her voice is a sexy purr, and it immediately appears best not to let Janice even suspect who the caller is.

"Brethren," I improvise, "what's up? I and the wife here in my work room typing."

"Charlie love," Sandra purrs through the line, "is she beside you?"

"No. What..?"

"Good. Keep it that way." Her voice gets even sexier when she continues: "You see, great lover-writer, I'm lying in bed and the phone is taped to my ear and cheek so my hands are free to roam. And I'm all naked, except for red silk stockings and black high heels. I'm on my back with my feet up on the head board." I recall the sight of her in that same get-up and position recently.

Heat fills my balls and great dick, but wanting Janice to think the caller is male, I manage to calmly say: "Look skip, I-man truly busy now."

Without missing a beat, Sandra keeps me trapped by saying: "I'm massaging my breasts, feeling your hands instead of mine." Her thick breathing fills the pause. "Uuuhh...so sweet. Nipples hard as rocks, and hot, so hot."

The phone is suddenly comfortably nailed to my cheek. I see the glorious breasts and amazing nipples. I turn the swivel chair so that Janice cannot see my face, "Ohhh," Sandra is groaning, "ohh...hands moving down...slowly...slowly over stomach...and belly to...to...oh my lover...uhhh...wish you were here."

I can neither speak nor hang up. I see her lovely hands crawling down the pretty curve of her flat, well-toned belly.

"Fingers of both hands in the hair...at...crotch...uhh...ohhh"

I see — and feel the texture of — the thick mass of dyed red hair at her beautifully formed crotch.

"Ohhh Charlie, my cunt is...hot and...wet. Feet still up on head board, pillow under ass. Uhhh...Right forefinger and its mate...going up...up hot...wet...pulsing pussy. Ohh uhh...Left forefinger on stiff clit. I ride the fingers...they're your fingers...Huhh...uhh...Uhhh won't last long. Must...must ride...faster...riding faster...faster...ohh-uhh."

Steaming in my underwear and pants, it's taking all my willpower to remain calm and watch Janice from the corner of the eyes; although Janice is about twenty feet away across the room and busy typing, she'd almost certainly realize that something is greatly amiss if she approaches me now. A quick glance shows that Janice has paused in her typing and is looking at me. Praying that she'll remain at her typing task, I mumble a few vague "Yeah/True" into the phone. My great dick is beating against my underwear and pants. It's as if I'm standing over Sandra watching her masturbate. Now her thickened voice flows down the phone saying: "I...I can't last...longer I'm coming...com...uhh uh yes uhh...yes uhh...yes oh ohhh." I see her shuddering in the throes of a powerful orgasm. My breathing begins to thicken. I hang up the phone, filled with a churning mix of sexual excitement and self-disgust.

Janice asks, "Who was that? You look agitated." Thank God, she remains at her desk.

I hunch over my typewriter, unable to type, and afraid to risk even just a one-word answer or a glance at her. Lust, having kicked away most of the self-disgust, is roaring and leaping inside me like a wild cat threatening to burst from its less than sturdy cage. Many throbbing seconds pass before, still avoiding Janice's eyes, I am able to grumble irritation at an imaginary caller: "It was just a hard-head fellow who thinks I've got money to waste on pipe dreams."

"Ignore him." She returns to typing.

For the first time in a decade I feel a strong urge to masturbate. But I will not give in to the urge, and it'd be futile to ask Janice for sex. I force myself to resume typing, cursing Sandra for the lascivious witch that she is; but after typing one sentence I pause and think: Tonight I shall visit her and teach her a lesson, give her a long hard fuck that might be the end of our immoral affair.

Having just driven into one of the best and newer shopping plazas here in Kingston, intending to buy a few items for the wife, I was about to get out of my car but has been held in place by the sight that has me wondering if the eyes are playing tricks, if I'm really seeing Mrs. Barrett and Hope Blackman getting into a car along with three muscular young men.

Yes, it's them all right.

Twisted emotions explode inside me. Thank Jah, I'm alone.

Although I haven't seen either of the two bitches in years, both of them are easily recognizable by these eyes that saw too damn much of them years ago. Seeing them now kills most of the jubilation from the news my agent delivered over the phone this morning. Within the three days since the New York publishers of my first novel got a copy of the typescript of the second, they've made a verbal offer of a huge advance and promotion perks that my agent rightly accepted without awaiting word from the other publishers who are considering copies of it, a contract will be ready for signing within the next eight days.

So, Mrs. Barrett has moved into bisexuality; now that old age is looming near her obese body, bedding her must be quite a chore. And no doubt, Hope Blackman, who is now in the mid-thirties, is more sadistic than ever. Two insatiable women; the younger one driven by a dominating sadistic streak, the older one greedy for orgasms as for food. Wonder how the three young men are stomaching those two bitches?

I shudder at the thought of going to bed with either of those two females now. Both at once is unthinkable.

There are shameful sexual memories of the two bitches. I attempt to weaken the shame by focusing on the fact that they weren't friends back when each had me on her own short chain, so I didn't even have to think of the obvious horror it would have been to be with both of them together.

How I wish I could erase the bitter disgraceful memories. Dear Jah, the horrors I have endured to rise in the world before I walked into your light.

CHAPTER 36

CHARLIE LOOKS BACK

I awoke with a slight headache. The sun hadn't risen as yet to overwhelm the dawn of that Monday morning, which would be my fourth day in Mrs. Barrett's home. The spirit was exactly what it had been when I had fallen asleep last night — a tight mix of bitterness and hope. Now I wondered aloud: "Must every female who offers me help view me as a sex toy?" I sighed and thought: Help is necessary, so I must endure Mrs. Barrett's annoying appetites.

I felt both older and younger than my eighteen years.

The previous night, after announcing that I was to go see one of the island's top two publishers at ten the next morning, Mrs. Barrett had then gone on to make it clear that I was to be her stud in exchange for the comforts of her home and her ability to help me realize the dream of great literary success.

It wasn't that I was exactly averse to begin bedding middle-aged women, although Mrs. Barrett's desire for me was a powerful surprise. But, although it turned out that she knew how to arouse a young man who was less than enthusiastic, even in the dark her obese body was a bit repulsive. Lying there at dawn that Monday morning on the comfortable bed in the cosy room she had given me, I hoped she'd always keep her sexual desires confined to the darkness in her bedroom and never ask me to tongue her huge, flabby, watery cunt.

Still, I mused, a woman her age wasn't likely to want sex regularly. One hectic night occasionally should be enough for her. And distasteful though each time would surely be, all in all, it'd be a fair enough price to pay. Yes, her help would make it much easier for me to be a big success before age thirty.

Pushing aside the thin coverlet, I thought how naive I had been when we met last week. But, it was damn good that a friend of hers knew the Blackman family and had been able to get me an interview so quickly to see daddy Blackman at his Blackman Publishing Company. This was a great stroke of luck that could become a firm foundation for a literary career. The interview was set for ten o'clock that morning, and I was willing to do just about anything to land a job with Blackman Publishing Company.

It was early summer, the sun had just risen fully on the city, and the mild headache I'd awaken with was still present. I stretched and swung my feet onto the thick oval rug by the bed. The room was airy and spacious. The chest of drawers and dresser were nice Jamaican antiques. My modest wardrobe took up only half of the wall closet. The wallpaper was a nice blue, white and pink design, and I had a bathroom to myself.

I put on slippers and then moved to open the thin curtains and the louvre windows. Cool, early morning air and mellow sunlight danced into the room. I took a few deep breaths. The mild headache disappeared. A damn nice little private community, I thought, standing there looking out the windows of my latest bedroom. If I got a job from Mr. Blackman that morning, within four years I should be able to live a fairly comfortable life without having to endure sexual exploitation.

I began a forty-five minute routine of Kung Fu exercises. At the end of this workout there was still no sound of Mrs. Barrett. I went to the adjoining bathroom for a long bath and shower, pleased about having a bathroom for myself. But the moment I eased down into the tub of warm water I was overwhelmed by the distasteful memories of the previous night.

"I just love to have supper in front of the telly," Mrs. Barrett had said last night when she pushed a laden trolley to a stop by my perch on the antique sofa in the softly lit living-dining room. Night was about to begin devouring the fleeting dusk, and we'd had a typical afternoon Jamaican Sunday dinner, so a big supper was welcomed. I was watching television. The lady was in a long dress and freshly perfumed, but my senses were tuned to the mouth-watering smells coming from the vast supper on the trolley. Charlie, I thought, she certainly was a gluttonous eater but she was also a fine generous cook and a kind motherly figure.

Meantime, the lady had turned on a lamp by the sofa and fixed its shaded glow on to the trolley. Then she sat down beside me and said through a huge smile: "Guess what? Minutes ago a friend phoned to say Mr. Blackman of Blackman Publishing Company said he could use a young man who loves literature and wants to be a writer. You are to report to his office at ten tomorrow morning for an interview!"

Excitement blasted away my breath and propelled me up from the sofa. "Oh, Mrs. Barrett, a job with Mr. Blackman will be better than a university degree in English! I don't know his sons but they're Calabar old boys of long ago. How will I ever be able to repay your kindness and great help?"

"That won't be hard," she laughed, chins and immense bosom jumping in all directions, her fleshy brown face aglow in the soft light. "Just work hard at your career. After we eat I'll tell you the other way to please me. Now sir, let's have some supper."

I sat down saying, "Anything to please you." Sex was the furthest thing from the mind. She beamed and began dishing out the mouth-watering homemade sour sop ice cream, her uniquely spiced ginger beer, a glowing carrot-cornmeal pudding, banana bread, and cheese sand-wiches. Joy over her amazing news made it easy for me to overlook her fast-paced gluttonous eating. Later, I wheeled the empty dishes to the kitchen. The moment I rejoined her on the sofa, she placed one of her ton-heavy arms around my shoulders and said: "I know you are a strong young man." Her tone was gentle. "And I want to help erase your mem-ories of the terrible time with that horrid Fraser woman. I may be a bit on in years, but I can teach you how to kill young women in bed. As old-time folks use to say, 'the older the moon the brighter it shines'." She drew my head to her immense, warm, perfume-powered bosom.

I was speechless with disbelief and despair. Refusing her advance could mean losing all chance of a job with Blackman Publishing Company, losing my secure haven in her home and having a hard time getting set up in a life anywhere close as good. So, of course, I meekly allowed her to haul me up from the sofa and propel me ahead of her upstairs to her room like a dumb animal. We went silently. Her room was semi-dark with the soft glow of a pink-shaded floor lamp and outside light filtering in through the lace curtains. She didn't turn on any other light but there was enough lighting for me to absentmindedly identify the antique furnishings while she hurriedly undressed me and then her obese self in the dispiriting silence of her thick breathing. Limp with despair, I kept my eyes away from her shadowy flabby rolls and loose mounds of flesh. She pushed me onto the huge bed. The bed cried out when she eased her short, mammoth self on it. Her hands immediately moved to the limp Mr. Dickie. Her heavy breathing was the only sound in the room. I closed my eyes and pretended that she was one of the young adult lovers back in my hometown. This made it easier for her competent hands and mouth to arouse me quickly enough.

"What a beauty," she breathed huskily when Mr. Dickie was stiff. I decided that I had best get the job done quickly as possible. So I began applying hands to her flabby flesh, adding a few kisses to her ear-lobes and shoulders. She purred with delight and said: "Ah, so my great stallion is no virgin, eh?"

Without further ado, I got her flat on her back, lifted up the sack of flesh hanging down over the target, and drove into her with all my power. But the power was lost in her folds of flesh and cavernous cunt. Like diving off a bloody building I thought, and wondered if I'd be able to give her an orgasm. Fortunately, within a minute I recalled a claim gleamed from listening to older men discuss sex in my hometown. "Bridging" they called it. I now commenced to try it by easing over Mr. Dickie against one side of the huge watery cunt.

"Yes!" she exclaimed, "Just like that!"

Eventually, after a lot of sweaty hard work, she had a grunting orgasm, during which she almost squeezed the life out of me.

Of course, I was nowhere near climax but was close to exhaustion. Finally, her laboured breathing turned to contented little sighs, and she stopped imprisoning me in her mountains of flesh, allowing me to ease off her. I was sweaty, and, miraculously, still rock hard in a curiously detached manner, sprawled on my back in the huge bed. She said: "You deserve a special treat."

She moved to kneel on a thick rug beside the bed, hauled me to her, wrapped her immense flabby breasts around my balls, and commenced to blow Mr. Dickie.

It was a nice enough treat that led to a climax after a reasonable period. Less than a minute later, she stopped me from executing a hasty escape from her bed. Then, after a while, her eager caresses and my fantasies of an Afro-American actress got the great rod hard again. I fucked her doggy fashion on the thick carpet. She growled, barked, and whimpered like a dog.

Now, sitting in the tub of warm water, I shook off the less than thrilling memories of the night, returned to the promising Monday morning and with a huge sigh, began to scrub away the stink of the night.

She was downstairs in the kitchen when I went down for breakfast.

"Good morning, Mrs. Barrett," I said, feeling too embarrassed to meet her eyes.

"Morning, my amazing young stallion," she replied chattily. "You're truly great, in more ways than one. I'll soon have a hearty breakfast ready to give you power for the ten o'clock interview with Mr. Blackman this morning."

Blackman's Publishing Company occupied a robust, old, two storeyed building on Half-Way-Tree Road, one of the major streets in the heart of Kingston. The building was brightly painted. Downstairs held the store-rooms and the work areas of the clerks, a general secretary, editorial assistants and part-time readers. Upstairs housed a conference room, the offices of the Junior Editor, Miss Hope Blackman; the Editor, Mrs. Jerrel and the Publisher-Owner, Mr. Blackman.

When my watch ticked ten minutes before ten o'clock, my feet were moving up the worn stone steps of the wide, ancient stairway, and at the top, I sat down in one of the visitors' chairs in the little office occupied by Mr. Blackman's half-Chinese secretary. I felt more eager than anxious. At ten sharp, the little secretary showed me into Mr. Blackman's neat, luxurious office and withdrew.

Seated in one of the world's biggest swivel chairs behind a huge uncluttered desk, and wearing a rumpled grey suit, the man appeared smaller than he actually was. He was slim, grey-haired, light brown complexioned, and in his mid-seventies. His probing eyes hinted at a sharp wit and uncommonly alert senses — I'd soon learn that he was much stronger than the average man of his age, and that he was a product of humble origins who had amassed wealth honestly but not without having twisted a few arms. Now, as I advanced across the carpet towards him, he pointed at a chair in front of his desk and said in a clear, firm voice: "Sit."

"Good morning, Mr. Blackman," I said.

Leaning back in his great swivel chair, he said: "So you are the Calabar man who wants to be a writer, and would first like a job in publishing." He wasn't smiling but appeared amiable enough.

"Yes sir."

"I'm interested in young men who want to be fiction writers. We need more in Jamaica. Our island has a great mass of poets, but in this age poetry doesn't turn much profit, so we rarely touch it. Non-fiction is fine, but I'd love to see Jamaica begin producing more fiction before I die, that's why I've began using short stories and novel excerpts in our quarterly general interest magazine. Anyway, my interest in you is also partly due to the fact that my two sons are Calabar old boys."

"I've heard about them but have never seen them," I said, cracking a tiny smile, offering up silent thanks for the power of old school ties — Mr. Blackman's sons were men in their early thirties, older than their sister, Hope. One of the sons managed the family's music recording and distribution business, which was located downtown; the other son ran the family's five fast food outlets that were scattered about the city.

After a few moments, Mr. Blackman continued: "How old are you?"

"Eighteen, sir,"

"Why a job in publishing now instead of Sixth Form or university?"

"Sir, I think I have the language talent to command the written word, plus a powerful imagination and good understanding of human character to write fiction, just like the many successful fiction writers who either didn't go to college or never did any form of writing course. Plus, there is the financial problem."

With a nice smile and a few lively nods he remarked: "Well, it certainly is a good sign that, unlike most people, perhaps even the majority in the literary world, you already realize that the art of fiction writing isn't a natural talent like having a good voice or a natural flair for creating musical sounds via instruments, or painting and carving, etc."

Obviously the man saw writing as I did.

I added: "So one isn't born to write, and doesn't really learn to write. You can develop the skill if you have the three necessary ingredients and are willing to spend the time necessary for you to become worthy of publication."

"The right outlook." (His smile was a powerful tonic to the self-confidence that I had the ability to become a top world-class writer.) "So, you took English Language and Lit in the GCE O' Levels?"

"Yes, sir."

"Okay. We'll put you on trial until you get your exam results." He pressed a button on the console on his desk. "You'll be a sort of glorified handy-man and messenger for now. If your exam results are good you'll move on to other tasks like proof reading and library research."

"Thank you, sir. I'll do my best."

"I expect nothing less of my workers," he said evenly. "Fifty dollars a week, for now. You are to begin today. Your hours will be eight to four."

The pay wasn't exactly what I'd hoped for. But the hours and the man's attitude made it a good enough start in the world I wanted to top.

"A bit of advice about your desire to be a writer. Avoid the party crowd, except as an observer of human behaviour. Keep away from womanising, fatherhood, and even thoughts of marriage until you have a good book in the stores."

I nodded and said: "I'll do exactly that, sir." And I honestly wanted to live that picture.

The door opened without a knock, and the light that lit up his mildly wrinkled face was a dazzling neon sign announcing someone very dear to him.

"What's up, dad?" a mellow voice behind me said.

"Here's the Calabar man I mentioned who wants to be a fiction writer. Break him in."

I turned and beheld a ravishing, light-brown complexioned beauty of medium height. She was obviously in her mid-twenties. Her short, floral dress heralded lush curves. This was Hope Blackman. Charlie, I thought, be on good terms with this one and your job is safe, and advancement will be brisk.

"I'm Hope Blackman." She had an impish smile, dimpled cheeks and mischievous eyes. "Your name?"

"Charlie, Miss."

"Come along, Charlie. Ta ta, dad dear."

"Okay, love."

Hope sailed out of the office ahead of me, rolled through her dad's secretary's domain and floated down a short corridor without a backward glance. I was labouring to keep my eyes off the lovely rear-end and legs. We entered a roomy office that had sky-blue walls, green and black carpets and a half-red, half-purple ceiling — I immediately guessed correctly that this odd mix of colour was her choice and reflected a highly eccentric character. The large desk was cluttered with piles of manuscripts and several books. A red and black cigarette holder was perched on an ashtray sitting on one of the books. Instead of going to her desk, she went to sit on the narrow, floral divan by the bright yellow blinds lining the wide sweep of tall windows. She kicked off her shoes and planted her pretty feet on the thick wall-to-wall carpeting. There was an amused twinkle in the eyes of her pretty face. Her dimples were like two shadowy caves.

There was a loud screech of tires out on the street. My eyes flicked to the windows. Hope didn't bat an eyelid. She crossed her sleek brown legs and said: "Come closer," I obeyed. She continued: "Dad seems to have taken a liking to you but you'll find that I'm the one you'll have to please to keep your job and get help from him with your dream of becoming a writer." Her eyes were roving all over me in a calculatingly greedy manner, so I wasn't much alarmed by her haughty tone and words. But, to be on the safe side, I kept my eyes away from the generous flow of thighs on careless display. "Dad said I'm to break you in, and you're a big, handsome, strong looking boy."

Our eyes locked. Something about her eyes made me uneasy. I glanced off at the small glass-front bookcase beside her desk. But immediately my eyes were jerking back to her, as she'd leaned forward from her seat on the divan to take hold of my crotch.

CHAPTER 37

I froze, gaping at her, and then resisted the rapid urge to trying stepping back out of her firm enough hold on my crotch. Her eyes were focused where her impertinent hand was.

"My my," she purred, "it does feel as heavy as it looks." She looked up into my face, ran her tongue seductively over her lips, began squeezing my crotch gently and said: "If you can use this thing well, your job and dad's help are secure."

My composure returned. "You can find out easily enough," I remarked, nodding, still standing in her grasp. The first tingle of pleasure stirred me. It'd be great to fuck her regularly, I thought.

"Mmm. It's growing." She tossed her wavy abundance of glossy, black shoulder-length hair, aimed a cheeky grin up at me and changed her gentle squeezing to a firm massage. I gave in to the pleasure. Mr. Dickie swiftly became hard in his bindings. She removed her caressing hand and said excitedly: "Let's see it now."

Without delay I pulled my pants and hauled out the great sugar-cane joint.

Blood flushed her light-brown neck and face. Her dark-brown eyes jumped at Mr. Dickie.

I killed the urge to laugh, certain that she wouldn't have appreciated it.

"Oooh, whooo," she breathed through puckered lips. "Even bigger than I thought."

"Aren't you afraid someone might walk in without knocking?"

"No one will." Her tone was husky, her eyes glued to the great rod. "I'd like to touch it. But I won't. Big banana, if I touch you I might have to begin devouring you here and now." She looked up and said curtly: "Put it away. You're to come to my apartment this evening."

I packed in Mr. Dickie and zipped up, trying not to appear too self-satisfied. Things were looking bright.

With a crooked grin she remarked: "Smiling, are you. Well, even if you have enough sexual experience to match your exceptional size, you're certain to find me a bit different. We'll soon see how you fare in my bed."

"We'll see," I nodded cheerfully enough, despite a little worry that she might be some kind of perverted sadistic nympho. But I briskly drowned this troubled thought by drinking up her curvy beauty and telling myself that she would be no match for me where sheer brute force was concerned, positive that if she was into inflicting pain on her lovers, I could easily overpower any such attempt with me.

She got up from the divan and moved to sit in the swivel chair behind her untidy desk. She beckoned me to sit in the chair by her desk, and began outlining my non-sexual duties.

I was to be a general handyman and messenger for her and the editor, Mrs. Jewel, plus unofficial security for the premises during work hours.

After her crisp outlining of these duties, Hope made it icily clear that I was to always address her as Miss Blackman and never do anything to let our co-workers suspect we were lovers.

Everyone at Blackman Publishing Company quickly accepted me. They were all kind and appeared to appreciate my penchant for making people laugh. Of course, it was possible that some of this popularity was due to the fact that most of my orders would always come directly from Hope. There were a few lovely ladies I would've gladly bedded but it appeared best to avoid any other involvement there as long as I was secretly screwing Hope.

At first, it could be said that my most important duty was to fetch and return reference books from the city's head library. Later, after I got impressive exam results in August, I was allowed to work with the editorial assistants in checking reference books for important facts and with proof-reading; and occasionally, I'd lend the clerks a hand with mail orders for books and the quarterly general interest magazine the company published.

On that Monday when I first set foot on the premises, the first task was to go downstairs and fetch Hope some coffee. It turned out that I had to brew a fresh pot, and this was a blessing — Hope was delighted by the coffee, and by the end of the week all the company's coffee lovers including Mr. Blackman and the editor, were praising me as a great coffee brewer. But by the end of that first week I was also nursing a secret loathing for Hope Blackman, and I dared not offend the bitch because she had the power to give either a great boost or a huge blow to my constantly ballooning ambition for fame and fortune.

CHAPTER 38

Hope and a girlfriend occupied a two-bedroom apartment on the top floor of a new five-storey building that was just half mile away from my perch at Mrs. Barrett's. So it didn't appear odd that after work that first day I got 'a lift home' in Hope's car and would thereafter often leave work in similar fashion. I still had my bicycle and enjoyed riding, and the journey to Blackman's Publishing Company wasn't far, but I disliked riding on the busy roads like those leading to work.

Hope's flatmate, Cherry, an insurance sales agent, wasn't home that first evening when we arrived at their comfortable apartment. Without either delay or a word, Hope led me through the oddly decorated living-dining room and down a short passage to her room. In the mellow daylight, the decor of her bedroom stunned me, despite the eccentric colours of her office.

The bedroom was a mad riot of colours — red, purple, green, silver, gold and blue. The wall-to-wall carpeting was in three different sections, two of which were solid colours, while the third section had a multi-coloured pattern, and the wallpaper was of a similar crazy mix. The ceiling boasted stripes and rectangles of black, silver, gold and blue. But all wooden surfaces were carved and stained the same reddish-brown.

"Strip and stop gawking," she commanded, tearing off her own clothes.

Out of the corner of an eye I beheld the unveiling of her ample, well-rounded bum. She turned on a tape deck and faced me with her lovely nakedness. Her skin was even-toned and golden-brown all over. Perfectly proportioned body, big juicy nipples, and thick, glossy, black hair at the great junction. Mr. Dickie lurched at her. "Truly," I said, running eyes all over her, "you're one hell of a sexy lady."

"Obviously. No sexier woman in town," she said haughtily. "And you're a sexy young man, especially that giant size thing of yours."

"Ever had one as big before?" I asked with a wee touch of menace, advancing at her.

"A few, plus one a bit bigger. But they were all fully-grown men." I embraced her. She ground her body against mine, saying: "I can handle any man and will handle you when your thing is fully grown a few years from now."

Aiming to immediately establish physical supremacy, I used my strength to shuffle us closer to the bed and then toppled us to the pink and red quilt, rolled to the top and glued my mouth to hers. But the moment our lips met, she countered by raking her modest talons down my back. I knocked aside her arms and rolled away from her. "Hey!" I exclaimed firmly but without true anger, although my back stung. I was propped up on an elbow. "How'd you like it if I get real rough and dirty?"

Without any hint of fear, she sat up and licked the fingers she had raked me with. There was a strange far away gleam in her eyes. Her lips settled into a twisted little smile.

I frowned. Was she some kind of mad woman or what?

"Please remember I'm your boss always." Her tone was sweetly acerbic. "Want to keep your job and stay out of prison for abusing a lady; you plant it in your mind that where our fucking is concerned you're my boy servant. Of course, I'll give you special rewards for the sexual work. Now lie back and do as I bid." That eerie far away gleam in her eyes twinkled beneath cocked brows. She now looked older than her mid-twenties. Part of me wanted to storm out of the apartment, but the importance that my job and her dad could be to the dream of literary success had a greater pull.

Swallowing indignation, I gave her one last great scowl and lay back on the bed.

"That's my pretty boy." Her voice was triumphant in a cool manner. "My handsome, young stud."

She now began the process of straddling my face, flooding the room with dismay. My erection dwindled. "Tongue me a bit," she commanded.

Cursing luck, I reluctantly set to the task, thinking of the joys, power and freedom literary success would bring. Thankfully, she rode my tongue for just about a minute before she moved aside, glared at my deflated dick and snapped, "So you're one of those who hate giving head, huh? Shit! Finger me then." I was happy to apply fingers, while she got with the task of using her hands and lips to revive Mr. Dickie to iron hardness. She accomplished the task quickly enough and immediately straddled the great rod, batting away my hands from her hips and shooting me a silent glower — we were facing each other. I resisted the urge to try hurting her with a few powerful upward thrusts although her shrewd insistence on keeping my hands from her hips would've lessened any such attempt. In silent ecstasy, she rode me at her own pace, giving herself nearly total command of her ride. Finally, being wary of offending her, I stopped trying to take hold of her hips. After a while, she began bouncing faster and faster, but remained silent, and quick shallow breathing was the only sound she emitted during her long, eerie, eye-rolling orgasm. Still, despite the less than pleasant circumstances, the tightness and muscle-grabbing movement of her cunt propelled me to a nice climax just as her long drawn-out orgasm was ending.

I would soon learn that Hope was always silent once a dick entered her cunt and that she didn't want to be held anywhere near her hips. She never had sex with me in any but the superior female positions and, occasionally with both of us on our sides. Unfortunately, I was never able to repay the sadistic bitch with a truly rough ride.

Her flatmate still hadn't arrived home when I left their apartment at the end of that first visit. Before leaving I had taken a shower, smelt fresh for the brooding half-mile walk home in the warm dusk now ruling the evening and the city.

There were clear signs of impatience on Mrs. Barrett's fat, wrinkling, brown face and in the tone of the "Good evening" she released when I walked in through the open front door. With a plastic smile plastered on my face, I thought: Thank God she and Hope Blackman weren't acquainted. But how the hell was I to cope with an obese unattractive middle-aged doxy and a sadistic young bitch?

I sat down on the sofa and chattily told Mrs. Barrett about the decent angles to the job I'd landed with Blackman Publishing Company. Her bad mood instantly turned cheerful — of course, the view I presented downplayed Hope's influence on my job. I lied that many evenings would catch me working late and that Mr. Blackman had made it clear that he disliked employees making or getting personal calls that weren't for an emergency.

After this little chat, I washed my hands and then we moved to the dining table for a vast delicious dinner. I was truly hungry, so I ate a bit faster than usual. But the lady still outpaced me, even though she had been eating when I arrived, but this was the least of my troubles. I wasn't blind to the near certainty that her heavy dose of expensive perfume, thick make-up and the long, false lashes she kept fluttering, were placards announcing that she was after a second straight night of sex, contrary to the prayer for her to desire sex no more than once a week.

The moment I ate the last morsel, she snatched a bottle of champagne from a covered bucket. Her grin was a huge messy thing. I joined her in toasting my job and future, hoping that good luck would make her drunk — there was to be no such nice fortune of drunkenness. When the champagne bottle was empty, I declared sincere tiredness.

"No problem," she said cheerfully, her fleshy, wrinkling face flushed, points of light dancing in the widened eyes, "I know just the thing to revive you before we go to bed." She winked lasciviously. "A massage will do the trick, dear boy. Go up and take a bubble bath first."

When I emerged naked from the bath and strode into the adjoining bedroom, the middle-aged glutton was sitting on my bed. She was fully clothed. I surrendered to a massage. And, to give the witch due praise, she did know how to give a good massage with those fat hands of hers. She revived me enough for me to voice earnest thanks, although I was worried that she might now undress in the brightly lit room.

"Come thank me in my room," she whispered. We left my room and went to her darkened room. When we got into her bed, she brought down a bit of joy by saying: "Dear Charlie, I won't ask for two nights straight regularly; don't want to weaken you."

The following evening, Hope Blackman again ordered me to accompany her home. This time her flat-mate was at their apartment, sulking with a marijuana spliff when Hope and I arrived, obviously not enthused about meeting me.

Within the next hour, I'd realize that Hope's flatmate was madly in love with Hope, greatly afraid of Hope, was in awe of Hope, and had been a slave of Hope's domineering bisexuality for the past ten years.

CHAPTER 39

Cherry had been Hope's ardent lover and best friend since high school. She was only a year younger than Hope, but whereas Hope looked her mid-twenties age, she looked eighteen-nineteen. She was a product of the ordinary middle class, and acted as if Hope's moneyed background was character strength. A tall, thin, yellowish-brown complexioned, mixed-heritage girl with a handsome face and short hair, her world revolved around Hope. Although taller than Hope, she appeared to be looking up whenever she gazed down into Hope's face. She had sex with men and other women only on Hope's order.

"Cherry, dear, here is my new stallion," Hope said, when we entered the apartment. Cherry gave me a plastic smile and a robot-like nod. Hope took a deep drag from Cherry's marijuana cigar and returned it, along with a long pinch that left a nice print on Cherry's cheek. Cherry managed to smile through a wince, her bum squirming in the floral armchair.

Hope flopped down on the orange sofa and said, "Cherry, build me a spliff. Charlie, you take off my cow-girl boots." With her boots propped up on a purple hassock, she was like a bossy queen. "Cherry and Charlie, a perfect match for me."

Swallowing my pride, I knelt to the assigned task, while Cherry sat in an armchair rolling a marijuana joint.

Hope was saying: "Cherry, don't you worry about his great size when your eyes behold it. I won't let him hurt you."

"I'm not afraid," Cherry said, trying to sound and appear cheerful. I felt like an electric vibrator. Cherry gave Hope the fresh marijuana joint and a light, then went off to the kitchen.

"I could do with a spliff," I said, having taken my first smoke with a non-religious cousin during the previous summer holidays in the country, plus with friends at school. I knew I had the head for it and that it'd make my stud job easier. Hope handed me a little tin of the weed and a packet of paper. While rolling a spliff, I decided that it made sense to begin doing more smoking as a means of soothing the exploited ego. When I lit the joint, the first deep drag felt like a healing to the soul.

Hope launched into a brief history of her relationship with Cherry. It wasn't funny, and didn't end until after Cherry returned with a tray on which sat three glasses, a jug of fruit punch, and plantain tarts and muffins.

"Hurry with the smoking and eating, you two," Hope commanded. "I'm starved for sex."

I drank a glass of juice, ate a muffin and a plantain tart, then returned to smoking until Hope finished her spliff and rose saying, "Come along now, bwoy an' gal (her upper-class accent gave the dialect phrase a comical ring), time for fucking." She floated off, leading the way to her room. Cherry was on her heels. I was rearguard.

The moment she entered the room, Hope set the tone by undressing briskly. Cherry and I followed her cue. Cherry's thin, near-flat chested body, was a modest sight beside her heavy breasted and far curvier mistress.

"Charlie, watch me and Cherry get each other ready," Hope said. Cherry favoured my half erect dick a glance; her eyes registered worry before she briskly returned full attention to the haughty princess.

I sat down on one of the three brightly coloured ottomans in the room and watched the ladies get into hot action on the bed. They quickly settled into the sixty-nine position — Hope atop, of course. It was an interesting sight that got me rock hard.

Before long, Hope moved away from Cherry and told her how to position her body, and then ordered me to shaft Cherry doggy fashion. I rolled on a condom.

"Be gentle with her," commanded Hope, who was now reclined on her back on the bed, her ass on a pillow, with Cherry's head at her crotch, Cherry kneeling on the carpet.

As gently as possible, I gripped Cherry's thin hips and gradually eased the first third of Mr. Dickie into her moist cunt. But she still cried out painfully and raised her head from Hope's cunt. Hope scolded her briskly.

Cherry quickly settled down, and returned her mouth to Hope's crotch. But it was obvious that poor Cherry disliked big bamboos. Moved by pity, I didn't give her Mr. Dickie's full length, I jammed gently and caressed her clit tenderly — like myself, she was a victim; I was handcuffed by ambition, she was chained by a crazy love. We settled into a nice rhythm. Within twenty minutes or so, Hope was into the gasping-French-words throes of an orgasm, driven there by her vast lust and Cherry's tongue and hands. When Hope sighed in the aftermath of her climax, Cherry immediately begged her to make me stop; Cherry appeared as far from orgasm as I was. The mistress of the scene ignored Cherry's plea for a break, kept us engaged in the same position for another five or so minutes before ordering a halt. The moment my erection backed out of Cherry, the boss lady ordered me to lie back on the bed. Then, to my dismay, she said: "Cherry, let him soothe you with his tongue."

Dispassionately, Cherry moved into position, while her bossy bitch mistress got ready to straddle my great rod. Meantime, I was quelling indignation.

Hope eventually had one of the long, drawn-out, eerie, eye-rolling orgasms she'd always have whenever Mr. Dickie was inside her.

Despite the sweet squeezing movement of Hope's cunt during her long orgasm, I didn't soar near climax, Cherry didn't climax either, and she moved aside the moment Hope's orgasm ended.

Hope wasn't interested in a third climax that evening, so she allowed me to go cool down with a shower; Cherry definitely was not interested in any further sexual contact with me.

Night had already taken control of the city when I completed the easy walk home. Mrs. Barrett didn't require sex for a third consecutive night — thankfully, she'd never ask that of me. We simply ate heartily of her good cooking, and then sat down in armchairs with reading materials in the well-lit living room, both of us facing the running television, and occasionally exchanging brief, banal chitchat. I went off to bed leaving her reading a new novel.

The following evening was wonderful. Hope didn't require my stud service after work and was actually kind enough to ask if I wanted to meet her marijuana supplier. Just after four o'clock we left our coworkers still toiling at their desks, got in her car and drove directly to the marijuana den, which turned out to be near my nest with Mrs.

Barrett. Hope introduced me to the dealer, collected a parcel and drove away to go prepare for a lesbian orgy set for that night.

The dealer owned the house, and lived there with his family. He was Joe to everyone, and had high connections in the two major political parties. When one went to this upmarket den, you simply walked or drove in through the constantly open gate to the back of the house where you bought little joints or parcels of two ounces from the dealer or a pleasant young man, one of whom was always on the back porch. If you desired to smoke on the premises you simply mounted the two flights of stairs that ran from the back porch up to the smoking room. That first evening, I went up to the smoking room.

It was a real high-class marijuana joint. This first visit of mine was also the first to a marijuana den and I'd never imagined such a fancy place for smokers. Of course, prices at this remarkable den were quite a bit higher than what I knew marijuana sold for in my hometown and the city's ghetto areas. But it was perfect for me — safe from cops and robbers, and near my most recent home.

I would become a regular visitor to that pleasant smoking room and within its lively friendly walls, I would meet a wide variety of people (mostly males) from the middle and upper classes, including quite a few middle class Rastafarians, who'd slowly rekindle my dormant interest in Rasta doctrine.

That Friday, last day of my first working week, Hope ordered me to report to her apartment at 7:00 p.m. "I want to ride you just before I hit the town tonight," she added. It was just after 10:00 a.m. and I had just entered her office with coffee. I nodded, praying that Mrs. Barrett wouldn't want an early fuck that night.

I left Mrs. Barrett's home at 6:40 that evening for the walk to Hope's apartment — I had told Mrs. Barrett that I was going to a party but would return early, and she had gruffly declared: "Don't disappoint me by staying out later than eleven-thirty." Minutes later, I was strolling through brightly lit middle class avenues. The few girls out walking were in male company. My thoughts were of the future when I'd have riches and fame to please myself.

A smug-face Hope, wearing a short leather dress, let me into the apartment.

Cherry was huddled pathetically on the sofa emitting desultory sobs, her tear-streaked cheeks bruised, her lips swollen. She appeared lost in baggy overalls.

"Damn it, Cherry, will you cut out the damn sniffling now," snapped Hope, "or must I give you another thrashing?"

Shock had me rooted where I first got full view of the battered Cherry, who now responded with: "Please, don't hit me again this evening. But...but I can't help crying...how she...been telling everyone she intends to...to take you away from me." She sniffled and dabbed at her puffy eyes with a towel.

Hope heaved a sigh that was a mix of exasperation and narcissism, and then declared: "Cherry, by now you should know I will never want another girl for my flat-mate, and that a teenager can't interest me for more than a few weeks, no matter how pretty she is. My dearest lover, by Monday Lena will be nursing an aching cunt and a welted ass, and wishing she'd never met me."

Cherry gazed reverence up at her goddess and reached out a hand to stroke the goddess' thigh. I felt like an intruder. Hope ruffled her slave's hair and said: "Let's go milk Charlie before we hit the town."

"Darling, I'd rather not," pleaded Cherry. "You go ahead. I'll fix a light meal."

"Okay, dear," Hope agreed. "And do something about your swollen lips."

Cherry jumped up, smiling.

"Come along, Charlie," Hope commanded, striding off without a glance at me. With a mental glower, I went after the sexy bitch.

When I returned home after eleven that night, having just spent over two hours at a go-go club, Mrs. Barrett was watching television. Hope Blackman had claimed my juices only once, then I had a quick smoke and a light meal with her and Cherry, followed by a walk on my own to the go-go club, where I ran into a former schoolmate and had joined his little group for drinks — a tonic drink and two beers for me — and lots of cheerful leering at the go-go dancers on stage. Now, minutes after arriving home, it was fairly easy for me to follow Mrs. Barrett to her dark room and give her the long fuck she was eager for.

The following morning, I awoke just before eight, happy that it wasn't a workday; and it was nice to know that only rarely would I have to work on Saturdays. After a huge breakfast with Mrs. Barrett, who had obviously done quite a bit of eating earlier and was now dressed for a shopping trip, I mounted my bicycle with Joe's marijuana haven in mind. It was now just after nine o'clock. The early July sun was already intense on the city; riding was certainly cooler than walking. At Joe's den, I spent roughly an hour up in the smoking room enjoying two little spliffs, drinking a soda, losing a dollar to the one-arm bandit gambling machine, and listening to the talk of other customers drifting in and out of the big, airy room. Saturday was always busy at Joe's place.

On that first Saturday visit of mine, I realized just how diverse the racial mix of middle class and rich marijuana smokers was in Jamaica — Afro, Euro, Oriental and the wide array of mixed heritages that are part of the Jamaican reality. The age scale ran from sixteen to over seventy. Quite a few female smokers came by, mostly young and escorted.

It appeared that I was the only person present who didn't know anyone else there but I got enough smiles, friendly nods and cheerful greetings to put me at ease with the certainty that making friends there would be easy, and made me wonder why the city streets and the whole world couldn't all be as pleasant.

When I rode away from Joe's place, heat waves were shimmering above the avenue's asphalt. I was dripping sweat as I pedalled through the guarded gateway of the walled townhouse complex in which I had the sex-for-easy-living nest.

Riding pass this new nest, I saw that Mrs. Barrett hadn't returned home as yet. She'd handed over a spare key days ago, but I was now headed for the pool. The moment the bicycle arrived by the pool area, I saw a sexy black complexioned lady who set the blood boiling. Minutes later, I was emerging from the male changing room and her eyes met mine, just for a fleeting moment.

CHAPTER 40

In the water, on the pool's tiled apron and on the covered veranda-like area of the pool house, there were nearly thirty members of the gated community. It was now after eleven o'clock. The sun was blazing but everyone in sight appeared cool and cheerful.

Every eye was on me when I stepped out of the male changing room and strolled on to the roomy tiled area surrounding the big rectangular pool, which was near the community's high, formidable back fence. I was the latest addition to the community and hadn't made any friends in the nine days since taking up residence with Mrs. Barrett, who wasn't exactly the friendly outgoing type. I was wearing my tightest swim trunks, which got what I wanted — the attention of the big girls and ladies. I was hunting a temporary lover or two who wouldn't have any power over my future.

In keeping with the skin colour reality of this gated upper-middle income enclave, most of my neighbours at the pool were brown-skinned. But of all the females over fifteen there, the loveliest had skin darker than mine. There was an arresting aspect to her beauty that boosted my usual low-keyed interest in ladies over twenty-five; she looked to be roughly thirty years old. Her jet-black complexion was alluring as one's favourite cool drink in that roasting sunshine. She was in a white swimsuit, matching swimming cap and large, dark sunglasses. She was sitting on the edge of the pool, her feet in the water. I stood across from her flexing my muscles, giving her sly looks and pretending to be oblivious of her glances. I closed out the whispers, giggles and lust of the other females. Was the foxy lady married?

Mr. Dickie began stirring towards erection mode. I killed this unwelcomed possibility by diving into the pool for a swim among the frolicking teens and the few adults doing laps. I swam one lap and was instantly lured to a corner of the pool by an amiable greeting from Ronald, the mulatto youth who lived next door Mrs. Barrett; his family was the only one in the community to whom Mrs. Barrett had given me a formal introduction. He was about seventeen and had two younger sisters who were showing great promise of beauty.

Ronald, two of his pals and two girls, were sitting close together on the edge of the pool. I exchanged greetings and names with them, then swam away because the lady I desired had just left the edge of the pool and was now sitting down at one of the vacant tables on the tiled area. It appeared best to cast caution to the sunshine. I swam to near where my desire was seated, hauled myself out of the water, headed directly for her table, and called up my most winning smile when I drew close to her.

Leaning under the big pool umbrella covering the table and three chairs, I saw that her black skin was like a magical combination of the finest silk and the most brilliant diamond — perhaps the term "diamond- black" would be the best description. "Good day, ma'am," I said politely, with a respectful nod of the head, no lust in my eyes; in fact, for unknown reasons, I was now too nervous to harbour any great lust. "Mind if I join you?"

"A pleasant day to you." Her smile and voice were pleasant but not encouraging in terms of a sexual quest. "You're welcome to sit."

"Thanks." I sat down across from her. Despite the strange unexpected anxiety, it took a lot of will power to keep my eyes from the magnificent breasts straining against the modest top of her white swimsuit. She took off her sunglasses. Her lovely, big eyes added glitter to the intense soon-to- be-midday sunlight. Her glossy face was pretty to the exceptional point where you were likely to weep gratitude the first time she allowed you to touch it. Your first kiss to her rich lips would certainly make your heart miss a few beats.

The radiant, even toned blackness of her face sparkled even further when she said: "You're a new addition to our little community, or just a visitor?"

I gave her Mrs. Barrett's name, and immediately rolled out the little green lie that Mrs. Barrett and I were using to explain my presence in her home — that Mrs. Barrett's late husband and my departed grandfather had been good friends via a farming interest in St. Mary and she was now interested in helping my literary dream. This nice fib was helped by the fact that Mrs. Barrett was a childless and highly reserved woman whose few close relatives were all resettled abroad. My new desire nodded and said: "I don't know Mrs. Barrett well. The age difference and all that. But she appears to be a nice lady." One of her lovely hands gestured alluringly, and her entire manner suggested that she wasn't averse to hearing more about me.

I gladly told her I was a new graduate of Calabar high. And, having lost most of the strange anxiety born when I had greeted her, it took a lot of willpower to control the urge to reverently feast eyes on her awesome beauty while giving her a rosy edited view of my rural origins and times with the Chens and Miss Fraser. I ended this edited tale with the nicer facts about my job and determination to be a writer.

"Song and fiction writing. A challenging ambition — two awesome roads," she said earnestly. "I admire people who have the guts to go after artistic careers. In high school I dreamed of becoming an actress. But by the time I graduated I was too afraid of the difficulties that artist careers pose to persons without a sound inheritance. I settled for the lesser dream of law."

"You must be some lawyer," I said, ignoring the inviting glances from two pretty teenage girls in bikinis strutting on by from the pool, "and no doubt you'll become great someday."

Her smile cooled the intense summer heat to soothing warmth. "I suppose my regular clients think I'm good. Perhaps one or two even think I'm 'super good,' as the kids today would say."

I grinned with pleasure; and then, realizing that both her hands were now lying on the table, I glanced down and saw that there was no wedding band. My heart leapt, the half erect Mr. Dickie swelled further. I swallowed the last of the uncanny anxiety and, in a voice that couldn't be overheard, said: "I think you're super sexy."

Our eyes met and locked. Her neat brows were elevated. "Ahh," she said in low tones, "making a pass at one who has a daughter almost as old as you." She appeared torn between amusement and disapproval.

"Really?" Her amazing figure and smooth belly didn't suggest a teenage daughter. "I suppose it's possible."

"I'm near thirty-three. She's sixteen. Most likely she'll soon arrive here; about an hour ago she left for her grandparents' house just across the street from our little community. So mind your manners."

Despite her show of displeasure, the recent signs of amusement and the absence of a wedding band had my guts loaded with anticipation. "And her dad?"

"We divorced years ago." She appeared to be getting truly cross at me.

"The loveliest divorcee," I whispered, and paused while a group of teens flirted by, all of them greeting my companion, who responded cheerfully. Despite her touch of ill humour, excitement had me pulsing all over. I resumed: "That you're the loveliest mother is obvious for all to see. And...and it means that I'm justified to dare make a pass at you."

She laughed. I had played the right note. She was back to being half amused by my boldness. She nodded and murmured, "You really are no ordinary youthman. I'm Patricia, you are?"

"Charlie. And, although self-praise isn't the best recommendation, I'm exceptional in more ways than one."

A puzzled sigh rolled out of her. "I shouldn't be having this talk, have never done anything like this before." She paused, frowning uncertainty. Her whole aspect shouted honesty.

"Well," I coaxed softly, "I'm an eighteen year old who has quite a bit of experience with older women, because I've always been a lot bigger and bolder than my age group."

She flexed her brows and said: "I already noticed." Then she released a sigh that I couldn't read.

"It'd be nice to learn a thing or two from the world's most beautiful lawyer." Was I going too fast?

"If it's law lessons..." She paused as two pre-teens raced by dripping pool water. Then she murmured: "Yes, I'd gladly give you some law lessons."

Her smile spurred me on towards defeat or glory. "As long as the lessons are at your home, or somewhere more private."

"But, then again, maybe you're quite a few years too young," she said thoughtfully, eyes narrowed. "Younger males have never interested me, you know. Honestly."

Certain her words were one hundred percent honest, I murmured: "What I lack in years is in another length." Our eyes were locked, and she began chuckling. I continued, "Come on, why not let's go start lessons today, huh? Men of your age are free to teach eighteen year old girls, why shouldn't you do likewise?"

"Mmm. Uhhh, here comes my daughter and friends."

The daughter, Julie, was a bit too plump for a sixteen year old but showed promise of someday becoming at least nearly as lovely as her mom. Her two friends were plain girls.

Patricia made the necessary introductions and said: "Julie, dear, I'm going now. Coming?"

"Later," Julie said. "This girl needs a good swim now." Patricia disappeared into the female changing room without any word or sign of interest in me.

Having donned shorts and a vest in the male changing room, I was outside sitting on my bicycle when Patricia finished changing her clothes and emerged from the pool house. She was now wearing a short cotton dress. With only an exchange of smiles, we walked off together, me pushing my bicycle. On the short walk to her front door we had a relaxed chat about her law career.

When she let us into her neat home, she became a bit tense, and, with her typical honesty, her first comment was a rueful: "Never thought I'd ever be attracted to one so much younger." Her smile made it clear that I wasn't yet certain to get the treasure. "Mmm, but an eighteen year old who appears better built than most grown men is heady stuff." She chuckled self-mockingly.

I grinned, moved by her noble honesty, and said: "You won't be disappointed." I gently took her hand and literally led her upstairs (her home was one of the two bedroom units, identical to Mrs. Barrett's town house). Her bedroom boasted black stained furnishings, beige carpet, pink bedside rug and light-blue walls. The curtains and lamps were white.

The sweet and melancholy memories of Patricia are too sacred and terribly self-defeating for me to think much about the exquisite sexual aspect of the wonderful affair we would enjoy for over two years. All I will allow is that I fell in love with her the moment I beheld her glorious nakedness in the bright sunlight flooding through the thin curtains of her bedroom the day we met. Her sexual skills were below average for a thirty-two year old mother, but love made our pleasures in her bed that very first day superior to anything I had experienced before. It was clear that sex and romance hadn't been major issues in her life since her divorce had gone down nearly six years before; her daughter and career were her joys. I knew she spoke truthfully when she declared that I was the first lover she'd ever taken without having gone through weeks of dating.

On average, Patricia and I would have sex once or twice a week — mainly on Saturdays and Sundays while Julie was out, plus furtive night meetings at two of the city small hotels. At the end of our very first sexual contact, she made it perfectly clear that we could continue as lovers only if I were diligent about keeping it secret and realized that we were nothing like a steady couple; I immediately knew that any declaration of love would've made her uneasy and quite likely ruin our affair. I instantly resigned myself to nursing love in silence, although it was my first taste of being in love — what I'd felt for Miss Simpson, and Ava and Ava's friend, Kimberly, paled greatly in comparison. I was wise enough to quickly realize there was no chance for a serious open affair with her before her daughter was at least on the verge of getting a college degree. I knew my secret love was strong enough to face this long wait. I lost the urge for any great effort in seeking other lovers, and the sadistic urges receded to occasional dreams of revenge against Hope and Mrs. Barrett.

I kept visits to Patricia's home at a minimum. She took my advice not to try becoming closer friends with Mrs. Barrett, who didn't appear the least bit jealous. Of course, I made certain she didn't even suspect that I had any sexual link with Mrs. Barrett or Hope Blackman.

Patricia and I laboured to give the impression that our friendship was a matter of mutual literary interest — together we began practising the crafts of song and fiction writing, her role being mainly that of a sounding board and spell checker. She was bliss; my heaven. She was as important as the dream of international literary success. But wretched fool that I was, my badly exploited male ego would ruin that first and greatest chance at life-long happiness.

Meantime, in those first weeks after Patricia and I became lovers, Julie and I quickly built a good friendship. This meant that neighbours, and perhaps even Mrs. Barrett, thought that I was after Julie. In these first weeks, I didn't think Julie suspected I was her mom's lover. Months later, I'd have reason to think that for quite a while Julie had at least developed a nagging suspicion of the truth.

From the first weeks after meeting her and her Mom, at times I would sense that Julie desired me. But, of course, I had no intention of dishonouring my love for her Mom. I made certain not to do or say anything that Julie could mistake as sexual or romantic interest in her; and I did the same with her friends.

That year, 1981, ended with me still chained in the frustrating sexual attachments with Mrs. Barrett and Hope Blackman, while nursing the strongest possible love for a wonderful thirty-three year old lawyer. This love for Patricia was so powerful I'd have willingly humoured her with the occasional bit of oral sex. But when I mentioned oral sex, Patricia said: "I'm basically a traditional African lady, with a biblical touch. I dislike oral sex. It appears weird to be kissing a man's private, so I don't expect a man to put his head between my legs. In any case, there can be no doubt that clothing and such make private parts a haven for germs."

"We're so alike!" I exclaimed joyously, and pulled her to me in the hotel bed. We settled into a quiet, satiated cuddle. I told myself that I must become a successful writer and then ask her to marry me.

Of course, the great fear of my heart was that she might fall for a successful man of her age group before I acquired fame and riches. But I managed to keep this thought from becoming a regular companion.

For a while, I was tempted to arrange for Patricia and Daddy to meet, but I quickly realized that Daddy would've read the truth about us. Patricia agreed it was best that Daddy shouldn't even know about her half-pretend literary role in my life. I, of course, went to great pains to ensure Hope Blackman never met Patricia or suspect I had such a lover — the bossy, nympho bitch would certainly have slyly done something to ruin my good romantic fortune.

In early March, 1982, Mr. Blackman presented me with a Honda CB100 motorbike to make my tasks as messenger and carrier of reference books more efficient. I was allowed to keep it on a liberal basis — Blackman Publishing Company paid insurance and licence fees, stood the cost of all major repairs, gas used on company jobs, and a steady supply of tires. I was already fairly knowledgeable about the riding and caring of motorbikes, thanks to two cousins and an uncle in my hometown who'd had bikes for years. Within a month I was happily zooming about the city. By this time, too, my salary had increased a bit and I was doing more checking of facts on manuscripts up for publication, and more proof reading. I was still the one who did most of the coffee brewing, as I was by far the best hand at it there at Blackman Publishing Company.

The motorbike promptly got me into paying regular visits to Blackman's Recording and Distribution Company, which was located downtown. Old Mr. Blackman had a healthy mistrust of talking delicate business with his two sons on the phone, plus he liked having their opinions on certain manuscripts. He rarely visited the premises of the businesses he'd given them to manage, so from the very first week when he gave me the motorbike, he began using me as a messenger with his sons' offices. Before long, Hope Blackman grudgingly nudged her brother who managed the music business into quickly allowing one of the company's most promising young singers to record two of the four songs I'd penned since graduating from high school the previous summer. It was a great help that Hope's brother liked me, and respected his father's upbeat opinion about my writing talent. While the young singer and one of the young producers loved those two songs, which I had written to the beat of two old catchy Studio One reggae rhythms — Hope's brother and the senior producers had healthy doubts about the project. Hope had her brother thinking she was enthusiastic about the songs, but with me she privately made it clear that she was largely indifferent and was just handing me a bonus for stud duty. My charm and Hope's influence prodded her brother to release one of the songs with solid promotion in early September of that same year, 1982. It immediately made a nice entry on to the local charts and was highly popular in the dancehalls. This nice success prompted Hope's brother and his top producer to put greater effort into releasing the other song. This one exploded stronger than the first, establishing the singer as a new star.

Of course, Patricia, my friends in the city and back in the hometown, Daddy and all close relatives, old Mr. Blackman and his sons, and my co-workers, were all ecstatic about this bit of brisk success. I was thrilled but couldn't help thinking it a bit unfair that the singer and producer were reaping all the public acclaim, a feeling that increased my desire to write popular fiction. Mrs. Barrett and Hope Blackman avowed delight in this success of mine, too, but it was clear that each of these two witches was hoping that it would be a long time before I'd become successful enough to escape her exploitive grip on me.

That same year also saw me making a step forward in fiction writing.

Patricia had a good typewriter at home, and together we began getting me to embrace the art of fiction writing. From reading about successful writers, I had become inclined to use pencils for early drafts of a story before typing the ultimate product. So I had the tools, the drive, and the vital encouragement of my love, Patricia, and my employer, Mr. Blackman. Patricia suggested I concentrate on short stories first. I took her advice, locked away the months old feverish attempt at a novel, and wrote three short stories that year. Each of these short stories went through several drafts and countless fiddling. Mr. Blackman liked one and accepted it for publication in that year's final issue of the quarterly general interest magazine he published. I submitted the other two to the kind, aging gentleman who was the literary editor at the island's top Sunday paper — both were accepted. One was initially returned with a suggestion for improvement, and one was published in December, which meant that, I had two short stories on national view that month.

By this time, my doubts about the bible had been weakened by the words and deeds of the Rastafarians I reasoned with at Joe's marijuana den, plus the actions of Christians like the literary editor at the Sunday paper. I resumed moving towards the light of Rastafari. But it was a slow growth.

I was now nineteen years old, and it felt damn good to be told that two popular songs and two published short stories were powerful proof that with diligent efforts I could accomplish my goals. But I knew there was a hell of a hard way to go before I'd be able to earn enough money to support even a modest middle-income life and be free from the clutches of Mrs. Barrett and Hope Blackman. I would then need a little fortune and plenty of public respect to ask Patricia to make our affair public by way of an engagement. It wouldn't do to burn any bridges yet. Thankfully, Mrs. Barrett continued confining our bouts of sex to the darkness of her bedroom, was still satisfied with one or two nights per week, and kept her word about not demanding sex two nights in a row; and Hope Blackman wasn't making any new distasteful sexual demands. Life was acceptable and loaded with golden promises. My inbred stamina and Kung Fu exercises, a strong interest in eating a balanced diet and a low interest in alcohol, meant that my hectic sex life wasn't likely to affect the nerves.

The following year began with the appearance of what would be the best year of my life. It almost flowed nicely on this best-ever-note right to its very end, with more modest nation-wide successes with one song and four short stories.

But there was to be no nice finish to that year. My battered sexually exploited ego and blatant teen provocation, would combine to bring about a horrible change in life that would unleash the mild sadistic nature I had been keeping in check for several years. When it escaped its cage it would become a beast that would override even my drift towards the caring humane life of Rastafarian livity.

CHAPTER 41

On that unforgettable Saturday afternoon in early December, 1983, I stopped by Patricia's home, aching to see her pretty face and hear her wonderful voice — when I had last talked to her the previous evening, she had said she'd be home all day Saturday; but now she wasn't present. At home alone was Julie. She had bloomed into a cheeky, sophisticated eighteen year-old college student, and was now much trimmer than she'd been at sixteen.

I was on the Blackman Publishing Company motorbike, riding in from visits to my tailor and a friend, when I eagerly stopped at Patricia's home. Julie said Patricia had gone out unexpectedly. I began turning away from the front door. Julie said: "Charlie, come in a minute, please. I'd like your opinion on something important." Nothing about her tone and body language hinted at even mild flirting. I followed her inside; hoping that the delay would end before the threatening rain came pouring down, as Patricia's absence now highlighted the need for some food. But, as the evil forces wanted it, immediately rain came out of the overcast sky, and my bike was under the porch-like roofing that covered the dual car parking space at the front of the town house. So, with a sigh, I sat down in an armchair in the living-dining room. Then Julie flopped down on the sofa at an angle that caused most of her thighs to be on display under her mini skirt.

The rain poured down outside. I moved my eyes away from the nice legs.

Julie grinned impishly and asked with sauciness: "Charlie, don't you think I'm old enough for a real sex life?"

I was startled, and began regretting having stopped by. Something in her twinkling eyes made me wonder if she suspected or knew I was her mom's lover.

"Well," she prompted in purring tones, "what do you think, dear Charlie?"

I couldn't help noticing that she had begun a neat bout of flashing of her red covered crotch. The rain was pouring too hard for me to leave. I thought of moving to another chair but anxiety and fear of appearing foolish glued me where I sat. "Julie," I finally managed to say, "you're an eighteen year-old college student. You must know what you want."

"That's not a helpful answer," she declared, batting lashes provocatively. Then she pouted invitingly, before asking: "Do you think I'm sexy?"

Thunder rumbled mightily. Lightning lit up the sky. I had no intention of intimacy with this daughter of my true love, but lust was drawing near the defences. "What are you playing at, Julie?" I asked, gazing into her searching eyes, hoping that my gaze was of a firmer no-nonsense note than the tone of the question.

She feigned bewilderment, brows puckered, her hazy eyes gazing from under lowered lashes.

"Come on, Julie, don't waste our time," I accused sternly, now the angry but wary older brother.

Her response was a grin and a pert: "You're just over a year older than me, right, so, tell me, why do you treat me as if I'm a child?"

I gave her what was intended to be a puzzled frown, while silently praying for the pouring rain to ease just enough for a hasty retreat.

"Perhaps," she declared dramatically "just maybe, the girls here are correct when they say the fact that mom is the only female you often smile with and talk to, must mean that you either dislike or fear girls."

I was startled into an eye lock with Julie — perhaps I even gaped foolishly. It hadn't occurred to me that my casual but reserved manner with all big girls and women would've had me looking like a prude, a stuff-shirt or a homosexual. I hadn't wanted to risk making Patricia jealous or causing her to think I had playboy instincts.

Julie ended the deep, heavy, thick pause by adding: "He is oh so tall, handsome and sexy, they say and oh so heavy in the pants. But is he a fairy or a wretched masturbator?"

"Shit," I blurted, further dismayed by the picture Julie was presenting.

With a mocking grin, Julie declared: "Sometimes I think you and mom are involved sex..."

"Julie!" I exclaimed. "Friends, that's what we are. Our mutual writing interests override the big age difference."

"Yeah," Julie said. "I see it. Lately I mostly agree with the majority of girls who think you're queer. Fairy Charlie. Is it younger boys or older guys?"

I glared at her indignantly. No young, hot-blooded, Jamaican heterosexual male, could be cool about a young lady calling him a fairy.

She said, "Mom won't be back before evening, and this rain won't allow anyone to come by now." Immediately she sprang up with legs apart, used her hands to raise her mini-skirt above her waist, began to gyrate her hips, and purred, "Come prove that you're neither a homo or a big limp dick."

This was too much. I leapt to my feet, taut with anger and desire for justice. Thunder rumbled. My heart drummed mightily. Rain roared. My blood surged. Julie moved closer, mini skirt still held above her waist. She used a hand to snap the waist of her little red underwear. My dick lurched to attention. She was less than six feet away.

"Oh," Julie cooed triumphantly, gazing at my tented pants front, "I've awakened him. He does lust at girls. But is he one of the shy masturbators?"

"I can discipline you and all your friends!" I snapped.

"So you say. I have condoms. Let's go see if your big thing is good." She turned, and with her mini-skirt bunched above her hips, moved off with a lusty hightailed wagging of her lovely rear-end. "Come along, big front, or my friends will hear that you're just a big masturbator."

I lost it completely, exploded beyond control, steaming with sexual indignation. My love for Patricia became a shrouded thing, that cherished jewel was wrapped and locked away for a time till I completed the necessary task of showing up the inferiority of the fake version. Reality was the need to discipline this infuriating young lady.

Julie's colourful bedroom, with its wall posters of Hollywood actors and Jamaican reggae stars, appeared to be the perfect place for a disciplinary fuck that rainy afternoon. She undressed quicker than I did — she had a lovely body. Then she turned to her dresser and opened a drawer. When she twirled towards me there was a condom in her hand. I was now naked and iron erect. Her eyes bulged, her saucy grin changed to a gape.

"Scared or what?" I mocked. "Ever saw such a man, Miss Julie?"

"It is huge," she breathed, full of the mix of fascinated greed and fear. Her eyes were glued to the mighty rod. Then she looked up into my face and said pertly: "Why should I be scared? I'm eighteen, and babies come out of where it's going."

I took the condom from her and, while rolling it on, said: "Mr. Dickie will teach you a lesson, but he won't hurt you too bad."

Grinning anxiously, she moved to sit on her bed. For some unconscious reason, I became aware that the rain had eased off.

But it was too late to back out now. Manly sexual honour was at stake. I joined her on the bed and began massaging her slightly plump belly and lightly haired pelvis. And instantly, before so much as a fingertip touched her pum-pum, the room door eased open. Then, after a second that was frozen and eternal, from the figure poised in the doorway there came a horrified half-whispered: "Oh my God."

CHAPTER 42

I rocketed away from Julie, my body trembling, the mind stupidly wanting to ask my beloved how she'd arrived in the rain, as if she didn't own a car and had a covered parking area attached to the front of her home; then, just as idiotically, I was remembering that the rain had eased up while I had been putting on the condom. My chest became a ball of fire. My eyes were riveted on Patricia. She was rooted in the doorway. Her black face was green with horror, her lips and hands trembling nearly as badly as my whole body was.

Time regained life in an ominous rumble of thunder. I had a vague notion that Julie was now huddled under her coverlet, and that I should begin getting dressed. But I was rooted in a mixture of dread, regret and the wish that I could either weep or die.

Patricia's features changed from horror to pure hatred. "Get out!" she hissed. "You beast! Don't ever come near me and my daughter again, you hear!"

The depiction of hate in her tone and eyes immediately told me there was no hope of ever getting forgiveness for having defiled her most sacred trust. To her, there could be no possible excuse for a lover to touch her daughter — she was perfectly correct in this.

Instantly, I saw that Julie's provocative words and action had not given me any justification for betraying love. I should've simply used words to counter Julie's mockery — my indignantly lustful reaction had marked me as a stupid boy — certainly not the dignified mature man that Patricia deserved.

In a haze, I gathered my clothes and stumbled from the room, avoiding Patricia's eyes. I dressed in the gloomy passage and then fled downstairs. The rain had eased away completely. I rushed out through the front door to my motor bike. Of course, just then, I couldn't face Mrs. Barrett or anyone I knew well. Under the overcast sky, I rode to the string of shopping centres on Constant Spring Road, parked the bike and commenced to wander aimlessly among the crowds of late-afternoon Saturday shoppers on the walkways of the plazas. For nearly an hour, the thought of suicide was like a nagging ache in my brain, but I'd always viewed suicide as one of the greatest acts of cowardice. Eventually I ended up drinking beers and absentmindedly munching salted nuts in the gloomiest corner of a restaurant-lounge on the top floor of a three-storey mall. I remained there until nightfall, mechanically drinking and munching, brooding regret, self-hatred and acceptance of a loveless future. Then, seemingly unable to get drunk, I journeyed home to the nest at Mrs. Barrett's, told her I was ill and went upstairs to bed. She brought some tea, water crackers and a little dish of honey to my room; and after I insisted there was no need to summon a doctor, she withdrew with a worried frown that suggested I looked near death.

For the following eight days, my dick was eternally limp and greatly shrunken; at times I wished it'd remain like that forever. To keep Mrs. Barrett and Hope Blackman from making sexual demands during this time of death, I visited a doctor on the third day, and then sternly lied to the two bitches that the Doc had said my libido was overworked and needed tonics and two weeks complete rest. Mrs. Barrett accepted this lie with a brisk purchase of tonics and a cool warning that young ladies can kill a young man. Hope's reaction was an angry warning that I had better stop sleeping about, as she'd turn her dad against me if I ever again allowed myself to become too weak for her insatiable, bisexual cunt.

That Christmas and the 1984 New Year passed me by in a fog of gloom — to Daddy and other close relatives, and to close friends, I lied that I had a case of bad backache. I felt twelve instead of twenty.

After the horrible self-defeating episode with Julie, I avoided mother and daughter like the plague. I didn't even glance at their home when riding by, didn't walk by at all, and stopped going to the community pool, tennis courts and clubhouse. I began hurrying out of the community at sunrise and staying out till after nightfall. From the two young men in our walled community with whom I was somewhat friendly, I learned that the buzz in our townhouse enclave was that Patricia had finally found out I had been bedding Julie. My response to this news was a non-committal grunt. This touchy situation ended rather quickly, as Patricia and Julie moved out of the community two weeks after the day of horror in Julie's bedroom. Their exodus from the walled enclave made life more bearable.

Luckily, during this wretched, depressed period, my appetite for food didn't drop far below normal level.

Over three months would crawl by before my eternal heartache receded to a level where the midnight tears and the nightmares of an angry machete-armed Patricia ceased. And by that time, I again began having sadistic fantasies about females I especially disliked such as Mrs. Barrett and Hope Blackman; this fresh onslaught of sadistic fantasies was more powerful than the other attacks I'd had over the years. I quickly plunged into the one-night stand business with females aged sixteen and over who were keen to have sex without at least three serious dates. I didn't go in for anything horrible like battering, drawing blood and such; this sadism was a matter of trying to use stamina and my unusually huge dick to make the girl or woman beg for an end to the gallop, at which point I'd become more excited and ride her harder till I climaxed. I became a pretty vile twenty year old.

Meanwhile, in the walled town house enclave where I nested with Mrs. Barrett, I began making sexual advances to the young ladies who had been close to Julie, as they were partly responsible for the temptation Julie had exploded in my face. All of these young ladies reacted in a wary manner, obviously uneasy about Julie and her Mom's abrupt move from the community. There was also the fact that I was the community's odd ball. In any case, my sexual advances to these young ladies were kind of half-hearted, as I really was not enthusiastic about risking a bust up with Mrs. Barrett because of parental anger over a ravished daughter. Life became a kind of drunken haze. I began drinking more and smoking less marijuana. This drinking was done overwhelmingly at nights, mainly weekend nights, and only very rarely did it go beyond a heavy tipsy state. I was like a mad dog on a long leash, tied up by an intense ambition.

I began spending more time shut up in my bedroom at Mrs. Barrett's home, writing new works and studying the advice and works of those writers I admired most. Seventy-five percent of this time went to fiction writing, as fiction held out greater promise for both wealth and fame, especially fame, which was as important as money to me.

During this debased phase, peace and contentment came only when I was writing. There was a feeling of serenity and control when writing, whether short stories or songs; I was still concentrating on short story writing, as I wasn't yet ready for the ultimate plunge into novel writing.

Meantime, success with songs and short stories on the local market continued, but the monetary rewards were meagre. Still, the modest fame as a song and fiction writer sent me many an easy girl and adventurous woman, including a few young, upper-class, married ladies. More importantly, Mr. Blackman's respect for my work grew, causing him to urge Hope to give me more proof reading and editorial tasks.

In the first half of 1985, two broad strokes of good luck germinated vigorously. First sprouting was on the third day of January, when my high school pal Mark returned from Christmas vacation in New York bearing a copy of that year's US published Writer's Market. Within two or three days, I promptly sent off three of my more cosmopolitan short stories to a top men's magazine and two medium range general interest magazines in the USA. All three magazines responded before mid-April. One of the general interest magazines responded with a rejection slip, but the other two sent letters of acceptance with pre-publication offers; the offer by the men's magazine was extremely generous by Jamaican standards. I knew that those two sales constituted a great feat for a young writer residing outside the USA. In early May, I got the two cheques and felt so damn proud I was reluctant to take them to my bank — at that time I had a bank account with between seventeen and twenty thousand Jamaican dollars, a nice little sum for a poor twenty-one year old youth. But despite my elation over the two overseas sales, I kept the news secret from all but Mrs. Barrett, Daddy, my few close friends, and the high school teacher who had been my first literary mentor. The reason I told Mrs. Barrett the good news was that she had been at home alone when the postman had delivered the letters from the magazines.

The second germination of good luck, was meeting the hottest new Jamaican international reggae superstar in the smoking room at Joe's marijuana den.

Ras Micka was a singer who had just signed an impressive deal with one of the top British recording companies. We met on a Monday evening in early February. Mr. Blackman himself had told me I could leave work an hour early, and I'd ridden the company motorbike straight to Joe's place. That time on a Monday evening — about half past three — was a slow period for marijuana sales at Joe's old mansion, so it wasn't odd that there were only three of us customers in the smoking room when a beaming Joe ushered in Ras Micka and his dark complexioned British girlfriend. The superstar was in white jeans, a long sleeved T-shirt, and black running shoes. His tall locks flowed down from under a black beret. His girlfriend was wearing an African print dress and matching head wrap. I stood, overjoyed to be seeing my favourite singer up close. He had been a star on the Jamaican charts for the past three years. Over a year ago, he had rocketed to fame in the U.K. — number one on the singles charts, number seven on the album charts — a triumph that immediately pulled him to London, and since then, he had hit the top ten of the British charts with two other singles and a second album. Now he was a star all over Europe, while also making good headway in the US.

Joe introduced me to the superstar and mentioned that I had penned a few local hits.

"Name them," Ras Micka said to me. "I not on the rock fo' the past fourteen months but I-man keep in touch with the music here."

I named my three modest hit songs, and the fourth that had been less successful.

Ras Micka slapped my shoulder and said: "I know three an' like them all, me Idren." We sat down across from each other at one of the tables in the clean, cool smoking room. He pushed out a chair for his girlfriend to join us. The other two customers were right at our shoulders. Joe gleefully set to cutting up marijuana he said was on the house, and shouted down for one of the kids or his wife to rush up some fresh orange juice. Ras Micka was saying: "I lookin' fo' some young writers. I-and-I write most of I songs, but I agree with I-man new producers that I should begin workin' with a wider range of lyrics."

"I have a fresh one here," I said, taking the neat, hand-written copy from my pouch. "But I must tell you that I am not a musician, care nothing for instruments. I write lyrics to good Studio One rhythms and my own little hummings." I told him which Studio One rhythm the lyrics in hand had been written to.

He took the neatly folded sheet of paper from me. Silence took over the room while he read the words. When he looked up again he was smiling, his eyes rich with respect. He said he loved the words and thought the Studio One rhythm I had written them for would be perfect with a few variations — he was good on guitar and keyboard.

Everything about Ras Micka made it easy to trust him. I had no qualms about telling him to keep the lyrics he'd just read. I immediately rushed down to my motorbike and roared the short journey to the nest at Mrs. Barrett's to fetch the four other new songs I hadn't yet shown to anyone. When I returned with those four sets of lyrics, he selected three. I waved aside his offer to draft up a kind of contract. So when he left the island that weekend, he had four of my new songs on verbal trust, while I had good memories of the three times we had smoked and reasoned together about music, his Rastafarian faith, and my little doubts about the bible. Also, immediately after Ras Micka flew out of the island, I began feeling little pangs of self-disgust with my lifestyle, especially the humiliating ties to Hope Blackman and Mrs. Barrett. Within two months, these weak twinges of disgust began growing into knives of anger and shame. It began to appear that I should be able to accomplish my goals without having to endure being exploited by Mrs. Barrett and Hope Blackman, or any other person. Once again, I began spending a lot of time among Rastafarians, and resumed giving serious thought to the bible, God and the Rastafarian Faith. The result was that each week saw me drifting closer to acknowledging the truths of all three.

Before my twenty-second birthday arrived that June of 1985, the heady pleasures of the sadistic one-night-stands began a gradual weakening; and the idea for a blockbuster novel began taking shape in my head. When this birthday arrived, I seriously began thinking about making the exodus from Mrs. Barrett's home. I had enough money saved to rent a nice furnished studio apartment for a year, plus other expenses. But my salary was meagre, and I also wanted to cut ties with Hope Blackman, even at the risk of having her turn her dad and brothers against me. At times, it appeared that chopping the sexual link with Hope was more important to my dignity than moving away from Mrs. Barrett.

At this time, June, 1985, I made my second foreign submission and mailed two stories to US magazines. I was optimistic about both stories, and equally confident that if they were rejected I'd get more sales in the near future; so I continued keeping the two earlier successes secret from the Blackmans and the literary editor at the local Sunday newspaper that was publishing my short stories on a regular basis. Blackman Publishing Company's quarterly general interest magazine was also using my stories regularly but the monetary reward was as insignificant as that from the local Sunday paper.

Five months after Ras Micka had returned to England, I got letters from him and his British born manager, who had Jamaican parents. Both letters said Ras Micka's next album, which was set for release in four to six months time, would contain two of the four songs I had given him. This was fantastic word, again I only told a chosen few: Daddy, my closest friends, and my major marijuana dealer, Joe, who had introduced me to Ras Micka, and I admonished them all to keep the news secret until the album hit the streets.

Then about five weeks after the remarkable news from Ras Micka and his manager, the star's British recording company sent me a letter confirming that two of my songs would be on his album, and stated that they'd welcome some lyrics from me.

It was clear that I'd soon be in some nice money.

I clearly recall that it was on a windy Wednesday that I got this explosively motivating letter. The Saturday of the coming weekend would be the last one of August, and it appeared the perfect day for a great undertaking, so I went out in the morning and rented a furnished studio apartment near Joe's marijuana den. That night was a time of merry but quiet packing up of all I had at Mrs. Barrett's home — the lady went out at dusk and didn't make any sexual advances when she returned just before ten. The next morning, my brisk moving out stupefied her — I ignored her pleas and grand financial promises. With a stoic face, I got on the Blackman Publishing Company motorbike and rode off behind the taxi bearing my writing equipment, manu-scripts, books, magazines and adequate wardrobe.

CHAPTER 43

The studio apartment, my first real home — was on the top floor of a little three-storey apartment building and was reached by an outside staircase. A bank of tall windows and a fairly high ceiling made the room airy. An arched alcove served as a tiny kitchenette, and there was a bathroom so small you had trouble turning around. Light tones of paint and loud, floral-patterned chintz-covered furnishings were the dominant features. The sofa opened into a bed at nights. The cheap, dismal furnishings didn't dampen my delight in the sturdy old desk and the fact that the building was at the end of a quiet dead-end street in a nice middle-income neighbourhood. Words cannot describe the incredible sense of freedom, the bubbly joy and ballooning self-confidence this move filled me with from the moment of arrival. Perhaps the best description of the heady delight and pulsing self-esteem lay in the fact that very evening I went for a carefree ride on the Blackman Publishing Company motorbike and gave away five hundred dollars to beggars in the streets, despite my limited funds. Then I returned home, did half-hour practice of Kung Fu, cooked a light dinner, took a singsong shower, ate and began working on the novel that had been oozing out of the great literary beyond to take form in my head during the past few months.

Less than two weeks after this change of address, I got a letter from Ras Micka announcing that one of my songs was to be the title song for his upcoming album and would be released as a single within four to twelve weeks (the single was released two weeks after I received the letter), and that he could wire me a loan. I was lucky enough to be able to immediately contact him in London by phone; and, as a precaution against possible delays in getting royalties from his recording company, I accepted a loan from him.

Of course, this bomb of further good fortune exploded the highest of spirits through me. And when roughly twelve days later I got a letter of acceptance for a short story from a US magazine — after a run of three rejection slips in recent weeks — I decided it was time to end the humiliating sexual link with Hope Blackman.

I confronted the bisexual bitch in her office at work and coolly gave her my decision, a firm declaration that wasn't rude. After an initial show of mute incredulity and surprise, her reaction was to rise from behind her desk and hiss that if I didn't report to her apartment that evening I would lose my job and not be able to have any more work published in the Blackman Quarterly, nor get any of my songs done by singers signed to her family's recording company.

I knew that her father and brothers thought she was an angel of goodness. So, after calmly allowing her to have her say, I chuckled aside the little sadness accompanying the thought of losing the job and links to her father and brothers, then threw the keys of the Blackman Publishing bike on her desk and went home to do some writing. I didn't bother returning to Blackman Publishing Company after that day. And, disappointingly but not surprisingly, none of the male Blackmans tried to get my side of whatever story the bitch told them.

Four Sundays later, the Jamaican Sunday paper that was publishing my short stories laid out a nice feature about my successes with US magazines and Ras Micka. Two weeks later, old Mr. Blackman used a messenger service to send me a letter and a contract for a collection of short stories. I turned down his offer because a clause in the contract could tie me to him for years. Plus, with three stories sold to top US magazines within less than a year, and with the immediate explosion in Jamaica and Britain of the newly released Ras Micka single that I had penned, it was clear that some 'nice' money was coming my way, while the sales to US magazines meant that most US publishers and literary agents would be willing to look at any of my fiction.

Unfortunately, there were more hard knocks waiting around the corner in ambush.

That year would end with intense work on a few new short stories, my first novel, and two songs, while enjoying the continued success of the cover single of Ras Micka's new album and the instant success of the album itself. I wasn't interested in finding another job, as my bank account and the royalties due from songs would be enough to allow me to write in comfort for at least another two years. I was also confident of selling more fiction on the US market.

It appeared certain that ample success was close. When 1986 began, my sadistic one-night-stands were becoming rare, and I stopped going with prostitutes. Also, it appeared best to avoid sexual links with the ladies in and near my little apartment building. The year would see me getting some royalties from the two Ras Micka songs I had penned — unfortunately the star was in such demand all over Europe and in several major North American cities, he wouldn't be able to make more than one rushed five day visit to the island; still, he and his producers would use two more of my songs that year. This great year would also see me selling three new stories to major US magazines, plus selling the British rights of four stories to top UK magazines. By the time I turned twenty-three that June, I was quite a little local celebrity, having been interviewed by the national papers and a monthly magazine, with nice pictures each time, plus brief appearances on two television music shows. Some girl or another would usually be all over me wherever I went, recognizing my face or introduced by one of my growing circle of fans, expressing delight in either my short stories or songs done by Ras Micka. But I was no longer into one-night-stands, wasn't much for sex now, and had pretty much lost all my sadistic urges, while I was determined to avoid a serious relationship until real success arrived. I was taken up with writing and the search for the true God.

Still, I did enjoy a steady enough flow of lovely females in the seventeen to forty age bracket, and was now into short affairs. None of these affairs went beyond a month. And it appeared best to continue avoiding all the females in and nearby my little apartment building.

That crucial summer of 1986 also saw me taking a grave view of the modest AIDS alarm. Unlike the average Jamaican man, I stopped having unprotected sex and I had stopped going with whores months ago. It was a golden summer and the future appeared perfectly level.

At the end of October, I completed the second draft of my first novel. The gut feeling was that it was of high international appeal but needed some minor changes. It was time to begin the search for a literary agent in the USA.

Over the next few days, I spent many hours musing through the literary agent section of my 1986 Writers' Market. I selected a female agent in New York, then immediately mailed her proof of the US and UK short story sales and an outline of my novel. Like most US/UK literary agents, this lady didn't consider work by writers who haven't at least sold one short story to a major US or UK magazine. I mailed her this big letter towards the end of the first week of November, so it amazed me to get a reply from her on the last day of the month. Her response declared that she had read two of my stories that had been published in US magazines, and that she had a special liking for Jamaica and expected the growing international appeal of reggae music to boost interest in Jamaican literature. She also loved the outline of my novel, and would be willing to look at two or three new short stories. Man oh man, her response got my self-esteem dancing up at hurricane pace, made me so high there was no urge to smoke, drink or fuck for days.

Two days after receiving her magnificent reply, I mailed three short stories to her. Then I gleefully began typing the first third of the novel. Roughly three weeks later, just before the Christmas holidays, a thick envelope arrived from her. Inside the envelope there was a letter praising the stories and declaring that she'd already sold one, "over lunch", felt confident of a sale for another, and was returning the other with suggestions for improvement. Enclosed were also a cheque and a two year contract giving her the sole right to be my agent during that time.

This incredibly quick response immediately dashed me off to the nearest photocopy shop, where my modest fame and glib tongue, charmed a young lady on staff to rush up a copy of the first third of my novel, which I mailed the next morning along with the signed contract.

The festive holidays saw me remaining in Kingston instead of making the usual visit to the little hometown, and I didn't do much partying. I concentrated on putting the finishing touches to the novel.

Two weeks into the New Year, a telegram arrived from my agent. It said that she loved the first third of my novel, but that I should not be too hasty about sending her the rest, that I should go slowly, and if necessary, she could loan me some money.

I soon learnt that she was a wealthy heiress who loved her career with a fierce passion, although she wasn't interested in piling up another fortune. She had just a small group of writers that she chose by whim, and she wasn't interested in expanding beyond being a one-agent agency.

When she flew down to Jamaica in March of that year, 1987, "to meet my next star writer", I would find out that dear, honest, kind-hearted Jane Andrews was also into abusive sex.

CHAPTER 44

At the time that Jane first set foot in Kingston, I had recently become convinced of the truth of Rastafari, and was embracing the common Rastafarian tradition of the ancient Nyabingi life. Nyabingi encourages living as naturally as you can manage to do, like using some form of vegetarian diet and avoiding as many manufactured goods as you can. Jane's reaction to my new lifestyle (livity, in Rasta talk) was that it would make me appear like a Bob Marley of Jamaican fiction. I was indifferent to this feedback, for I viewed fiction writing and Rastafari as two separate worlds.

I met her at the airport. A curvy thirty-two, she was of medium height, had pale blue eyes and even paler skin. Her narrow face was plain. The glossy, thick cascade of natural platinum blonde hair ended in an inward curve just above her elegant shoulders. On that day, our eyes instantly recognized each other from the photographs we had exchanged by mail. An engulfing smile filled her face as we moved towards each other after her emergence from customs. Her attractive body was spilling out of a short summer dress, but a sexual attachment was far outside my mind and plans.

I was in jeans and a short sleeve shirt, my uncombed hair under a beret.

"Hello, Miss Andrews," I beamed. Here was a lady who could get me into the big times. I held out a hand.

She ignored my dangling hand, planted her feet wide, hands on hips, frowned at me a moment, then rolled her eyes and said: "Is this the way my next super bestseller greets me?"

A bit embarrassed, I grinned aside the awkward moment and rebounded with: "Hello, Jane. I was just pulling your leg."

"Is that so?" Her eyes twinkled, matching her soft, airy tone. "In any case, let me show you how I expected to be met." She stepped forward, threw her slender arms around my neck, went up on her toes to plant a firm kiss on my mouth, her nice bosom hard against my chest. Her kiss threw the Wednesday morning and the world out of whack — contrary to plan I began seeing her in a sexual manner. "There," she said, after taking a step backward, her graceful neck angled backward.

"Some welcome," I said, aware of stares from the thin crowd near us in the cavernous airport lobby. On another level there was the thought that it was best to keep the newly born sexual angle locked down, as I certainly didn't want to do anything to endanger the business link with this lady agent, and I loved the idea of a small, high profile one-agent agency instead of a big one. "Glad to have you in Jamaica."

We collected her small suitcase and headed for the taxi I had waiting. When the taxi was moving out of the airport's parking lot, she said: "I'll be spending at least two weeks here. Part vacation — I've wanted to see the homeland of reggae and Bob Marley — and will take a leisurely look at your novel and short stories."

"That'll be good."

"I expect to see the sights beyond the Marley-Reggae thing, though."

"Will gladly see to that. There's so much to Jamaica, even a month-long, no-work vacation wouldn't be enough."

"I'll trust you to treat me to the best." Her smile glittered mightily.

I delivered her to a New Kingston hotel and left her to nap until the noon period. When I returned, it was five before the hour. She was already up, looking fresh in shorts, T-shirt and sandals. We lunched on the balcony of her eighth floor hotel suite, looking down on the busy boulevard that's the heart of Kingston's chic New Kingston area. It was a leisurely lunch, during which we exchanged basic background information. She was the only daughter and youngest of four born to a powerful New England industrialist and a New York heiress. Her brothers all held managerial positions in their father's business empire. Her parents disapproved of her career and life-style, especially her rejection of several "wealthy" proposals. But she had inherited two trust funds and valuable real estate from her grandfathers, and was in no need of her parents' wealth.

"My mamma almost had a fit when grand-dad, her father, who was of middle class origins, left me nearly half his fortune as a trust fund," Jane concluded with a husky chuckle. "I was eighteen years old, fairly well-behaved and doing well in college. Since the reading of grand-dad's will, mamma and I have been at odds, and I quickly became a naughty girl." She gave me an impish grin. "Now, I'd like some good Jamaican grass and a look at your work at your place."

We left the hotel and took a taxi to Joe's marijuana house. Jane was delighted with the layout of Joe's place and more so with the higher priced marijuana on sale there; fresh sensimilla (marijuana specially cultivated so that seeds are rare in the mature buds). We didn't stay long in Joe's high-class smoking room, as I was eager for Jane to begin looking at my work, and she appeared equally eager for the task. With cold sodas in hand against the strong heat of the late afternoon, we walked the short distance to my apartment.

"Nice studio for writing," Jane said when we entered through the front door. Then she asked for the bathroom. I pointed her to the door of the miniature kingdom. Ten minutes later she made a devastating reappearance — she emerged without T-shirt and bra, her nice breasts jiggling invitingly.

Lust and wariness tore the world. She was damn sexy, especially for a pale complexioned Euro, but was she a sleep-about or hard-drug user who might be carrying the HIV from New York?

In husky tones she declared: "I want you before starting on your manuscript."

My Rastafarian belief allows a modest flow of casual sex with women who aren't complete strangers or other men's wives, and Jane's avowal had muted my wariness, so I immediately turned to close the curtains and began undressing. But a condom was a must and there'd be no cunt tonguing, even if it meant losing her representation. She began peeling off her shorts and underwear. "Wow!" she exclaimed when I turned my nakedness on her, erection grinning at the ceiling. She stepped closer, her eyes glued to the mighty rod. "I once had one almost as big. He was a blue-eyed blonde." She grinned up into my face and quipped, "You exercise it with weights, or what?"

"Lady, you're something, too," I declared truthfully, and leapt to turn on my cassette player, glad that the cassette inside was over a hundred minutes of slower paced lovers-rock reggae songs. When I turned to her again, she was taking something from her handbag. Next moment I froze. In her hand was a silky looking whip with a forked end.

"Don't be alarmed," she grinned. "I get no pleasure from hurting men. But I do love to be whipped, slapped, shaken, dragged, but nothing to injure my face or break bones and such. I've been building a Jamaican fantasy since I fell for Marley's music and the reggae beat years ago." She winked. "That's why I read your first letter the day it arrived, instead of allowing it to wait its turn in the box of queries from would-be clients."

Relief was pouring down, but it was laced with a strong dose of uneasiness. Would whipping her revive my past sadistic tastes?

Reluctantly, I approached her and became aware that her upper thighs, belly, hips, bum, breasts and back were decked with scars, most of which were faint, the legacy of her delight in feeling pain. She dropped the whip on the thick oval rug I'd bought a week ago and knelt beside the whip, her arms on the sofa, and breathlessly implored: "Whip my bum first."

It appeared best to forget about opening the sofa to its bed status. Reluctantly, I took up the whip and gave her pale ass a lash.

"Harder!" she begged, wiggling the target.

I could feel the old sadistic devils trying to break free of their tombs, could hear them urging me to give myself over completely to this new sadistic delight. I raised the whip and gave her bum a lash that made her squeal: "Yes! Oh Yes! But harder!"

Half hour or so later, we lay spent on the thick rug, my face against her sweaty neck that bore a nice sample of fresh teeth marks. I was frightened by the drunken-like passion I had just given vent to, scared of the sadistic prospects of an affair with this crazy lady. I had every intention of putting my sadistic demons to eternal rest. Now this literary agent was threatening to hand them new power. Was I never to have a great degree of control over destiny; was it fated that my life must always be largely subjected to the sexual whims of insatiable women?

Pulsing righteous self-loathing, I rolled away from Jane, leapt up, hauled on my boxers, sat down on the sofa and firmly said: "Jane, even if we must part company, no more of this crazy sex for me."

She sat up on the rug, frowning.

I continued: "I'm not trying to tell you how to live. But Rasta don't do certain things. So, if you want, I'll get you hired playmates while you're here. But no more of it for me, see." Our eyes were locked.

Disappointment clouded her face. Then she heaved a long sigh that ended in a tiny grin. She declared: "All right, at least I'll have the memory of our fantastic time. Plus, I have always believed that dildos and vibrators are as good as live dicks, and I've had both that are bigger than you." She paused to grin wider; I flashed one too. She resumed: "I'm not religious but I allow folks theirs. In any case, one of the main reasons why I hardly travel outside the New York, Hollywood, Vegas, London circle is that I get most of my lovers via a certain international establishment operating in those cities. Since I got hooked on rough sex over ten years ago, I've avoided strangers and acquaintances who have no reason to respect me. So there's never any great danger to me. See?" Her pause was another grin. I nodded, recognizing the good judgment in how she got her abuse. She resumed: "I also go with dominating females. So, having sampled you as the Jamaican man, and seeing that I'll be here for only two weeks, I think I'll just like for you to find me a few strong Jamaican ladies to pleasure me for a price. But you will have to be on hand to make certain none of them gets carried away and hurts my face, lower legs, arm, shoulders and neck, or break any bones. You'll be a sort of pimp and keeper."

"Keeper?"

"Kind of a bodyguard who remains sober and alert while I have a wild sex party."

"It's a deal, Jane." I was delighted to remain in her literary stable.

She got up from the rug and said, "Get out the rest of your novel while I get dressed."

I moved towards my desk to get one of two photocopies of the typed novel, thinking that it was okay for a Rasta man to act as pimp and keeper to an unbeliever, just as it had been okay for the ancient Jews to sell pigs and strangled meat to unbelievers.

CHAPTER 45

Next day, Thursday, another bright spring day, the early afternoon caught me cheerfully setting out from Jane's hotel to visit a friend who, despite being a faithful, religious, one-woman man, was an authority on the city's nightclubs and sex life. He should be able to help me find two or three strong girls from the go-go club scene to satisfy Jane's craving for action that night. Since our lone sex act at my apartment the previous day, Jane had been engrossed in reading my novel and discussing certain points about it with me. Roughly an hour ago, when we sat down to lunch in her hotel suite, she had declared the novel a definite international hit, a verdict that placed me in rapture; it was during this merry lunch that she had voiced her desire for two or three strong girls that night; and after lunch I had phoned the friend to whose home I was now headed. This friend, a college educated marijuana smuggler of middle-class background who was four years my senior, lived in a popular section of the city's mansion-dotted hills. He was on the front veranda when I got out of the taxi at his gate. He called off his sleek pair of Dobermans and I strode up the driveway to the white two-storey house, which was occupied by Donald, his woman and their maid.

"What the writer saying, Charlie?" he said when I stepped up on to the veranda and sat down. He held up car keys and added: "Sorry to say, but after your call, I-man get another call about some urgent business. I have to leave within twenty minutes. But you can come along if you want to meet a few corrupt cops." His black face flashed his dental-enhanced smile.

"Seeking quick advice, me Idren," I said. We had met at Joe's marijuana house just over two years ago, and we didn't see each other regularly, but an easy binding friendship had developed between us. "Thing is, the US agent arrived yesterday. She just announced high hopes for I novel…"

"Congrats, man!" Donald enthused, grinning triumph. "I knew you're it, me Idren."

"Thanks for the faith and encouragement, Brethren. The thing now is that the lady has weird tastes. She wants I-man to find two or three girls who'll give her rough sex tonight. But no street whores."

He chuckled. "You sure land a wild agent, me supe. But Rasta have to do business with all types, as the world is for good and bad till the King establish the new Israel."

"Seen, Iya."

"I know just the woman to arrange things." He went inside to phone her. In minutes he returned and gave me the name of a young, female nightclub manager.

At half-past eight that night, Jane and I entered one of Kingston's better second-rate nightclubs.

The club was upstairs a two storey building. When I had visited this club several hours ago for a chat with the manager, who was a young bisexual female, it'd been near empty of patrons and bright with light, and the music had been low. Now, Jane and I entered to weave through a fairly thick crowd in semi-darkness, and there was a voluptuous dark skinned go-go on a little spotlighted stage gyrating to loud pop music. I asked one of the scantily clad waitresses for the manager. She pointed to the bar.

"Hello again, Charlie," said the manager, Carmen Wright, when Jane and I approached her. She was a trim, hard-faced brown woman in her late-twenties, now looking fairly attractive in a tight pants suit. "This must be the lady in question."

I nodded and introduced Jane.

"Fine," Carmen said. "We can get down to business in my lounge room."

Jane said, "I'd like a double gin first."

"What for you, Charlie?" Carmen asked. "On the house." I declined her offer. She called to the lanky bartender: "Smithy, a double gin."

Fifteen minutes later, Carmen, Jane and a curvy, young go-go dancer were walking ahead of me down a short, dimly lit passage. The three women entered a brightly lit room. Pleased to note that the only door had a key but no bolts, I immediately locked it and pocketed the key, then declared the rules for the rough sex Jane craved.

"Why you pocket the door key, Charlie?" Carmen asked, frowning, her hand on the bottle of whiskey on her desk, her words underlined by the hum of music and noise from the club's public area.

"Charlie is my keeper," Jane explained, flopping down on the bed. "He must be free to come and go, keep an eye on our party."

"That's reasonable," Carmen said. "Plus, any friend of Donald is okay."

The go-go dancer, whose voluptuous black body was spilling out of white knee-length boots and silver string bikini beneath an open robe, beamed at me and exclaimed: "Hey, wait a minute; I'm certain it was yuh in a newspaper interview some time ago, the writer guy who write Ras Micka biggest hit single? An' short stories? I adore those set in the country."

"Yeah," I said, "You're correct." I had no intention of mentioning that Jane was my agent and Jane didn't broach the subject. Carmen gave me a calculated look of respect.

"How come yuh don't use Rasta talk?" the go-go asked. "Because of the writin'?"

"Yeah, and the fact that I-man is the only Rasta present. Overstand?"

"Yes, sir, Natty Dread writer." Her grin offered friendship.

Carmen was saying: "Anyone for whiskey? There's ice and soda."

"None for me," Jane said, lying back on the bed and unbuttoning her shirt.

The go-go, whose name was Moreen, shed her robe. Her oiled black body glistened in the bright lights. She had strong legs, a big firm bum, trim waist and heavy upright bosom. She went to fix herself a whiskey at Carmen's desk.

Carmen was undressing — her lean brown body had small, hard looking breasts, and a lumpy bum that was almost flat. From a desk drawer she took out two dildos, an electric vibrator, ticklers and two mean looking whips.

I sighed, feeling an uneasy twinge in the gut.

Carmen strapped the bigger dildo to her waist, and took up one of her whips. She approached Jane, flicked the whip and sneered: "Come on white gal, strip!"

Jane jumped up, grinning and began shedding her unbuttoned shirt and pants. Moreen, now clad only in boots, joined the scene. The twinge in my gut spread to my balls.

Two minutes later, Carmen and Moreen had Jane face down on the bed with a pillow under her pelvis. Carmen was laying down some mighty lashes to Jane's pale bum, while Moreen was tugging a tight handful of Jane's hair and tweaking a breast. Jane was groaning and squealing, and sort of humping the pillow under her hips.

Despite a touch of distaste, I was on the verge of an erection. I got up from the couch and did the sensible thing — beat a hasty retreat from the room and locked the door behind me.

Thankfully, when I returned to Carmen's rest-room-office, the three females were sprawled across the bed, their naked bodies sweaty. Carmen and the go-go were on their backs. Jane was on her belly, her welted bum being stroked by Carmen. And believe this, the three of them were actually chuckling and snorting about male misconceptions of female sexuality.

"Jane, time to go now," I coaxed, sounding more calm than I felt, eager to be away from that place of devilish temptations. "Near eleven now, and we need to be off early in the morning for the trip to Dunn's River Falls."

"Yeah," Jane responded and sighed contentedly. "I've never been happier; I won't need any action before Monday or Tuesday."

For the next three days, Jane didn't mention sex. We were totally into discussing my novel, sightseeing, Jamaican feasting and smoking. But Monday evening when we returned to the city from a day of sightseeing in the island's breathtakingly beautiful eastern parish of Portland, Jane declared interest in another trip to Carmen's nightclub lair the following night. I, of course, was honour bound to set up the foul date.

Consequently, nine o'clock Tuesday night caught me labouring to appear dispassionate in Carmen's brightly lit lounge-office, while Jane, Carmen, and the go-go dancer from Thursday night's scene, plus an older go-go who shared Jane's delight in accepting rough sexual treatment, were all happily converging on the big, iron-framed bed to begin their foul games with whips, handcuffs, ankle-cuffs, a piece of velvet wrapped rope, dildos, vibrators, ticklers, and a velvet covered paddle. Carmen and Moreen would be handing out the punishment to Jane and the older go-go dancer.

Things went pretty much the same as on the previous occasion. The one exceptional incident was that on the last trip, I got madly turned on and actually went near the bed and began reaching out towards Moreen's lovely bosom, the tombs of my sadistic devils close to splitting open. I was saved from further madness by the sound of a mighty fart erupting from the older go-go, whose hands were handcuffed to the bed head and had her face being gleefully ridden by Moreen, who was also applying pinches to her victim's bosom. I backed up and fled the room with what little dignity I could manage, riddled by self-disgust and dread of Jah's wrath. Mercifully, when I returned fifteen minutes later, the action was truly over and there was no mention of my near fall from grace.

During the remaining eight days of Jane's fifteen-day stay in Jamaica, she requested two more visits to Carmen's nightclub lair — she didn't voice any interest in action anywhere else or with a man. Each orgy included the two go-go dancers of the first two trips, and Carmen, along with a tall, muscular, middle-aged lawyer friend of Carmen — this lawyer lady had a big clit and loved using whips.

Resisting the sadistic magnetism of those last two disgusting orgies dragged me close to a nervous breakdown. But, meantime, Jane's good opinion of my writing kept the self-esteem buoyant enough when we weren't at Carmen's club, and there was enjoyment in showing her many of the abundant sightseeing wonders of Jamaica. She was especially fond of the caves, arresting water-falls, river rafting, picturesque white sand beaches, and restaurants that served only Jamaican foods, including Rasta ital cuisine. She appeared blind to my unspoken anguish over being keeper at the orgies.

I was relieved when Jane flew off to New York with a copy of my novel and several short stories. But, in one of life's amazing turn of luck, in the weeks after her departure, I came to the glorious realization that the agonies of being her keeper had rid me of the sadistic devils of the past. By some subconscious chemistry, the tombs and their foul occupants had been bombed to nothingness. Since then I've not felt any sadistic twinge — absolutely none. Good came out of evil; and I've come to realize that it was an example of the law of physics "To every action there's an equal and opposite reaction," a natural law that applies to all aspects of life.

Three weeks after her return to New York, Jane phoned to announce that she had obtained a hefty advance and good terms from a major US publishing house for my novel — this advance was way beyond my dreams, and the biggest ever for a first novel by an Afro writer. Then one day later, I got a letter from her that was signed by a friend of hers who was a White House official and directed to one of the top diplomats at the US embassy in Jamaica, intended to ease the way for me to get a US visa quickly. Suddenly, at the age of twenty-three, I was fairly rich and close to international fame. It had happened much quicker than I had dreamed of.

If only I hadn't lost my mother and Patricia, the love of my life.

CHAPTER 46

Without any undue delay, my second novel was published in hardcover, a much quicker publication than I expected in February when I mailed the manuscript to Jane. But the spirit is low on this bright Friday in New York City, although just an hour ago the editor who oversaw the final editing and printing of the book, phoned to tell me that it's already exploding all across North America and Britain. Noon is coming up, and tonight the publishers will be hosting here in New York city, the first party of a North American and London promotional campaign.

New York is embracing good weather here in early October. From this leased Park Avenue two bedroom penthouse apartment, the brilliant sunlight has the city looking golden bright and lively, opposite of my feelings. I turn away from the vast window. The subtle yet arresting furnishings and colour scheme of the living room fails to have its usual soothing effect.

And my soul does need comforting. In the midst of the luxury of ballooning wealth and mushrooming international fame, I am in a shroud of gloom. A powerful time-bomb dilemma has dropped into my world, and that's why at the end of the coming ten city, sixteen-day promotional tour for the new novel, I shall take a vast risk with my wife. She may well respond with hysterical threats of either suicide or a divorce that'll severely limit me access to our son. But, I think, and pray, that the right tone and words will make her agreeable enough to grant me the request I shall ask of her: time for regaining ample peace-of-mind by finding a way to disarm the secret time-bomb disaster, and thereby regain the morals I've lost these past ten months, and then move into the long over due phase of becoming a truly upright Rasta man. Of course, I cannot tell her or anyone else about the secret calamity.

My nearly eleven week old depression is rooted in the fact that my sister- in-law, Sandra, is roughly six months pregnant.

Sandra claims I'm not the father. I know differently. That budding belly, which she managed to hide from me until midway in the fourth month, is mine. We haven't touched each other since the day I became aware of the pregnancy. She hasn't tried getting me into bed — but she delights in giving me views of her radiantly triumphant face and modestly big pregnant belly by visiting her sister more regularly. I've lost all desire for her.

What a fool I was not to have realized that Sandra would quickly challenge her sister by becoming pregnant for me? In fact, it's almost certain that last December when she used her nakedness to goad me into becoming her lover, her major aim was to become pregnant with my second offspring before her sister did.

Dear Jah, please don't let the child resemble me. The scandal would someday affect both the unfortunate child and the son I already have.

The front door opens. My son's merry voice flows in from the entrance hall, cutting off the gloomy thoughts. "Daddy!" he squeals, and with typical near-two-years-old zestful vitality, he explodes into the living room ahead of Janice and his Afro-American nanny. As usual, his presence brings a good degree of joy. There's a little flag in one of his fists. I scoop him off the carpet.

"What have you in hand, my prince?"

He holds up the little USA flag and chirps: "A uncle ham...'lag!"

His Mom, the nanny and I laugh. He laughs along, too. "Uncle Sam," Janice corrects. "Uncle Sam flag."

The sixteen day promotional tour is over, and we're back in New York City on this chilly October night. Janice, our son and his nanny, myself and the rest of the promotional tour party flew in from London yesterday afternoon. Now Janice and I are on the balcony of our leased penthouse.

Our son and his nanny have retired to bed. Tonight I must tell her of my decision concerning our marriage for the next three months or so. But I'm undecided about the best way to broach the dangerously delicate subject. But I must do it tonight...now.

"Janice," I begin, reaching across the ashtray table between our arm chairs to hold her gloved hand, glad that the balcony is bright enough for me to be able to see any hint of hysteria in the coming minutes, "By this you should know that nothing would make me abandon you and our son." She nods, her eyes narrowed on me, simultaneously worried and trusting. I continue truthfully, "But I now find myself so disgusted with my weakness for other women, so ashamed of living below true Rastafarian morals, that I need to be alone for four or five months to use prayer, fasting and meditation to cleanse myself. I'll phone you daily and come spend at least one weekend each month, then return to you a more faithful husband."

Our eye-lock fills the city night. Jah be praised, there's no hint of hysteria in her eyes. Jah, please don't let her find out about the terribly sinful affair I had with her sister.

"Charlie, I...thank you for bearing with my dislike for sex." Her voice is relatively calm. Her breathtakingly lovely beauty-queen smile comes forth. "Okay. I trust you. I'll give you four months. A call every two days and one weekend visit each month will be enough. Well, tomorrow our son and I will return to Jamaica. Seems best for you to start immediately."

"Thanks for understanding." What sweet relief, and I shall truly use the time away from her to improve my morals plus formulate a plan for dealing with her sister's pregnancy. "Let's go to bed now. It's getting too cold out here for a Jamaican couple." We stand. I hug her close. Dear Jah, please don't let her find out that I got her sister pregnant. Please keep Sandra from telling anyone the truth.

An hour ago I placed my wife and son aboard a midday flight to Jamaica. Now I'm in Jane's big, elegant, thirteenth floor Third Avenue office. Her eyes are fixed on me across her wide neat desk. I've just told her what Janice and I have agreed to.

"Why must male writers be such fools?" Jane finally snaps.

Her anger isn't surprising. She respects Janice a lot, and adores Jason. Being an astute Jamaican man, my response is a cool wordless gaze.

"Good God, Charlie, when will you realize that she truly loves you? If I find a man or woman to love me that much you can be certain that'd be the end of my sleeping about. How can you not love her? What does it matter that she isn't a great intellect, seeing that her charm and beauty help to keep the press happy?"

"I told you already, Jane, I married her because she's the woman I got pregnant and she wanted a stable home life for our child." I would never tell anyone the whole truth. Jane says: "Well, she allows you to screw around to your heart's content. So you shouldn't need time away from her for more..."

I interrupt with the truth: "Jane, believe I-man, the time away from her will not be for screwing around. It's to cleanse I soul. The aim is to be a more upright Rasta man and a better husband."

CHAPTER 47

CHARLIE LOOKS BACK

Seconds after Janice's shuddering orgasm, mine exploded with a rare intensity that made me want to weep and hoot simultaneously.

Then, spent and rejuvenated, I lay there a moment before rolling off her to lie on my back right beside her. For a while, we remained there holding each other in silence. I was wondering how she aroused such great passion in me regularly, seeing that she was not a highly experienced lover.

I had often pondered this thought since we became lovers four months ago in New York City.

Charlie, perhaps the answer is rooted in the fact that she is a reigning Miss Jamaica and first runner-up at the international level? But Charlie, you've had other beauty queens, beautiful superstar actresses and one of the world's top songbirds, and didn't feel any great passion with the ones who weren't skilful in bed. The top gossip writers have dubbed you with variations of "The big, wild, honest, Jamaican playboy writer."

Janice cracked my thoughts. "Charlie, you're such a wonderful man. I love you, my handsome dreadlocks." Her tone was soothing velvet.

I answered her with a kiss. Thankfully, she resettled into comfortable silence. I was determined that I'd never lie about love. I had been limiting myself to one affair at a time and always began each affair with a candid avowal that good times was the aim, declared clearly that long-term relationship and marriage weren't in my plans, and I ended each relationship when boredom entered or the lady started talking about true love. Janice hadn't yet asked if I loved her, but in the past few weeks she had used the sacred words "I love you" quite a few times. Soon I'd have to give her the standard affair ending speech.

On that warm May night of 1990, we were at my mansion in Beverly Hills, Kingston, Jamaica. I had bought the house seven months before, but had spent very little time there, having been constantly off touring the world to promote the paperback editions of my novel, increase interest in my short stories, and weave fame as the world's "best-hung" fiction writer. The past two weeks, since Janice and I returned to Jamaica from a ten-week whirlwind world tour, was the longest stay I had made in my grand half-furnished house. We weren't living together but she was spending most nights at my house, although there were many Jamaicans complaining via the media that a reigning Miss Jamaica shouldn't be having such a bold affair. Most of these people who were now frowning on our affair in Jamaica had accepted our recent whirlwind tour abroad because I'd arranged for the Jamaica Tourist Board to tag along and reap some benefits at the expense of myself and my publishers, and Janice had had a chaperon.

Our sex life felt good — actually a balanced mix of devastating pleasures and mediocre enjoyment. She allowed me sex regularly, and was a fairly good pupil.

Still, even after four months as lovers, I almost never gave her the full length of my giant dick, and rode her gently, sensing that anything more would hurt her — in the three years since the task of pimp-keeper during my abuse-loving literary agent's first visit to Jamaica, I had developed a great horror for hurting any female and had become skilled at giving each lover what she could endure. I also honoured Janice's dislike for sex in bright lights and daylight, although I myself had always enjoyed "brightly lit sex."

She was a fairly good companion as well — cheerful, had enough wit and intelligence, graceful, was a good listener, and such a true princess of various social modes that she had saved me from a few blunders during our recent hectic world tour. No trace of real boredom had yet entered our affair and it felt damn good to at last be involved with a celebrated Afro lady of exceptional beauty and awesome grace who wasn't into oral sex. It was also good that she was a fellow Jamaican.

Still, I mused, now that our relationship was four months old, her talk of loving me meant it was time to end it. I wasn't in love with her.

But, strangely enough, the next moment I was punched by a powerful need to tell her of my greatest fear. And before I could stop myself, the secret that I'd never uttered before now poured forth in the

Jamaican patois of my youth: "Janice, yuh think mi stupid to fear that I woulda go mad if a get a woman pregnant an' she abort it?"

There was a taut stillness in the dark bedroom. Then she stroked my brow and cooed: "Nothing stupid about that, my dear."

I got this curious feeling that the darkness of my bedroom was getting brighter. Although I now wondered why I had voiced my most secret fear and was feeling a little twinge of regret, a superior power forced me to add: "My mother died while having an abortion."

In the little silence that followed I was aware of two things: the pain of having lost my mother early in life, and Janice's eyes glowing oddly in the darkness.

Then Janice's eyes lost the unreadable glow, and she purred: "Oh my love, that must have been horrible. But you survived. You'll be okay, everything will go well. Life will be good." She kissed my throat, caressing my locks.

I was torn between gladness and regret over having told her the great secret.

Ominous barking by the dogs next door cracked the silence and vibrated the darkness. I wondered if thieves were on the prowl. Minutes of silence drifted by, Janice holding me close; while regret and gladness warred in my heart. There was simply nothing to utter. After a while her breathing suggested that she'd drifted from our silence into sleep. My mind went back to the day in January, just over four months ago, when we had met in New York City.

CHAPTER 48

We met in a Manhattan bookshop where I was cheerfully executing a scheduled two hour autographing task. It was a clear Saturday afternoon, highly welcomed after a night of snow and an overcast morning. I was signing hardcover and paperback editions of my first novel, and bookmarkers — the hardcover edition had spent months in the top ten of the major international bestsellers lists; while the paperback edition had been the number one international bestseller for over two months, and now, in January '90, was still hanging tough on the bestsellers lists. The busy bookshop was fairly crowded where I sat in an ornate chair behind a table at the back of the shop, and that's why I didn't notice Janice until she was near the front of the line. In addition to the line, there were a number of fans, press folks and gawkers, hanging around enjoying the cake and coffee made available by the bookshop and my publishers. I recognized Janice the moment our eyes met — I had been present when she had won her beauty title, Miss Jamaica, had since seen pictures of her via the Jamaican and international media, and had been thinking about meeting her in Jamaica. Her smile and beauty gave me a great rush of lust. But there were still five or six folks ahead of her in the line. I sped up the autographing.

"Hello there, my favourite Miss Jamaica," I beamed, when Janice and her chaperon were in front of me. Man, she looked lovely, a lot more beautiful than any of the other beauties in view. She made her red jeans and black sweater appear like the fashion every woman needed. My mouth watered and Mr. Dickie jerked to hardness. How good that I'd recently dismissed my last lover, a pretty, young, blonde French heiress.

"Sorry, I can neither rise to bow over your queenly hand nor rub nose African fashion."

She and her chaperon laughed; onlookers smiled; two journalists wrote briskly. It gladdened the heart to note that the chaperon appeared young and easy going. Janice said: "Really, I'm so happy to meet my favourite bestseller." Her mulatto face was flushed.

"I'd love to talk with you two ladies over a late lunch or UK-styled tea," I coaxed, taking their books. "Just another ten to fifteen minutes and you'd be bringing some joy to a lonely writer."

'We'll wait," Janice said, glancing at her chaperon, who nodded a smile.

With a dancing heart, I autographed their books and then said: "I'll soon be with you ladies."

"Looking forward to it," Janice said. "We'll wait at the front of the store."

The chaperon nodded and said, "Thank you. No need for any great hurry."

I gave them my best smile and cheerfully set about rushing through the rest of the scheduled autographing. When the allotted time was up, there were still about twenty fans hoping for autographs. The store manager urged me to see to them. I stood to do this task briskly and then said a quick thanks and goodbye to all, sidestepping the press folks who were hoping for one of my regular news-making Jamaican-Rasta styled comments on just about any subject.

Janice and her chaperon, Deanne, were waiting. I greeted them heartily, and was happy to hear that they were travelling by taxi, then steered them out of the bookshop to the chauffeured limo I was using that day, compliments of the bookshop and my publishers. It was a short drive to the top-flight restaurant where I had a table reserved. By the time the maître d' had us seated, I knew that two days ago the ladies had begun a four day vacation in the city, staying with Janice's aunt, after a Jamaica Tourist Board one week promotional tour that had ended here in New York City. They had come to the bookshop because they'd read that I'd be there. During our late lunch we talked about my work, and Janice's beauty titles and her half-hearted interest in model- ling beyond the Jamaican scene — she disliked the idea of using diet to cut down her sexy figure to be more like the average supermodel. Then we sat around awhile discussing Jamaica's economic problems.

That evening, Janice and I had a late dinner at one of Manhattan's best Italian restaurants. Then we went to a nearby nightclub that featured a short comedy act before dancing commenced at ten. Wearing a short, blue, off-the-shoulder dress, she outshined all the other fabulous ladies at the restaurant and club, and she was a good dancing partner. She had only one more day in New York, while I had business with my publishers scheduled for the next few days. I was determined that since her chaperon had allowed her out alone I must take a shot at bedding her that very night, as during the remaining months of her reign as Miss Jamaica, she'd be expected to live a chaperoned life most of the time. At just about half-past-eleven when we were at our table taking a break from the dance floor, I said: "Janice, I'd like to have a nice talk with you. How about my hotel?"

She hesitated just a moment, her eyes searching mine, before smiling and agreeing: "Let's do that."

The hotel was just ten minutes away by taxi, and my suite had a well-stocked bar. "Champagne?" I asked, the moment her lovely ass touched the sofa in the sitting room.

"Just a fruit drink, please." Her tone was a bit unsteady. "And, Charlie, I ah...doubt that any other man in...the world could...well... get me to his hotel room after just one date."

Our eyes locked within a broad moment of my lust and her anxiety. Sensing that her avowal had been honest, I bowed, beamed and said, "I'm honoured by her majesty's favour."

She grinned. I turned aside to pour the fruit juice. I hoped she was good in bed, for I was one playboy who didn't relish the role of sex teacher.

Bearing our fruit juice, I joined her on the sofa. Without a word, she downed her drink briskly, looking at me steadily. I followed suit and took her in my arms. She didn't resist. Our lips met for a long kiss. Then I stood and lifted her like a virgin bride and carried her to the bedroom. I told her I wanted to see her naked in bright lighting, and she didn't protest. Naked, she was beauty beyond imagination. But she gasped and shrank fearfully when my erection jerked into view.

"Don't be afraid," I coaxed, putting on a lubricated condom. "Just tell I-man if it get painful, so I won't give you more than you can bear. See? Trust me. I rule it." I turned off the bright light.

Later, after we had our orgasms and were lying beside each other in the dark, she declared: "I never thought I could endure...and enjoy such a big one. And you were so gentle all along. Next time I won't be afraid. I trust the Natty Dread."

I was truly moved, despite bewilderment over her unusual effect on me, and the fact that I hadn't given her more than about two-thirds of my giant erection. My self-esteem and ego ballooned. I was ready to accept her as my next steady lover. "Can you stay all night?"

"Would love to." Her tone was wistful. "But my aunt would worry and disapprove, even if I called her now, and she'd blame Deanne." Her fingers were in my dreadlocks, which were still short after over three years of growth. Her inability to spend the night filled me with a disappointment that was a bit unsettling. "Okay, we'll get you home when you're ready," I said, wondering what was happening to me. Roughly half hour later, we left the hotel, ferried her home by taxi, and I returned straight to my suite of rooms.

It was now after 2:00 a.m. I was feeling too alive for sleep, had no desire to write and wasn't interested in going out or reading or drinking or television; and there was also a new gnawing confusion about the strangely heady interest in Janice. It felt as if Janice had netted me with an evil spell that was weakening now that I was out of her presence. A little voice began whispering intermittently: Well, at least she's an Afro woman, and a Jamaican at that.

I phoned my agent, Jane, who was up toiling over another client's manuscript.

Jane wasn't surprised by this late night call. She had grown accustomed to receiving them. "Janey, dear, I-and-I cannot sleep, want no drink, and is bloody confused over a most naïve reaction to that reigning Miss Jamaica."

"Oh. Where is she? When did you meet her?" She sounded like an excited older sister, which was typical of our client-agent relationship. "Surely not before today?"

After relating about the bookshop meeting and the late lunch that had followed, I ended by saying: "Jane, I must be getting old at twenty-six, or is it plain stupid? I mean, what's special about a half-intelligent beauty queen who is no great lay?"

"Dear silly man," Jane responded, "I'd say you and the lady have been arrowed by cupid."

"Ah, Janey, come on," I snorted. My chest contracted and a picture of Janice's smiling face filled the world. "Me, in love? I know love won't come again. And as for Miss Jamaica loving me, Bah! My millions and international fame has her dazzled, that's what."

"Time will tell. Meantime, bring her and her chaperon to dinner here at four tomorrow...oops, midnight passed nearly three hours ago, so I mean today."

Humouring her request appeared harmless. "I'll try." We hung up. I felt a lot more normal and began viewing Janice's strange effect on me as one of those inexplicable realities of life. An affair with her certainly wouldn't affect my health and writing. It'd be okay to just go with the flow of it. In time it'd work out.

I drank a double whiskey and was soon in a dreamland dominated by the irrevocable lost love of my life, Patricia, and my lovers of the past few years.

Janice and I had planned to spend the afternoon and evening together, and when I phoned her at nine that morning, she and her chaperon, Deanne, were thrilled by the idea of dinner at my agent's home. I lunched at the middle class suburban home of Janice's aunt, a plump, nonreligious matron who worshipped wealth and fame. Then, at half-past one, we cruised to my hotel where we had a brief chat until it was time to groom ourselves for dinner at Jane's nearby Park Avenue penthouse. In Deanne's company, Janice's effect on me was less overwhelming.

The overcast Sunday afternoon-early-evening was cool to New Yorkers but it was cold to us three Jamaicans. We used the limo for the short journey to dine with Jane, who was all smiles in a black pants suit and a fortune of diamonds when she let us into her posh penthouse. She immediately took to Janice. "Janice and Jane in charge of best-seller Charlie," Jane quipped shortly after our arrival. I ignored the quip and avoided looking at Janice.

The other six guests quickly fell under Janice's charming spell, too. They were my publisher and his wife, the publisher's bachelor chief editor, the chairman of the publishing group, and Senator Dooley and wife, who was Jane's cousin and an important shareholder of the publishing group. I should've known that Jane would go to great lengths to encourage me into an affair with Janice. Such an affair would be good publicity and would give Jane hope that I'd get married.

It was obvious that Janice and Deanne were greatly impressed by my standing in such exalted company. I felt humorously resigned to whatever Jane had planned, and I couldn't help feeling proud of the way Janice, literally the centre of attraction, conducted herself.

After the five-course French and American dinner, we returned to the comfortable living room, and the moment we were seated, the chairman of the publishing group instantly got into the matter of the evening:

"Dear Janice, you have just done a fine promotional tour for your country's Tourist Board. Now you and Charlie are obviously much taken with each other." His tone was eloquent. (I fixed eyes on Jane, who was in an armchair directly across from the love seat Janice and I were in.) "So you shouldn't be put out by the delicate suggestion I'm about to make, and the fact that dear Jane fixed this dinner for us to meet you. Poor Charlie didn't know we would be here." He paused amid the chuckles, his grin riveted on me. I gave him a mock glower.

My eyes met Janice's glowing pair. I couldn't resist returning her smile. I glanced at Janice's chaperon, Deanne, who appeared fascinated.

"The thing is," the chairman resumed, "our marketing experts believe Charlie's novel can stay on the bestsellers lists a lot longer and earn big bucks from foreign language rights, if we can get his publicity changed from playboy to a man in love." He grinned at me; I gave him a little frown that showed my surprise and doubt. He added: "If you and Charlie become a couple and allow us to whisk you around the world for say, two months or so, you and your country would gain a lot of free publicity. We'd make it up to your chaperon for whatever losses incurred while travelling with you and Charlie." He glanced at Deanne, who nodded and grinned at Janice. The chairman added: "We'll also settle with your Jamaican sponsors, and so forth."

"I'll do it," Janice said excitedly. "Yes! I adore Charlie and love my country!" Her hands now grabbed mine, forcing me to meet her eyes. I was thinking: How dandy it'll be to pretend to be in love.

"You certain about this?" I asked.

Her response was to kiss my cheek.

My publisher said: "Charlie, you go off with her tomorrow. Jane and I will begin taking care of those papers and ideas you were to meet with us about over the next few days. When you return this way we'll finalise things."

That night, when Janice and I were alone in my hotel bed, I pointedly told her that marriage and a true long-term relationship weren't part of my outlook. Her response was: "That's okay, Charlie. We've just met. If we're meant to be, time will show it. Honestly, I'm game for some fun with you, my favourite writer, seeing that it will also help our country's tourism and can get me some big international modelling jobs." The breathtaking smile on her very pretty face appeared honest.

So the next day, Janice and Deanne and I, were pounced upon at the Kennedy International airport by over a dozen print journalists, several top photographers and three television crews, a scene arranged by my wily agent and publishers. Janice and I got down to acting as if we were in love — she is more talented at acting than I. But we both kept to our agreement not to make any explicit verbal declaration of a truly serious affair — we said ambiguous things like, "We've just met and like each other alot" and "I certainly can't see beyond spending as much time as possible with her." We flew down to Jamaica and immediately caused a roar of excitement — the nation's and the Caribbean's first true international bestseller — a Rasta man to boot, and the top beauty queen in love! Most Jamaicans of all classes were of the opinion that our affair could and should be used to give the country some good publicity to weaken the rope of bad international highlighting of our drug smugglers and high murder rate.

The disapproving minority constituted the little pockets in the various classes and Christian churches who were fiercely bigoted against Rastafarian, plus the small percentage of Rastafarians fanatically opposed to any profound links with non-Rastafarians. Janice's liberal-minded, non-religious family were wary of my playboy reputation but refrained from pressuring her about it — her younger sister, and only sibling, Sandra, was the friendliest and greatest fan.

The beauty queen and I spent ten hectic days in our home-island, with Deanne always present to act as chaperon in the public eye. Then the three of us returned to New York, where Janice and I immediately became the star of the literary circuit, dining in many of the city's most distinguished homes, appearing on top television talk shows and getting featured in the best of the print media. After two weeks in New York, my publisher whisked us off for an eighteen-day tour of the rest of the USA, with Deanne and representatives of the Jamaica Tourist Board tagging along. Then our cheerful group was off on an eight-week Canadian, British, European and West African whirl. This merry tour was greatly productive — my book and Jamaica's tourist industry and Janice's international appeal got a great boost.

Pleasure ruled those weeks of our promotional world travel. Her beauty, charm and social grace were sources of pure delight. Sex was often good, especially when she was tipsy; she had no head for drinking and obviously preferred to refrain from drinking more than a little bit of wine. At the end of that whirl-wind promotional tour, we had returned to Jamaica with the intention of spending two months for her to fulfil local obligations as Miss Jamaica, while I'd see about completing the research that was necessary to make a serious start on my second novel.

Now, two weeks later, on this warm May night, Janice farted in her sleep, ending my retrospection and adding a brief stink to my bedroom. Charlie, I mused, you must end this affair soon, and ignore whatever your agent, publishers, Daddy, friends and the public say. There's something odd...well, maybe a month or two more with her might be good.

Three and a half weeks of mostly joy would dance by without either of us mentioning my dread of abortion. I quickly buried all thoughts about the momentous avowal and the divided emotions this declaration had caused me. Then she floored me.

CHAPTER 49

The knock down was delivered on a cool overcast Monday morning at the beginning of June — the weekend had poured out heavy rainfall each day, breaking the drought that had enveloped most of the island for the past five weeks. While having breakfast with Janice at the small table on the balcony adjoining my bedroom, I became aware of an unusual tension about her. But I was too focused on getting into some writing after breakfast to wonder about her nervousness. Instead, munching the last of my oats and raisins, I was wondering whether I should begin the second draft of one of several new short stories or make the first effort at song writing in nearly a year. Janice drank the last of her coffee and dabbed her sensuous lips. Her anxiety sprayed me across the little table and clouded the balcony. She still looked immaculate, having left me in bed to give herself a good grooming. Her red T-shirt and white shorts were quite revealing, her make-up skillfully applied, and red nails freshly buffed.

"Charlie," she began hesitantly, avoiding my eyes, "I'm about to make a demand I dislike." She now met my eyes and most of her anxiety gave way to resolve when she continued, "It's something I must do without any compromise. I..." She fell silent at the sound of the live-in maid coming to take away the breakfast things. Tension pulsed. The maid cleared up quickly and withdrew. Janice resumed: "I love you and know I shall never love another. Ordinarily, I wouldn't think of suggesting marriage; it's really a man's duty. But," her eyes took on a cold gloss, "seeing that I'm now nearly four weeks pregnant I must insist that we marry within the next eight weeks, or I shall have to do an abortion."

The world trembled and spun. I was hot as an oven and cold as ice. Marriage! Abortion! How could she be pregnant? I had used condoms up to just over a month ago, and she had always been on the pill. Marriage? Abortion?

"Charlie, my love," she resumed, reaching across the table to grasp one of my trembling hands, "I just cannot have a child out of wedlock." Her eyes were riveted on me but she also appeared to be viewing other pictures of life. "I'll give my life for you; will share you with other women — but not a child out of wedlock. I care not about losing my beauty titles when we marry. The gossiping won't bother me when the pregnancy becomes obvious soon after our marriage." She paused, her unblinking eyes now protruding with gleaming zeal. She leaned across the table before adding, "Charlie, marry me so we can have our baby. I'll obey you in everything. Just save me from an abortion!"

I shuddered, feeling a knife in the chest and ice at my crotch. In my head two voices filled the breathing pause. One voice wailed: Charlie, you mustn't allow her to abort your child!

The other voice roared: Charlie, you don't love her and you're not interested in a social marriage!

I took a deep breath and managed to call up a fairly steady placating voice to say: "I don't want you to abort our child. But it would be better if we marry after the birth. Move in with me now and let's get engaged." My mind filmed her breaking off the engagement due to my infidelities, a cool distant attitude, and social pressure directed at my Rasta life. "A rush marriage would be dull and wouldn't fool anybody. After the birth we can have a grand marriage." I wasn't exactly trying to trick her; just confident that by the seventh month of pregnancy, she would leave.

She withdrew her hand from mine, and stood; her face now prettily cold. "No, Charlie." Her eyes made a few rapid blinks and then returned to the unblinking state they'd been in during the past few minutes, and I now got the first hint of the madness lurking under her polished shell. "Marriage within the next seven weeks, or its abortion."

Although now indignant, I was too weak to roar or growl, or even to simply arise from the table. "I thought you were against abortion?"

"In most cases." Her tone was cool, her cold eyes holding my glare.

"And what about your claim to be on the pill?"

Her response was a pout and that cool unblinking stare.

"You did it on purpose, right? Perhaps because I was foolish enough to tell you my feelings on the subject of abortion?"

"No, Charlie. I began trying to get pregnant before that night, knowing that I'd abort it if you refused to see that I was born to be your wife."

The plain honesty of her words rendered me dumb for the moment. The avowal of my secret dread of abortion had only given her confidence that I'd marry her rather than allow her to abort my seed. Maybe her pregnancy even began days before my stupid avowal. "Tell me; is it my wealth or fame, or both?"

"I love you for what you are, including your handsome features." The tone was level, her face now back to the usual serene prettiness. "If after we marry you lose your money and don't write another famous book, I'll stay by you. I want to be your wife for better or worse."

I recognized that her ultimatum was beyond negotiation. Nothing could change her half-cracked mind. It was marriage or abortion. The heaviest and longest sigh gripped me. "As long as you accept that I'm not a one woman man, I guess we'll just have to get married."

Her smile filled the balcony, overrode the brightening sunshine of the overcast morning. "My dearest, I know you'll be discreet, and won't risk catching AIDS. You can have your affairs." She blew a kiss down at me and said, "Darling, I must go begin arranging things immediately; must call Mom and Dad now. Perhaps you should think about getting an engagement ring today or simply give me your school ring." Then she pivoted in her trained beauty-queen-model way and skipped towards the bedroom, leaving yours truly glued to his chair, his head bowed towards the table.

CHAPTER 50

At noon the next day, my radiant, beautiful betrothed, returned to our mansion from shopping with her mom and aunt, planted a kiss on my cheek and breezily handed me one hundred wedding invitations for inviting whosoever I desired at our wedding. The invitations were expensive and elaborate. Her parents' home was listed as the venue for the reception — obviously, the crafty beauty queen had ordered them days ago, the wedding, a Saturday affair, was just over seven weeks away. While I was glancing at one of the invitations, her mom expressed delight at the grand engagement ring I'd bought the previous evening — the marriage was to save my seed, so in for a dollar, why not an expensive ring? Her aunt was more interested in the fact that my mansion was only half-furnished and in need of decorating, clearly awaiting a wifely zeal. I responded pleasantly through grins they could read as besotted bliss or pre-nuptial anxiety. Before the three of them rushed out again, the two older ladies got me to reluctantly accept that Janice's parents would be footing the wedding bill, except for the limo and champagne I insisted on providing. Of course, the engagement and looming wedding was headline news in Jamaica, and got international mention. Just about everyone immediately guessed that Janice was pregnant. She surrendered her beauty titles. Most Jamaicans were delighted by both the news of our wedding and the thought that she was pregnant.

For the good of the life growing in her belly, I tried to help Janice's honour by word and deed, despite my indignation over her trickery. Within a few days after the devastating execution of her balls-capturing

247

marriage trick, I cooked up the perfect little lie for us to tell everyone: we avowed loudly that we simply needed to marry that summer before work on a second novel and certain overseas obligations bogged me down for at least a year — oh how she gladly threw herself into proclaiming this falsehood high and low. Also, I decided to refrain from even simple flirting until after the marriage and honeymoon.

Oddly enough, immediately after Janice roped me into the marriage agreement, her usually friendly younger sister became less affable towards me in subtle ways that Janice didn't appear to notice. This new attitude from the twenty year old Sandra made me realize that she was jealous of her older sister. At this time, too, I began hearing that Sandra had been sleeping about wildly for quite a few years. Until roughly two days before the day her older sister had chosen for hauling me to the marriage altar, Sandra would be coolly polite when she was unable to avoid me. Then, suddenly, with the wedding day now directly in our face, Sandra reverted to being my ardent fan and the friendliest of Janice's relatives. I was too worried about the looming nuptials to try reading this latest change in Sandra's behaviour.

Daddy, my step-mother, other relatives and friends, business associates and ardent fans, all thought I should be happy to have such a charming woman madly in love with me and enthusiastic about becoming my wife. If only they knew the truth. But I simply couldn't bring myself to give even just a hint of the reality to Daddy and my few truly close friends, who all thought that my brief bouts of low spirits were typical husband-to-be jitters. Whenever they kidded me about losing the play-boy life, I'd grin and think about manoeuvring Janice towards a peaceful divorce within a year or so after the birth of our baby — any divorce or separation would have to be amiable, for I wanted to have easy access to my child.

Two weeks after she exploded her marriage bomb, Janice and I flew up to New York in search of wedding bands and to face the international spotlight. My dear literary agent and publisher viewed the engagement and coming wedding as great publicity. I went along with the press conferences and interviews they arranged, Janice and I sticking to our loud claim that the sudden marriage was mainly due to heavy writing and business plans I had scheduled for at least a year after the summer ended. As I'd expected, the international press and New York socialites saw no reason to respect our privacy; they were quick to ask if she was pregnant — she did a fine job at delivering the answer I'd prepared for this crucial question, arching her lovely brows and declaring through a generous smile: "Time will tell." She and I had to voice this ambiguous answer many times during that hectic four-day stay in New York City.

The wedding day dawned cloudy and rolled up in overcast mode but turned sunny by the time the afternoon church ceremony began in one of Kingston's oldest cathedrals. There were over two hundred guests, including roughly fifty local celebrities and quite a few from the international literary and music circuits. The bride, wearing an expensive French gown, was so damn beautiful when she entered the church on her father's arm that many male guests lusted openly and I couldn't help feeling a touch of pride. The tricky young witch was so lovely you didn't take much notice of the superb diamonds and magnificent emeralds I'd bought her recently. But, I would've gladly given her away to any of the unmarried men present, if she'd agree to having our baby and allowing me unlimited access after the birth. Thanks to days of meditation, I declared the "I do" without any noticeable hesitation.

At the wedding reception on the gaily-decorated lawns of her parents' home, I also did well with my little deceitful speech about being very happy and feeling extremely lucky. The cake cutting and feeding, kissing, first dance and picture taking went well too. But then came the tense, fairly wordless eight-mile limousine drive to the aerodrome. Now that we were out of the public eye I felt a bit depressed, a limp arm around her shoulder and, as a curtained glass separated us from the chauffeur, I refused to acknowledge her one attempt at a kiss. She was clearly uncertain how to counter my obvious melancholy; this bizarre just-married drive was followed by a silent and mercifully quick flight in a hired small plane to the island's tourist jewel, Negril, where we were to spend four days at a magnificent hotel.

Draped in a sheer, black silk negligee over red crotch-less lace panties, the bride emerged from the bathroom of our luxurious bridal suite and smiled a path into the brightly lit bedroom. I was already naked in the big heart-shaped bed, torn between the urge to give her the hardest fuck of her life and the desire to continue humouring her for the sake of "our pregnancy". Along with the fact that I was about to get the first clear view of her belly since she declared herself pregnant, her loveliness and ecstatic smile and proclamation that she'd gladly make love in the bright lights filled me with a rush of forgiving ecstasy, so I fed her champagne and gave her the tender sex she preferred.

The wedding night turned out to be quite satisfying, and was a prelude to what would happen during our two-month Jamaica, Pacific Islands and Japan honeymoon. The far east was meant to lessen the level of interest there'd be when it became obvious to all that she'd been pregnant from before the wedding. Throughout this grand honeymoon vacation, her passion and companionship were so satisfying and pleasing, that I began picturing us remaining happily together to raise a big brood of kids.

Foolishly, I didn't see anything significant about the fact that she got tipsy every night of our honeymoon. I too, drank more frequently than usual. Hell, it was a honeymoon.

Her five month pregnant belly was prominent by the time we returned home to Jamaica at the end of September. I was fairly happy, looking forward to the birth of my firstborn and to making an earnest attempt at being a fairly faithful husband. I was also awaiting the right time in the coming weeks to tell her of my desire for us to raise a big brood of kids. But on our first morning back home she dropped another powerful bomb on me.

CHAPTER 51

C harlie, I'm glad you enjoyed our long honeymoon and have no great resentment about our marriage," she began in a cool distant voice when I awoke and sat up in our bed on that first morning back home. I was feeling proud of having woken up with an erection; she was already up. "Now there are certain facts I must declare." Her eyes went to the ceiling, while the first chilly pangs of troubles fingered my spine and deflated the erection. "One: I don't like sex regularly, that's why I prefer it when tipsy; but I am cutting down on the regular drinking I've been doing since we met, and I expect you to continue being gentle when we do have sex. Fact is, I don't like sex that much" — her voice remained coolly distant, and she was still gazing at the ceiling, while I gaped at her — "partly because I know that regular orgasms are bad for a woman's complexion."

Utter incredulity gripped me.

She coolly continued with, "When I say no to sex, don't try to insist. You can have other girls, but no long-term mistress, and do nothing to embarrass me. I know you're cautious of diseases." She paused, eyes still fixed on the ceiling.

I was too shocked, confused and disappointed to move or speak.

She resumed in the same cool, distant voice, "Two: don't think about moving out or divorcing me after our child is born. If you ever cause us to enter a divorce you'll lose free access to our child, even if I kill myself after the divorce."

Her mention of suicide chilled me completely, and became one more leash on my manhood.

She continued: "Three: You must be nice to the people I like, just as I'll be nice to your friends. You must not leave me alone all day or all night when I ask you not to." She now paused and met my incredulous gaze. The obsessive wifely sentiments and hint of insanity in her eyes kept me flabbergasted. She added in a voice that was warmer and less distant: "Charlie, you are mine. I'm yours. I'll obey you in every other way. I intend to spend the rest of my life with you. But cross me unfairly and I'll tear you to pieces in a divorce court."

Utter stillness filled the bedroom and the sunny morning. Nearly a whole minute must've crept by before I was able to jerk free of the gluey incredulity and say, "Janice, what...really, what's this all about? Rastafari..."

She was already leaving the bed, her nice five-month pregnancy leading the way, and she favoured me with the tolerant smile doting mothers give their petulant children. Her soothing response was:

"Darling, later I'll give you a written copy. Just remember nobody can love you more than I do. I'm your slave. I have no intention to try ruling or changing you, or to try having any great impact on your manly freedom. Make arrangements for my protection and you'll always be free to go out most nights. Now I must go dress." She smiled dotty devotion and floated away towards the bathroom.

For many moments I remained there in bed trying to fool myself into thinking it was all a nightmare and that I'd soon awake into a far more pleasant reality. But I had to quickly groan aside this foolish hope and accept that the nice dream of a tolerable marriage created by our pleasant honeymoon was now in pieces. The reality was that I had landed me in a nightmare marriage with a crafty, half-mad, beauty queen who didn't like sex. And it was obvious that escape from this matrimonial prison wouldn't be easy, as my Rastafarian belief demanded devotion to one's children, while my former renowned playboy life would be a great disadvantage in a divorce court against a well-liked beauty queen.

Roughly forty-five minutes later, we were downstairs at the dining table having breakfast prepared by the live-in maid. I was now back in fair control of my wits, and highly indignant. Of course, my devotion towards her pregnancy meant that I wouldn't be as hard on her as the tougher instincts wanted. But it appeared necessary to shake her up a bit. My first comment was: "Well, wife, you've made your demands." I was labouring to keep a fairly level tone. "Now I have a few laws to lay down."

"Sure," she said calmly, smiling over her cup of coffee.

"First, I want at least six kids over the next eight to ten years."

Instead of the dismay I expected, she actually beamed and declared: "Both my grandmothers had over five children. I'll gladly have as many as possible — we can afford them. And the women in my family don't lose shape because of repeated pregnancy. Exercise and proper diet — especially limiting alcohol and meat — will keep me in shape." Her voice was excited. "I wouldn't mind adopting if we fall short or want to simply keep raising as many as possible."

I gulped some of my mint tea, thinking that she must have already decided to carry out a secret plan to ensure that she wouldn't be able to get pregnant more than two or three times. Then I immediately buried this thought, reminding myself that I mustn't be crude, and said: "As the wife of a prominent Rasta you should cease wearing pants and make-up."

"I won't mind giving up pants and make-up," she responded cheerfully. "I'll even grow locks to please you. But, darling, I cannot pretend belief that there's a God. Anyway, I like make-up but it actually helps to ruin one's skin."

Defeat punched and kicked me so powerfully that against my better judgement, I actually said: "Well, on second thought, given that you still don't believe there's a God, you stay as you are." At least my tone was level.

"Okay." Her eyes were on the bowl of cornflakes and wheat cereal she was arranging. "But I do want to give birth at least three times."

"Fine." My appetite was gone, killed by her calm reaction to my discarded laws. Fuming, I got up and left the dining room.

Within the following five to eight days, my lusty sister-in-law was now friendlier than ever towards me, and was into flirting whenever we were alone for even just a few minutes. I ignored the flirting, responding gravely, and tried avoiding her as much as possible, for the bible declares it a great sin to have sex with sisters. Meantime, in those tense days after the return from our honeymoon, I began work on a second novel, and quickly hunted out a competent older couple to keep Janice's company at nights when I was out having fun with my other young ladies. The weeks crept by. Janice became more swollen in pregnancy. But she remained beautiful, continued causing lust to flush male faces whenever she made one of her increasingly rare ventures out of our mansion, which she was redecorating in a tasteful, artistic manner.

I must admit that Janice was — and has remained — a dutiful wife out of bed, keeping an immaculate well-ordered home, plus taking keen interest in my wardrobe and health. Our diet was balanced and rich in the natural foods I and all Rastafarians favoured. Janice and the cook threw themselves into vegetarian recipes from all parts of the world, so meat didn't grace our table more than three times each week. Regularly, our wonderful meals together made me wonder how to get her to realize there was a God and that the bible was the word of God. My soul hoped for her to eventually see the Light of Rastafari and lose her absurd notion about orgasms. My efforts to lift her from her non-religious ways were met by calm smiles or placating sentences like, "I respect your belief, my dearest, but religion isn't for me." If two days passed without me eating heartily three times each day, she would become flustered.

I had always kept up my Kung Fu exercises and fighting skills — she cheered me on by mooning about my "beautiful" muscles and "majestic" movements. Then there were the regular massages, a job she was truly good at.

Of course, the result of all this was that by the end of the seventh month of pregnancy she'd become an enigma. Occasionally I thought I despised her. Most times I only pitied her. I could not ignore her remarkable beauty and charming grace, couldn't help being delighted by those rare nights when she allowed passion to guide her.

Our son came along one rainy evening late in February, 1991, putting a greater seal on our marriage and making me a cock-proud father.

I had to endure several anxiety-filled days and agitated nights because a fairly difficult birth left Janice and the baby in danger of complications. The birth took place at one of Kingston's best private hospitals, and they ended up spending nine days there. Janice's parents, Daddy and my few close friends were a great source of consolation during those nerve wracking days.

On the day Janice and our son came home, the doctors declared them free of any danger and this filled me with such happy relief that, despite not feeling any greater spiritual affection for her, if my wife had asked, I might have promised to stay with her always and make a great effort to become sexually faithful.

During the following four weeks, I would experience tender, forgiving sentiments that were the closest I had and would ever come to loving Janice. Towards our son, it was complete unconditional love — since day one, there was no doubt that there was nothing I wouldn't endure for his well-being. Because of his fascinating presence, happiness dominated life and made work on my new novel begin flowing quick and easy. I had to accept that his precious birth had linked three futures irrevocably, and would possibly cause me to remain with his mom for more than a decade.

It was clear that until he reached adulthood, I couldn't ever be happy if I didn't have free and easy access to my son.

I was almost like a puppet in Janice's hands and matters weren't helped by the fact that I couldn't help desiring her notably sexy body. I truly tried to weaken this lust for her, but for a highly sexed creature like I, having to live with such an exceptionally beautiful and graceful woman meant wanting her body despite being mostly torn between pity and dislike for her. Separate bedrooms would not have helped and might have even made me desire her more. She renewed our irregular sex life when Jason was nearly four months old, and I, wanting to avoid getting a second child from her, pretended to be blind to the fact that she was quietly using an oral contraceptive. Thereafter I've had to use great willpower to refrain from trying to force myself on her regularly.

By the time our marriage was a year old, I had more or less adjusted to its bizarre complexity, able to laugh with her regularly enough, especially when our little prince was present. In the eyes of the world, we were a happy couple. And now that the marriage is two-and-a-half years old, we are still viewed as a happy couple. But, any day now, it could all become a terrible mess.

CHAPTER 52

Looking down from the master bedroom window on the bustle of New York's Park Avenue on this clear January day, I am confident that from now I'll be able to resist any sexual advance from my sister-in-law — I ended our ungodly affair five months ago but it's obvious she intends to try renewing it someday. The regular fasting, more frequent prayers and daily meditation of the past three months of travelling alone have definitely strengthened me spiritually. From now on, my life shall be more upright in Rastafari. My morals have risen far above the debased levels that caused me to fall prey to the bold advances of my sister-in- law. The great problem now is what to do about the child she gave birth to a few weeks ago, a child I haven't yet seen and who she is proclaiming to be "fatherless" — her parents and my wife are aghast at this claim.

During these past three months I've been fairly chaste, avoiding the former lovers and hordes of would-be lovers, and was able to convince the press that the travelling was a promotional and research thing, and not about ending my marriage. Honestly, the thing I've missed is seeing my son daily. So this lonely tour will end with my return to our home for his second birthday, and then no more travels for a long time without him and his mom. But what's to be done about his newly born half-sister, my unfortunate daughter?

Shit, if the truth comes to public light, my wife might choose to massacre me in a divorce. I'd gladly give her half my assets but that would not stop her from knifing me via our son.

Oh Rastafari, forgive the terrible sin committed with my sister-in-law, and help I to handle the touchy result without causing further problems in my complicated marriage.

The best solution, of course, would be paying Sandra to quietly hand over the baby to my wife for us to nurture as a "fatherless" niece. But it's almost certain the bitch will want to keep the baby out of spite.

Whatever happens, I hope the truth can remain secret.

The doorbell is ringing. I turn away from the window and trudge through the apartment to the front door.

It's my agent, and she appears on the verge of tears.

I quickly let her into the apartment, sensing bad news, asking: "What's wrong?"

Hands in her pants pocket, head bowed, she walks in without answering. I follow her to the living room. The mind is whirling with the dread that something terrible has happened to my son.

My agent sinks to the sofa, raises teary eyes and says: "Janice...your wife...she has committed suicide. White rum and sleeping pills."

I'm dumbfounded. But instantly in my heart, I know the suicide is linked to the daughter of mine that her sister gave birth to and there's a great surge of relief that my son is safe.

Just over three hours later I'm on a packed flight to Jamaica. The suicide, executed just about five hours before my agent delivered the news, hasn't hit the streets as yet, so I'm grimly granting the requests for autographs from fellow passengers, half of whom are Euro-Americans on their way to a Jamaican vacation, but I cut all attempts at small talk by signalling to a non-existent bad tooth.

At Kingston's international airport, a bigwig fan-friend gets me through customs quickly and loans me his car with a driver after I tell him of the suicide. The night is overcast and feels too chilly for Jamaica. I know that it shall be a long night of sorrow for my dead wife, because although I didn't love her, my heart is now heavy with grief and I would've rather endured a lifetime with her than to have her go like this.

At my home, I find the two maids, my sister-in-law and her favourite female cousin and my son's nanny, all teary eyed in profound grief and seemingly expecting me to work some magic that'll drag Janice from death. I learn that my son is asleep in his nearly two year old ignorance of the true meaning of death, and that my secret daughter is also asleep up in the nursery. The others do not seem to know the baby girl is mine, but I'm still convinced that my wife's suicide was due to her having somehow learned the secret. I also learn that my mother-in-law collapsed at the news of Janice's suicide and is under sedation at home with her worried husband. I instantly go up to the nursery with Sandra trudging behind me. I turn on the overhead lights. My son is peacefully asleep on his bed. I turn to his outgrown cradle for the first look at my daughter. I take a good long look at her chubby sleeping features, turn to her haggard looking mother and, seeing that we are truly alone, declare: "I know she's mine. But thank God it looks as if she'll resemble your family."

Instead of answering, she covers her newly-lined face and sobs. Moving pass her, resisting the urge to immediately ask how she drove Janice to suicide, I turn out the bright lights and leave the room. Tomorrow will be soon enough to go about getting her to admit what the gut tells me occurred.

Tomorrow will also mean viewing Janice's body, plus facing the cops and the media. Now I must go downstairs for a bottle of whiskey and instantly return up the stairs to my workroom. There's a fierce need to be alone for awhile.

Pouring a glass of whiskey at my desk, instinct prods me to open the drawer that has a combination lock, the correct entry numbers for which I have told only one other person, my dead wife. I open the drawer and freeze. The light from the desk lamp shows a note atop the little pile of short story manuscripts. No doubt, it must be Janice's suicide note.

The note reads:

Right in front of her lesbian lover she declared you're the father!

I entered her apartment to find them entwined on the living room rug, in midday!

The baby right beside them! And when I called them disgusting, she laughed and said you're the father. I will not wait until the world knows and it kills my patents! Suicide, our son Jason, and the baby girl, will be my revenge!!!

The fact that there's no signature adds vast power to the chilling last sentence. My hands tremble; the world rocks. I silently curse Sandra and I for having had an affair. Damn Sandra for declaring the secret in front of her lesbian lover. It's almost certain that if Sandra had voiced the secret to Janice when they were alone, Janice wouldn't have felt driven to suicide: instead, my departed wife would have tried to keep it secret between us and use it as further power over me. The reality now is that, as the suicide note paints it, most likely the world will eventually know how sinful a sick prick I've been. Then later in life, my son and daughter will learn the truth and despise me.

I get up from my desk, turn off the lamp and begin pacing the dimly lit room. The terrible note is heavy in my hand. I quickly decide to destroy it. Nobody else will ever know of its existence. Perhaps I can use money, guilt and threats to let the truth remain secret between Sandra and her lover and I?

CHAPTER 53

The sunny Jamaican midday is forlorn here at home. My wife was buried three days ago, ten days after her suicide, and by then I had good reason to believe that Sandra's lesbian lover would be true to her tearful promise to remain silent about my fatherly links with Sandra's daughter and the truth behind Janice's suicide. The guilt torn lesbian didn't want to accept the money, but I convinced her to accept it as half loan and half investment into her little restaurant. Meanwhile, the police closed the case as suicide based on the medical reports and my declaration of us having sexual problems. Yesterday was Sandra's birthday and last night she committed suicide, via the same white rum and sleeping pill method her older sister used.

The suicide note Sandra left her parents declared that she could not bear facing another birthday without her sister and was asking them to allow me to raise her "fatherless daughter" with my son.

So now I must again approach Sandra's lesbian lover about keeping the truth about my daughter secret. Part of me believes that, as I could never commit murder, whether directly or otherwise, the best solution is to take the chance of marrying her; creating a matrimonial cage for the sinful truth about my departed sister-in-law and I. This holder of the deadly secret is a year younger than my twenty-nine, and a true fan of my work, and I believe her claim that she is really bisexual but has been mostly lesbian in the past four years.

I'm alone in my dark bedroom. Sandra's funeral was yesterday. How my heart ached for the agony being borne by the bewildered parents. Both daughters, their only offsprings, and were still so young, suddenly gone by suicide within fifteen days.

If only I could go back in time to straighten out this dreadful folly.

In keeping with her last request of her parents, I'm already in possession of the daughter by Sandra. This daughter, who I must raise as a fatherless niece is now in the nursery with my son, both of them under the care of the nanny. Two days ago, I did what now appears the only sensible thing, I asked Sandra's lesbian lover to marry me and be mother to the children. She accepted my proposal after several open-mouthed seconds of shock.

The bizarre engagement will remain secret for the next four months. We shall begin dating a month from now. She's ready to become my secret lover right now but I have no nature for that; within a week or two I should be ready to begin finding out the secrets of her body, and begin enduring the punishment that life with her will be.

WITHDRAWN
No longer the property of the
Boston Public Library.
Sale of this material benefits the Library

Printed in the United States
209375BV00001B/129/A

9 789768 184979